J.H. V4

MW01277558

COMMITMENT

AN ACT OF COURAGE, KINDNESS, PROMISES AND POWER BUT SECRETS THREATEN TO DESTROY EVERYTHING

COMMITMENT

AN ACT OF COURAGE, KINDNESS, PROMISES AND POWER BUT SECRETS THREATEN TO DESTROY EVERYTHING

R.C. CORD

CITY HOUSE
PUBLISHING
WASHINGTON, DC

PAPERBACK ISBN: 978-1-7349258-3-8
HARDCOVER ISBN: 978-1-7349258-4-5

Published by: City House Publishing
WASHINGTON, DC

Cover by: Lisa Monias
www.SouthRiverDesignTeam.com

PRINTED IN THE UNITED STATES OF AMERICA

To my muse, J.A.K.

Commitment is an act,
not a word.

— Jean-Paul Sartre

CHAPTER 1

The lone figure of a bearded man in his mid-thirties walked from a run-down house on A Street to the Capitol Mall. He was dressed in army fatigues, and wore a field jacket and regulation military cap. He walked with a purpose as if going to an appointment.

He performed this ritual almost every Sunday morning, regardless of the weather, and this day it was damp and cold. He adjusted the scarf more tightly around his neck and fastened the top button of his field jacket. The sky was a foreboding, ominous gray, the depressing color of late winter. It matched his mood.

He walked a block over to Capitol Street. It would have been shorter to just walk straight up A Street, but he liked the feeling of approaching the Capitol between the Library of Congress and the Supreme Court Building, so he took that route.

Because it was early and there were no cars, he cut diagonally across First Street, then walked past the north side of the Capitol and on down the stairs to the fountain. It was dry and empty except for some leaves and old snow collected in the corners, hidden from the warmth of the sun. He continued as always, taking the right-hand path along the north side of the Mall.

He had grown to love the quietness of Sunday mornings, and this ritual was like going to church for him. The men he would visit that morning were his brothers-in-spirit.

When he reached the top of the promontory where the Washington Monument stands, he stopped. He looked up to the top of the obelisk projecting over 500 feet into the sky and seeming to disappear into the gray cloud cover. He remembered when he had walked up the 897 steps to the top. He had counted them. He was 12 years old then.

His eyes followed the edge of the marble down to the circle of flags surrounding its base—one for each of the fifty states of the Union. Then he looked to the Jefferson Memorial, pondering the strength of the man whose statue stood within. He walked on along the north side of the reflecting pool toward the somber, seated figure of Lincoln. Joggers passed him, exhaling foggy clouds of breath. A few remembered him from previous Sundays and waved in recognition, but he was oblivious to them.

When he came to the path leading off to the right into Constitution Gardens he took it, and his pace slowed almost to a stroll as he looked over the large pond to the small island. Stones bearing the names of the fifty-six signers of the Declaration of Independence rested there as a memorial to the creators of the country and the freedoms for which he, too, had fought.

But this was not his final destination. As snow started to float down in heavy wet flakes, he walked on among the trees that surrounded the Vietnam Veterans Memorial. When he reached the bench that faced the black, reflective marble wall he sat down. Because there was no memorial to those who had died in the Operation Enduring Freedom war in Iraq, this bench had become his pew every Sunday where he remembered and honored those who had fought with him and had become his brothers, but didn't make it home. Their names were not inscribed on the wall, but they were members of the only family that he'd ever had, and he wanted to be with them. A lump came to his throat and his eyes misted over. He put his cold hands in the pockets of his field jacket and looked up at the sky through the bare branches of the tree above him. He was a lost soul.

He turned his attention to the flagpole and the sculpture of the Three Soldiers next to it. Snow had begun to accumulate on their shoulders. Then, he noticed a figure lying on one of the other benches. He watched the body for a few moments as it lay motionless. Then it occurred to him that, if the person had been there all night, he might be suffering from hypothermia or be dead.

He got up and walked over. When he looked down, he was surprised to see a young woman. She wore a long brown coat with a brown muffler wrapped around her neck, and a wool ski cap on her head, pulled down over her ears. She had tucked her legs up under her coat, and snow had begun to cover her.

He reached down and touched her shoulder. When she remained motionless, he looked around wondering what to do but saw no one. Gingerly he placed his hand on her shoulder and began shaking her. Her eyelids fluttered open slowly and he breathed a sigh of relief. Her eyes were brown and she looked up at him but didn't move. Then she saw his uniform, slowly raised herself to a sitting position and rubbed a sleeve across her face.

"Are you a guard?" she asked.

"No, I'm not, but you can't sleep here. Have you been here all night?"

She looked around but didn't answer.

He sat down on the other end of the bench and said, "Look, if you're in trouble, maybe I can help."

Still she didn't answer.

"I can help you get home. Where do you live?"

She looked off toward the Wall. "Nowhere."

He leaned against the back of the bench, and she turned her head toward him and said, "I don't want any help."

He noticed her worn wool gloves. They had holes at the tips and her hands were balled fists inside, the fingers of the gloves hanging loose. "Do you have any money?"

She looked away and shook her head. Her long brown hair spilling out from under her cap looked straggly, as if it hadn't been washed for a while.

He cleared his throat. "Look, I haven't had any breakfast," he said, although it wasn't true. "Let me take you to a place across Constitution Avenue." He pointed in that direction. "It's a couple of blocks from here. Great coffee and eggs. I'm on my way there."

When she remained silent, he pondered and looked up at the falling snow. "You can't stay here."

She hesitated apprehensively and finally stood up.

The snow was starting to collect on the grass as they walked past the statue and the flagpole, down the wet sidewalk on Henry Bacon Drive, across Constitution Avenue and farther on to the cafe. By the time they arrived, the snow was falling more heavily and they brushed it from their coats as they entered.

He led her to a booth by the window and helped her remove her coat. He put it on the seat of an empty chair along with his field jacket and sat down opposite her. Rubbing his hands together, he asked, "Coffee?"

She looked away, out the window, expressionless. "I'll have hot chocolate, if that's okay."

He gave the order to the waitress, then turned his attention back to her. "My name's David. David Madison."

She made no reply as she looked down at the menu. She was surprisingly attractive in a brown wool sweater. He guessed she was in her early twenties. Her fingernails were long and the polish chipped. She wasn't a vagrant. She looked like someone from a good home. Her face was a bit gaunt. He wondered when she'd last eaten.

The waitress brought their coffee and hot chocolate, and they both ordered.

She removed her wool cap and gloves and placed them in her lap. Warming her hands around the cup and breathing in the aroma of the steaming chocolate, she took her first sip. Then she brought her eyes up to his and said, "My name's Darlene."

He relaxed. "Where are you from?"

"Connecticut. New Haven."

He nodded. "I know it well. Went to school there. What brought you to D.C.?"

She gazed vacantly out the window. "I followed someone."

He remained silent, hoping she would continue on her own, but she kept staring at the falling snow. Finally, she said, "I left home when I found out I was pregnant and came here to find him."

David stirred cream into his coffee. "What happened?"

She watched the snowflakes falling more rapidly, obscuring the buildings across the street. "He has no interest in me. He says it's my fault. He refuses to believe he's the father."

"There are ways to prove that these days."

Darlene turned her head back toward him. "He wants me to kill the baby."

Her fierce expression startled him. "He'll pay for an abortion?" he asked.

"No. He says the government will do that. He refuses to take any responsibility himself. He says I should have the abortion and go back to Connecticut. No one will know the difference." She gave a humorless laugh. "As though it would make no difference to the child."

"What are you going to do?"

She looked straight at him. "I've thought of killing him. Not the baby...the father."

Startled again, he said, "What would that solve?"

"It would rid the world of an irresponsible man who would kill a child."

They stopped their conversation and remained silent as the waitress served their food and refilled his coffee. When she left, he said carefully, "You were responsible, too, you know. You weren't married."

"You're supposed to be married now before you have sex?"

"It kind of complicates things when you aren't, doesn't it?"

She looked at him accusingly. "Are you married?"

"I wasn't making a judgment, just an observation."

"He always said we would get married."

They ate in uncomfortable silence for a while. Eventually she looked up at him. "I wasn't really thinking, you know, of killing him or the baby." Then she added, "Abortion's a convenient word. It eliminates any guilt."

He scratched his beard. "I understand that for a lot of women it doesn't eliminate the guilt, it magnifies it."

They waited as the waitress refilled their cups. When she finished, he asked, "When is the baby due?"

"In four months."

He poured cream into his coffee, kept stirring after the cream had dissolved. "I could help you."

She set down her fork, leaned back against the booth, and eyed him suspiciously.

He took a sip of coffee, avoiding her stare. "I own a house on the other end of the Mall, past the Capitol Building. I rent out rooms. There's a vacant one. It's not much to speak of, so it's not rented. But you could use it for a while."

She thought for a moment and said, "That's nice of you, but I don't think so," and resumed eating.

He waited until she finished and the waitress had cleared the table. Then he said, "What are you going to do?"

She placed her hands around the cup, staring into it. "You know I couldn't pay you."

"I said it was nothing to speak of. I haven't found anyone who wants it."

"And you want nothing in return." It was a statement, not a question.

He kept his eyes trained on her. "Only that you have a healthy baby and get back on your feet."

She looked up at him. "You've asked me a lot of questions. Tell me about yourself."

Surprised, he leaned back and folded his arms. Then he clenched his jaw, his face taking on a "no trespassing" expression. "I don't talk about myself."

"You're too young to have served in Vietnam or the first Gulf War. Why were you at the Memorial?"

He turned his head away. "I'm more comfortable there among the dead."

"You're not. You're here."

His eyes came back to her. "Not really."

She met them. "It sounds like we both have a problem on the inside."

Her look had a tenderness he hadn't seen before, no longer distant and complacent. "Maybe so," he admitted. "But my liberation won't come in four months. I have to live with it for a lifetime."

"No, you have it backwards. I'm the one who has to live with this for the rest of my life. Your problem is in your head—or your heart. Mine is in my womb. I hate one man. You hate yourself and the rest of the world."

His eyes flashed in anger until he noticed her fingers tapping nervously on the table. "Look I'm only trying to help you. You need a place to stay."

She took a sip of the hot chocolate. "I have to know who I'd be living with."

His hands opened reflexively. "You misunderstand. There are five other people living there. It's what you'd call a boarding house. One of the renters is a woman, a nurse, someone you might be able to confide in."

She shook her head. "You don't understand. If I accept your charity, you'll constantly be trying to help me. I wouldn't just be living there. I'd become your problem to fix. It's not your problem, it's mine."

He nodded in understanding. "Okay, then let's have some ground rules," he said. "I don't fix your problem, and you don't fix mine. We'll start from here. Say I've run an ad for the room to rent. You're responding to the ad. The rent is one dollar a month, due at the end of each month. If you like the room, you take it for those reasons."

She studied him for a moment. Then she put the cup down, took the ski hat from her lap, and pulled it over her head. "Okay. Let's see the room."

CHAPTER 2

True to his word, David treated Darlene just like another tenant. She saw very little of him, and when they passed each other in the hallway, he greeted her with a perfunctory smile and a nod.

She signed up with a temporary agency and earned enough money as a secretary to buy food and a few clothes. Before the month was over she climbed the long staircase to the third floor and knocked on the door of his attic room. There was movement inside and she caught her breath as David opened the door.

His expression revealed his pleasure, as though a long-expected guest had finally arrived. He opened the door wider and said, "Come in."

Darlene didn't move. His appearance had changed almost beyond recognition. He was clean-shaven with a new haircut and dressed casually in a pair of brown loafers, old brown slacks, and a white shirt rolled up at the sleeves.

"I've come to pay the rent, plus one month's deposit." She held out her hand with a pair of one-dollar bills between her fingers.

He took it, surprised. "Thank you."

When he gestured for her to come in, she hesitated, then crossed the threshold into his private world. It was a large artist's studio, occupying the entire third-floor attic. Although neat and tidy, it smelled of oil paint. A skylight and dormer windows brought warm sunlight into the room, illuminating an alcove where a large easel stood with a cloth-covered painting. Off to the right was another alcove with a large desk in the middle facing into the room. Shelves filled with books lined the three walls around it. The alcove to the left had a leather sofa and chairs with an antique cocktail table on an oriental rug. The walls had hooks where paintings should have been. She glanced around and noticed several canvases leaning against the wall. There was no TV anywhere.

He saw her looking at the paintings. "I took them down and am working on new ones." He put the two dollar bills on the desk, then motioned toward the sofa. "Sit down, I'll make some fresh coffee... and hot chocolate."

She smiled that he remembered.

There was a series of doors in the wall next to the stack of paintings and he pulled them open to expose a Pullman kitchen.

Not ready to sit down yet, she looked around the room. "You're redecorating."

He concentrated on spooning coffee into the coffee maker and called out to her as he opened the refrigerator and took out a milk carton. "The off-white makes the room bigger and brighter. How do you like it?"

"It's nice, but I'd like to see it with the new paintings."

Pouring milk into a pan, he asked, "So, how have you been? You look great."

"Thanks to you."

"How are you feeling?"

"I can feel her kicking...or him."

"There's a little life inside of you."

"I know. It's hard to believe."

"Nancy downstairs jokes that you can tell the sex by how hard they kick."

He indicated for her to sit on the sofa and took the chair opposite her.

Settling into the worn leather cushions, she looked at him. Not only his physical appearance had changed. "You look good," she said. "What happened to the fatigues?"

"I put them away. I met someone about three weeks ago who made me realize the importance of not wasting my life." He thought she still looked a little gaunt. "You need to eat for two now, you know."

"Have you been back to the Memorial?" she asked.

This time the "no trespassing" expression didn't appear on his face and he answered directly, "I've said goodbye to that for a while. It was time to return to the living."

"I'm glad, David."

It was the first time she had ever said his name. He was surprised how good it made him feel.

When he went back to the kitchen to finish fixing the coffee and hot chocolate, she stood and walked over to the bookcases. Three of the shelves on one wall were filled with CDs, mostly classical music and jazz, arranged by composer. The other shelves were filled with literary classics, books on astronomy, science, and architecture, old law books, music, art, history, photography.

She slid her hands along the books caressing the bindings, and said, "Is there anything you're not interested in?"

Bringing two cups to the coffee table, he gave a slight laugh. "Not really. Maybe spectator sports. They're a surrogate's life. Except for tennis and sailing. I used to sail a lot when I belonged to a club at school."

Darlene noticed a cardboard packing box in a corner of the alcove. His framed Yale diploma sat on top of some file folders. She picked it up. "You graduated summa cum laude from Yale Law School?"

He tensed and a breath escaped him. "Look, that's no big deal. I have a photographic memory, and I only need four hours sleep a night."

She returned the document to the box. "You're lucky."

"It's more of a burden than a blessing, I'm afraid. My mind never seems to rest. It's unusual. I don't feel or think like a normal guy."

Returning to the sofa, she said, "I know a lot of normal guys. One of them is the father of this child." She stroked her swollen belly.

He put his feet on the coffee table. "I haven't accomplished anything."

"Graduating from Yale summa cum laude isn't an accomplishment?"

He took a sip of coffee. "No, it's not. What you do with it is an accomplishment. I've done nothing."

"But, think of the possibilities!"

He wagged his finger at her playfully. "You've just broken the rule."

She smiled. "You're right...sorry." Taking in the smell of the hot chocolate, she took a sip. "It's good."

He smiled at the little compliment, basking in the pleasure it gave him. He got up to get some biscuits. "Look, I'm going out of town for a few days," he said. "If you want to use this place, it's bigger and has a kitchen. And if you want to read, you can."

She wagged her finger. "Now you're breaking the rule."

He held up his hands. "Touché. But please, feel free. The fridge is full."

"Thanks. It's a nice offer. I'll think about it." She got up. "I'd better go now."

He wondered if he had made a mistake.

She walked toward the door, hesitating when she reached it. She kept her hand on the doorknob, as though she didn't want to leave. "Thanks for the chocolate," she said.

"You're welcome," he replied formally.

Stepping out into the hall, she started to close the door, then stuck her head back in and said, "Maybe I will."

CHAPTER 3

Over the next three months David took Darlene out on weekends. They promenaded on the Mall enjoying the delicately exuberant riot of the pink and white cherry blossoms, although Darlene preferred the small, budding oak and magnolia trees in the nearby park. They reminded her of the new life sprouting inside her. She also liked the concerts of the National Symphony at the Kennedy Center and began to feel for the first time in years that someone cared for her.

One sunny Sunday morning David knocked on the door of her room. He called softly, "Are you ready to go?"

There was a rustle inside and when the door opened, Darlene's smiling face greeted him. Her belly had grown even larger. He took her hand and walked her down the flight of stairs.

On the first floor, a short, ordinary looking woman stepped out of her apartment into the hallway. She was dressed in a tailored, navy blue suit and carried a large bag over her shoulder.

"Hi, Nancy," David said. "Off to your shift at the hospital?"

"Oh, hi!" Her startled look turned to pleasure when she saw them. "How's it going?"

Darlene gave a slight laugh. "Tiring."

Nancy smiled knowingly. "Of course." She touched Darlene's arm. "Can't stay—I'm late for my shift at the hospital. But I'm off tomorrow. Come down and see me. I mean it. We can go shopping."

David interrupted. "For baby clothes?"

Nancy glanced at him. "What does this guy know about having

a baby?" she teased.

"Not much!" David grinned affectionately as he held the front door open and let them go ahead.

As Nancy passed him she squeezed his arm and whispered, "Take good care of her." Then she hurried down the steps and headed toward the Metro station.

Darlene held onto David's arm and used the railing to maneuver the porch stairs to street level. They took the short route to the Mall.

When they arrived, they stopped at the first bench and Darlene sat down. "It's getting a little strenuous."

David joined her. "I understand. We can take our time." He crossed his legs and looked at her. "How are you feeling?"

"I'm fine."

"You're not eating enough." He smiled. "You have two mouths to feed now."

"You always say that."

"I have to. You never listen to me. Did you ever listen to your father?"

Her face dropped and she gave him a wry smile. "Never."

Looking out over the lawn where some children were kicking a soccer ball around, she changed the subject. "Where do you go all week?"

He put his arm on the back of the bench. "I've been looking for a job in New York."

Her face brightened. "That's wonderful!"

The soccer ball came rolling toward them. David stood up, stopped it with his foot, and kicked it back to one of the boys. Darlene joined him and they resumed their walk.

"What kind of a job?"

"A friend of mine in New York owns an art gallery. I'm trying to sell some paintings. He thinks they're worth something."

She chuckled. "Such modesty. Your new paintings are beautiful. They're more cheerful than your 'Black Period.'"

"I have you to thank for that."

"It's nothing compared to what you've given me." She stopped and sat down again at the next bench. "We won't get very far at this pace."

He rested one foot on the wooden seat and grinned at her. "I've come a long way, Baby, since I met you."

She laughed, but he could see that it was forced. "You look tired, let's go back."

She gazed up at the Washington Monument thrusting into the blue sky dotted with clouds. "It looks so white."

"It looked gray to me not long ago."

Suddenly, she leaned back and scrutinized him. "Is that why you wanted to come here to the Mall? To say your last goodbye. You'll move to New York soon, won't you?"

He smiled at her. "Not until you've had the baby."

"And then what?"

He looked away at the line of people waiting to get into the monument. "And then we'll figure it all out."

When she didn't say anything, he touched her shoulder. "While I'm gone next week, I want you to use my apartment. The refrigerator's full, and you need to gain more weight. Promise me."

She smiled up at him. "Okay, I promise."

He returned the smile. "I'll be back in a few minutes."

Darlene watched him walking toward the Lincoln Memorial, then taking the path that led to the Vietnam Veterans Memorial. She wondered what would happen to him now. She knew his life was getting back on track, but what about hers? She looked up at the white clouds. Some were piled high into puffy masses of softness, and she wished she could reach up and touch them. One of them looked like a little boy lifting up his arm. Was he holding a balloon or was he reaching for one that had escaped? Maybe he was hoping for a helping hand? Was it David's?

Suddenly, she felt like a veil caught in a gust of wind, carried upward, her body light as the clouds, no longer bothered by its weight and fatigue.

For the first time she felt the blessing of a child and she looked forward to the moment when she would hold it in her arms.

CHAPTER 4

When Darlene arrived home from work and opened the door to her room, she saw an envelope on the floor. It was addressed to "Darlene and the Baby." Although she was exhausted, she couldn't help but smile. Sitting on the edge of the bed, she opened the envelope and withdrew a shiny new brass key.

She wanted to check out David's place upstairs, but it had been a long day and she felt too tired. What strength she had left drained from her body. She leaned back with her head on the pillow and fell asleep in seconds with the key clasped in her hand.

It was dark outside when she woke up two hours later. There was a dim glow in the room. The lamp on the small end table by the window was on a timer to make sure she would never be surrounded by darkness.

She turned on her side and looked at the room David had given her. It was more like a large walk-in closet with a window at the end, framed by old-fashioned white curtains. Besides her small bed there was just enough room for an easy chair next to the end table and a tiny closet behind the door. It was all she needed.

She loved this little space with its slightly musty smell. It was her protective cocoon, her refuge during the incubation period of her child and journey toward motherhood. She loved the smallness of it. Just enough space...like the space inside her safeguarding the life that was forming there.

She felt the key in her hand under the pillow and wondered

if she should use it or just stay in her safe little world. Her eyelids slowly closed as sleep overcame her again.

When she awoke this time, it was almost midnight. She was still dressed and felt weak and nauseous. A trip down the hall to the bathroom didn't help much. When she came back to her room, she stood in front of the door, swaying. She still had the key in her hand and remembered her promise to David. Knowing that she had to eat, she took the stairs to the next flight up. Still feeling dizzy, she slipped the key into the door lock and went inside.

The room was pitch black and she felt along the wall for the light switch. When she flipped it, the studio was suddenly bathed in bright light. The easel still had a cloth covering the painting on it, and she fought the temptation to lift it and take a look. She already felt like an intruder. Coming to David's quarters alone at night seemed a surreptitious breach of privacy, although she didn't quite understand why.

She walked over to the bookcases and adjusted a dimmer switch until the light became a warm glow. She saw a note lying on the desk in David's handwriting, and she sat down in the old, leather swivel chair and read it: "Don't let the food spoil in the refrigerator." She smiled. It was so like him!

Suddenly, the telephone on the desk rang, startling her, as though she had been caught trespassing. The phone rang again. Panic seized her and she started to tremble. The next ring seemed louder, shriller. Suddenly, she imagined the face of her father staring at her from outside the window. Another piercing ring and he was in the room, advancing on her, shouting, "I know you're pregnant, and you can't hide."

Paralyzed and desperate, she wanted to cry out when the answering machine clicked on with David's voice, "Hi, leave a message," followed by a beep.

Then she heard David's voice again, sounding more natural. "Darlene, if you're there, pick up the phone. I'm sorry to call you at this hour, but I'll be delayed a little longer. Are you all right?" After a pause his voice resumed more urgently. "Darlene, are you there?"

She grabbed the receiver. "David, David!"

"Darlene, are you all right?"

"Yes, yes." Relief overcame her and she laughed as her nightmare seemed suddenly unreal.

"What's wrong?"

"Nothing, nothing's wrong. I was just startled. It was just like a nightmare, that's all." His voice became apologetic. "The answering machine is new. I just got it because I've been out of town so much. I'm sorry to wake you at this hour."

She rested the elbow of her free arm on the desk, cradled her forehead in her hand. "I found the key...fell asleep...then came upstairs...." She laughed again. "I didn't expect the phone to ring."

"You sure you're okay?"

"Positive." She felt a little embarrassed at her irrational reaction. As she leaned back in his desk chair, she had the sensation of having his arms enfolding her. "Where are you?"

His voice registered relief. "I'll tell you when I get home, but I need another few days. I'm so glad I reached you. How's the baby doing?"

"Fine." She rubbed her bloated belly. "I can feel him. He's kicking up a storm."

"You talk as if you're certain it's a he."

"He...she, it doesn't matter. What matters is this life I'm carrying inside me. Oh, David, if you could only feel what it's like."

"I wish I could. But I called for another reason. Nancy Watson is concerned. She doesn't think you're eating right and wants you to see a doctor."

Darlene laughed. "You sound like a worried dad." There was a silence at the other end of the line. She bit her lip, wishing she hadn't said that, and was relieved when he spoke again.

"Nancy's good, you should follow her advice."

"I'll do that," she said quickly.

"Nancy will make an appointment for you and let you know. Promise me you'll go."

"I promise."

"Good. Got to let you go!... Get some sleep. Goodnight, Darlene. I'll call you tomorrow."

Hearing a tenderness in his voice, she responded in kind. "Goodnight, David."

She put the receiver back in its cradle. What was he thinking after their past months together? Did he want to be the father? She felt almost too tired to move, but forced herself to go to the sofa and lie down. When she settled in she pulled up her blouse and rubbed the naked belly that held her child. She wished it were David's. She pretended it was.

CHAPTER 5

David entered the 21 Club in Midtown Manhattan. Known for its power lunches for New York's business, media, political, and entertainment elite, the dining room at dinner time was a bit more sedate. It was still early, and there were several empty spots among the well-dressed couples and larger parties.

He noticed Katherine Coyle waiting for him at a table for two on the far side of the room, toying with the glass of white wine in front of her. No doubt a Chablis which she always ordered whenever they came into New York during their Yale days. She looked cool and unflappable. He realized it was their table and felt a pang of anguish, followed by a jolt of anger.

When she waved to him, he hesitated, then waved back and crossed the room to her. She was wearing an elegant, navy blue dress. To his surprise, the gold pendant he'd once given her as a birthday present was dangling from her neck. As he hovered briefly above her, he smelled her familiar perfume and felt momentarily distracted, as if all the time that had passed were suddenly erased. A fleeting look of apprehension crossed her face until he took the seat opposite her.

During the ensuing silence, he looked at the woman he had loved but not seen in 10 years. She was as beautiful as he remembered. The blonde hair was different—still long but styled more fashionably. Then he noticed the small, thin worry lines at the sides of her blue eyes and the corners of her mouth. Perhaps, her life had been less rosy than he'd imagined.

"It's been a long time, Katherine," he said.

Fidgeting with the gold bracelet on her wrist, she replied. "I've been thinking about how to start this, but I haven't found the right words."

"I think the line in the movie goes, 'Yes, it has been. Too long.'"

She drew her hands down into her lap and lowered her head. "That didn't help."

"It wasn't meant to."

When she maintained an uncomfortable silence, David decided there was no point in postponing the confrontation, but the waiter came up asking, "May I get you a drink?"

"Glenmorangie on the rocks," David ordered. When the waiter disappeared, he said bluntly, "Why didn't you wait for me?"

Katherine blushed and her expression changed from embarrassment to entreating. "You were shot down. We thought you had been killed. Then, when you recovered, you re-enlisted."

"I had a job to finish," he said vehemently. "I had an obligation to serve my country when it was attacked. Three thousand people died!" He lowered his voice and continued, not hiding the bitterness, "I wanted to marry you, but you put it off."

Her eyes kept imploring, and the words tumbled out. "You asked too much. You wanted to have it both ways. You loved flying more than you loved me. I couldn't live with not knowing whether you would be alive the next day."

"So you married my college classmate."

When she didn't reply, he tried sarcasm. "How is Bradley? Do you come here with him often? Sit at this table?"

Her face hardened. "As a matter of fact, I never did. What I did do is file for divorce."

David tried to hide his surprise. "Why?"

"He was whoring around!"

David winced. Katherine had never been so direct and vulgar when he knew her.

Noticing his reaction, she said softly, "I thought he'd be more like you."

He snorted. "I never knew that lack of discernment was one of your shortcomings."

"I made a mistake," she pleaded. "I was so young. I listened to the men in my life. I wish I hadn't."

His tone remained harsh and unforgiving. "It's always obvious in hindsight, isn't it?"

She sighed. "Yes, it is."

"How could you do it?" he asked plaintively. "When I found out that you had married Bradley...you, who had gotten me through... you were what I lived for...."

She looked up into his eyes. "I am truly sorry I hurt you."

But when she searched his face for a sign of forgiveness, he turned his head away. They sat in silence for a while, not looking at each other. Finally, she clutched her purse and said, "This was a mistake. I think I should leave."

As she started to get up, David clasped her arm. "Don't go. This isn't what I intended. I apologize."

She hesitated and stared at him.

Taking a deep breath, he said, "I thought I had put the past behind me, but it came back at me all at once." He ran his fingers through his hair. "I didn't mean to hurt you either, Kathy. Please stay."

It touched her that he'd used his old name for her, and she settled back in her chair. "I can't imagine what you went through. It must have been hell on Earth. But I'm glad you made it back. And I'm glad you asked to see me again."

"Then let's move on," he said, willing himself to relax.

The waiter, who had kept a discreet distance, now approached their table with the Scotch in a crystal tumbler. David pointed questioningly at Katherine's nearly empty glass, and she nodded yes. The waiter bowed with a small smile and left.

David took a gulp of his drink and looked around. The room hadn't changed. The red leather booths, paneled walls, long bar, and realistic paintings on the walls gave a feeling of permanence. Letting

R . C .   C O R D

his eyes settle on Katherine, he asked, "So what are you doing now?"

"I teach a graduate course in political science at Columbia— what really goes on behind the scenes in Washington."

"Those jobs are hard to get. How did you swing it?"

She looked a little embarrassed. "My father–"

"Of course, the senator pulled some strings."

Her eyes flashed resentfully. "How do you think Bradley got elected to the House and then the Senate?"

Raising a hand, David said, "I understand. But if you divorce him and anyone comes forward about his...extracurricular activities, who'll stand by him? Won't that kill his chances for reelection?"

She gave a bitter laugh. "All his affairs are consensual. He's a philandering adulterer, not a predator, and he's never gotten on a soapbox touting family values, so no one can accuse him of being a hypocrite."

The waiter returned with Katherine's wine. David finished off his Scotch and held up the empty tumbler. When he started to look at the menu, Katherine took the opportunity to study him. He was still boyishly handsome, but more mature somehow. His hazel eyes were more penetrating than she remembered, perhaps because of what he'd seen in the war. He looked a little heavier, but still solid and athletic, and she found him even more attractive than before. How did everything go so wrong? It was David who had been her father's choice to succeed him, but in his absence, somehow Bradley had convinced him that he was the better man. Why had she listened to them?

He noticed her scrutinizing him and said casually, "See anything you like?"

She scanned the menu. "They have the rack-of-lamb for two tonight. Are you up for it?"

David hesitated, then agreed. "Why not?"

When the waiter returned with his drink, David ordered, pointing to the special.

"Excellent choice," the waiter said and collected the menus.

As he left, David scanned the ceiling which had the celebrity gifts hanging from it—model trucks, cars, and airplanes; sports paraphernalia; and other gifts from famous diners. He thought he saw some new ones. All that was missing was baby toys.

"What about children?" he asked.

Katherine shook her head. "We didn't have any. At least that's a blessing." She took another sip of wine. Then, she tilted her head slightly in a way he always found alluring and asked, "What are you doing now?"

"I'm going to have a showing of my paintings at Frank Gannovino's. You remember him from Yale? He was one of our classmates. He has a gallery in New York now, in Chelsea."

Surprised, Katherine said, "I thought that was just a hobby for you."

"Well, it's become more than that." To cover his insecurity, he asked, "What about you? What will you do after the divorce? Being a college professor isn't in your pedigree. Four generations of Cunninghams will turn in their graves."

She laughed for the first time. "You know me too well. You're right, politics is in my blood. I think I'll go back to Washington."

"You'll work for your father?"

"Probably...until I get my feet wet again, then I'll find another place...on my own. There are a lot of good people in Washington," she said, smiling indulgently when he scoffed.

"What will Bradley do now? Will he fight you?"

"Not unless he wants Daddy to go to war with him." She toyed with her wine glass again, turning it at its base. "He's still good looking you know. If you don't believe me, just ask him—he'll tell you. He's already lined up an heiress to marry—old Connecticut money. He'll use her wealth and connections to run for reelection to the Senate and will probably win again. She grimaced. "She'll get the title, he gets the money and power. They'll have three kids and live happily ever after."

"Do you know the heiress?"

She smirked. "Everyone does."

David leaned back, taking her measure—her intense, blue eyes, the slightly squared shoulders, the soft, tempting swell of her breasts. She could still stir him, he realized, but he no longer harbored any romantic feelings for her. Those were distant memories in his past, and he figured, like his dead comrades, nothing could resurrect them. He looked around the room at all the diners eating and deeply involved in conversations, and a feeling of serenity came over him.

"I'm thinking of getting married," he said.

Taken aback, Katherine raised her eyebrows. "Thinking of it?"

He feigned innocence. "Isn't that what one usually does?"

"One usually falls in love first."

He took a sip of his drink. "I owe her a lot."

"Love isn't a debt, David."

"She is pregnant."

Katherine looked at him intently. "Do you love her?"

"I will. Maybe I already do."

"Maybe?" She narrowed her eyes. "Don't be a martyr, David. I've been there, and it doesn't work. Eventually she'll hate you for it. You can't fake love. In the end, you'll both regret it."

They stared at each other for a long moment—a stand-off. Finally, Katherine broke away and sighed. "It's too late for us, isn't it?"

David's lips tightened. "I'm afraid it is."

He saw her disappointment as her hand unconsciously grasped the gold pendant. She took a long sip of wine.

When she had recovered, her voice was huskier. "You once wanted to change the world, to make things right that you believed were wrong. That's why you studied law. You were brought up the opposite of Bradley. He was handed everything. You worked for everything, joined the ROTC to put yourself through Yale. Don't you see? You're too good to be a painter."

He gave an uneasy laugh. "You mean 'not good enough to be a painter.'"

"Take it that way if you want, but my father thought you could do great things. You can still fulfill that dream." She reached across the table and took his hand. "The David Madison I knew was never a quitter. Dad could make you a congressman just as he made Bradley."

David shook his head. "If I did that, I'd want to do it my own way."

"That's not how it's done in politics. You know that. It takes connections, backers, promoters, and a well-orchestrated campaign. That's what we once planned together."

He squeezed her hand lightly and then withdrew his. "It's not for me, Kathy. Not anymore."

Before she could respond, the waiter arrived with their entrée.

CHAPTER 6

He could see that the light was on in his apartment as he climbed the stairs and knew that Darlene was there. He knocked softly on the door, then opened it. "Darlene?"

But it wasn't Darlene who waited for him. It was Nancy, still wearing her white nurse's uniform. It was the first time she didn't greet him with a smile. Instead she got up from the sofa and said, "David, I'm so sorry."

He looked at her in bewilderment for a moment, then the realization struck him. He dropped his travel bag. "What's happened to Darlene?"

Tears started to well up in Nancy's eyes. "She died, David." She bit her lip, trying to hold back her emotions, and shook her head. "It was the cancer. She was so weak."

David stood frozen in his place. "Cancer," he mouthed the word. "Cancer? She had cancer?"

Nancy moved toward him. "Yes, liver cancer. You didn't know?"

Shaking his head, he staggered toward the sofa and cried out in anguish, "I should have been here!" Then he collapsed on the couch and held his head in his hands.

Nancy sat down next to him and grasped his arm. "I rushed her to the Georgetown hospital. She kept calling for you. They had to do a C-section, but she didn't make it." She took his hand in both of hers. "I thought the baby was yours. I put you down as the father. I hope I did the right thing. I didn't want there to be any questions. It was a premature birth. The boy is in an incubator."

When he looked up at her she said, "She had a son, David."

Grief overcame him. "I never told her that I was going to marry her. That I wanted her child to have a father. She never knew that she was loved. I was going to tell her, but I always thought there was time." He started to weep.

Nancy put her arm around him. "I'm sure she knew that, David."

He shook his head in despair. "I almost told her that night on the telephone. And now she's lost, gone, and there's nothing I can do about it anymore."

"We aren't gods, David, we can only delay death. The doctors did everything possible."

He sobbed, "But I didn't." Trying to gather himself, he looked at the paintings on the wall through teary eyes. They conveyed a new feeling, a sense of hope. It was Darlene's influence. She had inspired him.

"I don't know how she lived this long, David," Nancy said kindly. "It must have been her determination to give life to the child. She wanted him to be named Grant."

That seemed to reach him somehow. His expression turned from pain to resolve. "Then his name is Grant. Grant Madison. You did the right thing," he said.

"Thank you," Nancy whispered gratefully.

He closed his eyes, expelled his breath, and they sat in silence for a moment. Then David turned to her. "Have you reached her parents?"

"Yes. Her father is a professor at Yale. They'll be here tomorrow."

He got up and started to pace. He ran a hand through his hair. "I'll let them know that I was going to marry her. I'll get a job in New York. New Haven is only an hour and forty minutes from New York. If they can take care of him at first, I'll go up there on weekends. He'll have grandparents and a father and grow up like a normal kid—as normal as possible."

CHAPTER 7

David waited in the lobby of the hospital, pacing more like an expectant father than an expectant son-in-law. He knew nothing about Darlene's parents except that her father was a professor of biology at Yale University. Where would he start with them? He had to have a plausible story when all the questions came. Where did you meet? She was already pregnant when she left home, so he would have to have gotten to know her in New Haven, before she joined him in Washington. Why hadn't they married before the boy was born? Once you start lying, where does it stop?

He looked up eagerly each time the big glass doors to the lobby slid open. They'd want to know his plans. If he sold his house in Washington, D.C. and managed to sell his paintings, he would have enough to get started in New York. He'd hire a nurse or sitter. Other single parents made a go of it, and so would he.

The doors opened again and an older couple walked in. It had to be them—the professorial beard, the rumpled tweed sport coat with patches on the sleeves. Edward Langley was a large man, somewhat overweight and balding to the point that only a ring of hair above the ears remained. He strode confidently into the lobby, not like a quiet, modest academic, but as the bombastic intellectual who used his physical size to dominate and intimidate those around him. David imagined that he was the type of professor who was more interested in himself than his students, more intent on preaching an ideology than in teaching.

Laura Langley wore a modest gray dress that ended below the

knee. It was appropriate for her age and, no doubt, made her immune from criticism of the women she associated with by assuring them that she would never outshine them. She had a slim figure, and her face, though etched with worry, suggested that at one time she had been quite beautiful. David wondered if she was trying to hold onto a debutante past because she had sublimated her own ambitions in order not to compete with her husband.

It was a familiar picture, and he could understand why Darlene had fled from them. What he didn't expect and gave him pause was the expression on Edward Langley's face. It wasn't remorse or anguish, but fury. He marched up to the reception desk, his wife in tow.

When the receptionist turned toward him, David walked over and extended his hand. He said, "I'm David Madison. I'm Grant's father."

Edward Langley looked at him pretending not to see his hand. "I want to see my daughter. Where is her body?"

David saw the distraught look on Darlene's mother's face and said, "I'm so sorry."

Giving him a frosty stare, Langley said. "You knew her for what, maybe a year? Got her pregnant, and now you're sorry?" He continued with contempt in his voice, "We raised her for twenty-two years. I witnessed her birth, actually saw her come out of the womb. And you're sorry?!"

Darlene's mother touched his arm. "Edward…please!"

David knew there was no point in trying to talk further now. "There's a nurse who was with her," he said. "Let me get her. She'll explain what happened."

He went to the reception desk to have Nancy paged. When she came through a set of automatic doors from an inside corridor, he heaved a sigh of relief and said, "It's worse than I thought, Nancy. Try to explain to them. He wants to see her body."

Nancy nodded. "The loss of a child is the most devastating thing that can happen to a parent."

"I understand that, but they're blaming me. Tell them I was going to marry her."

She took a deep breath. "Let me do what I can."

She walked over to Darlene's parents and spoke softly to them. The balled-up tension never left Langley's body, and when he and his wife followed Nancy through the door, they passed David without so much as a glance.

CHAPTER 8

The next time they met was on the 30th floor of a skyscraper on East 57th Street in the New York office of Eggleton, Baker, Schienig & Cooper. David and his attorney sat waiting in the conference room whose floor to ceiling window overlooked Central Park. The opposite wall was of thick, plate glass. A veiled drape hung at the sides that could be closed to offer privacy from the modern reception area.

David drummed his fingers on the black, marble-topped conference table. He'd been excluded from Darlene's funeral, as expected. The summons he received three days later in the mail was a curt announcement indicating the time and place of the meeting, written on the stationery of the law firm.

The only lawyer David knew was a fellow Marine who had become a real estate attorney, and he'd asked him to come along for moral support. Mac sat beside David and swiveled side to side in the black and chrome chair. "It feels like I'm sitting in a sinkhole," he commented. He reached below the seat, released the lever, and raised himself to David's height. "I think they do it deliberately."

David turned to him. "Nervous?"

Mac, who had attended closings as a junior partner in a small law firm, slid his damp hands down his pant legs to wipe off the sweat. Running a finger inside his collar and stretching his neck, he said, "They could at least have offered us some coffee."

There was tension in David's voice. "It's their way of letting us know how insignificant we are to them."

Mac pointed at the glass wall. "Yeah, it makes me feel like I'm in a fishbowl, waiting to be fed...or starved at their whim. I'm a real estate lawyer, for chrissake."

"You'll be fine. You're a war vet. You've survived worse."

Mac sighed and nodded. "What do you know about this guy, Langley?"

"I've checked him out since I met him at the hospital. He's a big deal at Yale, tenured professor, Nobel Prize in Biology, a list of publications as long as my arm, million-dollar research grants. All the credentials you need for an ego the size of the Washington Monument. He's used to getting what he wants."

"He's hired one of the biggest law firms in town." Mac gave a half-mocking laugh. "I'd have a better chance of winning the lottery than being hired here—as a janitor."

The conference room door finally opened and two attorneys ushered the Langleys into the room. They were both wearing hand-tailored, blue pinstripe suits and red satin ties, but one outfit was five times as expensive as the other, befitting the difference between named and junior partner. Langley, in contrast, had on another rumpled jacket and his wife wore a sedate gray tailored suit.

David and Mac stood up. The older, silver-haired attorney introduced himself as George Eggleton, but did not shake hands. He took the chair at the head of the table and said, "Please be seated."

The younger attorney closed the drapes, then took a chair next to the Langleys across from David and Mac. He placed a yellow legal pad and fountain pen in front of him on the table—the designated note-taker.

When neither Langley nor his wife looked at David, only their attorneys, David realized that, as far as they were concerned, they had settled everything among themselves already. For them, this was the end, not the beginning of a negotiation. He put one hand flat on the table and forced himself to relax.

Eggleton cleared his throat, as if to say, "We shall commence now." When he spoke, his voice was deep and carried a sense of authority. "The Langleys wish only to do what is best for the child. They will take custody and raise him as their own. You," he looked at David, "will be relieved of all responsibility, both financial and personal. Simply put, you can go on as before, as though you were never entangled in a relationship with...with..."—he searched for the right word—"the deceased." He put on the all-knowing demeanor of a judge. "The Langleys will adopt the boy. It's the best solution, given the circumstances."

David closed his eyes and sat quietly: a moment of silence for Darlene. That's how he thought of it, an acknowledgment of the absent mother as the fate of her son was about to be decided. When he opened his eyes, he said, "That's not what Darlene would want."

Edward Langley's face began to turn crimson. "We know who you are, Madison," he spat out scornfully as his two fists came to the top of the table. "You're a destitute derelict. Do you think you have a snowball's chance in hell of getting custody of that boy? You've taken away our daughter. You never married her. You're giving me back her son."

Mrs. Langley tried to soothe her husband. "Edward, she died of cancer."

Her intercession only increased his fury. He turned toward her, pointing a finger at David, and exploded, "A condition that I'm sure he provoked."

David realized that his dream of giving Grant even the semblance of a normal life with a father and grandparents was just that—a dream. He understood their grief and anger. They thought he was the guilty party. He wanted to explain that he wasn't that person and that Darlene had changed his life. But if he told them the truth, he would never be able to keep the commitment he had made.

So he calmly said, "I understand how you feel, but my name's on the birth certificate as his father." He phrased it that way to make the point without lying. "I want what's best for Grant, too. I know I can't raise him alone, not yet; so I'll agree to custody with visitation rights, but not adoption." He looked directly at the professor to drive home the point that there could be no negotiation on this issue.

Langley rose up in his chair and was about to explode again, but Eggleton reached over and restrained him with a hand on his arm. "Let's step outside."

After they left the room, Mac looked at David in amazement. "You can handle Silverhair and Junior without my help. Why am I here?"

"Because they'll think that they can push me around if I don't have a lawyer. And I need you to review the papers."

"Are you willing to agree to the terms you've outlined?"

"Yes. I'll never get custody right now. All I can hope for is visitation. I'll take it a step at a time."

∝

Eggleton led the Langleys to his corner office. It was more of a suite and had views of both Central Park and New Jersey on the other side of the Hudson River. He sat on the corner of his enormous antique desk. Laura Langley sat at the end of the sofa as her husband paced in front of her. The junior partner stood discreetly by the door.

"All that a court will grant you is custody, Edward, at least temporarily," Eggleton explained. "He doesn't have the means to be a father, at least not at this point. But he's a decorated war veteran with no blemishes on his record. He can demonstrate that, and he knows it. He's smarter than I thought. If he wants visitation rights he'll get them, as often as once a week at the most. I think he'd agree to that."

Langley remained silent and continued to pace. Eggleton finally asked him, "What do you want to do, Edward?"

Langley stopped in his tracks and clenched his fists. "I want to kill the bastard."

The attorney scratched his nose. "I know how you feel, Edward, but you will have the child with you to bring up. It could be worse. He could ask for money. Then you'd know he wasn't interested in the child."

"I'd rather that he did."

"But he didn't. You have to deal with the facts. If you get custody you're in control. Let him have visitation. You have to remember he's the biological father. You don't want to go to trial on this. Agree to custody now and wait until he screws up, which I'm sure he will. Then a judge will see adoption into a good family, a Yale professor and Nobel Prize winner, as an ideal alternative to his bad influence. This guy may abandon the child, never visit, get in trouble with the police ...then we pounce."

Mrs. Langley spoke for the first time. "Maybe we've rushed to judgment. Maybe he really did love Darlene."

Langley snorted. "Love? Ha! He got lost somewhere in the chain of evolution and never made it to the human level. What could Darlene possibly see in him?"

He resumed pacing while the others waited for him to make up his mind. Finally, he stopped and said to Eggleton, "If he ever mentions the name of my daughter in front of me, I swear, I'll kill him."

Eggleton took a deep breath to conceal his impatience with the continuing outbursts. Then, he asked, "Do you agree, Edward? We take it a step at a time. Custody now, adoption later?"

Langley frowned in anger and spread his arms apart helplessly. "Do I have a choice?"

CHAPTER 9

The Sunday morning train to New Haven was practically empty. David nursed the cup of coffee he'd bought at Grand Central Station. He hadn't seen Grant since his first meeting with the Langleys. He had managed to sell his house on A Street and moved to New York, finding an apartment in Brooklyn in the Williamsburg-Greenpoint area. Since then he had been getting ready for a winter show at the art gallery, working on several new canvasses.

He looked out the window at the suburban sprawl of Connecticut towns, occasionally glimpsing the inlets of the Long Island Sound with the last sailboats bravely weathering the brisk late October air. He thought about the task ahead and dreaded the encounter with the Langleys. He had agreed to release Grant to the Langleys, but now that the court order had come through, he intended to establish a routine and make sure never to miss a visit with Grant.

When he got to New Haven, he took a taxi to Cold Spring Street where the Langleys had a large, three-story colonial house across from East Rock Park. The elm trees framing the street in an arched canopy were just beginning to lose their leaves. As he drove up, he saw a car leave the driveway and recognized Professor Langley driving off alone.

Feeling somewhat relieved he got out and looked around. Everything about the residence was perfectly neat, from the trim landscaping to the well-maintained exterior. The Langleys were undoubtedly comfortably set, but David wondered where he had gotten the idea that they were wealthy. Perhaps it was the expensive lawyer they had hired.

He paid off the taxi driver, walked up the red brick sidewalk, climbed the steps to the spacious front porch, and rang the doorbell. He worried for a moment that no one would answer, but after another ring Mrs. Langley opened the door. She greeted him with a polite half-smile, but her tightened lips betrayed how she really felt about him.

"Come in," she said. "We've never been properly introduced. I'm Laura Langley."

"David Madison." He bowed his head slightly.

The interior looked even neater than the outside. The aroma of a bacon and eggs breakfast still lingered. The dark wooden staircase leading to the second floor and the furnishings looked like a movie set from a 1950s family sitcom. He could imagine himself picking up Darlene for a high school date and her coming down the stairs all prim and proper. He understood better why her father disliked him—the man he believed responsible for his daughter's pregnancy and death—and why he had absented himself for the duration of the visit.

Mrs. Langley escorted David into the living room and to the crib where Grant lay quietly sleeping next to a wall covered with family photos. David looked down helplessly on the tiny baby, wishing that Darlene was standing by his side. "Hello, Grant," he said softly.

He felt awkward seeing the smiling photographs of Darlene on the mantle of the fireplace, knowing how much the Langleys resented his intrusion. He would have liked some indication of acceptance from Mrs. Langley, but she was like a pillar of ice. He wondered if, like her husband, she blamed him for the cancer that destroyed their happiness. Had she, too, convinced herself that, had Darlene been with them, they would have discovered her illness earlier, and she would still be alive. But David was trapped in the lie and couldn't reveal that someone else had made her pregnant and abandoned her, and that he had nothing to do with the choice Darlene had made.

What he wanted to tell Mrs. Langley was how much he wished that one of the photographs on the mantle would be of her daughter in a wedding gown and him as the groom next to her, and another with them holding their son. But all he could muster was, "I don't want to disturb Grant while he's sleeping."

Mrs. Langley studied his face as though she were trying to put together a puzzle. Perhaps his composure, vulnerability and good looks told her why her daughter was attracted to him, but nothing broke her icy demeanor.

She motioned toward the sofa and coffee table where a teapot sat on a silver serving tray. "Would you like some tea?"

"Please."

David took in the surroundings, the two chintz couches set perpendicular to the fireplace; Langley's chair and ottoman with a pipe in the ashtray on the lamp table; an arrangement of fresh white lilies on the coffee table that lent a fragrance to the room. It all conveyed a feeling of hominess that he had never experienced.

Mrs. Langley poured the tea and passed the china cup on its china saucer to David. "Tell me how you and Darlene met."

He took a sip, the hot liquid almost burning his lips, and began his contrived story of half-truths—about having gone back to Yale after serving in the Marines, meeting Darlene and her following him to Washington.

Then he decided to be honest and looked directly at Mrs. Langley. "I was distraught after the war. She was an angel that lifted me from the depths of despair and brought me back to the living." He blinked away the mist that formed in his eyes. "I never knew that she had cancer."

"She never told us."

"It happened so fast. I don't think she knew until Grant came."

There was a cry from the crib, and Mrs. Langley went over to it. She lifted the baby up and gently rocked him in her arms. He quieted quickly, reassured.

"Would you like to hold him?" She leaned toward David and transferred the baby into his arms before he could refuse.

Clasping him awkwardly at first, he soon relaxed and the baby smiled at him. His eyes were brown, like Darlene's.

David beamed proudly at Mrs. Langley. "What a beautiful grandchild you have."

She didn't return the smile. She stood silently watching David holding Grant, as if trying to convince herself that they belonged together.

After a long pause, she asked, "How is your work coming along? Have you sold any paintings yet?"

Grant's tiny fingers wrapped around David's thumb. He thought how impossible it seemed that the miniature hand would someday become as large as his own.

Distracted, he said, "I have a gallery showing after the first of the year."

When she didn't respond, he wondered if she cared at all. He almost expected her to say "Good Luck."

He nodded toward a box he had put on the sofa next to him. "I've brought something for Grant. Won't you open it?"

She glanced at the tag that read "To Grant Madison" without comment and removed the blue wrapping paper. "How charming. A little carousel with horses. I'm sure he'll love it."

She held it out toward David with the hint of a smile and took Grant from his arms. "Won't you hang it over the crib for him?"

Perhaps a thaw was possible after all, David thought.

❧

The next several visits went the same way. Professor Langley was always absent, and Mrs. Langley, well-mannered, had tea prepared.

She always asked about how things were going, and he always gave her the same answer, "I work on my paintings for the gallery showing and write legal briefs and appeals on the side to earn a living."

Her condescending smile suggested that it gave her a certain satisfaction that he was still living hand to mouth and confirmed her low opinion of him: he would not have been a suitable husband for her daughter and continued to be a less than an adequate father.

Late December was especially difficult. When David arrived, he noticed the redness around Laura Langley's eyes and knew she had been crying. It was her first Christmas without Darlene, and there was nothing for her to celebrate.

From the looks of it, the house was decorated as it always must have been before. A wreath hung on the front door. Inside, there were Christmas cards displayed on the mantle above the fireplace, and the tree next to it was covered with garlands and multi-colored lights. Some of the ornaments were handmade by a young child.

Laura saw David looking at them and said, "Darlene made one each year."

David nodded in understanding and handed her a small gift-wrapped box.

"Grant will love unwrapping it," she said as she placed it under the tree.

"No," he said, "it's for you."

She stiffened for a brief moment, not knowing how to reply, and finally managed, "How thoughtful of you."

⌁

The next time he came, the decorations were gone, and there was no mention of the gift, and with each successive visit they had less to say to each other. David usually strolled around the living room with Grant in his arms while Mrs. Langley knitted quietly or sipped her tea. He would stop frequently in front of the photographs and study Darlene's face, marveling how young, happy, and contented she looked. But there was something missing.

And that's when he conceived the idea how he would paint her. A portrait of her holding the baby she never knew.

CHAPTER 10

On a Saturday evening in February the opening at Frank Gannovino's art gallery in Chelsea was in full swing. Waiters moved effortlessly among the lively crowd, their trays filled with flutes of champagne and an assortment of canapés. People were gathered in clusters around a number of the paintings, engaged in animated conversations. There were even a few critics among them, some from important papers. It was a more than respectable showing.

David stood in the middle of the room next to a young couple at an easel displaying one of his paintings. It was a small canvas depicting a young boy dressed in shabby clothes holding onto a string with a red balloon floating above him. A photographer snapped a series of pictures—David alone at the easel, with his new patrons, shaking hands with the husband, then with the wife—while the group of people watching applauded. It was his first sale and he felt a moment of pride as he took the painting to a table, wrote an inscription on the back, "To Morey and Naomi Sapperstein, my Balloon Friends," and signed it.

Frank Gannovino gave him a thumbs-up and took over. He gestured to an aide to take the painting to be wrapped, and beamed at the new owners.

"Congratulations," he said. "You have made an excellent choice and investment. David is an artist you will hear more of."

David smiled to himself. Frank talked the way he dressed, with understated flamboyance. He always wore an expensive suit with an ever-present pocket square, never stuffed, but folded into different shapes, depending on his mood. This evening it was a reverse puff, orange with red edges—he was feeling especially effusive.

David surveyed the crowd. There was the novelist Fred Warner with a group of four women hanging on his every word. Somehow "handsome" didn't fit the stereotype of a successful writer, but for him it was an extra bonus. Everyone knew his reputation as a womanizer including, no doubt, the quartet of young women gushing over him. David gave a slight laugh as one of them excused herself and walked over to where a state senator was holding court in a small circle of admirers who looked sufficiently awed to be worth his time. David figured he was a member of the new political aristocracy who paraded their titles the way the British used "Lord."

The woman listened for a moment, then moved on. The senator looked after her, all but devouring her with his eyes. David wondered where her search would take her next. She found Paul Lehman, the hedge fund guru entertaining a group of bankers with stories he had told a thousand times, but they laughed anyway like orchestrated sycophants. She asked him a question and his answer brought more laughter. David wondered what she said but decided he didn't care.

He searched the room for someone who wasn't just preening and noticed a woman standing by herself examining his paintings. She wore an exquisite black Chanel dress, pearls, and lightly tinted sunglasses that she raised and lowered as she examined his paintings. Her auburn hair was cut in a chic, trendy bob, and her lips were glossy pink.

She took a champagne glass from a strolling waiter as David walked up. When the waiter offered him the tray, he declined.

The woman cocked her head. "You don't like champagne?"

"Not until after this thing is over."

She looked at him quizzically. "You don't like gallery openings?"

"Not really. It's a bit nerve-wracking," he said, smiling indifferently. "I'm the artist."

To his surprise, she nodded in agreement.

She took a sip of champagne and looked at David over the glass. "I like your work. You see things that no one else sees, and your paintings reveal that. You have a talent, not just for capturing a scene, but conveying its essence."

"You're not by any chance the reviewer?" David said, grinning.

She chuckled. "No, but I mean it."

David wondered if she was just posturing like the others and decided to find out.

"Enough to buy one?" he asked.

She took his arm and drew him toward a large canvas. Her touch was light on his sleeve, and he let himself be led. She stopped before the portrait of a seated woman dressed in a soft, white gown, her hands resting together comfortably in her lap, and said, "Since you ask, the answer is 'yes.' I'd consider this one."

The contrast between the subject of the painting and the elegant, sophisticated woman next to him could not have been greater, yet they both had a distinctive presence.

"Why this one?" David asked, intrigued.

"Because it captures an emotion. Most artists can't do that. They can paint a beautiful scene, but it's just a picture...without a deeper feeling."

"So what does it make you feel?"

She stood still before the painting for a moment letting it affect her. "Contentment," she said, turning back to him.

"Contentment."

"Yes. Does that surprise you?"

"No. But it tells me something about you."

She refused to rise to the bait. "Tell me about it," she said and took a sip of her champagne.

"It's called *Lady in Waiting*, a play on words."

Her eyes widened and glistened. "And what is she waiting for?"

He smiled, amused. "It could be the Queen, a man, a gift—

whatever you want it to be."

"What were you thinking when you painted her?" she said, studying him intently.

He glanced at her in surprise. "No one has asked me that before." He looked at the crowd, seeing no one in particular. "I'd rather not say."

"Why not?" Taking another sip, she gazed at him over her glass again. "Are you trying to keep the identity of your model hidden?"

He shook his head. "I don't paint from models. I paint what I see in my mind."

"It's that vivid?"

David said softly, "I painted what she was like on the inside— her character, her faith, her love."

Angling her head, the woman evaluated him. "So, tell me who she is."

He grabbed a champagne glass from the tray of a waiter passing by, breaking the spell. Raising it, he smiled and toasted, "To the *Lady in Waiting.*"

"Oh, no, that's not fair," she exclaimed. "You have to tell me."

He took a long sip and ran his fingers through his hair. Should he tell her the truth or fabricate a fictitious story. Opting for something in between, he said, "She is the woman I'm waiting for."

Leaning in as if seeing him in a new light, the young woman asked, "How will you recognize her when she appears?"

David tossed down the remainder of his champagne and said, "She'll buy the painting."

CHAPTER 11

When David arrived in a taxi at the Langley residence the next morning, he was surprised to see their car in the driveway. Figuring he was early, he looked at his watch, but it was the usual time. As he walked past the black Mercedes to the porch, he thought, *He should have left by now.* When he knocked at the door, it was opened almost immediately by Mrs. Langley. She let him in but didn't look at him.

Mr. Langley was sitting in the living room. He didn't get up and motioned to David to sit down in the chair across from him. Grant's crib wasn't in the usual place.

"I want to talk to you." He spit out the words distastefully. "Please sit down."

As David settled in the chair, Mrs. Langley started to leave the room, but her husband stopped her. "Laura, I want you to hear this."

She walked over to the sofa and reluctantly sat at one end.

Mr. Langley stared at David in silence as if he wanted to skewer him.

Letting his annoyance show, David said, "Are you here for the first time to insult me or to convince me of something?"

Langley recoiled slightly and cleared his throat. "I thought it would be productive if we spoke directly, but you can talk to my lawyer, if you wish."

Your lawyer at least would be more civil, David thought and said, "I understand how you feel, but neither your manner nor your intentions are going to change my position."

David wanted to see Mrs. Langley's reaction, but her eyes were fixed on the fireplace. "I have money put away—invested for Grant's education," he said.

Langley snickered. "It will take a lot of money to put him through Yale." He drummed his fingers on the armrest of his chair. "I have a proposition. I could make it worth your while...financially."

David took the affront calmly. "You want me to sell my son?"

Langley's eyes narrowed. "How crude can you be? I want to give him an opportunity you can never provide. I want to spare Darlene's son the miserable life you would give him."

"And I want Grant to have a normal life with a loving father and loving grandparents."

"Normal?!" Langley shouted. "How can you think that? You never even married his mother."

"No, but I planned to."

Langley jumped up in a fit of anger. "Did you plan to get her pregnant, too?!" His face grew redder. "And then wait for the child to be born before you married her because maybe she would have died before that happened and the baby with her?"

David tried to remain calm, but his voice took on a dangerous edge. "I'm on his birth certificate, not you. How will you explain that to him?"

Langley stepped toward him. "You smarmy bastard! You used her as your toy." He almost loomed over David, shaking with rage. "You'll get him over my dead body!"

Mrs. Langley stood up and stepped between them. "Edward, please!"

David rose. "I think I'd better leave." Then he asked Mrs. Langley, "Would you mind calling me a cab? I'd appreciate it."

When she nodded and went to the kitchen, he faced Langley and said firmly, "But nothing has changed."

Then he left. Walking down the porch steps to wait for the taxi,

David realized that Langley was right. The real father was a smarmy bastard and had acted like one. But if he told them the truth now, he would no longer have any claim on Grant. He thought, *Oh, Darlene. I know what you want.*

As the cab pulled up and he got in, he felt a pang of regret that he hadn't seen Grant.

✆

When he reached Union Station he was early for his train. He bought a newspaper and sat down in the waiting area, scanning the headlines and leafing through the first section, still irritated by his encounter with Langley. Finally, he stood up, folded the paper and slammed it into a trash container. He walked through the tunnel and up the stairs to the platform. As he peered down the tracks, his cell phone rang.

He looked at the screen and answered. "Hello, Frank? How many paintings did we sell?"

Frank hesitated. "Two, David, besides the one last night at the opening."

"Only two? How can I make a living at this?"

"Actually, you're doing very well. To sell three paintings before any reviews have appeared is better than most new artists can hope for."

David ran his free hand through his hair. "Besides *The Balloon Boy*, which two paintings sold?"

"*Friends Forever* and *Lady in Waiting*."

David was bewildered, but it made sense. They were his best works, the two he least wanted to let go. The image of the young woman at the opening came into his mind and he asked carefully, "Who bought them?"

"An older man. He paid cash and took them to his waiting limousine."

"An older man bought *Lady in Waiting*? Not a woman?"

"Yes, a distinguished looking gentleman. He reminded me of a butler on a PBS Masterpiece mini-series—without the British accent."

David heard the clanging warning bells of the approaching train and said, "Look, Frank, I have to go. I'll see you at the gallery tomorrow."

The doors opened and he stepped inside the railcar. He walked down the aisle between mostly empty seats. All he could think about was Darlene and not wanting to lose Grant.

CHAPTER 12

Living in his tiny apartment in Williamsburg-Greenpoint and sharing a small studio with several painters, David continued to struggle as an artist. The reviews had not been great, and his paintings weren't exactly selling like hotcakes. With his freelance legal efforts, knocking out briefs and appeals, he managed to make ends meet. It was frustrating that the work he didn't care about proved more successful than his artistic endeavors—several law firms wanted to put him on staff. But whenever he thought seriously about saying yes to a regular income and health benefits, Frank Gannovino called to tell him another painting had sold and David, inspired, renewed his creative efforts.

Once in a while, when he thought of Darlene, his mind would turn to the *Lady in Waiting*. He'd wonder who had bought it, on whose wall it was hanging, or if it was collecting dust in some attic. But as time passed, he stopped musing and dismissed any such thoughts immediately.

The one constant in his life he felt good about was Grant. No matter how discouraged or exhausted, David made the weekly trek to New Haven, even if it meant feeding his son a bottle, changing his diapers, or watching him crawl across the rug in the Langley's living room. His efforts were rewarded as Grant started to walk and learn to speak, although David was disappointed that he missed his initial steps and the first word coming out of his mouth. But it didn't really matter. Grant was precocious. With each Sunday visit he seemed to have acquired a new word for another object. Seeing his eyes light up as he recognized his "da-da" always made David's heart melt.

Along the way, Laura Langley's attitude grew more favorable toward David. Once in a while, she smiled in his presence.

As the summer turned to fall, David became increasingly frustrated with his life. He seemed at a standstill both financially and in his career as an artist. He couldn't imagine wasting another year if there wasn't any more progress.

Alone on Christmas Eve, he wrapped his painting of Darlene holding her baby and had it sent to Laura Langley.

When New Year's Eve came he thought about Katherine and the celebrations they had spent together. He considered calling her, but didn't, finishing another legal brief instead.

During an early February visit to Grant, David happened to see a front-page picture in the local newspaper showing the wedding of Bradley Coyle and an heiress from Greenwich, Connecticut. He realized it meant Katherine was single again and wondered how she was doing. He remembered her comment at their dinner in New York about Coyle's ambition and his relationship with a wealthy woman that could propel him further into the political limelight, but he didn't give it much thought.

Thus, a week later when he received a call from Senator Cunningham's chief of staff with a request to come to Washington for a meeting, it caught him completely by surprise. He had no idea how much his life was about to change.

CHAPTER 13

David left Union Station and walked through Senate Park toward the Beaux-Arts facade of the Russell Senate Office Building. The snow crunched under his feet and the oak trees looked like their branches might break under the heavy burden of an early March snowstorm. As he climbed the shoveled steps and headed into the impressive rotunda in the foyer of the building, he had a hunch why Senator James Cunningham wanted to see him. He had always found the senator a bit stiff and formal, a true New England blue blood who had only accepted him as Katherine's choice because he loved his daughter more than the Constitution. David thought the quick switch to Bradley Coyle more to the senator's liking. Until, that is, the day of Bradley's betrayal.

Inside, the columns and the high dome they supported were impressive, and David understood why the senator had used his seniority to obtain an office in the oldest and most prestigious Senate office building. He imagined he'd find him in a suite overlooking the park.

He wasn't disappointed. The large window in the cherry wood-paneled office framed the Capitol Building like a picture postcard. Senator Cunningham got up from his ebony desk and walked around it to enfold David's hand in both of his. "So good to see you again, David. Thank you for coming." Then he reached for the humidor on his desk, withdrew two cigars, and held one out to his visitor.

David shook his head. "No thank you."

The senator put David's cigar back. "Not smoking anymore?"

"Only occasionally."

The senator nodded toward an old leather chair as he snipped off the tip of his cigar with his engraved, gold cutter and returned it to his pocket. "Make yourself comfortable."

As David sat down he looked at his surroundings. Numerous framed photographs hung on the walls of the senator shaking hands with various presidents and foreign dignitaries. David studied the one with Pope Francis and another with the Dalai Lama as the senator puffed his cigar to life. Then he leaned back and looked at the man he once thought would be his father-in-law. He carried more weight now around the middle, and his hair had turned silver gray. The lines in his face were more deeply etched.

The senator took his seat behind the desk and fixed his gaze on him. "I'll come right to the point. I want you to run for Bradley Coyle's old congressional seat."

David smelled the sweet aroma of the cigar and almost wished he had accepted. "You've spoken with Katherine," he said. "Did she put you up to this?"

Cunningham contemplated his cigar. "Yes and no."

"What is that supposed to mean?"

The senator pointed the cigar at David. "You know I don't mince words, David."

"You know I don't either."

"She suggested you, yes; but I've always appreciated your talents."

"Then what is it about? You and Bradley Coyle?"

Cunningham's jaw hardened. "Yes! I put him in the Senate and he switched parties and divorced Katherine. I want you to take his old congressional seat."

David looked away at the wall with the pictures. "Katherine and I aren't...we haven't seen each other in nearly a—"

The senator cut him off. "This isn't about you and Katherine. I made a mistake." He leaned toward David. "I want to make up for what happened between us. What's between you and Katherine is between you and Katherine. There are no preconditions."

David flared up. "Where were you, Senator, when I got back from Iraq? I could have run against Coyle when he left the House to run for the Senate."

The senator stabbed his cigar at him. "Where have you been since you got back?"

"That isn't really your business," David shot back.

Realizing that he was pushing too hard, Cunningham said more gently, "I want to pick up where we left off and get you elected to Congress."

"Where we left off isn't where we are now. I am a single father with a son. That complicates things, doesn't it?"

"Only a little.... Actually, it could be an advantage...a widowed man devoted to his son, a veteran, Ivy League graduate." He took a puff on his cigar. "As I recall you made mincemeat out of Bradley in your Yale debate days. And now you're a war hero with three purple hearts, who demonstrated plenty of valor."

David smiled ironically. "I see that you have it all figured out, as usual. Except that I won't do it that way."

"Then what do you suggest?"

David stood up, went to the window, and looked out toward the Capitol and the Mall. It was as though he was gazing into his past, watching himself in his fatigues walk toward the Vietnam Veterans Memorial and encountering Darlene lying on the bench. It was two years ago when he'd met her. He remembered her words when she first visited his apartment and picked up his diploma, "But think of the possibilities!" So much had changed since then.

A feeling of angst welled up inside him. He had always believed that civilization progressed like a long climb up a hill. There were occasional bumps in the road, but forward movement was inevitable. Now there were horrific setbacks. The Middle East where he had fought for democracy had turned into a hotbed of hatred and terrorism. Unless stopped, it would revert to the Middle Ages, but utilizing the destructive tools of the twenty-first century. Russia had resumed an aggressive imperial foreign policy, attempting to undermine Western democracy with sophisticated cyberwarfare.

He thought about Grant and all the others of his generation that would be living in a future determined by people who only cared about themselves—selfish, greedy power grabbers. And in that moment he made a decision.

He turned away from the window and faced the senator. "What do I suggest? Honesty and issues."

Cunningham stood up. "All right. I can work with that." He winked at David. "I'll get someone to handle the dirty business of politics."

"I intend to change that."

The senator stepped over to him and placed a fatherly hand on his shoulder. "Let's not be naive. That isn't going to happen. We'll be lucky to get back to civility at some point."

David looked directly at Cunningham. "The one thing I am not, Senator, is naive. If Bradley hadn't defected and filed for divorce with Kathy, I wouldn't be here."

Senator Cunningham dropped his arm and cleared his throat. "And that's your opportunity."

When he held out his hand to shake on the deal, David hesitated. "I want to know where Kathy fits in."

"I've told you. That's between the two of you. Shall I ask her to come in?"

David looked surprised. "She's here?"

"Of course. She works for me, as my communications director. I thought she told you."

"We haven't seen each other for two years."

"Then you'll have plenty to catch up on. I'll leave the two of you to discuss it alone." The senator crushed out his cigar in the ashtray, pressed a button, and Katherine entered. He looked at his watch and walked to the door. "I have a committee hearing in a few minutes. Shall we all have dinner?"

David answered without taking his eyes off of Katherine. "That would be fine."

"Then eight at the Hay-Adams." He closed the door behind him.

They stood facing each other uncomfortably, frozen like two mannequins. Finally, Katherine broke the silence. "Well, what do you think?"

"I think that your father is very generous."

"I think he's very smart. You'll make a wonderful congressman."

"If I vote the way he decides."

She walked over to him, smiling, and straightened his tie. "If you vote for what you believe."

David removed her hands. "That may not always be the same thing. Look what happened with Bradley."

Katherine's smile disappeared. "Bradley changed sides. What do you expect?"

David walked to the window. The snow was starting to fall again.

"I expect to vote my conscience."

"Your conscience or your Constitution?"

He turned back to her. "The Constitution is my conscience. Otherwise, our democracy is at the whim of vacuous, ambitious individuals.

"Like Bradley Coyle," Katherine said.

"Like Bradley Coyle."

"Then we all agree." She looked around the room and announced, "Let's celebrate."

She walked to the wood-paneled wall behind the desk and slid a section back revealing a well-stocked bar.

David sat down at the end of the sofa, stretched his arm along the backrest, and watched her dropping ice cubes into two glasses and pouring Scotch over them. She looked remarkably beautiful, unchanged physically from when he had left her in New York, but more poised. Her movements were more fluid, too, and there was a cool confidence in her bearing he'd never seen before. *We have both been through a sea change*, he thought.

Bringing the drinks to the sofa, Katherine said, "What more is there to think about?"

"Us," he said, taking the offered glass.

She sat down at the other end of the couch, facing him, and raised her glass. "To us, then."

He ignored the toast. "You know what I mean. Was this the senator's idea or yours?"

She smiled. "Does it matter?" She leaned back with her arm reaching along the back of the sofa, her fingers almost touching his, and crossed her legs. "Is that something that we need to even discuss now? I'm committed to only one thing at the moment— your election. I've helped Dad with his most recent one, and I can help you with yours. All you need to do is ask."

"Then I'm asking, Kathy. I want you to run the campaign. But I'm also asking for only that, nothing more."

She slid her hand over his and squeezed. "So am I."

Somehow it felt like a trap closing and he withdrew his hand. It was a beautiful trap, though, he had to admit. And it did offer a solution to his problems. If he won the election, Grant would be his for good, and everything that had gone wrong until now would be made right, including his promise to Darlene. If he won, he could also do something for the soldiers who had been abandoned by their own country. Even those back from Iraq and Afghanistan were still dying, dying at their own hands. He could become their champion, their voice.

David raised his glass, touched it to Katherine's, and said. "We have work to do. I have to find a place to establish residency in my Connecticut district."

She smiled at him coyly as she took a sip. "I've already taken care of that."

CHAPTER 14

David walked into Frank Gannovino's Gallery. His friend, looking dapper as always even with his shirt sleeves rolled up, was installing a new collection of paintings. Two canvases already hung on the wall and Frank was supervising a crew to mount a third. The paintings were a riot of clashing colors—aggressive cityscapes with nothing revelatory about their subjects. On the wall opposite, David's delicate, understated, realistic paintings looked out of place among them.

Frank pointed aggressively at a workman on a ladder. "I've marked the place. Just hang it there."

When he saw David he smiled and called out, "How soon are you going to have more paintings for me?"

David joined him and watched the workmen struggling with the large polychromatic canvas. "Not any time soon."

Frank looked surprised. "What do you mean? I'm not taking yours down. I'm just filling the empty spaces."

David gave him a grateful look. "You're a good friend, Frank, but let's face it, my paintings aren't exactly in big demand."

His friend smiled at him. "I don't mind. I'm a patient guy."

"I'm not. I'm a realist. I don't think I'll ever make it as a successful artist."

Frank took him by the arm and led him away from the others, whispering intently, "That doesn't happen overnight. You can't base your career on one showing. You're an artist with great potential. We'll keep selling them one at a time."

David rubbed his forehead. "I don't have the luxury of time. I've got a son to take care of, and work as a freelance paralegal doesn't pay the bills."

Crossing his arms, Frank asked, "So what are you going to do then?"

"I'm moving to Connecticut and running for Bradley Coyle's old congressional seat. Senator Cunningham is pulling together a campaign and Katherine's going to run it." David smiled at Frank's astonished look. "I know, it's incomprehensible that I'd be running for public office, but Senator Cunningham is backing me, and I'll be near Grant."

Frank's eyes widened. "You're going to marry Katherine!"

Startled, David shook his head. "It's not what you think."

"Then what is it?" Frank said. He walked over to a painting of David's, entitled *Lost*. It showed a clipper ship on the high seas at sunset with a sailor thrashing in its wake, an island in the distance shrouded in dark, turbulent clouds. He pointed at the sailor. "Look at this. Does the captain realize that he's gone overboard? Will he be rescued, or does the ship go on without him? Does he make it to the island? This is about life. There's an emotion here that conveys more than the reproduction of a scene. You don't just see the scene, you feel it—it draws you in. You want to throw that all away?"

"I painted that before I met Darlene," David said. "It doesn't belong in someone's home. It's too depressing." He ran his hand through his hair. "Look, Frank, I need the money."

"Since when did you place money above everything else?" Frank scoffed.

Looking down at the old polished wooden floor, David said, softly, "Since I have a son."

If he thought that revelation would garner him any sympathy, he was mistaken.

Hands on hips, Frank said, "Do you know how many children Franz Hals had? Ten!"

David bristled, "Damn it, I want to do this. I can make a difference!"

"Make a difference or sell out?"

Their heated discussion attracted the attention of the workmen, and David lowered his voice, "What difference would my paintings make a hundred years from now?"

"I'll tell you. They'll hang in someone's home or in a museum, and for a moment, a little joy will enter the lives of the people looking at them. They'll connect with their emotions."

When David remained silent, he added, "The point is to fully express your talent, and then you'll create something to live on after you're gone."

"So I should bring up my son in poverty in order to be admired posthumously?"

Frank slapped his forehead in exasperation. "Marone!" He walked away raising his arms in the air, then dropping them to his sides as he returned to David, confronting him, his eyes blazing. "Okay, how much do you want for the whole lot...lock, stock and barrel? How much?"

David held up his hands. "Look, Frank, I can paint in my spare time. Do it as a hobby. Like other politicians who have written books."

"So who are you now, John F. Kennedy? Winston Churchill? You'll be a freshman congressman without any seniority. It would take years to make any difference, and by then you'd be one of them."

David couldn't help but burst out laughing. "Are you comparing my paintings to Churchill's?"

Frank picked up on the absurdity and joined in for a moment.

Then he said, "Don't laugh. Maybe your campaign will make your paintings more popular and more valuable." He cocked his eye at David. "That is, if you win!"

"Oh, I will win. I promise you that."

Seeing David's determination, Frank went back to *Lost*. He lifted the painting off the wall, carried it to the front of the gallery, and placed it on an empty easel near the window. "I'll make you a deal. For every painting of yours I sell, you'll paint me another."

David laughed. "Only if you double the price."

"That's exactly what I intend to do, Congressman."

CHAPTER 15

As the taxi pulled up in front of the Langley's house, David wondered if the black Mercedes would be there, but Edward Langley was nothing if not consistent. On all the weekends David had visited after their last altercation more than a year and a half ago, he had conspicuously absented himself. His wife, on the other hand, had gradually dropped her icy demeanor as she witnessed David's unwavering commitment and love for Grant.

She had even tried to apologize once for her husband's behavior. Nervously wringing a handkerchief in her hands, she had explained, "Edward never had a very good relationship with Darlene. I think he's been trying to appease his own conscience. He's always been vindictive. It was an insult to have offered you money. I think when he sees you, you remind him of Darlene and the past. When he sees Grant, he thinks of the future."

David paid the driver, slammed the door to the cab, and maneuvered his way around a snowbank. Noting that Langley's car was not in the driveway, he slipped on a patch of ice and fell down hard. As he got up he felt a pain in his wrist. He flexed it back and forth thinking, *I should sue the bastard.* Brushing the snow from his black wool coat, he took the steps to the front porch gingerly and rang the doorbell.

Laura Langley opened the front door with a look of concern. "Are you all right?"

"I'm fine," David said, and stepped inside. "Thank you for seeing me on such short notice, but it is necessary."

She gave him a weary smile. "I'm not sure Edward would appreciate this. He's in New York delivering a paper at a Society for the Study of Evolution conference." She glanced toward the stairs. "Grant is sleeping. We'll go up in a minute."

David removed his overcoat and draped it over the banister of the stairway to the second floor. When Laura led him into the living room, they took their usual seats on opposite ends of the couch. As he contemplated the comfortable surroundings, he once again felt a pang of regret—he wished he'd had such a cozy hearth when he grew up.

Pouring tea, Laura said, "You mentioned on the phone that there was something you wanted to tell me?"

David rubbed his sore wrist. "I've found a new position, Laura. I'll be busy for the next several months and have to cut back on my visits here."

To his surprise, she seemed disappointed. Fussing with her hands, she said, "I've grown accustomed to our visits. I was hoping they would continue."

He smiled. "Nothing would please me more."

There was sadness in her voice as she said, "Once I tell Edward that you have a good job, he'll realize that he can't keep Grant. You know that he's been counting on your failure."

David nodded. "Actually, I don't have the job yet."

"I don't understand."

"I wanted to tell you before it is announced officially. I'm going to run for Congress—for representative of your district. I've known Senator Cunningham for a long time. He's asked me to run. With him on my side I have a good chance of winning."

Laura brought both hands to her cheeks. "This changes everything."

"I was hoping you'd say that." They heard crying from upstairs.

"Ah, Grant's awake," Laura said. "But before we go see him, can I ask you for a favor?"

"Of course."

She smiled at him for the first time. "Can I be the first signature on your petition to get on the ballot?"

David grinned happily. "It would be an honor."

~

David looked up at the gold and white hexagonal pattern of the ceiling of New Haven's Union Station. The old turn-of-the-century lamps failed to light the waiting area adequately, but that didn't diminish his pleasure. Even though the meeting had gone well, something nagged at him. He wished he could have spent more time with Grant. But that wasn't it.

He grabbed a coffee and newspaper, then strolled through the tunnel and bounded up the steps to the platform for the Metro North train to Grand Central Terminal in New York City. He folded the paper and tucked it into the outside pocket of his coat and looked around. Suddenly, he realized what bothered him: Laura Langley had that same tired, worn look as the older woman commuter waiting near him. Taking care of Grant must be exhausting at this time in her life. She needed help. He needed to find an au pair for her.

He immediately thought of Nancy. Perhaps she would know of someone. He had attended her wedding last summer when she got married to Jack Sullivan, a doctor recently graduated from Georgetown Medical School, who, coincidentally, was about to start his residency at Yale New Haven Hospital in neurology. Nancy had no difficulty getting a job as a nurse as well. Considering her history with Grant and the secret she and David shared, there would be no one happier and more motivated to find the right person to help out. Laura would like Nancy, too, a selfless, capable woman who loved Grant as much as he did.

How could he ever repay her for what she had done for him and Grant? He knew that their love was all she wanted in return and decided they would call her Aunt Nancy.

He smiled at the thought as his train pulled into the station and a young woman nearby smiled back. When he didn't reciprocate further, she stepped into the railway car. He boarded the next car. There were several empty seats, and he took one by the window. The view of the soot-covered embankment walls as the train left the station wasn't appealing, so David took the newspaper from his pocket. As he opened it, he thought about the challenges he'd have to face when his bid for the House seat became public knowledge.

CHAPTER 16

A black stretch limousine with dark tinted windows was waiting for Stephanie Jordan as she walked out of the terminal at New York's La Guardia airport. The driver opened the door for her. He took her suitcase and placed it in the open trunk.

Stephanie slid into the back seat next to Bradley Coyle who barely waited for her to settle in before he kissed her aggressively.

She pulled back. "Wait until we have privacy!"

He leaned toward the front seat and said to the driver, "Plaza Hotel." Then he pressed a button, and the partition slid into place. "We have privacy," he said, reaching for her again.

"Brad...not here." She pushed his hand away.

"How about here?" He touched her breast and inched his fingers up her blouse.

Stephanie pulled his head toward her and gave him a quick kiss. "We have all weekend."

As the car moved forward, Coyle took her hand. "I'm sorry we couldn't sit together on the flight, but you know, it's better to play it safe," he said, chuckling. "The poor guy in the seat next to you trying to chat you up—if he only knew."

Stephanie squeezed his hand. "That's how we hooked up, Brad, remember?"

He glanced at her as they pulled into traffic on the Grand Central Parkway. She was a young reporter at a small town TV station when he found her, and look at her now—a nightly anchor on MBS in

Washington, elegant, sophisticated, not a blonde hair out of place. Well, not for long.

He grinned. "How are things at the Mostly Bull Shit network?"

Stephanie bristled. "That's not funny, Brad."

"I'm teasing," he said. Landing her a job at MBS, had been a stroke of genius. Not only did he plant a mole inside the network to do his bidding, he created a striking media figure who owed him big time and knew it.

She squeezed his hand again. "It's so good to get out of Washington for a weekend. What do you want to do?"

"Anything you'd like."

"How about a Broadway play?"

"Too risky. But we'll be lost in the crowd in a museum. Let's go to the Museum of Modern Art. Or the Guggenheim."

"Or both," she said. "It's going to be a perfect weekend."

When they got to the Plaza Hotel, Bradley dropped her at the Central Park entrance while he got out on the Fifth Avenue side. He registered and met her at the elevator. As they rode up to the sixteenth floor, Stephanie pushed him against the paneled wall and kissed him until the door opened. They hurried down the hallway to a pair of double doors. Bradley inserted the key card and they opened the doors into a lavishly furnished suite. The warm afternoon light streamed in through the tall windows. As Stephanie took in the view of Central Park, Bradley put his arms around her from behind, his hands cupping her breasts, his face against hers. She leaned back into him.

He pointed to a horse-drawn carriage ambling along Fifth Avenue below. "Let's have dinner at a hideaway restaurant tonight where the food is superb," he purred softly in her ear. "Then we'll ride in one of those carriages together until morning."

Stephanie turned, put her arms around his neck, and kissed him forcefully as he stroked her back and drew her more tightly against him.

There was a tap on the door and they pulled apart. Bradley reluctantly released her and let the bellhop in.

"Just put a suitcase in each of the dressing rooms," he said.

They both waited self-consciously as the porter followed his instructions. When he was finished, Bradley slipped a folded ten-dollar bill into his hand and ushered him out the door, locking it after him.

He went to Stephanie's dressing room and watched her unpacking and hanging up her clothes. He unbuttoned the back of her blouse and said, "You know where to find me."

She put a finger to his lips as the blouse slipped off her shoulders. "You really know how to impress a girl."

He took her finger into his hand and kissed it. "Don't be long."

In the adjoining bedroom, he undressed and put on a black silk robe. Then he lay down on the king-sized bed, turned on the television, and idly flipped channels.

Suddenly, he froze as he saw David Madison's face on the TV screen being interviewed.

"What the hell?" he burst out. "David Madison is running for my old congressional seat."

Stephanie, wrapped in a thin, white robe, came into the room. When she glanced at the television, something caught her attention and she sat at the foot of the bed to watch the rest of the interview. "This guy has a way about him—direct and to the point. Good looking, too," she commented. "He could be interesting in an otherwise uninteresting race. What do you know about him?"

"I knew him at Yale. He fought in Iraq and came back scarred. Forget about him." Bradley got up and went into the living room to the bar while Stephanie remained focused on the TV.

"Bradley, this guy is no lightweight," she called after him. "He's getting a lot of applause. You should watch this."

"I've seen all I want of him. He'll be a flash in the pan."

"He's not coming across that way."

"So just how is he coming across?" Bradley asked sarcastically, pouring two glasses of bourbon.

"Not like a politician. Like a man on a mission."

He settled into a chair. "You can tell all that from watching for just a few minutes, and don't give me that woman's intuition nonsense."

"It's my professional opinion. I think you should pay attention to this guy."

"The only one I want to pay attention to right now is you. Turn the damn thing off and come over here. We're here to get away from Washington not to watch it on TV."

Stephanie shrugged and clicked off the television. Moving to the back of his chair, she began massaging his shoulders. Bradley closed his eyes and she rubbed his temples. Gradually he relaxed and sighed. "That feels so good. I wish you could do that every night."

"Why not?" she said. Her hands moved up and rubbed his hair. "You could have me for good, you know."

He took her hand and pulled her around onto his lap. "Soon," he said, running his lips along her neck. "Soon."

CHAPTER 17

The August primary proved Stephanie right. David easily beat his opponents. Senator Cunningham's influence and Katherine's savvy handling of the campaign made all the difference.

But David turned out to be more than a dark horse candidate. Like Coyle, most of the local politicos, media heads and reporters underestimated him at first, until his cool confidence in interviews and charismatic passion in his speeches made them take notice. He worked without a moment's rest until the day of the primary, campaigning in areas of the district the other candidates ignored and achieved a surprisingly strong voter turnout among minorities. By then, his success was assured, but no one expected it to be such a resounding rout. Even Bradley Coyle finally took notice.

Two weeks after the primary victory, David walked along the corridor of the top floor of the Capitol Building where the doors were only marked with numbers. It was one of the better-kept secrets that ranking senators had personal refuges there away from the offices where they could escape from the public. David was more than curious. The summons from Senator Cunningham had not come as a surprise, but the meeting place did. When he found 309 he tapped lightly.

Katherine opened the door. "Come in." Noticing his puzzled expression, she explained, "This is Dad's 'hideaway.'"

Senator Cunningham was on the telephone pacing in front of the windows with the Washington Monument visible behind him in the distance. The room was paneled like his office, intimate and imposing, but also more personal and private. There were photos on the walls depicting his love for sailing, many featuring his 75-foot yacht, all sails flying from the two masts. The only dignitary in any of them was Buddy Melges, the builder of one-design racing monohulls, winning America's Cup skipper and Olympic sailing Gold Medalist standing next to a much younger Senator Cunningham at the cockpit wheel. Several trophies from regattas occupied a shelf and miniature boat models were scattered on a side table. In the middle of an antique round table stood a large Baccarat vase with a bouquet of long-stem white roses whose fragrant aroma wasn't quite able to extinguish the lingering cigar smell.

Katherine went to an ornate bar next to a glass door cabinet filled with books and poured Dewars into two crystal glasses. Handing David one, she smiled and said, "Most people don't know about the hideaways. Every senator has one in the Capitol building. You start in the basement and work your way up by seniority."

She took his hand and led him into a side alcove and showed him a Murphy bed concealed in the wall and an adjoining bathroom and shower. Then they returned to the main room to an upholstered sofa and chairs arranged as a conversation area. "They're not all as big or posh as this, of course," she said.

Senator Cunningham hung up the phone and looked at them matter-of-factly. "You've been accused of having an affair together while you were still married to Bradley." He focused directly at Katherine. "They're saying you resumed your relationship behind Bradley's back, and that's why he divorced you."

David's face flushed an angry red. "That's a bloody lie!"

The senator continued calmly. "Of course, it is—dirty tricks. It's to be expected. This is no surprise."

"But it irritates the hell out of me." David smacked his glass down on the bar.

Katherine sat down on the sofa and crossed her legs. "This is just a smear tactic cooked up by Bradley and his cohorts to derail your campaign."

David scowled. "I'd think that you'd be more offended."

"In two weeks it will be forgotten."

"That's not how I operate in this campaign, Kathy. I don't let fires burn out, I extinguish them."

The senator went to the bar for a refill. "That's not going to work. They plant a lie and keep repeating it until people believe it. And the press perpetuates it, effectively acting as their propaganda machine." He topped off his Scotch and raised the bottle toward David and his daughter.

They shook their heads.

Katherine pulled her legs up under her. "I'll just say it isn't true."

David scoffed. "Everyone expects you to say that. They expect that you'd lie to cover it up."

"It's his word against ours."

The senator took a sip from his drink and settled in one of the easy chairs. "David's right. Denials aren't enough. If you deny it, it just keeps it longer in the news cycle. Remember what Churchill once said: 'A lie gets halfway around the world before the truth has a chance to get its pants on.'"

"It doesn't matter. We're in a safe district."

David glared at Katherine. "It does matter. This isn't just about an election. It's about my character...and yours."

He walked over to the window and looked out beyond the Washington Monument toward the Lincoln Memorial. *Even Honest Abe had a lot of people who called him names*, he thought. Then he said, "I'll handle this with Coyle."

The senator frowned. "If Bradley walks his story back it would appear that he was persuaded, or worse yet, blackmailed. He'll never do that."

David continued to stare at the Memorial. "Yes, he will."

"I don't see how. The press runs on rumors, not facts. And he's their current golden boy."

David turned from the window toward them. "Just wait and see."

"How can you be so sure?" Katherine asked.

"Just a hunch. But give me a week, and I will be."

CHAPTER 18

Senator Bradley Coyle walked from his car toward the exit sign above the stairwell door in the underground parking garage in Roslyn. He would have liked a cigarette, although he had quit several years ago. Instead he paced, revolted by the filth and litter everywhere and the smell of oil and gasoline that pervaded the place. He tightened his tie and brushed his Brioni suit as though the dirt had settled on it. He was accustomed to the painted floors and pristine cleanliness of the Senate garage and the fleet of upscale Beemers, Audis, Mercedes, Cadillacs and Lexuses. Except for his own BMW there wasn't a single luxury car parked here.

He wondered why David had chosen this spot in Virginia, just across the Potomac River. When he received the note that his erstwhile friend wanted to discuss something important in private, he had been wary. But David had been insistent, and Coyle knew enough about politics not to leave loose ends dangling in the wind. Still, he was apprehensive.

When he saw David's yellow Jeep pull into the garage, he took a deep breath and composed his face into a welcoming smile.

David shut off the engine, got out of the car, and watched Bradley approach. It had been at least twelve years since he had last seen him. His former friend had always been glib and arrogant, but now he had graduated to a $5,000 suit and all the trappings of success, which covered the ruthlessness and self-centeredness at his core. What had Katherine ever seen in him?

Coyle greeted him with a practiced politician's charm. "I'm

surprised you wanted to see me...it's been a while." He dialed down his dazzling smile. "I think it's time to bury the hatchet, don't you?"

"It depends on where you want to bury it."

"What do you mean?"

"The last time you buried it in my back."

Bradley grinned sarcastically. "Get over it, David. You've got Katherine now."

"Not when you were married to her."

"I never started that rumor."

"I see." The easy smile on David's face turned dangerous. "Then I'll start a new one for you."

Bradley tensed. "I don't like playing games."

"You call this games? You want to play games to secure elections? Well, here's the game that will secure the presidency you want so dearly—for someone else. You've been having an affair behind your wife's back with a reporter who broke the story about Katherine and me on prime-time television for you. How would you like to deny that 'rumor'?"

Bradley straightened. "So, it's war you want."

"No, not war, just a level playing field. That's all I'll ever ask of you."

Bradley rubbed the Rolex on his left hand. "Okay...I'm a gentleman, and I'll give you the benefit of the doubt."

David's laughter echoed from the bare concrete walls. "Let's get the truth out on the table. I can easily prove your guilt and you can suffer the embarrassment and consequences, or you prove my innocence. I'm sure your current wife would love to hear the sordid details."

"What do you want?"

"Quash the rumor!"

David stared into Coyle's eyes until he looked away. Then David turned his back on him, got into his Jeep, and drove off without giving him another glance.

Coyle listened to the squeal of the tires as he walked back to his own car. He got in and sat behind the wheel with his lips tight and his brows furrowed. Straightening, he turned on the engine, reached for his cell phone and keyed in a number. When it was picked up at the other end, he said softly, "Honey, someone knows about us. So listen. I want you to set up a live interview with me to clear the air on Madison and Katherine. When I deny that I divorced her for an affair, and it appears that I'm protecting my former wife and my old friend, I'll look like a hero...and you'll get a few more points in ratings."

His smile turned predatory as he pulled out of the garage and gunned the engine. David may have won this round, but the fight was far from over.

Once Coyle exonerated David on national television, his numbers soared and his election was almost a foregone conclusion. Not only was he an articulate, good-looking candidate, voters liked his passion and straight talk. It didn't hurt that he was a decorated Iraq war veteran. He ended up beating his opponent by double-digits.

As David concluded his acceptance speech from the stage in the ballroom at the Omni Hotel in New Haven, he looked over the sea of cheering faces. Some he recognized, many he didn't, but they all had worked diligently and selflessly to get him elected because they believed in him. He wondered if the veteran who tipped him off anonymously about Bradley's tryst in New York was among them.

As he finished with his arms raised high, the cheering increased. The music, confetti, balloons and noise gave him a surreal and euphoric feeling. He had come a long way from his penitential walks in uniform down the Mall to the Vietnam Veterans Memorial. Darlene would be pleased.

CHAPTER 19

The next morning while David was having breakfast in his house near East Rock Park, an emergency call came from Laura Langley. In less than twenty minutes, he was rushing down the corridor of the Yale New Haven Hospital to Professor Langley's room. The antiseptic smell and whiff of ammonia brought back the bitter memories of Darlene's death and he felt slightly nauseous. He hesitated to go in, not knowing what to expect.

When he entered, he saw Edward Langley lying in the bed, hooked up to various tubes and monitors, his face ashen and drawn. His eyes were closed and he breathed evenly.

Sitting in a chair beside him, Laura Langley looked worried and spent. She stood up and approached David, touching his arm. "Thank you for coming. I'll leave you two alone."

He whispered, "Nancy's just down the hall."

When Laura closed the door behind her, David advanced toward the bed. The man who had been his angry enemy looked frail and powerless. Langley's eyes slowly opened, fluttering as they adjusted to the light. He smiled weakly as he recognized David. "I understand you won the election— congratulations," he said faintly. "What was the margin?"

"More than fifteen percent," David replied, a smile playing on his lips. "I understand it gave you a heart attack."

Langley laughed and winced at the same time. Then he cleared his throat and said, "I want to apologize to you. I needed to tell you while I still can. I've been such a fool."

This was not what David had expected. Feeling awkward, he tried to be gracious. "We all do things we regret. I'd be the first to challenge you for that prize."

"You're letting me off too easy," Langley said, his voice labored. He reached for the bed control next to his pillow and fumbled with the buttons until the mattress rose to a full sitting position. He frowned. "I've never been under the knife before. A quadruple by-pass isn't routine surgery. At least not for me."

"You're in one of the best hospitals in the country. I understand you're recovering just fine."

"I've had a narrow escape," Langley said pensively, his fingers fidgeting with the blanket. "When you realize how close you've come to checking out, you get a different perspective on life. You can be gone in an instant, but the world moves on indifferently, oblivious to your extinction." He sighed, then looked up purposefully. "Thank you for coming, Madison. There are some things I need to say to you before it's too late."

"Please call me David, won't you?"

Langley reached for the glass of water on the hospital table in front of him and took a sip through the straw. Then he said, "You have been a formidable opponent. You won fair and square, and you did it without rancor. Like you won the election. I wish I could say the same for myself, but I let hate make me irrational. I'm not proud of what I said and did." He took a deep breath and set the glass back on the table. "I've done some soul searching, David." He smiled as he used his first name. "I want you to have Grant."

At first David couldn't believe what he'd heard.

Langley saw his confusion and added, "Laura and I discussed it and we both agree it's best for the boy and the right thing to do."

An almost euphoric feeling overcame David. The nightmare was over. He sought the eyes of the man whose animosity had caused him so much unpleasantness, and the icy wall of resentment melted between them.

"I've been hoping you'd say that, Edward," he said warmly. "It's a far better gift than winning the election."

"It wasn't mine to give. I tried to take Grant away."

David smiled kindly. "You wanted what you thought was best for him and that's what counts. I think you'll make a good grandfather."

"Better than a father to Darlene, I hope. I missed most of her growing up. Don't you make that mistake."

"You know I won't."

Langley nodded slowly, then looked up with a guilty expression." I'm leaving everything to Laura. Then it all passes to Grant. You don't have to worry about his education. Darlene..." He bit his lip and blinked away the tears welling up. "Never mind."

"Yes, I think it's what Darlene wanted."

The tension left Langley's face. He nodded and smiled weakly. "You know what John Maynard Keynes said on his deathbed?"

"No. What was it?"

"I didn't drink enough champagne."

"I'll remember that."

Langley looked at David. "Well, neither did I." His smile broadened. "I've got some catching up to do."

David reached down, grasped his hand and gave it a light squeeze. "I intend to help you with that."

Langley pulled the bed covers up under his arms. For a moment he held David's eyes, conveying his respect for him. Then he said, "Now, go celebrate, before I croak. You've had two victories today."

"There will be a bottle of Champagne waiting for us to share as soon as your doctor approves."

As David started to leave, Langley called after him, "I want you to know something, Congressman."

David found the formal address amusing and turned back. "What is it?"

An impish grin blossomed on Langley's face. "I voted for you."

CHAPTER 20

David was well aware that as an inexperienced politician, he needed all the help he could get, at least for his first term in office. Knowing next to nothing about the ins and outs of how Washington functioned, he understood that the key to his success lay in hiring a staff that did. Fortunately, Katherine was a pro at it. While congressmen in Washington came and went, the better members of their teams often remained, snapped up by another congressman. Katherine as his chief of staff recruited the most experienced and dedicated scheduler, legislative director, press secretary, legal aides and interns to form an effective and dedicated team. David gave her carte blanche in hiring whom she pleased. Where he took full control was in bringing in experts and advisors in the areas he wanted to focus on—in particular, the issues surrounding veterans in the military.

Then, in the midst of the whirlwind of preparation, he got some unexpected news.

Considering the rocky beginning with the Langleys, David never imagined that his wish for Grant to have a father and loving grandparents would be granted, but Edward Langley's brush with death made him a changed man. After his discharge from the hospital, he took a health leave, whose end coincided with his retirement from his professorship at Yale at the end of the semester.

During his furlough, he and Laura leased their house in New Haven to a visiting English professor from Oxford and his young family. In consultation with David they decided to move to

Annapolis, Maryland, so that Grant would be closer to his father, yet far enough away from Washington's urban environment. Eventually he would enroll in school there.

An added bonus was the proximity to the Chesapeake Bay which would allow David to go sailing with him. Once the plans were settled, Katherine located a place on Market Street, a few houses up the brick sidewalk from the water with a large backyard and front porch that pleased Laura Langley. Edward took a visiting research professorship with a light teaching load at Johns Hopkins University in Baltimore.

David almost felt it was too good to be true. For the first time in many years everything was going his way.

On the evening of January 3, Senator Cunningham's townhouse was packed with guests. To David it almost seemed like he was back at Frank Gannovino's gallery showing. Trays of champagne glasses seemed to float above the heads of the crowd as strolling waiters tried to work their way through the throng of attendees. Only a few guests seemed interested in taking advantage of the lavish display of food in the dining room, but the bar was crowded.

Katherine touched her champagne glass to David's. "C'mon, smile. Tonight is supposed to be a celebration. You've just taken the oath of office."

David's smile was strained. "If I must."

"You must."

Over his shoulder, Katherine saw Bradley Coyle enter the room.

She forced herself to relax and with a practiced smile warned David, "Don't turn around, but Bradley Coyle just arrived."

He stiffened. "What's he doing here?"

"Daddy always invites all the New England senators to his pre-session party. It's a courtesy, even in these divisive times of Congressional gridlock. Some things you just have to endure in politics and let bygones be bygones."

David looked annoyed. "You didn't tell me he'd be here."

"I meant to."

"Meant not to tell me or just forgot?"

Katherine frowned. "Don't be unpleasant, David. You'll have to deal with him again at some point."

"This isn't the time."

She swirled the top of her champagne glass in a little circle. "Why not? We must keep up the appearance of civility."

He looked toward Coyle. "I don't like being blindsided. Don't ever do that to me again."

Visibly annoyed, Katherine said, "It's my house, David. You're my guest here." She moved abruptly away to a nearby group, her manner instantly changing back to gracious hostess with a ready smile.

David realized that she was punishing him for pushing too hard. He was the new kid on the block and his domineering manner had offended her. She should have taken him along and introduced him. Leaving him alone sent the message: *Don't tell me what I can and can't do.*

He felt a hand on his shoulder. It was Senator Cunningham. Next to him stood a gray-haired man. Katherine's father made the introductions. "This is David Madison. David, I'd like you to meet Senator Garrett from Virginia."

David was surprised at the contrast between the two men. Senator Cunningham was the perfect Boston Brahmin, lean and tall, with a thick mane of white hair and a chiseled face worthy of Mt. Rushmore. Garrett was more approachable, not as statuesque, with a ready twinkle in his eye.

"Congratulations, and welcome aboard. You ran a brilliant campaign," he said with a hint of a Southern drawl in his rich baritone voice.

"Thank you. That is a high compliment coming from you, Sir.

I've admired your career and hope I can accomplish a fraction of what you've done."

"Not without my distinguished colleagues. No one accomplishes anything here alone."

As Katherine stepped into their circle, Senator Garrett's eyes lit up. She tilted her head flirtatiously. "Now, Senator, you know the house rules. No politics tonight. David agrees with you on just about everything anyway, so there's no need."

Garrett slipped his arm around her shoulders and gave her a squeeze of acknowledgment.

She turned to David and touched his hand—he was forgiven. "Senator Garrett has a farm in Middleburg and raises horses," she said.

David became all ears. "What breed?" he asked.

The senator answered. "Thoroughbreds."

"I worked on a horse farm when I was a kid. They raised Thoroughbreds—the gentlest and fiercest creatures I have ever met."

"Then you ride?"

"After a fashion."

Senator Garrett seemed pleased. "We always start off the summer season with a picnic at my farm the weekend of the Kentucky Derby. Consider this a personal invitation."

"I'd love to," David said, "but I see my son on weekends."

"Bring him along. There will be many children there. He'll enjoy it."

Garrett turned to Katherine. "Will you be joining us this year?" She looked at her father. "Dad and I will be back in Connecticut hosting our own Derby party for some of our constituents. Besides, you know how I feel about horses. They're best admired during races from the window of the Jockey Club."

Senator Garrett laughed. "There will be races to watch, but there won't be any air conditioning," he grinned and tapped David's arm and said, "Come if you can." Then he moved on.

David watched him join another group assembled around Bradley Coyle. The junior senator from Connecticut laughed a little too heartily and looked downright uncomfortable as Senator Garrett stepped up and shook hands all around.

As Senator Cunningham excused himself as well, Katherine squeezed David's arm. "I didn't know you were a horseman."

"Horseman?" David laughed. "I was a stable boy."

"How did you stand the smell?"

"Why don't we go over to Bradley and I'll show you how."

Katherine put her hand on his arm. "David, be nice."

As soon as Senator Garrett left the group, David took Katherine's hand and led her toward Coyle. He saw them coming, excused himself from the others and strode over to meet them.

With a smirk on his face, he said, "How nice to see you, David. Lazarus has been raised." He looked at Katherine. "This is just like old times."

"Don't you wish," Katherine said.

"Ouch! And all I wanted to do is welcome your boyfriend to the legislature."

He extended his hand and David shook it. "Let's go outside for some fresh air," he said. When Coyle hesitated, he added, "I'm ready to extend an olive branch."

Katherine looked at the two men. They were both handsome, but Bradley's sophisticated demeanor was superficial—polished on the surface as though he wore make-up. The contrast with David's subtle ruggedness seemed the difference between a man and the imitation of one. "I need to get to the other guests. Will you excuse me?" she said.

As she walked away, the men moved in the other direction, out the French doors onto the open patio. It was a mild January evening and the snow had all melted. Beyond the stone balustrade was a formal garden with a white gazebo. They walked over to it in silence.

Bradley looked uncomfortable as they stood and faced each other. "What are you going to say that couldn't be said in front of everyone else?"

David looked at him with contempt. "Do I need to make a list?"

"Oh, come on, Dave. It was just politics. You'll need to develop a tougher hide if you want to make it here in Washington."

"You tried to smear us. I expected that for myself, but to drag Katherine through the muck was disgraceful." He set his empty champagne glass on the table. "Is there no cesspool you won't crawl through?"

Coyle's distorted smile turned into a sneer. "You're the one to talk after screwing my wife."

The next thing Bradley knew, he was lying on the ground, his lower lip throbbing. When he touched it he came away with blood on his fingers. Shaking his woozy head, he saw David disappear into the house and the doors close behind him.

Katherine noticed the self-satisfied expression on David's face as he walked up the stairs. She waited for Bradley to reappear. When he didn't, she left her circle of guests and went outside. The patio was empty.

Puzzled, she headed to the second-floor guest suite and found David in the bathroom standing over the sink. He was running cold water on his right hand.

She suppressed a grin. "David, you didn't!"

He looked at her in the mirror and said, "I did. It was the most satisfying punch I've ever thrown. One was all it took."

"Oh David, that's not how we do things here on the Hill."

He saw the twinkle in her eyes. "What better way to repay a debt."

"A debt? You didn't owe him anything."

"Let's just call it a debt of ingratitude. Haven't you wanted to do that to him for a long time?"

"Actually, yes," she said. "As soon as I finish with the guests I'll be back."

David walked into the bedroom. He thought about the possible repercussions and figured he didn't need to worry. Coyle wasn't about to cry foul and make himself the laughing stock of Washington. He looked at his watch. It was half-past ten. The party would soon be over. No one stayed up late during the week in D.C.

He removed his suit jacket and tossed it over the arm of a chair, slipped off his shoes, and lay down on the bed. Katherine would be up soon.

A short time later, the doorknob turned and the door slowly opened. Katherine gave him an approving look. "I didn't know if you'd gone to sleep."

He sat up on the edge of the bed. "Did you tell your father?"

"Yes. You're a hero. Daddy said he's wanted to punch Bradley in his 'panache' for a long time." She shook her head and her hair whirled about her shoulders seductively. "What is it with men and this macho stuff?"

"It's less lethal than women stabbing each other in the back."

She came up to him and stood between his knees, grabbing his necktie. "If I had a knife I'd cut this tie off." She loosened the knot and pulled it off, leaning forward so her breasts almost touched his face, then pulled back.

He put his hands on her hips as if to push her away but didn't. "Have you forgotten our deal?"

She looked down at him and tossed her hair again. "What deal?"

"Nothing personal."

"Okaaay." She turned her back to him. "Then just undo me and I'll go away."

He unloosened the clasp and pulled down the zipper of her dress to the arch of her back at her narrow waist. Then he released the hooks on her bra and rubbed her bare back.

She turned to face him and pulled in her shoulders so that the top of her dress and bra dropped down to her waist. Leaning toward him, she pulled his face to her bare breasts. He kissed her cleavage and rubbed his lips lightly over her nipples and heard her gasp.

Then he drew her across him and onto the bed.

CHAPTER 21

Several months later David strode purposefully through the pedestrian tunnel from his office in the Longworth House Office Building. He preferred walking outside to cross Independence Avenue to the Capitol Building, but it was one of those early May days when rain washed the last of the cherry blossoms from the trees. He glanced at his watch—he would make it on time. He stopped for a moment at the heavy wood-paneled doors of Room 334 where a sign next to it read: Committee on Veteran Affairs Hearing. Then he entered the room.

Katherine had gotten there ahead of him. He marveled how she was always on schedule, yet never seemed rushed. She stood at the center of the raised, horseshoe-shaped dais that faced and flanked the witness table. David saw her talking intently to Congressman George Smithson and wondered what she was saying to ingratiate herself to the powerful committee chair. Impeccably dressed in a dark blue suit and yellow tie, his thin hair slicked back, he carried himself with sophistication and a hint of swagger.

As David took his seat at the far end of the dais, he watched Katherine working her way through the group of congressmen and their aides mingling behind their chairs waiting for the hearing to begin. With practiced ease, she dispensed a compliment here, a quick laugh at a witty comment there, and the occasional physical touch. Their eyes followed her and David thought how lucky he was to have her at his side.

By the time she sat down behind him, everyone was settling in, eager for the hearing to begin.

From his high-backed leather chair, Smithson gaveled the meeting to order and thanked everyone for coming. With his papers organized in a perfect pile in front of him, he began reading, "We are here to address an issue of enormous importance and responsibility." He looked up momentarily. "Our veterans are dying, not in combat, but after they return home and try to reorient themselves into society. Every day, twenty-two end their lives by their own hand. That's over eight thousand suicides per year, significantly more than have been killed in the wars in Iraq and Afghanistan combined since the beginning of our operations in the Middle East!"

The spectators in the back of the room—reporters, veterans and guests—shifted uncomfortably in their seats.

Smithson's resonant voice rose in intensity. "Why? Why are we still losing our soldiers at their own hands in vastly greater numbers than at the hands of our enemies? And what can be done about it? This is a tragedy of epic proportions, and it must stop!" He paused to look directly at the witness. "You promised to make reorganizing the VA a priority, to give veterans easier access to health care, and yet, here we are again. We are looking to you for an explanation."

As Congressman Smithson introduced Paul Michaels, Assistant Secretary of the Veterans Administration, Katherine whispered to David, "Did you have any idea it was this bad?"

David nodded. "Yes. And I'm prepared to speak out about it when I get my turn." He looked at the assembled reporters and spectators. "It will take a while. The full committee is here, and I'll probably be the last member to speak."

Katherine touched his shoulder. "That's good. You'll get a feeling for how it goes."

"Mister Michaels," the chairman intoned. "May we have your opening remarks?"

"Yes," Michaels said with apparent confidence. In contrast to Smithson's chiseled features and refinement, he looked a bit flabby and out of his league, despite his expensive suit and haircut. He folded his hands and began reading from his prepared statement. "Mr. Chairman and members of the committee, the VA takes this issue very seriously. But I'd like to put it in perspective – not to minimize its importance, but to be sure that we understand the nature and complexity of the problem. There are one hundred and five suicides per day in the United States, and–"

"Mister Michaels," the chairman cut him off gruffly, "I am sorry to stop you at the very beginning of your testimony, but I will not permit you to marginalize this issue. This hearing is about the fact that our soldiers are dying in civilian life faster than in combat. This is happening on your watch, and we want to know what you are doing about it!"

Michaels' eyes narrowed and he leaned back defensively. "Perhaps you would prefer if I omitted my opening statement and proceeded to your questions."

"As you like," Smithson's voice had the brittle sound of breaking ice. "Since you are waiving your opening statement, I call on the ranking minority member, Congressman Forsman."

The congressman from Colorado nodded. "Thank you, Mister Chairman."

Katherine leaned forward and whispered, "This is going to take some time. Do you mind if I go to the office and come back later?"

David shook his head, and she slipped out of the room unnoticed, while he turned his attention to the proceedings.

As Katherine had predicted, the questioning was lengthy and mostly pointless. One congressman lobbed softball queries, another decided to grandstand for the cameras by uttering a string of clichés. David grew tired of the posturing but maintained a placid exterior.

Just as the chairman finally recognized him, Katherine slipped back into the room. Instead of returning to her seat she stood in the rear with some of the reporters.

David waited a moment, then spoke in a calm voice into the

microphone in front of him, "Mister Assistant Secretary, I am new to this committee but not to its work over the past three years. During that time how often have you appeared here?"

Mr. Michaels shrugged. "Perhaps a half a dozen times."

"Seven to be exact." David looked away from Michaels toward Katherine standing at the back. "I have watched videos of all of those hearings—and the testimonies by you and others, mostly employees of the Veterans Administration. The same questions are put to you, and your answer is always how your organization is making big changes to correct the problems that the committee identifies, but nothing gets fixed!"

He put on his reading glasses and shuffled the papers in front of him. "Let me highlight what has been accomplished during your administration. The suicide rate has increased from twenty to twenty-two men and women per day." He looked up and repeated for emphasis, "Per day," before resuming. "I'll give you credit for reducing the backlog of appeals for consideration of medical benefits, which doubled from two hundred and fifty thousand to five hundred thousand and used to take as long as ten years to settle. Approximately a quarter of the veterans who had to wait that long died in the process."

Katherine's eyes darted around the room. The reporters and spectators growing increasingly bored, suddenly became attentive. The Assistant Secretary kept glancing back toward his aides.

David turned over the page and continued. "But while the average wait time for veterans to see a specialist after a primary care physician has gone down as well, the rate of suicide among those under treatment for post-traumatic stress is approximately ten percent. Treatment for PTSD is usually limited to prescription drugs, with little follow-up by a trained psychiatrist or another qualified psychiatric assistant."

Murmurs swept through the hearing room, and David's fellow congressmen on the dais shifted uncomfortably.

He flipped through several pages as the scowling Assistant Secretary looked up at the tiered chandelier hanging from the ceiling. "I could go on, but my time is limited, so let's consider this: The budget for the Department of Veterans Affairs is second only to the Defense Department in size and has exceeded a total of a quarter of a trillion dollars over the past three years, including an increase of five percent over last year. Given those vast financial resources, I ask you, 'Are you satisfied with the performance of your department?'"

Michaels leaned forward toward his microphone. "I am never satisfied, Congressman. There is always room for improvement. That is precisely why we have restructured the entire department to deal with delays and accessibility. We are converting to electronic files to better serve our veterans, and we have instituted several pilot programs to–"

"Pilot programs?" David interrupted. "You are just now starting pilot programs that will need months of evaluation to determine whether they are effective while more veterans die?" Another wave of murmurs swept the room as David continued with irritation, "Aren't there a number of programs already, many of them started by former soldiers to help their fellow veterans, that show promise and success?"

Michael's face reddened. "We haven't had the time to evaluate them."

"Haven't had the time or haven't taken the time?"

Before Michaels could answer, David addressed Representative Smithson. "Mister Chairman, while we have been deliberating here, two more veterans have died at their own hands. Almost every hour another veteran commits suicide. Yet there seems to be no sense of urgency to find solutions to this intolerable situation." David cleared his throat. "Therefore, I recommend that a commission be formed to explore specific programs that work to reduce the unacceptable rate of non-combat casualties. If the VA doesn't have the time to do so, we will do it on its behalf!"

He looked down at the Assistant Secretary as he clicked off his microphone.

For a moment Katherine could hear a pin drop. Then there was an eruption of activity as some of the spectators applauded and the members of the press rushed out of the room to file their stories.

Katherine smiled and said under her breath, "Now you've done it, David."

Congressman Smithson pounded the gavel repeatedly until order was restored. "I thank the Assistant Secretary on behalf of the committee for his testimony. The committee will reconvene in closed session in two weeks. This hearing is adjourned. Have a pleasant weekend." He struck the table once more with extra emphasis. Standing up he turned toward his aide and said quietly, "Go over and tell Madison I want to see him—right now."

As he gathered his papers, Stan Forsman, the ranking minority member, approached Smithson angrily. "I can tell by the look on your face that you didn't know this was coming."

"No, I didn't." Smithson jammed his papers into his briefcase and snapped it closed. "But that doesn't make what he said wrong."

"Then we need to talk."

"I'll call you later, Stan, as soon as I finish with Madison."

He started toward the private door which exited to a back corridor as David approached. An aide held it open for them to pass through. In the passageway, Smithson said, "Come with me. I don't want you to meet the press just yet."

He led David down to the Capitol Subway. There was an empty shuttle car waiting, and he eased himself onto the seat opposite David. He crossed his legs, stretched his arm along the back of his seat, and said, "I'm not against what you did, Madison, but you should have run it by me first. I don't appreciate being blindsided by a freshman member of my own party!"

As the car moved forward to the hum of its electric motor, David said, "I wasn't sure where you stood."

"All the more reason to check with me ahead of time," Smithson retorted. "You need someone to cover your back. If you're going to stick your neck out, you have to be damned sure your head won't get cut off."

David looked at the state flags and crests hanging from the ceiling and walls above the walkway flashing past as the car gained speed.

Smithson continued, "I know you're something of a protégé of Senator Cunningham. You did your homework and were prepared, but if you want to accomplish something here, you have to build relationships and coalitions. You will get nothing done by yourself."

"Then we're fighting on the same side?"

"Yes. But I want to win. At the meeting of our committee we'll discuss referring the issues you raised to the Health Subcommittee and the eventual appointment of a commission, but this has to go through the proper process. Just be ready for the flack you'll be getting from the press and the other party. Stan Forsman will put on a fight like nothing you ever saw in Iraq."

David said contritely, "I get your point. It won't happen again." He looked the congressman in the eye. "But I want you to know that I'm prepared to lose my seat fighting for my fellow veterans. They shouldn't be dying when they come home. They risked their lives when their country asked them to go to war. They were trained to kill. Now we need to find a way to help them live."

Smithson nodded and slapped David's knee as the car slowed and came to a stop. "I like your spirit. You remind me of myself twenty years ago."

He got out and headed toward his office in the Cannon Building. David took the other corridor toward the Longworth Building where Katherine would be waiting. As he entered the lobby several television reporters descended on him, with bright, blinding camera lights accompanying them, and stuck their microphones in his face.

"Are you going to introduce a bill to eliminate the Veterans Administration?" a voice called out.

David did not break stride. "No, just improve it. We're going to take that up in the next committee meeting. Stay tuned till then."

"How did Chairman Smithson react to your stealing his thunder?" yelled a young woman reporter.

"The chairman and I are on the same page on this issue."

An older male reporter queried, "That was quite a debut, Congressman. What are you going to do next?"

David stopped and scanned the entire group of eager, aggressive faces, eager for the latest sound bite. He did not know their names or the media outlets they represented yet. "I came to Washington to solve problems," he said. "The VA isn't doing a very good job, that's obvious. I intend to do everything possible to give the veterans the medical care they rightfully deserve."

He used the momentary silence to slide into the elevator. As the doors closed, he smiled and said, "See you all soon."

When he entered his office, Katherine was sitting on the edge of her desk with her arms folded and legs crossed. The rest of his staff was gone. She was alone.

"It's Friday. I let them off early." She looked at him dubiously. "The chairman's secretary called. Smithson wants to see you in his office on Tuesday at ten. What happened?"

David chuckled. "I got a dressing down. But we're on the same side. We're going for the commission."

Katherine got off the desk and straightened her skirt. "Do you think for one minute that Congressman Forsman and Bradley Coyle are going to sit back and let the findings of a commission upset their big government apple cart? Even if it passes the House, it will never make it out of the Senate. I hate to burst your bubble, but you're tilting at windmills."

"Smithson doesn't seem to think so. Why else would he go for it?"

One hand resting on her hip, she challenged him. "Sometimes I don't know what to make of you. Why can't you just act like a normal congressman?"

"Because I have no intention of becoming one. I've got two years to accomplish something here."

"Commissions take time, David."

"The VA's a bureaucracy that moves like a glacier, while men and women are dying! A commission without a vested interest can speed the process. I'm not trying to do away with dedicated doctors and administrators who do their jobs. It's the rotten apples I'm after, the appointees and bureaucrats who see it as their little fiefdom and put themselves ahead of the vets. Maybe fear for their jobs will shake them up."

He went over to the closet and pulled a bottle of champagne from the small refrigerator and two glasses from a shelf above. "Let's enjoy our first small victory."

"You've only won the first skirmish, you know that."

"Every war starts with the first battle." He popped the cork, filled the glasses, and handed one to her.

She took it and raised it in a toast. "I must confess that I'm proud of you. I can't think of anyone else who would have had the guts to do that."

"Then let's celebrate." He clinked his glass against hers, took a deep swallow, and set it down. Then he slipped his arms around her waist. "When I saw you at the back of the room, I felt like I wasn't alone up there." He took the glass from her hand and set it next to his.

She smiled and put her arms around his neck. "I have a confession to make."

He looked at her lips. "Which is?"

"I was glad I wasn't sitting next to you. That way I could watch you, not just hear you."

He chortled. "That wasn't what I expected you to say."

"What did you expect?"

"Something like, 'I want to go away with you this weekend.'"

Bringing her face up to his, she whispered, "I want to go away with you this weekend."

CHAPTER 22

Bradley Coyle finished his lunch meeting at the Round Robin Bar in the Willard Hotel, but instead of returning to his office through the street entrance he went into the lobby and up the elevator to the sixth floor.

When he entered Room 610, the TV was on and Stephanie Jordan lounged on the sofa, her shapely legs stretched out along the cushions. The jacket of her white business suit was neatly draped over the back of a chair while her shoes lay carelessly tossed off on the carpet—the telling combination of prim and reckless that Bradley loved about her. *This is better than dessert*, he thought.

"I'm sorry it took me so long, but you know how donors want to be stroked," he said, grinning.

She ignored him, her eyes remaining riveted on the television screen.

As Bradley checked out what she was watching, his grin disappeared. David Madison, his nemesis, apparently had just finished grandstanding for a gaggle of reporters in the lobby of the Longworth Building and was disappearing into an elevator.

The camera focused on a news reporter in the foreground summing up. "After dropping a bombshell at the VA hearings, the question on everyone's mind is: What will the freshman congressman from Connecticut do next?"

Bradley groaned. "What's he done now?"

Stephanie glanced up at him casually. "He's calling for a commission to look into an investigation of the VA."

"Son of a bitch!" Bradley shouted and stomped to the minibar where he poured himself a glass of bourbon. "God damn that son of a bitch," he said again between gritted teeth. He took a big gulp and struck the counter with his fist. "Three months in office and Madison makes waves on the Veterans Committee." He took another swallow. "I should have made sure he never got elected."

"I tried to tell you," Stephanie said warily.

"I let him get away with it. I let him intimidate me in that garage. I never should have backed down." His jaw hardened. "Next time that bastard gets what's coming to him."

"What is it about him that sets you off?"

His eyes narrowed and he scowled at her but didn't answer. Instead, he swallowed the rest of his drink, went to the TV and punched it off. Then he looked at Stephanie lecherously, went over to the couch, picked her up, carried her into the bedroom, and tossed her on the bed.

"The last time you got mad at David Madison you played too rough with me, so cool it," she warned.

He pushed up her skirt and pulled off her pantyhose. As he zipped down his fly and started to move onto her she brought her leg between them and pushed until he fell back onto the floor.

"I said, 'Cool it, Bradley!'" She lay back on her elbows as he sat on the floor with his legs apart and his elbows on his knees, hands clasped.

"Now look who's playing rough."

"Just so you understand, Bradley."

He stood up. "What I understand, Stephanie," he said as his eyes swept over her bare legs with her skirt up near her waist, "is that you're the sexiest woman I've ever met."

She patted the bed next to her. "Come lie down," she said, in a husky voice, "and I'll show you what you'll be missing if you don't divorce Helen."

CHAPTER 23

The outdoor riding arena at Senator Garrett's farm had a panoramic view of the green, undulating hills of the Virginia countryside. Standing at the railing, David enjoyed the coolness of the pleasant breeze. White paddock fences crisscrossed the grassy slopes. Spring flowers dotted the meadows. Sunlight reflected off the wavelets on a small pond surrounded by willow trees, the tips of their branches drooping into the water.

As he took a deep breath inhaling the smell of horses, the laughter of young children caught his attention. They were riding ponies around the ring. A young woman was smiling and talking to Grant as she led him on a palomino, making sure he was safe. She wore a white blouse, brown boots, and tan jodhpurs, which accentuated her slim figure. Her auburn hair was tied in a ponytail.

"Who is the gal with all of the kids?" he asked Senator Garrett who stood next to him leaning on the top rail.

The senator laughed. "That's my daughter, Jenny."

David observed her with Grant. He had on a helmet and held the reins, doing his best to act as if he were in command—his back straight, legs parallel to the side of the horse, toes tipped up slightly. *She must have taught Grant how to sit a horse*, he thought.

Out loud, he said, "My son seems to have taken to her."

"All the children love her. She has a way with them," the senator agreed. "She should be married by now, but the right man hasn't come along. I'm afraid my career has narrowed the pool of candidates."

Responding to David's perplexed expression, he explained, "She doesn't like politicians, won't even go out with one."

David laughed. "Are we that bad?"

"In her mind, yes." He chuckled and started to head toward the stables.

Joining him, David took a glance back at her. "She's not coming with us?"

"Definitely not. She prefers children and horses; thinks we're all conniving hypocrites."

David followed Garrett inside to the stalls where several horses stuck their heads out from the open tops of the half doors. The smells of sawdust and manure brought back fond memories of his time working in the stables as a teenager.

"I suggest you ride Red," Garrett said, pointing at a large stallion. "I think you'll like him. He's an old thoroughbred that was left to graze on his own by an owner who abandoned him. When Jenny found him he was all skin and bones. She saved his life." He looked at Red fondly. "Let's saddle up. The others are waiting in the indoor arena."

David rubbed the white star on Red's forehead, talking to him in low tones. Then he opened the stall door and went inside. He ran his hand along Red's neck, over his withers, and along his back in gentle strokes, continuing to talk quietly, noticing his good balance and the muscular shoulder and leg. He examined the front of the legs and ankles. Satisfied, he said, "You're a beauty, big fella."

He led Red out of the stall, took the bit and bridle from the wall, and placed them gently in his mouth and over his head. Red stood still and didn't resist.

"Senator," David called over to the next stall, where Garrett was saddling his own mount. "Your daughter saved a marvelous horse."

"Yes. Red's become one of her favorites," came the reply, followed by a chuckle. "He'll give you a good workout, if you let him."

David brushed off Red's back, then placed the blanket and saddle. When he tightened the cinch, he noticed that Red had inhaled to fill out his sides. "You're not going to get away with that, big guy," he said smiling, and waited for Red to exhale. Then he retightened the cinch and let down the stirrups.

As he led Red from the stall, Garrett was waiting with a handsome black bay that stood twelve hands high but lacked the near-perfect proportions of his own mount.

"How long have you owned the farm?" David asked.

"For twenty-five years. I bought it when Jenny was three years old, and by the time she was five she was taking blue ribbons." His face clouded. "When her mother passed away, it became our life together."

They led the two horses by the reins to the arena where the other guests, weekend riders from around the area, were working out their horses.

David mounted and moved the reigns from side to side. Red responded immediately, acknowledging the commands. As David put him through his gaits, he quickly realized that someone, probably Jenny, had treated him with respect and care. Red wanted to please a skilled rider.

At the senator's signal, they all trotted single file toward the riding trail. Garrett looked back over his shoulder as David rode up to him. "How do you like your horse?"

"He has a nice temperament," David said.

"I didn't think he would make it when Jenny first got him, but he's a tough one. Now he's happiest when he can run, as though he knows how lucky he is to be alive."

David leaned forward and, stroking Red's neck and mane, said to Garrett, "Shall we pick up the pace?"

To the senator's surprise, he gave his heels a kick and surged ahead. Garrett soon followed and they rode side by side in a relaxed canter. By the time they reached the practice track they were galloping easily, well ahead of the others, and the senator shouted, "Let him run!" David gave Red his head and passed his companion at a full gallop. Red raced on the soft surface, completely at home on the racecourse. Everything came back to David as though he had never left the saddle.

As they entered the first turn, David held him back. "Easy, Boy. We've got a way to go."

The senator brought his horse up short in front of the low observing stand. He watched as David and Red came out of the turn. David was holding him at a comfortable pace, his head by Red's neck down low, talking steadily to him. Garrett marveled at David's skill as a rider, as though he had lived a lifetime in the saddle and enjoyed the romp as much as the horse.

As they rounded the far turn and came into the backstretch, David gave Red his freedom, letting him run his own race, not against anyone, but purely for the love of it. The thoroughbred's muscles flexed, his powerful legs reaching for the next stride. As they crossed the finish line, Red slowed and David led him into an easy canter to cool down. Red twisted his neck in a rhythm that tossed off the sweat and lather from his mouth. Breaking into a trot, he headed home like a champion aiming for the winner's circle.

The senator called over to them. "Congratulations. You won by at least six lengths. I thought you said you rode 'after a fashion.' That was a beautiful ride."

"I wanted to become a jockey when I was fourteen," David said, grinning happily. "But when you reach six feet two, that dream goes away."

"Well, keep winning races. The party needs you."

The rest of the riders trotted up. Several waved and called out, "Nice ride!"

"I think I'll take him back to the stable and rub him down," David said to the senator. "That was a pretty good day's work."

"Okay, I'll ride on with the others. We'll see you back at the house."

David had Red trot back in an easy rhythm. When they reached the stable, he washed him off, brushed him down, and tossed a blanket over his back. Red raised each leg as David picked the dirt and stones from each hoof, talking to him softly. When David closed the stall door, Red turned his head back toward him and whinnied. David acknowledged the gesture with a look of appreciation and said, "You gave me a wonderful ride. I enjoyed it as much as you did."

By the time David got back to the small ring, the ponies and the children were gone. Heading toward the house, he heard young voices, laughter, and noisy splashing. He followed the sounds around the corner to a sun deck and saw Garrett's daughter sitting on the edge of the heated swimming pool, her legs dangling in the water, watching the youngsters play.

Grant stood in the shallow end, laughing and splashing with the others. When he saw David, he waved and called out, "Hey, Dad!"

David smiled and waved back. Then he walked to a chaise lounge close to the pool and sat at its foot, facing the woman he wanted to meet. She was wearing a modest, one-piece bathing suit that struck him as sexier than any bikini she could have put on. Her long auburn hair was no longer in a ponytail and moved gently with each turn of her head. She wore no makeup yet looked vaguely familiar.

"Hi. I'm David Madison, Grant's father," he said.

"Jenny Garrett." She looked over at Grant. "You have a very nice son."

"Thank you for saying that and for taking care of the children."

"My pleasure."

David wrinkled his forehead. "I have to ask. Have we met?"

Jenny angled her head and gave him an evaluating look. How many times had she heard that before? "I don't think so. I would remember." Noting dirt on his jodhpurs and boots, and the sweat stains on his shirt, she said, "You're back early. How was your ride?"

He smiled. "Red's quite a horse."

"Not too much horse?"

"Why do you say that?"

The corners of her mouth puckered in amusement. "It looks as though you had a little trouble with him. All that dirt on your clothes suggests he might have tossed you. Don't be embarrassed. It's happened before."

David held her gaze. "Let's just say that I enjoyed the ride."

"Hey, Dad, watch this!" Grant jumped from the side of the pool into the water making a large splash.

When his head came out of the water, David grinned and called to him. "Nice one. But come on out. It's time to go."

"Aw, Dad...already?"

Getting up, David nodded. "Say goodbye to your friends and Miss Garrett."

As Grant climbed up the ladder, David gave him a hand. Jenny put a towel around him, then rubbed him dry.

When she had finished, David said, "Thank Miss Garrett for being such a nice hostess."

Grant straightened and said, "Thank you, Jenny. It was awesome!"

She smiled at him and tousled his hair. "Thank you for coming, Grant. I'm glad you had fun today."

David intervened. "We need to get going. It's a long drive back to Annapolis and Grandpa's and Grandma's place." He extended his hand to Jenny. "Thanks, again. And thank the senator for me, won't you?"

"Of course." She shook it earnestly. Then she smiled once more at Grant and said, "Take good care of your father."

CHAPTER 24

L ate Friday night Katherine and David were finishing up thank you letters to donors in his office. All kinds of documents and papers were strewn across his mahogany desk, the in-box was piled high with reports, and Congressional Records were stacked next to it. Yellow legal pads with ragged tops from pages torn off were scattered here and there, each with a different topic heading in David's unruly handwriting.

The clutter spread to a credenza off to one side which also displayed a small American flag and a framed picture of Grant, smiling. David's honorable discharge, medals and university diplomas hung on the wall above them.

Katherine sat at the front of his desk, munching popcorn from a small bag. She checked the iPad perched on her lap and handed him a letter. "This one goes to Mark Henshaw," she said. "You can congratulate him on his daughter's success as captain of the field hockey team at Choate Rosemary Hall. That's a prep school in Wallingford, Connecticut. He's a big booster."

"I know what Choate Rosemary Hall is," David said, irritated, as he wrote a special note in the margin. He scrawled his signature at the bottom and gave the letter back to her. "This paperwork is ridiculous. Can't you just finish these yourself and use my signature stamp?"

"No. These people can tell. For them, the personal touch is important," Katherine insisted. "If it comes from you, they're more likely to contribute next time."

"I spend hours a day at the call center in a little cubicle cold calling wealthy donors like a telemarketer, and now this," David said, exasperated. "Fundraising seems to be all I'm doing. That's not what I signed up for."

"David, you're exaggerating. If you don't have a big war chest, you can't hope to compete when it comes time for your reelection campaign. Plus, the party won't give you the plum committee assignments. There is only so much influence Daddy has."

She passed him another letter. "Stephen Marquette. Just got back from his annual safari in Africa. This year he shot a lion."

David made a face. "And I'm supposed to give him an 'attaboy' for that?"

Katherine balled up a sheet of scrap paper on his desk and threw it at him in mock anger. It bounced off his chest, and he raised his hands in surrender.

"I spend half of my time in pointless committee meetings and the other half signing papers that no one will read," he carped.

"Stop complaining," she said, holding out the bag of popcorn to him as a peace offering. "I don't burden you with all the stuff I take care of that you never get to see."

He shook his head, refusing. "I'm not complaining, only frustrated. I'm surprised that we get any legislation done at all."

Katherine was about to hand him another letter when David glanced at the picture of Grant and said, "I don't want to be here all night."

Eager to change subject, she asked, "What are you going to do with him tomorrow? Something special?"

"Nancy Sullivan is in town, visiting an old friend. She used to look after Grant in New Haven when the Langleys needed a break, and she's agreed to take him for the day." He hesitated for a moment before continuing, "Senator Garrett invited me to go to the Preakness as a guest in his box."

Katherine brightened. "That's wonderful! Why don't I come

with you? I'd love to go to the Preakness."

"Why? It's a horse race. You don't even like horses."

"The Preakness isn't just any horse race. It's one of the biggest social events of the year."

David felt a pang of guilt as the image of Jenny smiling mischievously entered his mind. He ran his fingers through his hair. "I'm afraid it's not possible. Senator Garrett's box is filled up."

Katherine's eyes narrowed. She knew what that unconscious gesture meant. He was uncomfortable or trying to work out something that bothered him.

"What are you not telling me?" she asked pointedly.

"What do you mean?"

"First, you try to talk me out of going and then you tell me I didn't have a choice in the first place."

David opted for denial. "Kathy, don't be silly. If you want to go so badly, I'm sure your father can arrange tickets."

Katherine flushed red. "Okay. What's really going on?"

Glancing away, David said, "People will talk."

"Well, let them talk."

He shrugged. "I just don't feel comfortable with us being seen together socially. People might think we're an item. You know our arrangement."

She stood up, fuming. "Nothing personal, you mean? Except when you decide you want to make it personal. Like our nights together!"

"Perhaps they were a mistake."

"Mistake? If I got pregnant, that would be a mistake."

"You're my chief of staff, Kathy, not my wife!"

She thrust her head forward, incensed. "What am I then, David, your chief of staff and chief lay?"

David looked up and held her eyes. "That was a cheap shot."

"Cheap or not, are you going to answer?"

When he didn't, she walked to the sofa, plopped down, and

folded her arms, smoldering. Dismayed that she'd gotten under his skin, David came around the desk and tried a conciliatory note. "I've always liked horse racing since I was a kid. The Triple Crown is the epitome of horse racing. This is the second leg, and I've been invited to it, that's all."

"And you want to exclude me from it." She refused to look at him.

"Look, it's Friday night and getting late. We're tired and hungry. Why don't we go to dinner? You choose the restaurant."

"Oh, we can dine out together, but we can't go to a horse race together?"

"Kaathyyy!"

"Well?"

David felt that she left him no choice but to dig in his heels. "You already know my answer."

Her face became a mask. She got up and took her place in front of his desk. Rifling through the remaining letters, she said, "If you really feel that way, then that's the way it is. You want to spend the day with Senator Garrett and his racing friends, fine. It's not worth arguing about."

Knowing how stubborn she was, David sighed and went back to his seat. He held out his hand, and she gave him the next letter.

"Richard Eagleton," she said. "He's a Marine."

"I remember," he said. "The first Gulf War, Operation Desert Storm."

CHAPTER 25

The white clouds dotting the vivid blue May sky made the perfect backdrop for a horse race. The noisy crowd of enthusiasts milled in the stands, anticipating the possibility of another Triple Crown winner. In over eighty years only thirteen horses had accomplished that feat, and because the Preakness Stakes at Pimlico in Baltimore was the second contest, the atmosphere was always charged with excitement. Would the Kentucky Derby winner prevail again? Or would the Belmont, the third leg of the Triple Crown, become just another horse race?

David looked across the track at the white tents where the wealthy patrons sipped Black-Eyed Susans, the signature cocktail of the Preakness, in the shade, soft grass under their feet. The hoi polloi, jam-packed and exposed to the sun in the infield area, were guzzling beer. He felt the rumble of the energized crowd from across the track and understood why Senator Garrett preferred having his box at the finish line, away from all the hubbub. He himself couldn't enjoy the excitement because the seats next to him were empty—Jenny wasn't there. He looked at his watch. It was 10 o'clock. The first race would start in half an hour, but the Preakness Stakes, the 13th race of 15, wouldn't run until six-thirty. It would be a long day if Jenny didn't show.

David didn't want to ask his host where she was, so he broached the subject indirectly, "Who else is joining us?"

Garrett, contemplating his racing form, said, "My daughter and some of her equestrian friends. I learned a long time ago not to make this a social occasion. Too many people I don't invite take offense, so I've made it clear that it's for family and racing enthusiasts only."

Relieved, David said, "Then I consider myself fortunate."

The senator grinned at him. "You deserve it. I haven't seen anyone ride like you in a long time."

"How about Jenny?"

"Well, yes, but she's been on horses since she was a child." He looked up toward the grandstand. "Here they are."

David eagerly followed his gaze to where a group of six people waved to the senator but, to David's disappointment, Jenny wasn't among them. They made their way down the stands, and the senator introduced each of them to David as they filed into the box.

Ed Wharton, the dapper president of the Middleburg Equestrian Club, was dressed in white slacks and a blue blazer with a straw hat that would have been more at home at the turn of the previous century. He was accompanied by his daughter, Susan, who was about Jenny's age, pretty and eager in an unsophisticated manner that made her seem younger than she was.

Jack Bowden, a professional horse trainer who had retired from racing, now managed the senator's farm, although David had not met him before. His old tweed jacket looked as though it should have retired with him. His wife, Mildred, wore a white cotton dress that looked just as dated, but she had a genuine smile, and David liked her immediately.

The same could not be said for Tony Mangione, one of the top ten polo players in the world. He came from a wealthy, old Italian family that lived and owned vineyards in Argentina. His easy charm and megawatt smile matched his reputation as an international playboy. No one seemed to know the young woman on his arm who had eyes only for him. Perhaps she was a model whose stylish clothes looked like they came straight from an haute couture house in Milan. Senator Garrett kept sneaking glances at her.

David would have liked to talk with Jack Bowden, but Susan

Wharton sat down next to him. "So, you're Congressman Madison," she said brightly. "I saw you on TV recently. You're the one helping the veterans."

"Yes, I'm trying to," David answered.

He was still wondering what had happened to Jenny when Susan leaned over in front of him and asked, "Senator, where are John and Jenny?"

"They'll be here," he said.

John and Jenny? David thought. As nonchalantly as he could, he asked Susan, "John?"

"Yes, John Ralston." She touched his arm lightly and leaned back. "Surely you know him."

Senator Garrett, concentrating on his racing form again, interjected, "He's an active supporter of our party. In fact, he contributed to your campaign, David." He circled a name with his short pencil stub and stood up. "Who are you betting on?"

David smiled apologetically. "I'm sitting this one out."

The senator shrugged. "Well, I'm going to place my bet."

As he left the box for the mutual window and the others joined him, Susan remained behind with David.

"John Ralston is one of the wealthiest men in America," she resumed their conversation. "How could you not know him?"

David responded, "Apparently, we don't travel in the same circles."

"You're here, aren't you?"

Amused, David said, "You're right. So, tell me about John Ralston. What does he do?"

"He's a corporate raider—he buys and sells companies, don't you know. That's probably why he's late, working on some deal. Whenever he makes a big score he buys himself a new toy—a yacht, a car, a new polo horse." She touched David's arm again. "You know, he plays polo."

Everyone except Jack Bowden came back to the box as the first race was about to start. It was a contest for three-year-olds and had a one hundred thousand dollar purse, in contrast with the Preakness Stakes at the end, which had a 1.5 million dollar purse. While the serious horseman bet each race, the social set dabbled, waiting for the big one.

David excused himself and made his way through the crowd, down to the paddock where Bowden was standing watching the next group of horses circling.

David leaned on the fence next to him. "You missed the race."

Bowden chuckled. "Not really. I stay down here and watch it on a monitor. Mildred places our bets. She can pick a winner almost as well as I can." His eyes followed a filly as it passed in front of them. "Besides, I can't handle the small talk."

"Then I came to the right place," David said with a grin.

Bowden glanced over. "I was in Vietnam. I know what you're trying to do for the veterans." He faced David directly. "If it hadn't been for horses, I'd be one of the head cases that never came out of it."

"Well, you had a marvelous career. What was your favorite win?"

"They were all favorites. But one loss topped everything."

"You're kidding."

"No. I ran a horse against Secretariat in the Belmont back in 'seventy-three when he won by thirty-one lengths. No one could touch him, but it was a privilege to have been in the same race." He chuckled. "I actually wanted him to win. Greatest horse that ever lived. Still holds the course record for all of the Triple Crown tracks." He looked toward the stables. "It was a different time then, classier, too, not like today." He jerked his head in the direction of the track. "It's a carnival now."

David nodded in agreement. "I prefer it down here, too."

Mildred came up to them smiling broadly. "We won, dear." Then she turned to David. "How did you do, Mister Madison?"

"Haven't bet yet."

115

"Do you know much about horse racing?"

"I was brought up on a racetrack," David replied, smiling.

"Good," Mildred said. "Then let's pick the next race together." They stood side by side at the paddock fence, studying their racing forms and the horses. David drew lines across the numbers of the entries he didn't like and made marks beside the ones that remained. Then they pooled their observations, made a decision, and let Mildred place their bets on number four, Dangerous, at 10-to-one odds. Although they lost, they made a good team, and by the time the seventh race was called they had finished in the money enough times to be well ahead.

When that race finished, Bowden said, "I'm going to the barns to see Gus and congratulate him on winning. He's an old trainer friend. I'll be back in a few minutes."

David waved after him and looked around. Leaning back with both elbows on the top rail, he saw Jenny coming toward him, and his heart skipped a beat.

She wore a sleeveless white dress and white hat that would have looked ostentatious on anyone else. Poised and confident, she stood out from the other women around her because of her understated beauty, supple movements, and happy expression.

She walked up to him, as though he was the only reason she was there and said, "Mildred said I would find you here."

"I'm glad you did," he said, trying to contain his excitement.

Her make-up had a natural look, and he found her scent intoxicating. Taking an open spot next to him at the fence, she scanned the horses in the paddock. "Have you enjoyed the races?"

"Jack and Mildred saved my day," David replied, meaning it.

She took a deep breath and said, "Look, I owe you an apology about Red. The Senator told me how well you handled him."

"No apology necessary."

"I shouldn't have assumed the worst."

"That I'm just another politician, or that I can't ride?"

Frowning, she said, "Now you owe me an apology."

"Only if it's not true. Which is it?"

She looked at him more seriously. "That remains to be seen."

Turning back to the paddock, she examined the circling horses, led by their handlers. The jockeys in their brightly colored silks with numbers attached to their jerseys were discussing last-minute strategy with the trainers. "Who's your pick for the eighth?" Jenny asked.

David pulled the racing form from his back pocket and reviewed it, scrutinizing each horse and rider as they passed.

Jenny studied him with interest. "So which one is it?"

After a long pause, David said, "Number six: Lucky Guy."

"What are his odds?"

"Four to one."

She looked over the parading horses with a connoisseur's eyes. "I like number seven. What are his odds?"

David checked his racing form. "Safire at three to one."

"I'll take that bet. He's more spirited."

The paddock judge called, "Riders up," and the jockeys mounted. Each contender was led out in single file to the gate by a lead pony and rider. The trumpet sounded announcing the race.

As David and Jenny joined the bustling crowd returning to the grandstand, she asked. "Where's Grant?"

"With a good friend," David answered. "She's taken him for the day. Nancy is like an aunt to him, the only person I'd give him up for on a Saturday."

When they got back to the senator's box Jenny introduced David to John Ralston and took the seat between them. The business tycoon had a handsome, well-tanned face, easy smile, and strong handshake. His fingernails were manicured. He looked to be in his late forties, early fifties, and there was a predatory quality about him—quick-moving eyes that sized David up.

As Ralston sat down on Jenny's other side, David noted that

there was no physical contact between them, no casual touch, no hands laid easily on the other's arm. It pleased him.

Suddenly, David flinched and struck his forehead. "We didn't bet!"

Jenny brought a pair of field glasses to her eyes as the bell clanged and the horses broke from the gates. "I did."

David looked baffled.

"I'm betting against you."

"What are the stakes?"

"I'll tell you when they finish." She kept looking through the binoculars. "Right now you'd better worry. Lucky Guy broke poorly and is dead last, two lengths behind the rest. Safire broke clear and moved beautifully to the rail in first place." When she offered him the glasses, he declined, shaking his head. "You don't want to watch?" she asked playfully.

"They still have over a mile to go."

She continued watching as Lucky Guy overtook the horse in front of him, moving out of the first turn into the backstretch, and gradually made his way into the middle. The crowd cheered louder as Lucky Guy took fourth position rounding the far turn. When the horses entered the homestretch, he made his move to the outside, and the crowd came to its feet. With a burst of speed Lucky Guy galloped into second place.

The crowd began cheering wildly as the announcer's voice rose, "It's Lucky Guy on the outside, coming alongside Safire."

Jenny dropped the glasses and started to jump up and down. Her small fists pumped in the air with every movement as she yelled, "C'mon Safire! C'mon, Safire!"

The crowd began to roar as Safire and Lucky Guy matched each other stride for stride, their jockeys madly whipping their flanks. Jenny grabbed at David's arm, pounded her fist against it, and shouted at the top of her lungs, "C'mon, Safire! C'mon, Safire!"

The cheering reached fever pitch as the two horses raced for the finish line.

The announcer's voice rose, matching the hysterical excitement of the crowd: "They're neck and neck—Lucky Guy—Safire—Lucky Guy—Safire—Lucky Guy—

When the two horses crossed the finish line, his voice dropped to a normal level, "And the winner is...Lucky Guy by a nose, Safire second and Presidential third."

The stands erupted in thunderous cheers.

Jenny tugged at David's arm and mouthed over the deafening din, "How did you know?"

He shrugged nonchalantly. "Beginner's luck."

Her eyes narrowed. "I don't think so." As things quieted down, Senator Garrett waved his winning ticket. The others were tearing up theirs, except for Jack Bowden, who knew his wife had another winning ticket in her purse but wasn't going to steal the senator's thunder. Instead he squeezed Mildred's arm.

Ralston nodded to David and started to congratulate Jenny's father.

David took the opportunity to lean toward Jenny and ask quietly, "So what did I win?"

"An apology."

He pulled back a little. "You already gave me that."

"Okay. I'll buy you a drink."

"Not good enough."

"Well then. You name the prize."

His eyes danced mischievously. "Dinner with a politician."

CHAPTER 26

The Middleburg Equestrian Club had an understated elegance— old wooden floors, antique furniture, oriental rugs, and cream-colored walls that harmonized with the horse paintings, polo and fox hunt scenes hung along the walls. An air of nostalgia pervaded the place.

"This is the favored country club for the equestrian set," Jenny said, as she led David onto the broad patio. She pointed toward a polo field in the near distance. "Shall we have a drink and watch the match from here?"

David felt that as long as he was with her it wouldn't matter what they did. "Sure," he said.

There were other, mostly older spectators sitting comfortably at the railing of the porch. The younger fans watched from the sidelines up close. David and Jenny found a quiet corner with a view and settled in.

"What would you like to drink?" she asked.

"I think champagne is in order." He signaled to the waiter.

"Don't rub it in," Jenny said. "I still don't know how you managed to pick the winning horse."

David gave her a Cheshire Cat grin as the waiter arrived. He ordered and sat back comfortably. "If you really want to know, I noticed that your horse burned a lot of energy before he got to the gate. What you took for spirit was nervousness."

Jenny looked at him with surprise. "Why didn't you warn me?"

"And miss out on having dinner here with you?"

She blushed and turned away toward the polo field. A rider struck the ball in full tilt with his mallet, sending it careening across the grassy expanse. The other players chased after it, urging their horses on, jostling for advantage. There was something exhilarating about their energetic grace.

Jenny glanced at David. He was watching with mild interest, but there was excitement beneath his placid exterior. "Did you ever play polo?" she asked.

"It wasn't exactly within my budget." His laugh sounded forced.

When the champagne arrived, they remained silent until their waiter opened the bottle and filled their glasses.

Then Jenny offered a toast. "To the winner of the race."

David clinked glasses with her and took a sip, savoring the taste.

Squinting against the rays of the setting sun, she asked, "Can you see the scoreboard?"

He looked toward the field. "It's the last chukka," he said. "So whom do we root for?"

"The blue shirts—John Ralston's team," Jenny said. "He's number four."

"Any relation to the dog food impresario, Ralston Purina?" David quipped.

She frowned. "Not funny!"

A cheer erupted from the small crowd watching the game from the sidelines, echoed by the viewers on the porch.

"Well, he just scored a goal. They've won. It must have been over-time."

"You should get to know John," Jenny said a little defensively. "He could be a big contributor to your campaign."

David slapped his arm. "The mosquitos are coming out. Let's go in to dinner."

He signaled to the waiter to bring the champagne bucket, took Jenny by the elbow and escorted her inside.

As they approached the restaurant entrance, the maitre d' came forward and asked Jenny, "Will Mr. Ralston be joining you?"

"No, it's just the two of us tonight."

Taking two leather-bound menus, he led them to a table. Along the way, several people already eating said hello to Jenny and mentioned they heard that John Ralston had scored the winning goal.

When David and Jenny were seated, David said, "So why has everyone we've met here talked to you about John Ralston?"

"He's been a big supporter of my father's campaigns for years."

"That doesn't explain why they're asking you."

She directed her eyes at the menu and said nonchalantly. "We're dating."

David's heart sank, but he kept his composure. "So, you're an item."

"I'm not sleeping with him, if that's what you're implying."

"I didn't mean to offend. He doesn't look like your type, that's all."

She continued to scan the menu, a bit annoyed. "What does my type look like?"

"Someone who doesn't get a manicure."

Surprised, she looked at him, then at his hands. "You'll have to reconsider that. Every congressman I know gets manicures. You don't even need to leave your office."

"Sorry to disappoint you, but I'm not your typical congressman."

She put the menu down and smiled wryly. "I'll say." Then she added, "I recommend the trout."

When the young man arrived with pad in hand, David said, "We're both having the trout...and balsamic vinaigrette dressing on the salad." He glanced questioningly at Jenny and she nodded her agreement.

When they were alone again, he said casually, "So, what do you do when you don't attend horse races and polo matches?"

She unfolded her napkin and placed it in her lap. "I'm a curator, at the National Gallery."

David was taken aback. "I never would have guessed!"

She looked up, challenging. "Why not?"

A melancholy expression came over him. "Before I became a congressman I was an unsuccessful painter."

Jenny's eyes narrowed, examining him. "Most painters are not a good judge of their own work."

"They were hanging on the walls of a gallery in New York for quite some time and didn't sell." He shrugged dismissively. "That's in my past. I don't paint anymore."

"Maybe you should. Everyone needs art in their lives, whether it's painting, poetry, or music."

The waiter came and served their salads. When he left, she said earnestly, "I'd like to see your work, David."

"Frank Gannovino still has them at his gallery in New York."

Jenny expressed surprise. "That's an excellent gallery. He only carries good artists."

David shrugged. "We're old friends from our days at Yale. I think that may have affected his judgment."

"Seriously, David, I wouldn't be surprised if you're selling yourself short."

He shook his head. "I've moved on. There was a point in my life when I needed art to pull me through, but now I have a job to do in Washington."

"One never loses the need for art. It's an aspect of life that begs fulfillment. Just like nurturing our spiritual side. Without a spiritual side we're not a whole person."

David speared a piece of artichoke heart with his salad fork and held it up. "Right now, this is all the fulfillment I need." He popped it in his mouth.

Jenny watched him thoughtfully. Then she said, "I have a proposition for you. Come visit me at the National Gallery next weekend."

David's fork stopped in mid-air. "What's the catch?"

"You have to do some homework and answer a question. If you could pick one painting in the National Gallery to take home and hang over your fireplace, which would you choose?"

David smiled. "That's not a fair question. What I'd want over my mantel isn't the same thing as what is a great work of art."

"I know. Just come prepared to answer the question."

"Since you're the curator, let me ask you, 'What's yours?'"

"I'll show it to you when you come."

David hesitated, even though he was dying to say Yes. "I spend my weekends with Grant."

She touched his hand. "Bring him with you. We have a program for children every Saturday at ten, introducing them to art. Then one of our instructors has them paint on their own. It gives the parents time to enjoy the museum unencumbered. Grant will like it. While he's having his lesson, we'll answer each other's question."

David smiled. "You've got yourself a date."

CHAPTER 27

The following Saturday morning David and Grant climbed the pale pink marble stairs to the entrance of the National Gallery. Grant made a game of it, jumping up the steps one at a time. Although David had a hard time holding on to his hand, he couldn't help smile at his enthusiasm and determination. When they reached the top, Grant leaned against one of the tall, neoclassical columns, and looked up in amazement at the smooth surface to the curled capital at the top.

"Big, huh? Are you looking forward to art with Miss Garrett?" David asked.

Grant came over to him. "She's nice."

"I think so, too." David looked at his watch. "We're early."

They sat down on the top step next to each other. Grant imitated his father, sitting with his legs apart and his hands clasped together, looking more like a little man than a three-year-old.

As they waited David thought about Jenny's attitude toward her father's colleagues. The intervening week of political infighting over the Veteran's Administration weighed on him. Every day the paralysis caused by small-minded bureaucrats and his callous opponents cost more veterans lives. Seeing Jenny would be a breath of fresh air after enduring the miasma of bloviators who paid lip service to how much they cared about their constituents but used their elected office to amass power and influence. No wonder she disliked politicians. He didn't think much of them either.

Not only that, but the constant pressure of trying to raise funds in order to please the House leadership and prove his commitment, as well as meeting with constituents about matters over which he had little control, ate up the rest of his time.

Grant started to get antsy, but then other children and their parents arrived and occupied his attention. By the time the huge center doors opened, there was a small, impatiently waiting crowd. Grant jumped up and he and David filed into the main entrance with the others.

As they waited to check in, Grant looked up at the dark, marble columns and dome and exclaimed, "Wow!"

When they reached the front of the line where two security guards stood near the admissions desk, Jenny was waiting nearby. She was wearing a simple tan blouse and dark blue skirt, and her hair was pulled back in a ponytail again. She waved and Grant rushed up to her.

"Good morning. Are you ready for some fun?" she asked, smiling.

Grant nodded enthusiastically. Taking him by the hand, she said loud enough for David to hear, "I'm going to meet your father in forty-five minutes in the American Gallery, number sixty-eight."

David was once again surprised by Jenny's unpredictability— treating his significance as incidental to her meeting with his son. He watched their backs as they passed the fountain in the rotunda, Grant pointing at the water, talking animatedly, happy to hold onto her hand.

He felt a pang of regret, witnessing what Darlene had missed, and he imagined for a moment that it was her taking Grant on a day's excursion. He looked at his watch. It was ten-fifteen.

David had gone to the National Gallery's website to pick out a painting he liked, but he wasn't happy with his choice. He needed to see it on the wall, not just as an image on a computer. So, he picked up a brochure at the desk and opened it to the floor plan. Then he headed toward the European Gallery in the West Wing, meandering under the vaulted, sky-lit halls and garden courts. Byzantine altarpieces, icons, and jewelry yielded to Dutch masters and other European artists.

When he arrived at gallery fifty-seven, he scanned the Turner marine paintings searching for *Keelmen by Moonlight*, the one he thought had possibilities. When he located it, he marveled at the way Turner used light and vivid color to add mystery to an otherwise commonplace scene, but it didn't feel like the right painting, and it was much too large for a mantle.

On the way to gallery sixty-eight, he looked for another that might work but didn't find any. He was surprised that Jenny had chosen the exhibit of American artists; but when he got there, he spotted a painting that immediately drew him. It was Winslow Homer's *Breezing Up*, which depicted a man sailing a small boat with three boys. The late afternoon light was just right, casting shadows on the sail and the boys relaxing in the natural surroundings. David could almost hear the waves lapping against the hull and the occasional luffing of the wind beating against the sail.

He looked at the man in the red shirt, sitting in the cockpit, working to get the set of the sail just right. He saw himself in the man, imagining how much he loved the sound of the water, wind, and waves. He was there with Grant and his two friends, whiling away the day in contentment, unaware of time. A touch on his arm, Jenny's soft voice and the fragrance of her Chanel perfume brought him back to the present. "I thought you might pick that one."

David kept his eyes on the painting, wondering at her ability to read him so well. Was he that predictable? "And why would I do that?" he asked.

"I had a hunch it would make you feel something, and it does—you are there, in the painting, sailing with them, aren't you? It's a great work of art."

Amazed, he turned to her. "How much will you take for it?"

Jenny smiled. "Sorry, it's not for sale."

"So which one is your choice?"

"Follow me," she said.

She led him through the rotunda, explaining that each gallery was furnished to represent the artists' eras. When they arrived at the French galleries, Jenny stopped in the archway that led into the room and fastened a rope cordon behind them to close off the gallery for private viewing. Then she took his hand and led him to a large painting above a Louis the Fourteenth fireplace on the far wall. The painting showed a young girl sitting next to her grandfather in his fishing dory, both her hands on the oar. The elderly fisherman with his pipe in his mouth and a foul weather hat on his head looked down at her tenderly, his big, worn hands pulling on the end of the oar. Her eyes were focused straight ahead, lost in a dream of her own. He squinted at the engraved metal plate below it: *The Helping Hand* by Emile Renouf.

Jenny still held David's hand as if to bring him into the painting with her so he could feel what she felt. It took time for her to break the silence. At last, she said, "It just came in on loan. I grew up seeing it at the Corcoran and had it hung here where I can look at it every day for as long as it stays with us." Her eyes went from the painting to him and she said, "I know you understand, because I saw you looking at the Winslow Homer in the same way."

He nodded. "Yes."

She took a deep breath. "There is something special about visual art that goes beyond words and takes place inside of us. It is like love, David, and you have the ability to convey it, to do what these artists have done."

He shook his head skeptically. "I wish I could believe that."

Jenny went on firmly. "Frank e-mailed me your portfolio, and even from looking at your paintings on the computer I know how good your work is. If you studied under the right people, you could become a successful artist. Talent is innate. You either have it or you don't. You have it, because the person looking at it feels something beyond just the picture. That's why the Impressionists are so loved. All the great artists can do that."

David gave a self-deprecating laugh. "Jenny, I'll never be a great artist."

"That's not for you to decide. History does that. What matters is that a painting never dies. We can never forget Renoir, or Turner, or Rembrandt, or composers like Beethoven or Chopin, for that matter. Great artists, painters and musicians never die." She became increasingly passionate. "It is something spiritual, David. You can't throw that away. It's too important."

He moved to a bench in the middle of the room and sat down. Running one hand through his hair, he looked up at her. "Jenny. You have to understand something. I made a decision. I'm a politician now. I deal with what's possible in the here and now. Frank gave me the same lecture, but I don't care what may happen after I'm gone. What matters to me is what I can do now. I believe I can make a difference."

A melancholy smile crossed her face. "I wish that were true, David, but you can't. It's a rigged system."

They stared at each other, no longer knowing what to say until a voice called from the entrance to the gallery. "Miss Garrett, Grant Madison has something to show you."

A young woman stood behind the rope cordon with Grant, who was holding a large piece of paper. His head barely reached over the velvet barrier.

"Thank you, Sandra, I'll take him now," Jenny went over to Grant, removed the cordon and knelt down in front of him. "Can I see your painting?"

"Sure." He turned the mat paper around.

She looked at the painting of a smiling woman and put her arms around him. The caption said, "Jenny."

❧

129

They walked through the gallery back to the entrance hall, Grant between them, Jenny holding one of his hands and David the other. When they reached the steps outside facing the Mall, Jenny knelt down and gave Grant a goodbye hug, then squeezed David's hand.

Grant pulled at his father's jacket. "Are we going to see Jenny next weekend?"

Jenny and David exchanged glances. For his benefit, she said to Grant, "I hope so."

She watched them descend the steps. Grant stopped halfway down to look back and wave. Jenny waved back.

When he and David were out of sight, she returned to the French Gallery and sat down on the bench facing Renouf's *The Helping Hand*. She was glad David liked the painting. She knew many art historians and critics considered it a sentimental work by a minor painter who was out of step with the Impressionist Movement of his time. But she had encountered it at a seminal moment in her life, when her mother, who loved art, had first taken her to the Corcoran Gallery.

The little girl with the intent, deadpan eyes staring straight ahead touched something deep inside Jenny. Looking like her twin sister, she seemed to know exactly how Jenny felt—unwanted and forlorn. The old fisherman's expression of tender love for his granddaughter moved her to tears.

Her father had never looked at her that way. He had married her mother when she became pregnant after a fling. There was no love between them, and their relationship swerved from hurtful arguments to silence and glacial indifference. As Jenny grew up, she felt that her father didn't love her and came to believe that he thought of both her and her mother as a mistake.

Then came the accident in which her mother died. Her father, who had been drunk at the wheel and swerved off the forested road when a deer jumped in front of the car, survived the crash unscathed. When the party bosses and other fixers covered up his part in the accident—it was in the middle of a hotly contested election—the resulting sympathy vote propelled him to victory.

Remarkably, it changed him. Whether it was feelings of guilt or genuine remorse Jenny did not know, but the senator took a greater interest in her while pursuing his career with passion. Although there was nothing he could do to bring her mother back, he did his best to make up for it. He sold the mansion in Bethesda and bought the farm in Middleburg, hoping that the horses and countryside would have a healing effect. While he never remarried, he continued to have liaisons and affairs of various duration, but Jenny became his icon of virtue and center of attention. They eventually reconciled, but an undercurrent of resentment on Jenny's part remained. She had never completely forgiven him.

In time, the painting became her touchstone for her romantic relationships. Jenny suffered her share of dreadful dates, but a few men held out the promise represented by the fisherman. In the end, most turned out to be as self-centered and success-oriented as her father and his political friends. None had come close to reaching the impassive little girl she still carried inside or could make her smile.

CHAPTER 28

Bradley Coyle and Stephanie Jordan were relaxing in bed in her luxury apartment on the eighth floor of a new condo building in Alexandria. He had a blissful smile on his face, like the proverbial cat that ate the canary. Stephanie was going to tease him about it when the doorbell chimed.

Untangling herself from the sheets, she said, "I'll be back in a minute. It's probably a messenger with details for Monday's program." Bradley watched her slip into a white silk robe and leave the bedroom. He leaned his head back on the pillow and looked up at the ceiling, breathing in her lingering scent, and reflected on how much pleasure it gave him to exert his powerful will to satisfy this beautiful woman. He would have to tread carefully, though, with what he had in mind.

When she came back she tossed a large, manila colored envelope on a side chair. "It can wait," she said casually. "Do you want a drink?"

"Fix us both one. There is something important I want to discuss." He grabbed the black robe from his side of the bed and followed her into the living room. It was newly furnished and its decor was minimalist, monochromatic contemporary—glass, stainless steel and white walls. The non-objective paintings provided the only touch of color.

She mixed martinis in a cocktail shaker and poured the contents into two iced glasses, dropping an olive in each with a practiced flick of the wrist. Handing him one, she asked, "So, what is it?"

He sat on the leather sofa, took a sip, and smacked his lips in satisfaction. "If only Helen could fix a martini like this."

"If you divorce her, you'd have one every night."

He patted the cushion next to him. "That's what I want to talk to you about."

She held her breath and tried to conceal a smile of anticipation but couldn't quite manage it. Sitting down, she said, "I'm all ears."

Bradley looked at her expectant eyes, paused dramatically, and said, "I'm going to run for president. Harry Morgan asked me to yesterday morning."

A moment of shock registered on her face, followed by a welter of emotions.

"You didn't expect that, did you?" he said, smiling.

Stephanie took a deep breath. "I expected something else."

"What?"

"That you were going to divorce Helen."

Bradley knew that would be her reaction. "I will eventually, but I need to win the election first," he said, seriously. When she did not respond, he continued, "I can't run while I'm getting a divorce, you know that. Besides, her money.... But after my inauguration, you'll be sleeping in the Lincoln bedroom until we get married. Imagine, the first wedding of a president in the White House since Grover Cleveland."

Her demeanor cooled considerably. "Is that a promise?"

"You bet it's a promise," he said eagerly. "You're my partner. We're going to win this election together, and then we'll drink martinis and you massage my neck and shoulders in the Oval Office." He gave her the broad smile of a practiced politician.

She stood up and walked over to the sliding glass door of the balcony and looked out toward the old town and the Potomac. After a moment she turned abruptly and faced him. "You really think you can do it, don't you?"

"Yes, I do. But I need your help."

She went back over to him and sat on his lap. Her robe fell open as she looked into his eyes. "Where do we start?"

He reached inside her robe around her naked back, pulled her toward him, and kissed her. "Right here."

Stephanie pushed him back. She drew her robe closed and fastened the belt tightly. "Bradley, I need to know if you're really serious."

"Let me tell you how serious I am." He looked at his watch. "The Senate Majority Leader will be here in a half-hour."

She jumped up as if stung. "Harry Morgan? Here? In my apartment?"

"Yes. He knows about us. I told him," he said deliberately, letting his statement sink in. "Without the Majority Leader, we can't win, but with him, we're assured of it."

"This is getting too personal. I don't want him here."

"That's the point, darling, it's going to get personal whether we like it or not."

"What are you driving at?"

"We start with David Madison. We have to diffuse what he knows about us. I'm not going to make the same mistake a second time. Harry Morgan will become your escort to social functions in D. C. Simply put, you two will become an item."

"At his age?! You've got to be kidding me!"

Bradley smiled at her outburst. "Precisely. Since his wife died two years ago, he's been a zero on the social scene. He'd like nothing better than to be seen with you. It'll restore his reputation. When I'm elected, he'll be the most eligible bachelor in D.C."

When she looked at him dubiously, he continued, "I'll take Helen to the same parties. He'll serve as a cover for our relationship, and being openly seen together with you will diffuse any claim that Madison might make. It would look like he was attempting to smear not only me, but Harry."

Stephanie stood there in silence thinking, squeezing the collar of her robe together at the neck. It made sense in a twisted, devious way. "Just one thing, Brad," she cautioned. "He keeps his hands to himself. Make sure he understands that."

"He wouldn't dare."

"If he does, I'll blow this thing apart, and don't think I won't."

Bradley raised his hands in surrender. "You can tell him yourself. The reason he's coming over is to familiarize himself with your part in this and to set out the terms and boundaries, so we're all clear about the arrangement."

Since Stephanie still seemed uncertain, he quickly added, "Look, there's more in it for you. You get exclusive interviews. You compile a book and we'll work on it together. Just leave out the parts about my prowess in bed."

When he saw a small grin appear at the corners of her mouth, he knew he'd won. "You'll become the talk of the town, honey, I promise you."

She came to him and laid her hand on his cheek. "There's only one promise I'm interested in, and I'm going to hold you to it."

Her piercing blue eyes said it better than words.

CHAPTER 29

David and Jenny were out riding with other equestrian friends gathered for their Saturday morning outing. David had been a little worried about their conversation at the National Gallery the weekend before. He was pleased to see the familiar twinkle in her eyes.

Red was frisky and David reigned him in, then touched his heels against him and broke into a trot next to Jenny.

"I'm glad you brought Grant. The Senator enjoys spending time with him, and Red's glad you came back to ride him again," she said.

"He's not the only one I came back for." He glanced to see if Jenny would take the bait, but she looked straight ahead and kicked her horse into a canter away from the others.

David and Red matched her pace as she led them through a winding riding trail that opened up to a meadow. They stopped and enjoyed the view. Except for the occasional call of a whippoorwill, the only sound was the creaking of leather as they shifted in their saddles.

Jenny took a deep breath and smelled the new-mown hay. "This is my favorite time of year, David," she said dreamily.

He studied her tranquil profile, her back erect—she could have graced the cover of any equestrian magazine. She wore a chocolate brown scarf at her neck that matched her helmet, riding boots, and the coat of Fanny May. Beige jodhpurs, and a crisp white blouse completed the ensemble that together with her alluring figure gave her a tempting sexiness. "You love this place, don't you?" he said quietly.

She hesitated, then said, "The Senator bought it when my mother died and he sold the house in Bethesda. I guess he thought we needed a change. I'd been riding for some time, and it was something we could do together. Before then I hardly knew him."

"How come you always refer to him as 'the Senator?' I've never heard you call him 'Father,' or 'Dad.'"

She leaned forward, turning Fanny's head. "Because that's who he is—a politician first and foremost," she said in a serious tone. Then her demeanor abruptly became light-hearted again. "Want to race to the pond?" she challenged.

"That depends."

"On what?"

"Whether we settle on the bet first or after."

She laughed. "After. It's more fun that way."

"Okay," he agreed casually. "But it could be dangerous...if you lose."

"I always expect to win, don't you?"

"No. Only if I've sized up my competition wisely."

"Good luck with that."

"We'll see."

They kicked their horses at the same time and bolted down the trail with Jenny in the lead. She took a jump over a log lying across the trail and looked back over her shoulder to see David clear it easily and in perfect form. She came to a fork and took the path that led to a field and raced across the green grass, as David did the same. Clearing a fence, she picked up a trail through the trees with David still close behind. She felt a recklessness and exhilaration that she hadn't experienced for a long time. As Fanny's head worked back and forth, mane flying, Jenny whispered, "Come on, Honey, we'll show 'em."

They galloped through a curve in the trail, over a narrow stream, and uphill to a flat, where Jenny went full out and pulled further ahead. Another fork led to a medium-height hedge and she jumped it easily. As she raced on, she heard a shout behind her, but paid no attention. It was an almost straight run to the pond and she let Fanny have her head, feeling the exhilaration again. Reaching the water's edge, she experienced a rush of adrenalin. She was so far ahead that David and Red weren't even in sight. She patted Fanny's neck and waited for them to catch up.

When they didn't show and there was no sound of hoofbeats, she became apprehensive. Then Red came trotting toward them, his saddle empty, and panic seized her. She turned Fanny's head and galloped back toward the last jump, praying under her breath that David was all right. Coming up to the hedge, she saw him lying on the ground, motionless. She swung her right leg over Fanny's neck while they were still moving forward, slipping her left foot from the stirrup. The momentum carried her forward as she ran to David's side.

His eyes were closed, but his chest rose and fell. "David!" she shouted, kneeling beside him. "David!"

His eyes fluttered open and looked up at her woozily.

"Can you move your legs?" Jenny said, catching her breath and trembling. She looked down at them as he wiggled them slightly. Relieved, she said, "Can you move your arms?"

He lifted them, then reached up around her neck and pulled her toward him.

Surprised, Jenny yielded, but when she saw him grinning, she struck her fist against his chest. "You beast!"

But David refused to let her go. At first, she resisted as her arms started shaking. She fought him for a moment, then dropped down on his chest. His arms enveloped her tightly to calm her, his warmth beginning to absorb her shivering. She clung to him and they stayed that way until her trembling stopped. Then he kissed her. When she pulled back there was a wildness in her eyes. She felt as reckless as during the race, dropped back down, and kissed him, pressing herself against him as he stroked her back. He slipped off her helmet and ran his fingers through her hair.

They lay entwined on the ground without saying a word for some time. At last, she pulled away, and sat upright. "Did you really fall off?"

David smiled as he stretched out, crossing his legs at his ankles. "You'll never know."

"I think I already do," she said, with mock indignation. "And here's something you should know." She smiled triumphantly. "I won the race."

"You mean you finished the race before you came back for me?" He feigned surprise.

"Of course."

He laughed. "So what do I owe you?"

She stretched out her arms and grasped his free hand, pulling him up. "You've already paid."

He smiled, thinking it was the kiss. He didn't realize it was his advice she referred to—to size up a person wisely before you bet.

CHAPTER 30

Katherine worked her way through the crowd of television crews milling in the hallway, anticipating the end of the committee meeting on Veterans Affairs. *Good, the hearing is still in session*, she thought. She didn't want to miss David's entire presentation. Not that she needed to hear it since she knew it by heart. He'd worked on it all week, prepping with her during the days and on his own at home at night, and on the weekend, taking time off only to be with his son. She slipped inside the door and joined the overflow of reporters standing jammed at the back of the room.

David was speaking, holding up a chart and pointed at it. "In the past three years the VA has had more whistle-blower cases filed against it than any other department of the Federal Government, almost sixty per-cent more than the Defense Department, and more than Defense, Homeland Security, and DOJ combined!"

There were murmurs from the assembled crowd, causing Chairman Smithson to pound his gavel repeatedly.

David used the opportunity to drop the chart and pick up a report. When the room quieted, he waved it dramatically and continued, "This GAO Report concludes that the VA's restructuring has moved resources around but, other than reducing wait times for veterans to see doctors, achieved little to improve their actual health care."

He let the booklet drop on the table with a thud as his voice rose. "It is unconscionable that the VA has done nothing substantial to address the serious problems our veterans face. Apparently, they are beyond its capability or desire to fix."

A hush fell over the gallery at the audacity of the young congressman.

Turning to Chairman Smithson, David finished, "Therefore, Mister Chairman, I now formally move that the matter be referred to the Health Subcommittee to recommend alternatives, including the appointment of a commission to determine specific programs that work. That is the only way to achieve true accountability and deliver the health care our veterans deserve."

A buzz went through the room as Congressman Faulk of Utah seconded the motion.

Smithson gaveled for order. "We have a motion and a second. Is there any discussion?" He scanned the faces of the committee members. "The chair recognizes the congressman from Colorado."

Stan Forsman, the ranking minority member, cleared his throat to conceal his irritation. "As you all know, my state is the home of the Air Force Academy, and there is no one more concerned about our veterans that I am. However," he leaned closer to the microphone, "I am adamantly—adamantly—opposed to a measure that will cause more chaos than good for our veterans and perpetrate further delays."

Representative Faulk raised a finger and, when recognized, said, "We need to provide our veterans with as good a medical program as we have as congressmen. Veterans should not continue dying at the present rate. We need to examine this with experts and make a determination based on the facts as quickly as possible."

Chairman Smithson tapped his gavel and looked at his watch. "I think that everyone has determined how they view this issue, and we will now vote on the motion on the floor." He scanned the faces around the table. "So, without objection—all those in favor?... Opposed?" Only three hands went up against. "The motion is carried. If you would like to sit on the subcommittee, please so inform me, and the subcommittee will meet after the summer recess." He tapped the gavel one last time. "This meeting is now adjourned."

David started to get up when a hand touched his shoulder from behind him and he turned. "Katherine, when did you come in?"

She smiled proudly. "Just in time to hear your last comments and the motion. I am so proud of you."

David took a deep breath. "I'm just glad we got it done! Now we'll really have to get to work."

As he stuffed his papers into his briefcase, Chairman Smithson came over and put a hand on his arm. "Well done." Then he winked at Katherine. "I'll handle the wolves outside the door."

She nodded to him. After he left, she indicated the private exit to David. "We better go out that way. There's a crowd of reporters out front, and you don't want to steal Smithson's thunder."

When they got there, Congressman Faulk intercepted them and offered his hand to David. "Well done, my friend. You've saved us a lot of work."

David shook it. "Anytime, but it's just the beginning..."

When a reporter approached, David and Katherine ducked into the hallway.

"Don't forget to enjoy the moment," she said.

Without breaking stride, he replied, "I won't, but seriously, here's what we need to do next. I want the names of every organization that has programs supporting our veterans, NGOs, foundations, private programs, whatever you can find. We need to select the ones that have the best programs in place and figure out why they work when others don't. I want this information to go to the new subcommittee."

She stopped and looked at him in amusement. "Anything else?"

"Isn't that enough for now?"

She took his arm. "Let's have dinner tonight and celebrate. Just the two of us. I'll cook."

David hesitated. "Not tonight. Another time. I'm pretty fried and want to rest and take it easy."

Katherine was surprised. "Since when did you ever want to take it easy?"

David looked down, avoiding her eyes. "Just tonight, okay?"

Katherine decided to be magnanimous. "Of course, David, I understand."

❧

When David got home to his apartment in the Georgetown waterfront complex, he called Jenny.

Had she been able to see through the phone, she would have been surprised by the sterile, contemporary interior of his studio apartment which revealed nothing about him. There were no pictures or paintings on the wall. A shelf held a few books, mostly dealing with politics, and a stereo sat on a glass side table with CDs stacked neatly underneath. The glass-topped desk resting on two black pedestals was neat and bare. Two nondescript overstuffed chairs sat in a bay window, and an opened Murphy bed temporarily trespassed into the living room space. The small kitchenette along one of the walls looked as unused as the ones in hotel rooms, although there was a coffee maker whose glass decanter was a quarter full. It was a place to sleep, nothing more. Even the usual pied-á-terre would have reflected something of the owner's taste and personality.

"So how was your day?" Jenny asked cheerfully.

"Major win. We got the veterans issue referred to the subcommittee that will enable us to recommend the appointment of a commission. If it all goes smoothly, we could have a report by the end of the year."

"That's great, David!"

"Thanks. We go into summer recess soon, and I have to spend the month in my constituency. The Langleys have their house back for the summer in New Haven, and Grant and I will be there until Labor Day. Can I see you before we leave?"

"I wish I could, but I'm off to Rome, Paris, London, and other European cities to finalize loans of paintings for a new special exhibition we're mounting on Western Art. I leave tomorrow."

"That soon?" His voice revealed his disappointment. "How long will you be gone?"

"At least a month. I have to visit a number of museums."

"Then you'll miss Grant's fourth birthday."

She responded, instantly distressed, "Oh, David. What shall I do?"

He decided to let her off the hook. "Why don't you send him a postcard from Paris, wishing him 'Happy Birthday' in French."

"Will that be enough?" she asked uncertainly.

"Sure it will. And send me a postcard from Rome."

"I'll miss you," she said softly. "I'll call you when I get back."

"Ciao, then. Don't forget the postcards."

Jenny laughed. "Ciao."

CHAPTER 31

It turned out to be an enjoyable summer break. The Langleys had returned to their New Haven home while the professor who leased it went back to London with his family, until his return at the end of August. Edward Langley never seemed to tire of Grant's curiosity, marveling at his rapid physical and mental development.

The Sullivans were there and they spent many an evening visiting or dining together, having cook-outs in the backyard. Nancy treasured her time with Grant, a substitute for the child that they couldn't have, and Jack became Uncle Jack. They took Grant to day camp to involve him with other children, which allowed David some time to relax on his own.

During the first week, in the quiet, warm afternoons, David would walk along the rocks at the water's edge of Granite Bay, recalling his days sailing from the Yale Corinthian Yacht Club and swimming at the adjacent beach with Katherine. They'd sail from the boathouse out of the cove toward Green Island and into the Sound. Watching the sailboats reminded him of Jenny and the Winslow Homer painting *Breezing Up* they had looked at together at the National Gallery. He wished he were in Europe with her.

When Katherine came up at the beginning of the second week, she talked David into holding a series of town hall meetings. He soon found out what a diverse district he represented. In New Haven and the surrounding towns—Hamden, East Haven and West Haven— the wealth and privilege of Yale University existed side by side with old ethnic neighborhoods, middle-class enclaves, and ghettos rife with poverty, gangs and crime. The small towns of Wallingford, Cheshire, Prospect, and Bethany, nestled among rural farms and mountains, had seen better times. Middletown on the Connecticut River with Wesleyan University, and apple orchards and dairy farms in the rural areas to the west, were also beautiful and economically depressed. And finally, Branford and Guilford, both upper-middle-class suburbs, though not as wealthy as Greenwich, Westport and Fairfield, offered scenic shorelines on the Long Island Sound and a modicum of financial stability.

In the town hall meetings, David took a different approach than during his campaign. He let his constituents do most of the talking while he did the listening. He expected them to express their anger about Washington's lack of interest in their concerns, their difficulties to make ends meet, their anxieties about the future—and they did. What surprised him was their passion, pride, and determination not to give up, and their love for their state and country. He saw great potential for positive results if he could appeal to them directly while working with the local politicians to define and achieve the changes needed. The people who attended the meetings appreciated that David came to see them with an open mind. When Coyle was their representative, they were lucky to catch a glimpse of him during his brief campaign stops in their communities.

David quickly realized that Katherine's political instincts dovetailed well with his ability to develop rapport with his constituents. He began relying more on her as she turned the tedium of Washington politics into opportunities to connect with the people who had voted for him. In the process, their relationship of mutual respect developed into mutual appreciation, and David realized how much he depended on her. The town halls always energized him, and afterward he and Katherine spent hours talking to his constituents one on one and building political relationships.

On several occasions when they returned to New Haven, Katherine stayed on for a day or two to relax. They spent time with

Grant at the beach and took him sailing on the Long Island Sound. It was a reprieve from politics for both of them.

At times Katherine flashed back to their Yale days and began to feel the old desire for David more intensely. Grant should have been her child. As she held her hands on his and trimmed the sails, she tried to pretend that he was. She told him how the wind made the boat move forward as it filled the sails while David manned the tiller and watched them together. Grant looked cute in his little red life vest as he sat pressed against Katherine and, for the first time in his life, David felt like he had a little family.

On one of their excursions as he maneuvered the boat through the wind, he called out, "Come about!"

Katherine placed her hand on Grant's head to protect him as the boom came across and said, "Watch your head."

They ducked to move to the other side of the boat, but the boom caught Katherine's shoulder and she slipped. David managed to grab hold of her before she went overboard, pulling her to him. She lay sprawled on top of him, convulsing Grant into a fit of laughter.

Katherine stayed in that position a moment longer, whispering under her breath, "Let's do that again."

When Grant continued giggling, she turned to him. "Now that, young man, is why I said, 'Watch your head.'"

At dinner that evening, Grant told the Langley's, Nancy and Jack the story of Aunt Kathy's sailing lesson, culminating in another fit of laughter. Everyone at the table joined in and Katherine, like a good sport, laughed with them.

Laura Langley watched the three of them together and thought of Darlene. What would her marriage to David have been like had she survived? She felt a pang of jealousy. Katherine seemed the woman who was taking David away from her daughter, although she couldn't deny that they seemed to be the perfect political couple. She doubted that Darlene could have been as good a match.

Nancy, who'd become something of a mother hen regarding

Grant, wondered how sincere Katherine's love for him was. But she had to admit that the boy took to her. Children usually sensed when someone wasn't sincere. David looked relaxed and happy, too, more so than she had ever seen him before. She was glad that his life seemed to be working.

That night after Katherine tucked Grant into bed and read him a story, she and David went for a sail alone.

The full moon illuminated a glistening path along the water from the bow of their boat to the shoreline.

"It's beautiful," Katherine said. She moved over and lay next to him on the cushions as he guided the tiller over his shoulder. "Too bad that I have to go back to Washington tomorrow. I wish we could just stay here like this all night."

"Well, your flight doesn't leave until nine tomorrow." He sensed her shiver. "Cold?"

"A little."

Reaching over her, David opened a seat locker and pulled out a blanket. She snuggled up next to him and he spread the blanket over both of them. Then she put her leg over his and an arm across his chest, leaned her head against his shoulder and closed her eyes.

After a few moments he said, "It's been a wonderful time, Kathy. I never dreamed that holding town hall meetings and getting to know the people like we have, could actually be fun. It was a brilliant idea."

"Shhh. Just listen to the waves slapping against the hull."

"I just wanted to tell you how grateful –"

"Shhh. Listen."

The waves, lapping against the boat in a seductive rhythm, and the warmth of their nestling bodies lulled them into an amorous trance. Katherine slipped her fingers into his open shirt and tousled the hair on his chest.

Almost in a whisper she said, "This means more to me that anything you can say."

CHAPTER 32

David returned with Grant to Washington from the August recess just before the Labor Day weekend. The Langleys had preceded them by a week and a half because the professor who rented their house wanted to get settled in with his family before the start of the fall semester. Nancy and her husband had been kind enough to help with childcare, giving David some time to himself while allowing him to spend the rest of his vacation with Grant.

Father and son had a good time together, looking at the dinosaurs in the Peabody Museum, visiting the Connecticut Children's Museum, and having hamburgers at Louis' Lunch. One day they hiked up East Rock and enjoyed the view of the city. Grant was a trooper, although David had to carry him for the final part on the way down.

The evening before they left, they invited Nancy and Jack out and waited in line to get into Sally's Pizza on Wooster Street.

When Grant got fidgety, Nancy picked him up and said, "It's worth the wait, you'll see."

After they got seated and ordered a "Tomato Pie" with pepperoni and a white clam pizza, David took Grant to the rear of the narrow room with booths on either side of a central aisle and showed him the original, coal-fired, brick oven, still in use after more than eighty years.

Back at the table, Grant sipped on his root beer until the waiter brought them the thin crust, oblong pies on two metal trays.

David sniffed at the clam pizza and said, "I've missed this—the best pizza in the world!"

Grant imitated his father, twitching his nose like a bunny, to the amusement of the others. Suddenly, he said, "I wish Jenny were here."

David felt a pang in his chest and said, "Me too."

Nancy ran interference. "I'd like to meet her sometime," she said and plopped a piece of pizza on Grant's plate. "Careful, it's hot."

David gave her a grateful glance as Grant had his first taste. His eyes lit up as he chewed and swallowed. "Hmm," he announced. "Best pizza in the world," and dug in, earning him approving laughter from nearby patrons.

For David, it was an uncomfortable reminder that he hadn't heard from Jenny in some time. She'd sent Grant a Happy Birthday postcard from Paris of the Eiffel Tower, as promised. He figured another, perhaps of the Colosseum in Rome or of London Bridge, was waiting for him at his apartment in Washington. But when he returned there and sorted through the mail that had piled up in his absence, there was none. He figured she was too busy or had used the opportunity of their time apart to pull back and let their relationship lapse.

Saturday morning, he took Grant to the Langleys in Annapolis and accepted their invitation to join them for a late breakfast.

Laura Langley had just placed a plate of pancakes in front of Grant when David's cell phone rang. Silencing it, he recognized the number. It was the Garrett farm—Jenny!

He excused himself and walked outside onto the front porch. Sitting on the wooden balustrade, he tapped the touchscreen. "Hi," he said in a husky voice.

"Hi!" Jenny sounded cheerful, as if she had never been away. "Did you get my postcard?"

"The one from Paris?" David cleared his throat. "Grant liked the Eiffel Tower."

After a brief silence, Jenny said, "Well?"

"Me, too."

"I'm glad."

Another silence.

Then David asked lightly, "Are you back for good now?"

"I wish. I fly out to Santa Fe Monday, but I'd love to see you and Grant. Can you come to the farm tomorrow?"

David didn't hesitate. "Absolutely. We'll be there by mid-morning!"

"Great! I'll have brunch ready."

There was another awkward moment when both faltered, neither sure how to best end the call.

Finally, Jenny said, "See you then."

"OK."

He broke the connection. "Short and sweet," he thought. But his heart beat a mile a minute.

Driving to Middleburg, both David and Grant became more excited the closer they got to their destination. When they pulled up to the farmhouse, David could see Jenny was at the corral saddling a horse. She looked up at the sound of the Jeep arriving.

He barely managed to say, "There she is," before Grant jumped out and ran to her.

She knelt and hugged him. "Did you have a fun summer?"

"I learned to sail with Aunt Kathy!" he said enthusiastically. Jenny frowned. Who was Aunt Kathy? Was that David's chief of staff? Naturally she would be there.

David walked up and gave her a peck on the cheek which she returned. They looked at each other, unanswered questions passing between them.

"You look well-tanned," she said.

"We had a good time sailing. It was a nice respite in the

Connecticut sun when we weren't holding town hall meetings," David said as he picked up Grant and placed him in the saddle.

He walked next to her as she led Grant's horse by the reins. "How were Rome, Paris and London?"

"Paris has changed. There weren't any artists sitting along the Seine painting anymore, and the love locks on the Paris Bridge have been taken down."

David smirked. "I can understand why. It's not exactly the right setting for contemporary art, and the love locks probably got out of hand."

Jenny pushed him away playfully. "Go talk to Dad. He's waiting for you by the pool, wants to know how things went for you back home. We'll meet you there in a bit." She turned and handed the reins to Grant.

As David walked away she looked over her shoulder at him, thinking how good it felt that they were back together again.

After the riding lesson and brunch, they spent the rest of the afternoon playing with Grant in the pool. Following dinner, they all settled in the library surrounded by leather-bound volumes on dark cherry wood shelves. Senator Garrett read a biography of Daniel Webster. Jenny read to Grant, nestled together in the corner of the sofa. She had her arm around him as he listened attentively to the story about a boy and a special horse, looking at the pictures and turning the pages of the book. David smiled. In the amber lamplight it looked idyllic, like a 19th-century painting come to life.

As the senator began to doze off, David quietly went to his desk, took out a pencil and paper, and began sketching Jenny and Grant. He kept glancing up, trying to capture Jenny's natural sensuality and her empathy for Grant.

After Jenny finished the story, Grant wanted to hear it again, and she complied. Halfway through, he yawned and fell asleep. David set down the nearly finished sketch, went over to the sofa, and gently took Grant from Jenny's arms. "I'll take him upstairs and put him to bed," he whispered. "Don't go away."

When he returned, Jenny stood by a window with her back to him. The senator was getting out of his chair.

"If you two don't mind," he mumbled drowsily, "I think I'll retire and finish this book in bed." He went over to Jenny and kissed her on the cheek. "Good night, my dear." On his way out, he stopped in front of David, placed a hand on his shoulder and said, "He's a mighty good boy."

After he left Jenny turned to David. Her eyes searched his face, mystified.

"What?" he asked.

"I looked at the sketch you made of us. It's lovely."

"I got back into practicing a bit this summer. Some drawings of sailboats on the wind in Granite Bay," David said, self-consciously. "It's not even at the hobby stage."

"I wish you wouldn't sell yourself short," she said. "You know how much I'd love to see you get back to painting." She held up her hand. "But I won't push."

"Thank you," he said. "I guess the August break was relaxing enough, I started to miss it—a little."

"Well, maybe you'll find after a while that being a representative is not so demanding that you can't do both."

David stood before her, a bit awkwardly. "Maybe."

Jenny took his hand. "How about some fresh air?"

They walked out the French doors, down the porch steps away from the brightly lit house. The full moon cast a soft, ethereal light on the trail ahead as they passed the stables. Jenny gave an involuntary shudder.

"Afraid of werewolves?" David asked jokingly.

"Only wolves on two legs."

"Then I assure you that you are safe in present company."

"How disappointing," she said coyly and pointed ahead to where a log lay across the trail. "That's where you fell off your horse."

He laughed. "I didn't fall off, I vaulted off."

"You deceived me."

"I bet you're just as capable of deception."

She tilted her head at him. "Haven't you lost enough times to give up wagering against me?"

"It depends on the prize."

"Oh no!" But there was laughter in her protest, and she gave him a sidelong glance. "I don't trust you."

"What if the prize were a painting by David Madison?"

Jenny stopped, suddenly serious. "David! I don't want you to kid me about this. Does this all mean that you'll start painting again?"

"It depends on whether you win or not."

She eyed him suspiciously. "What's the wager?"

David looked around as they approached the pond. Then he pointed toward the raft in the center. "I bet you can't beat me to it." She gave him another suspicious look. "Why not? But we didn't bring our bathing suits."

"I've always wanted to go skinny dipping in the moonlight," he challenged, grinning.

"I haven't...but I'm game." She motioned with her hand for him to turn around. "I'll tell you when I'm in the water."

He waited a moment until he heard a splash, then stripped and waded in. The bottom of the pond felt soft and mushy and he leaped forward and started to swim toward Jenny treading water.

As he got within several lengths of her, she yelled, "Go!" and took off.

He swam behind her watching the moonlight reflecting off her shining hair and arms as they came smoothly out of the water with each stroke. He started to catch up but stayed close behind her until she reached the ladder just ahead of him.

When she climbed up onto the raft, her panties and halter were dripping wet.

"Why you deceptive little cheater," David called out in mock indignation.

She ran her hands over her wet hair and wiped her face. "So, what are you going to paint?"

"You," he laughed. "In the moonlight—but without a stitch of clothes."

"Ha! Fat chance."

"I have an excellent imagination." He swam under the raft and hovered in the air pocket under the wooden planks, treading water and keeping still.

Jenny waited. She could hear his breathing. "David?"

"Yes?" his voice echoed off the metal barrels.

"I'm coming in."

Moments later the raft shifted as she climbed down the ladder. Her face and glistening hair appeared between the drums, haloed by the moonlight.

"Now, about the Madison painting," she said, mischievously.

Then she wrapped her arms around his neck and pulled him against her body. The water from her hair dripped onto their faces as his arms enfolded her and they kissed.

Jenny was in her office late the next day after the National Gallery had closed, getting ready for her flight to Santa Fe the next morning. She was dawdling and she knew it, but her thoughts kept drifting to the previous day and evening—Grant, the sketch, David, the kiss, their bodies wrapped around one another in the water.

When the phone rang she was still thinking about him and answered cheerfully, "Jenny Garrett."

The receptionist's voice announced, "Allyn van Arsdale for you on line three, Miss Garrett."

Surprised, Jenny's eyes darted from the flashing button on the telephone console to one of the pictures on her credenza. It showed two young women on horseback smiling broadly, holding their ribbons. They were dressed exactly the same—black velvet jackets and boots, white jodhpurs, and white blouses with crossed ties at the neck. With their black felt helmets tucked under their arms and brunette hair pulled back in a bun, they looked like twin sisters.

"Thank you, I'll take it," Jenny said.

They had met at Smith College and become fast friends. They both had lost their mother at an early age, Allyn because of an acrimonious divorce and Jenny because of the fatal car accident. Considering their fathers' backgrounds and personalities, they had made a pact that they would not marry a doctor or a politician. Allyn was the first to break their agreement, marrying an orthopedist from a well-to-do family. They had two young daughters and what seemed like a storybook marriage. But then things went sour.

Sighing, Jenny pushed the flashing button, making the connection. "Hi Allyn," she said with more cheer than she felt.

There was a momentary silence, then, "Jenny?"

Her friend sounded upset. "Sorry, I was distracted for a moment. How are the girls?"

"Anxious to see you," Allyn said, unable to hide her distress.

"Then it must be Jim. Did you patch things up?"

Allyn didn't answer but Jenny could hear her sniffling.

"What's happened?" she said softly.

"I'm filing for divorce," Allyn blurted out.

"I thought you were still in counseling. Did Jim...?"

"Yes. He's having another affair, despite his promise of fidelity. I've done everything to save this marriage, but it's no use. Men are such liars and bastards," Allyn went on, her voice dripping with bitterness.

"Some men," Jenny said gently.

"Show me one who isn't!" Allyn had her back up.

"John Ralston."

"Then why didn't you marry him?"

"Because I didn't love him."

After a brief pause, Allyn said, "I should never have broken our pact."

"C'mon, Allyn. We were young girls then, and plenty foolish."

"But we were right!" She sighed. "Oh, Jen, it's so humiliating."

"I understand how you feel, but you know that's nonsense."

"Yes, but I can't seem to help myself."

Jenny tried to reassure her. "It'll take time, but you will get your confidence back. Remember, you are a beautiful woman." When Allyn started to protest, she added, "I would hate for people to stop mistaking us for sisters!"

Allyn started to chuckle in spite of herself. "And here I was hoping you'd commiserate with me."

"If that were the case, you wouldn't have called me," Jenny said judiciously.

"You're right!" Allyn expelled a heavy breath. Then she asked, "So who are you dating?"

The sudden turn caught Jenny by surprise. "Uh...no one in particular."

"It's been more than two years since you broke off your engagement. How much longer are you going to act like a wallflower?"

"Let's not make this about me. Tell me about the girls."

For the next ten minutes they chatted. Jenny was pleased that by the time they ended the call, Allyn was laughing and sounded like she was back on firmer emotional ground. But after she hung up, Jenny realized that the conversation had left her at sea about David Madison. Although she found him maddeningly attractive and admired many of his qualities, including his artistic sensibility, she didn't know all that much about him. If she pursued a more serious relationship with him, would she end up feeling disappointed and betrayed like her best friend? Maybe there was more to their youthful pact than she thought.

CHAPTER 33

After his return to Washington, David was chagrined with the lack of progress he made with the Veteran's issue. Lengthy budget negotiations that ended in deadlock forced continuing resolutions to fund the government because no one wanted to take responsibility for shutting it down. An ongoing investigation in both the Senate and the House into misspending billions of dollars by the Defense Department captured national attention and preoccupied many of his colleagues. With both parties grandstanding and blaming one another, the legislative wheels came to a grinding halt for some time, frustrating David further.

It was mid-November before Congressman Hunter as subcommittee chairman, under pressure from Congressman Smithson, was able to put the subcommittee hearing on the docket.

Katherine slipped into the subcommittee hearing room and sat in back behind a reporter from the Washington Record. She tapped him on the shoulder. "Ted, I heard raised voices from the outside. What have I missed?"

Ted Fullerton leaned back and whispered over his shoulder, "Stanley Forsman has been fencing with David Madison for the last half hour. Forsman's been interrupting Madison's questioning and David's having no part of it. The chairman keeps gaveling Forsman out of order."

Katherine craned to see the witness. From where she sat, she could make out the barest hint of a profile. But the close-cropped hair, dark complexion, and crisp marine uniform suggested it was

Lance Donovan, and his deep, resonant voice clinched it. Here in the committee room, it sounded even more commanding than in the two conversations she had with him on the telephone about his program for veterans in Chicago. He was working with 60 ex-military men and women and 200 street gang members to address the rising murder rate in the city—the highest in the country—as well as deal with post-traumatic stress. Rebuilding derelict houses in the ghettos with the veterans and youths working side by side gave both groups a purpose and resulted in remarkable changes in behavior and attitude. She had been impressed both with the project and his ability to articulate its practices and goals, and had recommended him to David immediately. She was looking forward to meeting him in person.

David said, "You have told us a powerful story of recovery and change, Mr. Donovan, and I commend you for the results you have achieved."

"It is just the beginning, Congressman. We hope to expand and serve more people in need."

David smiled and continued, "I'm sure you will. Have you ever contacted the VA with information about your project?"

"Yes, on several occasions."

"And what did they tell you?"

"We never got a hearing. It wasn't until your office phoned me that I was given an opportunity to speak about it."

Stanley Forsman, looking disdainfully at the black man over his reading glasses, interjected, "Mister Donovan, are you a personal friend of Congressman Madison?"

If Donavan was surprised at the interruption, he didn't let it show. "Yes. I served with him for a time in Iraq."

"I see," Forsman, said smirking. "Well, that clarifies things."

Murmurs of confusion rippled through the committee meeting room. Katherine was puzzled, too. What was Forsman after? She scanned the audience to see the reactions. Some of the reporters took it in stride, as if it was just more of the same bickering. Many faces seemed nonplussed.

David's voice brought her attention back to the committee table. "Before we go on," he said, "I want to make clear that there is nothing sinister in my having served with Mister Donovan and his appearing here. When we did an extensive search for organizations that are actively working with veterans who suffer from PTSD, his program came highly recommended, with personal references of support from a number of veterans' groups and the city's mayor."

"That remains to be seen," Forsman retorted and Chairman Hunter slammed his gavel down with a piercing smack. His annoyance was evident. "The guests we have invited have graciously offered to come to Washington to testify, and they should not be subjected to discourtesies."

"Then proceed," Forsman said, with a smug expression on his face.

Congressman Jenkins seated next to the chairman leaned over to him and spoke in his ear. Chairman Hunter nodded and turned to the witnesses and spectators. "My colleague reminds me that we have had a full morning and that some of your stomachs, if not your heads, may be grumbling by now." To approving laughter, he continued, "Thank you, Mr. Donovan, for your enlightening testimony." Then he struck his gavel again. "The subcommittee will recess for lunch."

Ted Fullerton stood up and turned toward Katherine. "Any idea what Forsman is doing? Doesn't he know he's making a fool of himself?"

"No, I don't," Katherine said. "It's like he's on a mission to torpedo David, except all his missiles are misfiring."

Bradley Coyle paced in his office like an angry bull looking to gore someone. The large TV monitor on the wall opposite his desk showed the C-SPAN feed of the crowd breaking up in the subcommittee room.

Stephanie Jordan who was seated on the sofa, dressed in a smart gray business suit, shook her head and said, "Forsman certainly didn't make a dent in Madison's reputation with that performance. Next to your rival, he looks and acts like a snotty kid."

"Thank you for stating the obvious. I had no idea he would be so incompetent!"

"I think you're underestimating David Madison," Stephanie suggested.

"No...I overestimated Stanley Forsman." He stopped at his desk and picked up the phone. "Doris, send someone to Forsman's office and have him come to see me—pronto." He slammed down the receiver. "We're going to have to fix this."

"I can't cover that one up."

"Yes, you can. Make it look like Forsman's suggestion about a cozy relationship between Madison and Donovan is a story."

This was one of the moments where Stephanie wished she hadn't given up smoking. "It's a non-story and you know it. Madison refuted it effectively," she insisted. "You're exaggerating this whole episode. Nobody watches C-SPAN. The worst thing you can do is try to turn it into a story."

Bradley rubbed his temple. "So what do you suggest?"

"Stay the course. Forsman bungled this one for himself. Don't help him get out of it. It's his problem. We just keep hammering Madison for just using the vets to get elected. I'll throw it in every time he makes a splash, like tonight. If we say it enough, it will stick."

Bradley smiled for the first time all morning. "You're right."

Stephanie rose and tugged at her skirt. "I'd better leave before Forsman gets here."

As she checked her hair in the mirror near the door Bradley grabbed her from behind and pulled her against him. "I do need you, you know."

She leaned into him and looked at his eyes in the mirror. "How did you mean that? For my body or my brains?"

"Both," he said, smiling.

She pulled away and faced him, pressing a finger to his lips. "And don't you forget it."

When he opened the door for her, Stanley Forsman stood in front of them, poised to knock. The intercom buzzed behind them and Doris' voice announced, 'Congressman Forsman is here."

"Thank you, Senator, for the interview," Stephanie said coolly to Bradley. Then she smiled pleasantly at Forsman. "Nice to see you, Congressman."

As she left, Forsman glanced after her.

Bradley ushered him into his office. He motioned to the empty sofa. "Sit down, Stanley."

Forsman stood his ground. "Look, I've already had one lecture from Hunter, just now. I don't need another, even if I was doing you a favor."

To his surprise, Bradley was all charm. "Just cool it from now on. If you see an opening take it, but don't play the brute. It will get us nowhere."

Feeling somewhat relieved, Forsman tried to change the subject. "What was Jordan doing here?" He motioned with his head toward the door.

"I gave her an interview," Bradley said testily.

"Is that all you gave her?" Forsman said, grinning.

"I didn't call you up here to get a lecture on morality," Bradley said, trying to restrain his anger. "You're the one who screwed up."

Forsman glanced at the TV monitor. The subcommittee room had emptied out. "I think Madison has been coached. I don't see a way I can stop him in the subcommittee."

Bradley went to the window. "Don't worry about it," he said distractedly.

"You aren't worried? I think Madison is onto something big. America loves the vets. They're like Mom and apple pie. And he's beating the drum for how they're being mistreated."

"I said, don't worry about it."

"What are you going to do?"

Bradley grinned, a dangerous flicker in his eyes. "Poison the pie, Congressman. Poison the pie."

CHAPTER 34

David stood in front of the Art Institute on Michigan Avenue in Chicago looking up at one of the two, larger-than-life, bronze lions that guarded the entrance to the museum. They had been there for more than a century. He had spent a stimulating time in the Windy City already with Lance Donovan and he was glad he'd made the unexpected trip.

After the lunch break of the contentious subcommittee hearing, Forsman had been on his best behavior, refraining from any further interruptions. David didn't know why and didn't care. He was just happy to let the various witnesses describe their programs and respond to well-considered questions from the other committee members.

Lance Donovan had stayed in Washington for the duration of the hearings to meet with the other presenters and to catch up with David. The evening together had rekindled their friendship, and when Lance left for Chicago, David decided to join him on the spur of the moment and see his program in action for himself. His staff had been in a tizzy about his sudden change of plans, and Katherine had done her best to talk him out of it, but he'd been adamant.

It was a good decision. The reality was as impressive as Lance's account at the hearing. On Chicago's South Side, David had witnessed veterans and former gang members working side-by-side renovating derelict houses. Much of the building materials was donated by local construction companies. Talking to the vets and gang members and hearing their stories took David back to some of his own experiences in Iraq and allowed him to tap into a part of himself that had lain dormant for some time. Above all, seeing the men and women, most of them black and Latino, excited about their newfound purpose—to be able to serve others in a constructive manner—inspired him to want to see more.

When he had called Katherine and told her he was staying another day, she had protested, "It's a waste of time," and added, "What about Grant?"

David had dealt with her objections firmly. "He'll be fine. I'll be late, but I'll get back for the weekend. I have to do this!"

He was glad he had insisted. By going back and meeting some of the same people again, he gained a better understanding of the difficulties they had to overcome. It gave David a new perspective on what was required to make projects like theirs work. The last thing he wanted to do was to get Congress to authorize funds and watch the program end in failure.

After a final lunch, Lance had dropped David at the Art Institute.

As he started to mount the stone steps to the entrance, he suddenly felt reluctant. He'd concocted the idea of surprising Jenny when he found out she was working in Chicago, but what if she was too busy to see him when he walked in on her unannounced, without an appointment?

Fortunately, when the security guard picked up the phone and checked with the curator's office, it turned out she was in the members' lounge having lunch. The guard handed David a map, pointed straight back past the heavy white marble main stairs, and instructed him where to check his coat and travel bag.

When David reached the museum café and the members' lounge next to it, he spotted Jenny right away. She was seated at a table by a tall window with long, cream-colored, sheer curtains, talking with another woman as they finished lunch. Jenny's white, high-necked blouse and brown slacks contrasted with the other woman, who was more plainly dressed. Jenny's legs were crossed, with her foot behind her calf.

When she reached for her coffee cup, she saw David staring at her. The serious expression on her face immediately vanished, replaced by a sparkle of delight in her eyes. The other woman turned to see the reason for her joy and smiled.

David and Jenny's eyes locked for a moment. Then she looked away and spoke to her lunch partner who quickly finished her coffee. She slipped a notebook into her briefcase, shouldered her purse and after touching Jenny's arm, left.

As Jenny went over to David, he grinned like the fox that had just entered the chicken coop. She kissed his cheek. Her soft hand on the back of his neck sent a shiver of pleasure down his spine.

"Okay, wipe that look off your face," she said. "You surprised me and I'm pleased."

He kissed her cheek in turn. "So am I."

"How long are you here for?"

"Only a few hours. I had a meeting about a veteran's program. I have to get back for the weekend with Grant."

Jenny retrieved her purse and grabbed his hand. "I've been stuck inside here for a week. I need a breath of fresh air. Let's go outside." As they walked through the Impressionist gallery, David touched her arm. "We can't go without looking." He stopped in front of Renoir's *The Rowers' Lunch*. "I love this painting."

"He painted happiness—with color and light, and scenes that invite you in," Jenny offered in explanation. "You almost feel as though you want to pull up a chair and be welcomed into their conversation."

David nodded, not taking his eye off the canvas depicting two young men and a woman in a trellised gazebo.

Jenny tugged at his arm. "Renoir's making me jealous. We only have a few hours, so let's make the most of them."

He smiled at her. "And I thought I was going to have to drag you away."

They retrieved their coats. Holding hands, they descended the entrance steps to Michigan Avenue and headed north.

"Where are we going?"

"Just up the street. Not far." She squeezed his arm. "It's my turn to surprise you."

David looked around, then his eyes settled on the Millennium Park ice rink, a large outdoor facility at the McCormick Tribune Plaza. "No, not that!" he exclaimed.

"David, I've been watching them skating from the museum restaurant all week. We must." She saw the look on his face. "You don't skate?"

"I've done it once or twice."

"So you aren't Wayne Gretsky. Who is?"

"Where did *you* learn to skate?" he tried delaying the inevitable. "On the pond at the farm when I was a little girl."

"I tell you what. When the pond freezes over, I'll skate with you."

"David, don't be ridiculous," she said. "If you can fly a plane, you can ice skate."

"I wouldn't land a plane on ice." He cleared his throat, continuing to stall for time. "Why don't I just watch."

"A New Englander who doesn't skate? Who will teach Grant?"

He was about to say, "You can teach him," but thought better of it. "Okay, if it means that much to you I'll give it a shot."

They got skates at the rental window and sat on a wooden bench to put them on and lace them up. Jenny finished first and stepped into the rink, gliding out onto the ice. She looked a little uneasy herself and David wondered who was going to lean on whom.

When he was ready, he hobbled over to the entrance. As he took several steps onto the ice, his legs flew out from under him, and he landed splayed out on his back. When he opened his eyes and looked up, Jenny was standing over him laughing.

"Some help you are." He reached for her hand and she pulled him up.

"Lesson number one is you don't walk on the ice, you glide," she explained, demonstrating by pushing off with her left foot and gliding on the right with her knee slightly bent.

"Now you tell me." He feigned displeasure. "Hereafter, let's have the lessons first."

She took both of his hands and held them crossed in front of them as David followed her skate strokes.

"Not bad for an old flyboy who's used to having his feet off the ground," he said, as he became more confident.

Then she turned and began skating backwards holding his hands in front of her. When she turned to come back next to him she stumbled and fell, sliding on her stomach.

"Nice swan dive," David commented. "Works better on unfrozen water."

She brushed the snow off her front, trying to hide her embarrassment. "You tripped me."

"Sorry, I can't take credit for that, although I can't say I wouldn't like to."

When they skated to the center, she tried to show him how to skate backwards and he ended up on his backside again, earning him another round of her laughter.

"Maybe we should stick with the basics," she said.

"I'll tell you what," he said, taking her hand. "If we make it five times around the rink without falling, we quit while we're ahead."

After five times they stopped counting and continued more confidently until the Zamboni came out to refresh the ice surface and interrupted their simple routine. They left the ice with the other skaters and turned in their skates.

As they headed back toward the museum, it began snowing in

heavy flakes that stuck to their overcoats.

"Wasn't that fun?" Jenny said, grasping his arm and holding it tightly against her.

"Only when I was watching you, sliding headfirst across the rink," he answered, grinning,

"A gentleman would never have mentioned that."

"I'm a congressman, not a gentleman, in case you forgot."

"You were a good sport, though. Shows character."

"Is that what it was? I mistook it for stupidity."

She cackled with glee. "You did look a bit foolish."

"Only when you pushed me backwards."

They strolled past the Art Institute and continued on to Grant Park. By the time they reached Buckingham Fountain, the snow had begun to accumulate. There were other couples and families with children who were making snowballs. Suddenly, the Christmas lights illuminated the fountain and the center rock formations, where alternating light bulbs simulated falling water. It was a magical moment.

David and Jenny started to walk around the fountain, arm in arm, watching the children toss snowballs at each other.

Two benches ahead, a prone figure lay on a bench, snow accumulating on a brown overcoat. David stopped in his tracks. For a moment, he thought it was Darlene. Then his vision adjusted and he relaxed.

"What is it, David?" Jenny asked. "You look like you've seen a ghost."

Just then an errant snowball struck him from behind. As he shrugged it off, he said, "Nothing. I was thinking about Grant."

Jenny gave him a sidelong glance, but his smile reassured her. "What was his mother like, your wife?"

David clenched his jaw. Then he said, "She was the most generous person I ever met, until you."

Startled, Jenny looked at him searchingly. She saw he meant it and put her arms around him. "You'll always be honest with me, David, won't you?" she asked.

"Yes," he answered, and drew her close to him.

CHAPTER 35

It was late Friday night when David got back to his apartment near Washington Harbor. Everything was dark as he opened the door and stepped inside, but he knew immediately that he was not alone. He was instantly on alert, but when he turned on the lights, he found Katherine sitting in one of the bay window chairs.

Relief mingled with irritation. "Kathy, what are you doing here?"

"Waiting for you."

She took her empty glass to the kitchenette to fix him a drink and freshen her own. "How come you're so late?"

"My flight from Chicago was delayed."

She hesitated, as the ice cubes tinkled into the glass. "I was worried when you didn't get back."

"Sorry, I didn't think it was necessary to call you."

She went over to the sofa, handed him the drink, and raised her glass in a mock toast. Then she sat back down tucking her legs under her as her skirt slid above her knees. "So, what did you find out walking around a Chicago ghetto for two days that you couldn't get from the hearing?"

He responded more crossly than he intended. "A lot more than sitting in a comfortable chair asking questions."

Unintimidated, she pointed to his formal attire. "Didn't you look a bit conspicuous in a suit?"

He gave a slight laugh. "Not with Lance beside me."

Katherine looked concerned. "You could've been in physical danger!"

"You have to spend time with people to understand them. How can you be a good representative if you only live in the Washington bubble?" He motioned with his glass around the room.

"Sometimes I don't know what to make of you. Why do you court danger unnecessarily?"

His eyes bore into her for an instant. "You know better than to ask me that."

When he noticed the sheaf of documents on his desk awaiting his signature, Katherine saw his questioning look and said casually, "Leave your receipts so I can take care of your expense account."

He started to reach into the inside pocket of his suit jacket but stopped himself. Two tickets to the Millennium Park ice rink would open a Pandora's box of questions. He glanced down at the papers then looked over at her seriously. She was wearing a white silk blouse and nothing underneath.

He took a sip of the scotch, considering, and said, not quite meaning it, "It's late. I don't want you going home alone at this hour."

She gave him a coy smile. "Is that an invitation for you to drive me home or for me to stay the night?"

He came over and set the drink on the end table. "To drive you home."

She looked disappointed. "Why don't I just stay here." It was a suggestion not a question.

He sat down in the chair opposite her. "Those papers didn't need to be signed tonight."

She stood and moved over to the arm of his chair. As she leaned down, she loosened his necktie and undid the top button of his shirt, then she said seductively, "I thought you'd appreciate my working late."

His arm wrapped around her as she leaned down to him and he could see the top of her shapely breasts inside her blouse. The smell of her perfume aroused him. It had been some time since he'd been with her and she was as alluring as ever.

"What does that have to do with it?" he said softly.

Katherine ran her hand through his hair. "Tomorrow's Saturday. Won't you be with Grant?"

"I see Grant every weekend."

"Will you take me with you?"

He pulled back, the mood broken. "I thought you didn't care to spend that much time with him."

"It's not that. It's the work," she attempted to justify it. "We can have dinner at that restaurant you keep talking about that looks out over the bay."

He sighed. "Look, it's been a long day."

She remained with her legs suspended over the arm of the chair, and leaned forward, letting her blouse slip open.

"Kathy, I really do have to get up early."

She hesitated for a moment, then stood up and buttoned her blouse. "I can drive myself home," she said, annoyed.

"No," he said, getting up. "You were worried about me. It's my turn."

She recovered her poise. "Promise me the next time you go to the Chicago ghetto, you'll wear your fatigues."

He laughed. "I got rid of those a long time ago."

"It's not something to joke about. I still don't see the point of your going there."

"The point," he said firmly, "is to do Lance's program in New Haven, Bridgeport and Hartford."

She stopped straightening her clothes and looked at him with interest. "Really?"

"If I can get the program successfully started there, Lance and I figured it could help him get more financial support and convert my work on the committee into votes next fall."

Her frown turned into a smile. "Those are the sweetest words I've heard you say since you walked in the door."

"If I'm going to do this, I'm going to play for keeps."

So am I, she thought. *So am I.*

CHAPTER 36

The holidays passed quickly as the parties began in Washington in early December and lasted through New Year's. Much to David's chagrin it was another lost month out of what amounted to a year of haggling with little to show for it. Committee hearings seemed to accomplish nothing but raise the ire of the members. It was all about posturing before the television cameras, both during the session and afterward. Devoid of meaning, nothing transpired until the next committee hearing. It reminded David of a royal court of the ruling class whose goal was self-preservation and self-aggrandizement, basking in the luxury of their privilege. In the gridlock of animosity that surrounded the Capitol the voters were the last to be considered until the campaigns began again.

Katherine and her father tried to reassure him.

"It hasn't always been so contentious here," Senator Cunningham told him. "But getting a major bill passed has always been a slow process."

"Maybe that's why so many people have such a low opinion of us in government," David replied, exasperated.

Soon he would have to begin running for reelection but, unless he got the commission appointed to examine and evaluate the VA and make recommendations for corrective action, he would have nothing to show except a failure of good intentions. Bradley Coyle knew this and was stalling the committee hearings through surrogates to paralyze him. And so another month went by.

David and Jenny attended the Christmas party at the National Gallery, but because it was a social affair, she had to mingle with patrons and donors and he hardly spent any time with her. A brief kiss was all they shared before she went to Middleburg and he departed with Grant for New Haven.

The Langleys came up for the Christmas holidays and stayed at the house of a former colleague of Edward's. David and Grant put up a Christmas tree together at his house that filled the living room with glowing lights, sparkling ornaments and the smells of pine cones and scented candles. The Langleys joined them for Christmas and shared in the excitement of a three-year-old boy opening his presents from Santa Claus and singing along with carols. It was David's first real Christmas, too, and he enjoyed the warm family atmosphere, pleased that it seemed to fill the void of another year without Darlene for the Langleys.

Katherine came up from Washington to organize a town hall meeting so David would get coverage on the local television channels. Attendance was low, but the event served its purpose—giving him visibility in his district. Grant spent New Year's Eve with the Langleys while David and Katherine went to several parties to mingle with some of New Haven's and Yale University's important movers and shakers. Finding a few like-minded donors among them—ex-military men and their wives who shared his passion for helping veterans—allowed him to recapture the excitement he felt when he started out in Washington politics.

As the evening wore on and he and Katherine became increasingly tipsy, she kept cozying up to him. After they watched the crystal ball drop in New York on a large TV monitor, they ushered in the New Year with a champagne toast and a lingering kiss, and one thing led to another. They went back to his house and spent the night together.

They both had a good time after missing close physical contact for so long. Even after several months' abstinence, the easy familiarity was a pleasure, as if their bodies were naturally in sync. Katherine was happy, but David was troubled by thoughts of Jenny, dismissing the potential conflict by turning to the new term in Washington, determined to push harder for what he believed in.

CHAPTER 37

A few weeks later, Jenny surprised him when she called him at his Washington apartment after an overnight snowstorm blanketed the entire northeast.

"Since the government offices are closed," she said, "I thought you might want to bring Grant out to the farm and go riding. It's an enchanting winter wonderland. Do you think the Jeep could get through?"

"I can't get to Annapolis and back, but what if I just come on my own?"

"Well...I don't know, I did invite Grant," Jenny teased.

"I don't blame you. Besides, I might walk into a barrage of snowballs when my back is turned."

"On second thought, that is a great idea. When can you get here?"

"Depends on the road conditions. Two hours, give or take. I'll definitely be there before noon."

It was stop-and-go to the Key Bridge and over it into Roslyn, but when he reached I-66 the traffic moved better than expected. Apparently, the salt plow trucks had been out early. But the airports were closed and Katherine was still in New Haven.

When he reached the farm, it was a beautiful scene of white with snowflakes falling as in a picture postcard. The long driveway to the house had been cleared and a sculptured snowman waved in greeting with its glove covered, stick arm. Jenny's scarf was over its head with the ends tossed around the neck. He grinned as he passed it and shifted into second gear heading up the drive.

An attendant with a snow-blower was working near the house but the tracks led him to the stables where he stopped and parked. The snowflakes were getting larger as the temperature was already warming up. He got out of the Jeep and tossed his parka on the back seat.

Jenny came out of the stable dressed in a white turtleneck sweater and tan jodhpurs. She was leading Fanny May and smiling.

Damn, she looks smart, David thought.

As he went to kiss her, Fanny May put her head between them. "She knows something I don't know," Jenny said. "You're making her jealous."

David reached up and petted Fanny's forehead. "What has Jenny been telling you about me that you don't approve of?"

"She can smell a politician a mile away."

"Well, Fanny May, you'll see that I'm different and you'll change your mind, just like your mistress will."

"No amount of carrots and apples will bribe her," Jenny said, "so don't even try."

"Horses are a good judge of character. Maybe you should let her decide." He patted Fanny's neck, and she pushed her nose against him.

Jenny noticed and scolded her. "Be careful or he'll charm you into a trap."

"Don't listen to her, Fanny. Make your own judgment. She has prejudices that distort her normally clear thinking."

Jenny gave him a disgruntled look. "Hmmm..."

Jack Bowden brought Red out saddled. David thanked him and mounted. Then they waved goodbye to Jack and trotted off side by side.

David stroked Red's neck. "I'm counting on you to change Fanny's mind about me," he said.

"You two can stick together, but so do Fanny and I," Jenny said.

She petted the mare's neck. "Don't we, Fanny."

"We'll see." He leaned down to Red's neck and whispered something, then sat back. "Where to?"

"First stop is the Red Fox Inn for some hot buttered rum."

As they passed the pond David smiled comfortably. "We forgot the ice skates."

"I bought you a pair as a Christmas present."

"Good grief. It's a good thing the ice is covered with snow."

"I've already provided for that. It will be cleared when we get back."

"No wonder spring is my favorite season." He changed the subject. "How did things go in Santa Fe?"

"Really well. As a matter of fact, I heard about a program in Texas that uses animals to rehabilitate troubled youths and veterans. It's a national organization that I thought you should know about. There's a professor at North Texas University in the psychology department who has become an expert on it. I've invited her to the farm to start a summer program here."

David brought Red up short, and Jenny stopped Fanny. "What's wrong?"

"Wrong? Nothing's wrong. That's such a marvelous thing for you to do."

"The Senator agrees, so we're going to try it. You can monitor it personally to see how it works."

"I'm flabbergasted."

"I want to start an art program for veterans, too—painting."

"Jenny, I never dreamed that you would involve yourself into this," he said admiringly.

"I think that what you're trying to do for the veterans needs to happen," she said frankly.

"I had no idea that you even knew about what happened at the hearings."

Ever since you met Lance Donovan in Chicago I've been thinking about it." Jenny kicked Fanny and Red moved forward with her. "I watched some of your hearings on C-SPAN."

"Then you believe in what I'm trying to do."

"That depends."

"On what?"

"Let's just say on how artfully you do it."

The snow began to turn to sleet, feeling like wet needles pricking their faces. Jenny raced ahead to a small outbuilding near the meadow where bales of hay were stored. She dismounted and lifted the latch as David pulled the heavy door open. They led the horses inside, dropped the reins and let both horses find some hay to chomp on.

Jenny turned her back to David and pulled off her wet, wool sweater, then took a horse blanket from a line and wrapped it around herself and hung the sweater on the line. She did it so casually, so naturally, without the slightest hesitation that it left him speechless.

He went over and put his hands on her shoulders, then turned her to face him, cradling her wet head and hair in his hands. He kissed her softly and felt her arms come around his neck. Their kiss became more passionate. He lifted her up and her legs wrapped around him as he carried her to a pile of loose hay and laid her gently down. He unclasped her bra and slipped it over her shoulders. As her head leaned back, her mouth opened, and she breathed deeply.

Then Fanny whinnied and she froze, sat upright as he pulled away, a concerned look on her face. "Someone must be coming." She quickly hooked her bra and wrapped the blanket tightly around herself and stood up.

David went over to the door and peeked outside. The sleet had stopped and it was snowing again as the temperature dropped precipitously. "False alarm," he said.

He looked back at her and she laughed. "You said Fanny May should decide. Apparently, she doesn't approve of you yet." Then she started to shiver.

David put his arms around her and rubbed her back. "You'll

catch your death of cold. Let's go back to the house."

✥

By four in the afternoon the snow had continued to fall and David felt he needed to leave if he was going to make it back to Washington before it got completely dark.

Jenny was disappointed but understood. "Drive carefully," she said and gave him a long kiss.

He drove off in the Jeep, watching her wave and getting smaller in the rear-view mirror until he crested the top of the hill and she disappeared from sight. He passed the snowman which had icicles dangling from his stick arms now, then turned onto the highway. An inch of new snow covered the road surface and, as the first hint of twilight descended, it glistened whiter in the cone of his headlights.

David thought of the moment in the barn when Jenny had all but given herself to him. Her playful unpredictability was as disarming as it was enticing. But how serious was she really? Did she accept that he was putting his painting on the back burner? Would his political career stand in their way? With Katherine there was no such conflict. If anything, politics brought them together. But how would she respond to another woman in his life? They had agreed on no commitment, but relationships always got complicated. And what about Grant? Both women were good with him, even if the boy seemed to prefer Jenny. Did he, himself, feel that way, too? All David knew was that he wanted to pursue Jenny, but he'd have to take his time.

As he drove on, he kept going over the various issues again and again in his mind, his whirling thoughts matching the whirling snow around him.

CHAPTER 38

David had been in Senator Cunningham's hideaway before, replete with photographs of sailboats and regatta trophies. But when he followed Katherine into the room, there was nothing leisurely or relaxed about the atmosphere. He immediately felt the tension in the air. He was surprised to see Christopher Steward, the National party chairman, sitting on the leather sofa next to Neal Neuman, the party's legal counsel. They looked like Mutt and Jeff. Steward, tall and thin as a reed was a nerdy but smooth political operator. Neuman, a former college football star, had bulging shoulders that threatened to burst his suit jacket at the seams. His overpowering physical presence often distracted people who didn't know him for his razor-sharp mind. David hadn't seen them since his victory celebration the night of his election.

Cunningham and Garrett sat opposite them in overstuffed, matching leather chairs. A map of Connecticut, divided up into red and blue areas, was spread out on the large coffee table. David recognized them as the voting districts of the last presidential and senatorial election.

Senator Cunningham rose and said, "Come and join us." He nodded to his daughter, "You know where the bar is."

Garrett chimed in, "I understand things went well at your last town hall meeting in New Haven."

"News travels fast," David said, noticing that the flat-screen TV over the side table next to the fireplace was on, tuned to one of the news channels. It was another sign in the senator's sanctuary that something unusual was going on.

Cunningham indicated the others, "You know these gentlemen, David."

They all stood up, shook hands, and sat back down.

As soon as David settled into one of the two empty chairs, Cunningham came straight to the point. "While your committee was in session, you probably missed the breaking news: Jeff Stevens may be dropping out of the Senate race against Bradley Coyle. Three women have accused him of sexual abuse during his last term."

Neuman leaned forward. "Stevens says he's innocent, that anything that might have happened was consensual. He claims he's being framed—pilloried in the press for sexual harassment."

Senator Garrett added, "We want to give him the benefit of the doubt, but we think he's toast."

From the bar, Katherine said curtly, "He's guilty."

Everyone's eyes turned toward her. Neal Neuman asked, "How do you know that?"

"Because I know a woman, not one of the three who came forward, who rejected his advances."

"What did he do?" Senator Garrett asked.

"Put his hands where they don't belong."

"And what did she do?"

"She slapped his face and he never touched her again."

"Perhaps he took notice and stopped a long time ago," Garrett proposed.

Katherine's voice would have frozen molten lava. "I'm afraid he didn't."

The room fell dead silent. No one wanted to ask the obvious question: How do you know?

Her father's face registered both surprise and shock. Finally, he said, "Well, that settles it."

Katherine brought David his drink and sat down in the chair next to him as if nothing had happened and said, "So who do you think should replace him?"

"That's what we've been talking about," Senator Garrett said, exchanging glances with the others around the coffee table. "We think this development presents an opportunity to tip over Coyle's applecart."

Steward waded in, "If Coyle loses his bid for reelection to the Senate, he'll be damaged goods, and his party won't support his presidential aspirations."

Intrigued, David asked, "How are you going to make that happen?"

Senator Cunningham leaned toward him. "We don't, David, you do. We want you to replace Stevens on the ticket."

For a moment David was stunned. Then he chuckled and said, "You can't be serious. You want me to run against Bradley for his Senate seat?"

"That's what we're saying."

David shot up out of his chair. "This is crazy! I'd be a freshman representative in office for a little over a year running against an incumbent senator." He tossed back the remains of his drink and went to the bar.

"No one knows Bradley Coyle like you and Katherine," Garrett called after him. "We've got to stop him. You're our best shot."

As David poured himself another Scotch, he said, "It sounds like political suicide to me. I'd have nothing to run on. I haven't accomplished anything yet."

"Right now you have the attention of the press by shaking up the status quo with the Veterans Committee and the VA," Cunningham urged. "That is political gold. You can capitalize on your own momentum."

"All the more reason why I have to stay and finish the job. I'm just beginning to make headway. I won't desert the veterans now. Besides, it would look like I just used them. My constituency would see me as an opportunist."

He walked to the wall with the photographs of sailboats, and stared at them, but he didn't really see them. Instead, images of Jenny, Grant, the Langleys, Katherine, and Coyle tumbled through his mind.

"We'll put you on the Senate Veteran Affairs Committee," Cunningham kept pressing. "You can reconcile the bill in the Senate that will be passed in the House. Smithson will keep the House committee in line. You'd actually be more help in the Senate."

When David didn't respond, he glanced at Senator Garret.

His colleague took up the baton. "Look," he said loudly, "maybe David's right. He's not ready. It's probably too soon. Won't get anywhere if he's just a one-note candidate."

Hearing his name, David paid attention long enough to recognize the good cop-bad cop routine. He focused on a small photograph in front of him. It was a shot of the crew of one of Cunningham's regatta victories—himself, the senator, Katherine, Coyle and a few others. He had to squint to see the faces. How young they all looked during those Yale days, the picture of idealism.

He turned around and gazed on Katherine sitting in her chair, legs crossed. "What do you think, Kathy?"

She gave him a big smile. "Hello, Senator Madison."

His eyes narrowed. She had known all along and was in league with them. This was an ambush by an experienced team of operators who knew every trick in the book on how to get someone to do their bidding. Yet he felt surprisingly relaxed, knowing he was in good hands.

He walked to his chair and, putting his hands on the back, looked at their serious, expectant faces. "Say I'm in, what would we have to do?"

A knowing glance passed between Cunningham and Garrett, and the tension in the room dropped a few degrees.

Garrett took the lead and ticked off the items on his fingers. "Get you on the ballot, put together a crack campaign staff, introduce you as the new candidate—we need to make a big splash—come up with a winning strategy, raise more money fast..."

"Get Stevens to resign from the race officially," Neuman interjected.

"Let me handle that," Cunningham said, casting a dark glance in the direction of his daughter.

"I'll take care of all the legal requirements to get you on the ballot," Neuman said.

The foot of Katherine's crossed leg bobbed up and down. "I can put the campaign staff into place quickly. We'll get as many as we can from the House run and supplement them with Steven's old staff. Some of them are quite sharp and will be looking for jobs."

Steward piped up. "You've got the guts and the energy, David. There's no one I'd rather work with. I can guarantee the national party putting our money on you if you agree to run. It's a twofer. We gain a Senate seat and knock Coyle out of contention for the presidency."

"We'll need a lot more money to do that, though, and right away," Senator Cunningham interjected, getting excited. "All of the campaign materials will have to be changed—TV ads, flyers, stationery."

"Wait!" David yelled above the mounting din to get their attention. "You're asking for a huge commitment. I haven't given the green light yet. I need twenty-four hours to think this over." He ran his hand through his hair.

Chris Steward rose slowly. "Congressman, we don't have that much time. I need to meet with the party regulars to get the ball rolling. The switch has to be made as soon as possible, arranging for Stevens to bow out gracefully and keep going in a positive mode."

With all eyes on him, David withdrew into himself for a moment. It was a daunting challenge, but nothing seemed wrong about this. He could feel the small ball of excitement growing in his gut that had always accompanied him into battle. He looked up, eyes flashing. "Okay. Let's kick Coyle's ass!"

Neuman jumped up, pumped his fist, and shouted, "Yes!" He raised his hand for a high five slap. When no one took him up on it, he sat back down. "Old football habit," he said, grinning sheepishly.

No one cared. They were all too busy shaking hands and clapping each other on the back.

Katherine went to the bar and poured out six glasses of brandy and handed one to each of them.

Cunningham raised his glass. When the other's followed suit, he said, "To the next senator of the great State of Connecticut!"

Everyone joined his toast and tossed down the brandy.

Garrett placed his glass on the bar and rubbed his hands. "Okay, let's get to work. We're going to need a lot of money to match Coyle's war chest. I can have John Ralston, who is my biggest financial supporter, out to the farm on Sunday. If he says yes, our road will be a lot smoother."

He looked at Katherine. "Can you be there?"

"Of course," she said. "I'll get together a dossier immediately. By tomorrow David will know everything about him, down to the color of his underwear."

In the face of everyone chuckling, David pretended to be indignant. "Kathy, I'm not going to kiss his ass. Just get me up to speed on him."

"You won't be kissing his ass, but you'll know if there's a freckle on it."

"I'm only interested in what's on his mind and in his wallet."

Everyone laughed.

"On that cheerful note," Steward said smoothly, "Neal and I have a lot of work to do today." He and Neuman shook David's hand, then Katherine's. "We'll be in touch." After saying their goodbyes to the senators, they left.

Garrett stepped up to David and placed a hand on his shoulder. "You always make good choices, son. You're bringing up a really good kid. Jenny adores him. We'll see you on Sunday."

David said politely, "Give my best to your daughter."

Katherine stiffened as Garrett kissed her cheek. She hardly heard him say something about looking forward to seeing her there, too. "Wouldn't miss it for the world," she said absentmindedly, kissing his cheek in turn.

Garrett waved to his colleague and made for the door.

Senator Cunningham waved back and took David by the arm. He led him to the sofa and said, "Let's have a look at your state, shall we?"

As Katherine watched the two men pouring over the map of Connecticut, she felt troubled. When did David and Garrett's daughter meet...who adored Grant!? When did they spend time together? He always talked about going sailing on Saturdays with Grant. Was he lying or had she gone with them?

As she gathered the empty glasses and took them to the bar, she felt a flood of emotion—anxiety, hurt, and anger. She poured out three more brandies, thinking feverishly, *How long has this been going on?*

CHAPTER 39

The tea kettle whistled on the kitchenette stove in Jenny's studio next to her bedroom on the second floor of the farmhouse. Jenny dropped a tea bag into a large cup and poured the boiling water over it. Then she settled into the comfortable wing chair, relaxing as she sipped the Chamomile tea and enjoyed the scent of the burning logs in the fireplace.

When the telephone rang, David's voice was almost apologetic. "I know it's late but I wanted to tell you as soon as I had a chance."

She hit the speaker button of her cell phone. "I know what you're going to say."

"Your father told you?"

"Yes.... Congratulations."

"You don't sound pleased."

She placed the phone on the side table next to her. "I know you had to do it."

"I wanted to do it, Jenny. There's so much I can accomplish. A Senate seat will give me a national forum, and I don't have to run every other year."

It felt like he was in the room with her and she grasped the pink silk robe loosely at the neck. "I understand."

There was a brief silence as she sipped the tea, watching the fire.

"Where are you?" David asked.

"I'm just relaxing in front of the fireplace in my studio."

"So what painting do you have over your mantle?" he asked. When she didn't answer right away, he added, "You never told me at the National Gallery."

"A painting by a local artist I admire."

"That's nice," he said perfunctorily.

"Maybe you could paint one for me that's better."

"I won't have much time for that now."

"Pity," she said and, to take the sting out of it, added, "I understand you're all coming to the farm this weekend with John Ralston."

"Yes. Can you put in a good word for me?"

"Why don't you come out early Sunday morning before the others get here? Let's go for a ride together."

"I'd like that."

"I'll meet you down at the stable."

"Can't wait."

"Me, too."

Jenny ended the call and settled into the wing chair and put her slippered feet up on the matching footstool. The fire had started to crackle with some of the logs engulfed in flames. She smelled the Chamomile aroma, took a sip, and contemplated the *Lady in Waiting* hanging over the fireplace mantle.

She had been on the verge of telling David about her, and his other painting, *Friends Forever*, which hung in her office at the National Gallery. After their interrupted interlude in the hay shed three months' ago, they had seen each other on a regular basis, their busy schedules permitting—mostly on weekends with Grant on the farm and for a few dinners in Washington during the week.

As their relationship progressed and the magnetism between them became stronger, Jenny felt increasingly uncomfortable about keeping her ownership of the paintings a secret from him. She'd been trying to figure out how to best let him know, but now she was not so sure.

It felt like a lifetime ago since she first met David at the reception in Frank Gannovino's art gallery. He had been open, almost vulnerable, and refreshingly honest, observing the crowd with a distaste she had begun to feel herself. She had bought the paintings on an impulse through an intermediary and didn't expect to see David ever again.

Soon after, Jenny turned her back on the New York social scene and its aggressive, success and money-driven men, so confident in their superiority, yet shallower than they realized. She left two failed relationships in her wake, including a broken engagement. The handsome, dynamic attorney, who was a partner at a prestigious law firm, seemed different than the rest until she discovered that he regularly cheated on her. Wounded, she swore off men for a while and used John Ralston as her escort to keep them at bay.

So, when David showed up at her father's farm as a newly minted congressman, widowed and with a child no less, she was both surprised and standoffish. Yet somehow, he managed to insinuate himself into her heart and she had fallen in love with him.

Nothing since then suggested that he was anything like those charming, self-centered men she'd left behind, or most of the politicians she knew who lusted for power and had roving eyes, no matter how they concealed it. Her father had been one of them, and it took a personal tragedy for him to become different from them.

Jenny took another sip of tea. Yes, David was not like the rest. As a representative, he had managed to keep a semblance of balance, in part because of his commitment to be a good father to Grant. But would he be able to withstand the siren lure of power as he moved closer to its center? She worried that it was just a matter of time until he succumbed. His obvious anger when the subject of Bradley Coyle came up accidentally was troubling, too.

She gazed at the woman on the canvass. With her serene eyes and hands held in her lap, the *Lady in Waiting* looked so sure of herself. Her calm, confident demeanor had been a touchstone for Jenny in the early days when she was still smarting from the failure of her disastrous relationships. More recently, she used her presence to recover her own equilibrium after a hectic day. In her presence,

Jenny felt some of the contentment she radiated.

Feeling confined, she opened the door to the balcony for some fresh air. Looking out toward the trail that led to the pond where she and David had gone for a swim, she shivered. She realized that it was her fear that held her back. Having deliberately avoided a world where she had allowed herself to be badly hurt, she wasn't at all confident that she could handle it any better this time around.

As she stepped back inside, it occurred to Jenny that the man who managed to convey so evocatively the emotion she sought in a painting, deserved the benefit of the doubt. He might not emerge from his immersion in politics unscathed, but there was a good chance that his core would remain intact. Perhaps she needed to put her trust in the *Lady in Waiting* and take a risk again herself.

CHAPTER 40

Early Sunday morning on the way to the Garrett farm, David hardly took notice of the lovely surroundings—the gently sloping meadows, tree-lined country lanes, and white paddock fences. Instead, he spent much of the drive immersed in thought about the people who had changed his life dramatically since he met Darlene—the Langleys, his mentors in the House and Senate, Katherine, Grant, Jenny.

He had been surprised when Katherine offered to pick up Grant in Annapolis and bring him to the farm for the meeting with John Ralston. He thought Grant would be a distraction, but Katherine had persuaded him that it was important for Ralston to see him as a father. Being a single dad who cared and wanted to be a part of his son's life would play well. Also, driving from Washington directly to Middleburg would allow him to stay focused on preparing for the meeting with Ralston. He decided she was right and felt relieved after he had consented.

It had been a hectic week, crowded with planning meetings and strategy sessions about how to best launch his campaign in Connecticut. The announcement of his run for the Senate had set off a turmoil of news stories and TV interviews that had gone very well. Coyle's off-the-cuff remark to a reporter that he expected an easy win over the inexperienced freshman congressman had come off as pompous.

John Ralston was another matter. Katherine's dossier had been detailed and thorough on facts, as expected, but David didn't feel that he had a real handle yet on the man. David remembered him from the Preakness as a no-nonsense type with a strong handshake, and a lively, predatory look. He vaguely recalled a young woman in the box telling him that Ralston bought himself a toy whenever he pulled off a big financial deal.

With a net worth of $2.6 billion Ralston could have anything he wanted that money could buy, which included a penthouse in New York at the Pierre overlooking Central Park; a 175-foot yacht; a fleet of fast cars that had been custom-built for him by Ferrari, Maserati, and Porsche; a Learjet and a helicopter; and several strings of polo ponies. It wasn't that he liked money more than women, but that he liked them too much and never wanted to settle on just one. Although he had been linked with any number of supermodels, media figures, and movie stars, at fifty he was still unmarried.

Other than the fact that Ralston liked quality products, beautiful women, and life in the fast lane, David had no idea what made him tick. Perhaps the most important thing David didn't know—there had been no mention of it in the dossier—where did Jenny fit in?

When David arrived at the Middleburg farm, there were no cars in the driveway. He was the first visitor. He parked the Jeep and walked down to the stables, past white oaks that seemed to house an orchestra of songbirds, considering the noisy concert they were putting on. As he entered, he smelled fresh coffee from the tack room. Tiptoeing, he came up behind Jenny as she poured coffee into two mugs from a thermos. He kissed the back of her neck.

"Is that you, Tony?" she said in an affectionate tone.

"Tony!" For a second David was completely caught off guard. "Who is Tony?"

"Just a polo player friend." She turned around and faced him, wrapped her arms around his neck, and kissed him on the lips. "I saw you through the window."

He laughed at her trick, then turned serious. "I had to jump into the Senate race, Jenny. There was no other option. We have to defeat

Coyle now."

"I know." She leaned her forehead against his chest. "I'm just concerned for Grant. There's always something that gets in the way."

"I am too. Once the campaign gets into full swing I'll be tied up every weekend."

Jenny looked past his shoulder. "Where is he?"

"Katherine is bringing him."

Jenny's eyes widened. "Really."

"She suggested it herself."

"Well, apparently she has better sense than his father. You missed out on an opportunity to spend time with him. You won't see much of him today while you meet with John."

David felt rebuked, and the moment of intimacy was gone. Jenny handed him one of the steaming mugs. She looked at him over the rim of hers as they sipped the coffee.

"What?" he asked.

"Nothing," she said and went to get Fanny May from her stall. David put the halter on Red and led him out.

"Tell me about Ralston."

Jenny tossed the blanket over Fanny's back. "He's an old friend of the family."

"I know that, and a lot more. But what's his passion? What does he really care about?"

"Competition. Winning."

"Of course, but what's his interest in politics?"

As Jenny put the saddle on her horse, she said, "I'm sure you've done the research and know which candidates he has supported financially and what their political leanings are. But that's secondary for him. When John puts money on you, he expects you to do everything necessary to win."

"I figured as much. But why would he want to support me? Why would he put money on me in the first place?"

They mounted their horses and started out to the trail at a walking gait. Jenny stayed silent for a while. Then she reached down, rubbed Fanny's neck and said, "John feels that he owes my father. When he was young, he got into serious trouble and my father rescued him."

David waited as they sauntered on, hearing only the muffled clomping of the horses' hooves on the dirt path.

Before long, Jenny continued, "Middleburg has always been the place where a bunch of wealthy horse people settled. John was a poor stable boy like you, probably even rougher around the edges, and he took some money that didn't belong to him—a substantial amount— and he got caught. My father thought he deserved another chance and helped him get out of the jam. Then he got him a job on Paul Mellon's racehorse breeding farm and kept a watchful eye to make sure he didn't falter. Mellon later saw the same thing in John that my father did and gave him the opportunity to prove himself, starting at the bottom in his banking business. John has never forgotten what my father did for him.

As the horses continued at an ambling pace, David said, "So he values loyalty above all else?"

"No. The Senator taught him what it means to have personal integrity, that if you don't play by the rules, someday it will catch up to you. He was lucky because he was young. If someone cheats him today, they're through, and that includes not giving everything you've got. He hates corruption. That's why he'll back you and not Coyle. But you must give your all to win. A decent try isn't enough."

David smiled at her. "That's good to know."

Jenny turned in the saddle toward him and rested a hand on Fanny's haunches. "There's something else you should know that probably isn't in the file you have on him. He's not the playboy he's made out to be. He dates one woman at a time, and he's a gentleman. If it doesn't work out, he moves on. It just hasn't worked out yet."

"Is that what happened with you?"

Jenny blushed and shot David an angry glance. When she saw the searching expression on his face, she relented. "As I told you before, we are good friends. We've always been good friends."

"That's good to know, too," David said, although he didn't feel entirely reassured.

⌘

As David, Jenny and Senator Garrett sat on the front porch, sipping more coffee, they heard a high-pitched, whirring sound, as if a gigantic wasp was heading their way. Soon, a black, open-top Lamborghini zoomed up the driveway and came to a stop next to David's Jeep.

Another toy, David mused. *Must have closed another big deal.*

The man who extricated himself from behind the wheel was dressed in casual, yet perfectly tailored, tan riding clothes. He removed his driving gloves and tossed them into the front seat as Senator Garrett came down to greet him.

"John, so good of you to make time today," he said and ushered Ralston onto the porch, where David and Jenny stood in anticipation. "You remember David Madison from the Preakness."

"Of course, nice to see you again," Ralston said.

Except for the stubble on his cheeks and chin that looked like he had forgotten to shave, which was the current vogue, he seemed no different than before. David noted the same tan, quick eyes, easy smile, firm handshake, and manicured hands. Yet, the combination of overt and subtle displays of casual wealth didn't seem to add up somehow, and David wondered when the man's killer instinct would emerge.

Jenny kissed Ralston's cheek and handed him a bloody Mary. "I made a pitcher the way you like them."

Just then Katherine's BMW convertible sped up the drive without the roaring flair of John Ralston's seven-hundred horsepower Lamborghini.

Once again Senator Garrett acted as host and brought his visitors to the porch. Jenny was surprised to see Grant comfortably holding on to Katherine's hand as they climbed the steps together. She hadn't seen Bradley Coyle's ex-wife for some time and had to admit that her taste in clothes was excellent. Dressed in white slacks and a navy-blue sweater that accentuated her trim figure, she looked efficient and practical, and sexy in an understated way.

Garrett made the introductions. "John, I'd like you to meet Katherine Cunningham, David's chief of staff and campaign manager."

"Senator Cunningham's..." Ralston waited to be prompted.

"Daughter," Katherine said, extending her hand. "It's a pleasure to meet you, Mr. Ralston. I've heard a good deal about you."

"Please—John. Only good things, I hope." Ralston smiled and shook her hand formally.

"Of course," she said. She put both hands on Grant's shoulders. "And this is David's son, Grant."

Grant shook hands like a little man and waved to David, "Hi Dad," then raced over to Jenny.

Watching Jenny kneel and Grant flying into her arms, giving her a big hug, Katherine felt chagrined.

Meanwhile, Jenny asked, "How was the ride up?"

"We sang songs all the way," Grant crowed cheerfully. "Aunt Katherine taught me 'John Jacob Jingelheimer Schmidt.'"

"After we ran out of animals on Old MacDonald's farm," Katherine said with a smile.

David looked at her in amazement. In all the years he'd known her, this was a side of Katherine he had never seen.

Jenny felt a pang of jealousy. Since when had David's chief of staff become "Aunt" Katherine? Obviously, they'd had fun together, and she was pleased that Grant was happy. But she still felt a little hurt. She rose and shook hands with Katherine. "It's nice to see you again."

"Yes," Katherine said. "It's been some time. It was at the inauguration, wasn't it?"

She didn't wait for a reply, quickly moved to David and kissed him on the cheek. "Grant was a dream. He didn't make a fuss once."

"Thanks for bringing him," David said appreciatively.

Meanwhile, Grant tugged at Jenny's sleeve, bobbing up and down. "When can we go ride the horses?"

Jenny looked to the others. "Now is a good time. Senator, you want to come along?"

Casting a meaningful glance at Ralston and David, her father said, "Sure."

Grant shouted in delight and quickly said to the others, "Bye, Dad, bye, Aunt Katherine, bye, Mr. Ralston." Then he hopped down the steps and skipped toward the stables, singing at the top of his voice, "John Jacob Jingleheimer Schmidt! His name is my name, too..."

Jenny and her father followed more slowly, the senator calling back over his shoulder, "We'll have brunch at 12:30."

Ralston, taking in all the byplay with amusement, turned to David and said, "He's a bundle of energy, isn't he?"

"Yes," David gave a theatrical sigh. "I'll be hearing that song non-stop on the way back." He grimaced at Katherine with mock exasperation, "Thanks a lot!"

Katherine smiled sweetly.

Ralston laughed and asked, "I'd like to go to the polo club, show you my ponies. Interested?"

They both said simultaneously, "I'd love to."

Walking toward the cars parked in the driveway, David suggested, curious how Ralston would react, "Why don't we take my Jeep? Not exactly riding in luxury, but it will get us there."

"I've always wanted one of these," Ralston said, climbing up in back, leaving the front passenger seat for Katherine.

David settled behind the wheel and turned on the ignition. "To add to your collection of Ferraris, Porsches, Maseratis and the new Lamborghini?" he asked as he shifted into first gear and started down the driveway.

Ralston took up the gauntlet, and for much of the trip, the two men continued to fence amiably while revealing enough personal information to make clear that they had both read in-depth research on each other.

Ralston figured Katherine had done most of the spadework on his past. Watching her, he asked David, "How was your ride with Jenny this morning?" and was pleased to see Katherine's startled look.

David responded with a non-committal, "Fine."

After a pause, Ralston queried Katherine, "You didn't come dressed for riding. You do ride, don't you?"

"Only the horses on a carousel, I'm afraid," Katherine tossed back over her shoulder.

He chuckled. "Then you won't miss anything."

"I do like to watch."

David looked questioningly at Katherine as he pulled into the drive that led to the stables.

"Well then, we'll give you a little exhibition," Ralston promised. "How about it, David?"

"I've never played polo before, but why not?"

"Then I'll give you a quick lesson. Pull up to the second barn just ahead."

David parked in front of the white stable building with a green and white cupola on the roof. Inside, it was quiet except for the sounds of the horses moving in their stalls, drinking loudly or chomping grain and hay. Occasionally one of them struck a hoof against the wooden boards.

Katherine wrinkled her nose at the pungent smell and covered her mouth with her hand. "I'll wait in the bleachers," she said, and hurried outside.

Two horses stood in front of their stalls already saddled and tied to large rings attached to heavy posts by the stall doors.

"This is Jackman," Ralston said, stroking the white star on the forehead of the jet-black horse with white stockings to match the star. He stood sixteen hands with a shiny black mane and tail that gave him a commanding appearance. "He's scored more goals than any other horse I own." Ralston rubbed his cheeks affectionately.

"*He* scored?"

"Yes. He knows just how to position himself on the ball within my reach. He'll ride off another horse to keep me to the ball. Smartest horse I've ever been on."

Ralston patted Jackman and moved on. "This is Capella. Gentle as a lamb, but a real competitor on the turf. You'll ride her, David."

David stroked the neck of the chestnut mare. She was a hand shorter than Jackman but the determined look in her eyes matched his. David pulled the stirrups down to their full length and adjusted them a notch, then checked the girth. When he finished he unfastened the reins from the post ring and followed Ralston and Jackman out.

Ralston fetched two mallets and a ball from the tack room and handed David a pair of thin leather polo gloves. He put his hand through the mallet strap and showed David the hand grip. Then they mounted, waved to Katherine in the bleachers, and trotted toward the practice field.

David broke into a canter and worked the reins to get to know Capella's responsiveness and let her feel her rider's competence.

Ralston liked the way David took charge and seemed comfortable in the saddle. He swung his mallet in an easy arc as David rode up. "Like most sports played with rackets, clubs and sticks, it's all in the wrist," he explained. "So you can get accustomed to striking the ball, we'll pass it to each other using the face of the mallet head not the end." He demonstrated again with a fluid motion. "You don't need to worry about getting into position for now, Capella will do it for you. Just concentrate on hitting the ball." He swung the mallet and sent the ball downfield.

While they practiced Ralston explained the rules. David worked up a sweat, slowly getting the hang of it. After thirty minutes they took a break and rested the horses.

From the sidelines, two other players rode out onto the field. One of them looked familiar to David. Ralston waved them over and made the introductions. "Tony Mangione, Ted Wilcox—David Madison. You remember the Congressman from the Preakness, Tony?"

"Yes, I do," Mangione said, flashing his megawatt smile.

As they removed their gloves and shook hands, David examined the newcomers. Both were tanned, trim and handsome. Mangione displayed the confident charm of a seasoned professional athlete. Wilcox, who looked twenty-something, had the serious expression of an eager disciple out to prove his mettle.

"Shall we scrimmage for a bit?" Ralston suggested, not waiting for an answer. "You and Ted defend the north goal, David and I will bring the ball out."

For a while, they went back and forth, the horses' hooves thudding on the turf. Then Mangione took the ball away from David and scored. But on the next round, Ralston battled against Wilcox and the ball came toward David. Instinctively, he struck it with a resounding whack and it went fifty yards, bouncing between the goal posts.

David was as surprised as the others. He heard Katherine cheering from afar.

Ralston rode up to him and said, "Well done!" as they tapped mallets.

From that point on, the play became faster and more competitive. Mangione continued to move with practiced ease, crowding David off the ball at will, and scored twice, but Wilcox rode with greater intensity.

The next time he brought out the ball, Ralston passed it to David and they moved down the field toward their opponents' goal. Soon, David found himself locked with Wilcox, the ball at their horses' feet. As they battled to punch it loose, an arm struck David's face, almost knocking him from the saddle. David leaned back in and, as they continued fighting for the ball, snapped the end of the mallet into Wilcox's side.

"Foul!" Wilcox cried like a bully who whines when he's been humiliated. "Foul!"

David felt his face and wiped blood from under his nose.

Ralston and Mangione rode up, exchanging glances. "The horses need to rest," Ralston said diplomatically. "Let's call it a day." But behind Wilcox's back, he gave David a thumbs-up.

Mangione and Wilcox continued practicing while Ralston and David rode back to where Katherine sat in the bleachers.

"You pick things up quickly," Ralston said. "How can I get you interested in playing polo regularly?"

"I have to win the Senate seat first," David replied, smiling broadly. "Help me get elected and I'll play."

"That'll take more than beginner's luck sending a ball through the posts."

"If we have the same goals, we both win. We have to decide if we're on the same team."

"And how do we do that?" Ralston retorted, amused by the exchange of clichéd sports metaphors.

David pulled a folded and wrinkled piece of paper from his back pocket and handed it over. "It's a little worse for wear, but I'd like you to look at this. It's a copy of my candidacy announcement, the part about what I want to accomplish. Think it over. Then make your decision."

Ralston unfolded the paper and perused it. "Are you always this direct?"

"With me you get what you see."

"You know, David, I owe Senator Garrett a lot. If he asked me to fund your campaign, I would do it without a second thought. But now I feel even better about it."

They brought the horses to a stop in front of Katherine and dismounted.

"You guys look like you need a shower," Katherine said.

David glanced at his watch. "We'd better get back to the Garretts' farm." He took the reins of the two horses and headed back to the stables.

"The attendants will take them," Ralston called after him.

Walking to the Jeep, Katherine said, "You gave him quite a workout, John. Did he pass?"

"He's part of the equation," Ralston replied. "You're just as important to the election campaign."

"I'm flattered you think so," Katherine countered.

"Well, elections are like big construction projects. They need an expert builder who can realize the architect's vision. Madison and the senators may determine strategy and make the decisions, but someone has to execute them. As far as I'm concerned, you're as important as the candidate. You run the team."

"We only employ people of merit and integrity," Katherine said. "David attracts those kinds of people."

She caught Ralston staring at her intently and wondered if he had something more in mind than their overt conversation. Katherine had come to expect admiring looks from men.

"We're trying to accomplish something that hasn't happened in Washington for quite some time—working together for the good of our country," she said. "My father and Senator Garrett have made it their mission to restore a sense of decorum and respect. They both think David can help do that—lead a younger generation of elected officials to return to true service in government and put our country first, not just pursue their ambitions and ideologies at all cost."

"You've set a high bar."

"I'm sure you do, too. Have we cleared it?"

Ralston smiled at her, his eyes playing over her face. "Yes," he said. "I'm in."

❦

With Ralston committed to the campaign, the mood at brunch was celebratory, but while the political players would have liked to strategize, conversations remained light and casual because of Grant's presence.

Ralston told entertaining stories about the time he made a financial deal among several bigwigs from different countries who only spoke their own language, requiring four different translators and leading to confusion all around. Senator Garrett told of hanky-panky in the corridors of Congress—the G-rated versions, for Grant's sake— while Jenny rolled her eyes.

Katherine chuckled politely. Being on Jenny's turf was anything but enjoyable. She found her rival's intimate relationship with Grant especially irritating, knowing how much it meant to David. It would be difficult to find something as exciting for Grant as the Garrett farm. With a boy his age, how could anyone compete with horses?

So, as soon as brunch was finished, Katherine excused herself. "I need to get back to D.C. David and I have a meeting with the new staff members in the morning that I need to prepare for, and I'm meeting Dad for dinner."

As the others got up, she put a hand around David's neck. "I'll see you early tomorrow."

It didn't escape Jenny that he covered her hand with his and mouthed, "Thank you, Kathy."

Katherine tousled Grant's hair, gave Senator Garrett a peck on the cheek, and shook Jenny's hand politely. "Thank you for the lovely brunch," she said.

She reserved her warmth for Ralston, grasping his hand in both of hers. "It's been a real pleasure to meet you, John. Thank you for deciding to support the next senator from Connecticut."

He bowed smartly and looked after her as she walked out. Then he turned to the others. "I have to get ready for my polo match. I'll see you all afterward."

He caught up to Katherine on the way to her car. "I have a proposition for you," he said.

She tossed her purse onto the front seat of her BMW and leaned against the door, waiting.

"You're going to need a lot of help to beat Bradley Coyle—more money than I can give to the campaign, not to mention a brand-new approach." He watched for any sign of agitation at the mention of her ex-husband's name. When she remained calm, he continued, "Why don't you and David hold your next strategy session aboard my yacht? You can bring along whatever staff you need."

Relaxing, Katherine smiled politely. "That is very generous of you, John."

"Once I'm in, I'm all the way in." His smile became calculating. "If you like, you and I can head up the coast afterward for a couple of days before the campaign madness begins."

He saw a look of recognition come over her, followed by disappointment that he just confirmed he was like all the other men who had come onto her.

"Aren't you being a bit fast, John?" she confronted him.

He smiled roguishly and said, "I thought as much. Just stirring the water."

Realizing that he'd been testing her again, Katherine became annoyed. She opened the car door and settled in the driver's seat. Then she faced him and said, "Let's get one thing straight. I don't like games like this and I don't play them. I'll take you up on your generous offer, but that's all."

Ralston nodded. "I like your style, Katherine. It's a deal."

CHAPTER 41

Senator Bradley Coyle sat next to his wife at the table immediately in front of the dais where the President was giving a speech. He enjoyed these Washington fundraisers even if it meant having to endure an impossibly long, boring speech. He imagined himself on the podium thrilling the audience with his wit and charm, something that the current occupant of the Oval Office lacked in spades.

Shifting his eyes from the President to Helen, Coyle wondered if she was as bored as he was. If so, she certainly concealed it well, looking up at the President with rapt attention, laughing at his lame attempts at humor as if he were a brilliant stand-up comedian. *Pathetic*, he thought.

His mind wandered to the promise he had made to Stephanie. Well, that remained to be seen. Helen had the breeding that came with her background, a Mount Holyoke graduate with a wealthy father and the brains and poise to rub shoulders not only with the rich, famous and politically connected, but also the movers and shakers of the business establishment. He could not have wished for a better match for his political purposes. Even Katherine fell short of her in those areas.

Helen was far more important to achieving his ambitions than Stephanie could ever hope to be. But Stephanie was well placed in media circles, and her sexuality excited him. In many ways he had the best of all worlds—a great, if rather frigid power marriage and a stirring bedmate, who also could further his political career.

If he couldn't have them in one person, he certainly deserved this arrangement. In fact, he felt entitled to it. Because Helen was such a cold fish, he had convinced himself that his philandering was her fault, and he felt completely justified.

As the President finished his speech to rousing applause and a standing ovation, Coyle glanced at his wife. She was a beautiful woman and in her Oscar de la Renta dress no one else in the room could match her taste and stylishness. As he stood next to her, he imagined the accolades were for him. It was his destiny.

When the applause subsided, the President came down to their table, took Helen's hand, and whispered something to her that made her laugh. Then he shook Bradley's hand and leaned forward to murmur, "I understand you want to succeed me. I wish you the best, Senator. Just between us, we couldn't do better."

Soon, other important guests came up to be seen with Washington's anointed power couple, to touch the mantle of political success, and act like their close friends. Suddenly, Stephanie and Harry Morgan appeared in front of them and Bradley shook hands with her as though she were merely another admirer.

Helen looked at Stephanie without smiling, long enough to make the younger woman uncomfortable. Then she said, "It's so nice to see you again. Is this a new dress? How becoming." She touched her own expensive pearls while her eyes dismissed Stephanie's as inferior, relegating her to a lower position on the Washington food chain, the snub complete.

No one noticed except Stephanie as she blushed and kept a forced smile in place. Then she turned to Coyle and, with a deliberate edge to her voice, said, "Senator, perhaps you'll give me another interview soon."

"Bradley and I have talked about my doing TV interviews about the personal side of our family and domestic life as a human-interest feature for the campaign," Helen said with feigned politeness. "We'll be on several morning shows discussing our life together, our art collection, and our philanthropic activities. I believe that is outside of your purview."

Stephanie responded through pursed lips. "I do a hard news show, so you're right, it wouldn't fit in." She quickly turned to Bradley again. "I'll be in touch with your office about an interview next week." She forced a smile. "Always a pleasure to meet you, Mrs. Coyle. Good night, Senator."

Then she was gone and Coyle and Morgan stood looking blankly at each other. Bradley motioned with his eyes for him to go after her, but Helen intervened. She took Morgan's arm and said, "Come with me, Harry. I want to introduce you to someone." They moved off, leaving Bradley standing alone.

As he worked his way to the bar, the elation he had felt just a few moments before deserted him. He longed to be with Stephanie and wished she hadn't left so abruptly. He ordered a scotch straight and endured small talk with a number of wealthy donors.

Twenty minutes later, Helen came up to him. "Are you aware of the rumor going around?" she said under her breath.

He looked puzzled. "I have no idea what you're talking about."

"Let's go somewhere more private." She took Bradley by the arm and pulled him into a quiet corner of the lobby.

"What is it?" Bradley asked.

"Word is that David Madison has John Ralston funding him."

Bradley blanched. "Who told you?"

"One of my little birds. And if it's true, you better get ready for battle!"

His head spinning, he said, "What do you suggest?"

"Why don't you have your little floozy dig up some dirt on him." Bradley looked around to see if anyone was within earshot. Then he turned toward the wall so that no one could see the expression on his face and said, "That little floozy, as you call her, is Harry Morgan's latest conquest, and she'll be useful in my campaign. So lay off. You're reminding me of Katherine."

Stung, Helen retaliated. "I understand now why she divorced you."

He smiled dangerously. "You're forgetting why you married me."

"At the moment I'm deliberately trying to forget it."

He scowled. "Then I'll remind you. You love the power it gives you as much as I do, Helen, maybe more. The senator's wife, the endless perks, the lauding it over all the other wives. The invitations to the White House and trips on Air Force One; the treatment like royalty wherever you go, the celebrities you get to rub shoulders with, not because of who you are, but because of what you are— Senator Bradley Coyle's wife."

Helen ran her fingers along her hair and smiled to make it appear that they were having a little husband and wife tete-a-tete, but her voice was filled with bitterness. "You're right, Bradley. But you are such a complete ass."

Bradley's face flushed with anger. "I'm going to become President, and you will become the First Lady, if you play your cards right. If not, it's you who will be the complete ass."

Helen smiled contemptuously. "Do you really believe that?"

He gave her back an arrogant smile. "My dear, you have no idea. We're building a one-party system that can't be defeated, because we don't just control the government, we control the political process. The bigger we make the government, the more votes we control. We vilify our opponents as though they are criminals, accuse them of what we have done or accuse them of a conspiracy against us, and the public believes it, because the press is on our side. We can twist anything to our advantage because we have a propaganda machine that makes Tammany Hall look like pikers."

"And if you lose your Senate seat to David Madison? What then?"

His face became contorted and reddened. "Believe me, I won't. There is zero chance of that happening."

She smiled as though there was nothing amiss. "Well, you better keep that little trick of yours in line or you can kiss the Presidency goodbye, and me with it. Now, I want to go home. Why don't you get the limo, and we can go back to pretending how much we love each other."

CHAPTER 42

On Friday afternoon David left his congressional office early to drive to Annapolis. He hoped to make it to the yacht club where John Ralston had moored his boat in an hour, half the time it took in the rush hour traffic of people leaving Washington for the weekend.

Katherine and John had arranged a working weekend retreat aboard ship with David's campaign staff, the Garretts and Senator Cunningham. While the yacht traveled up the East coast, they would formulate strategy, map out rally stops, and plan fundraising events. The camaraderie they built would prepare them for the kick-off of David's campaign on Monday in New Haven.

He wondered how Jenny and Katherine would get along. Since the first of the year he had been ramping up the fundraisers in preparation for reelection to his congressional seat and he and Jenny had not seen each other as often as he would have liked. Now, he would have to raise far more capital to fund a Senate run, playing catch-up, and there was likely to be even less free time. He'd been able to spend several idyllic Saturdays at the Middleburg farm with her and Grant since the snowstorm, and they'd gone out after dinner for an impromptu evening at a gallery walk in the Adams Morgan art district. There was the time at the farm a week earlier, but that had been mostly consumed with getting John Ralston aboard.

At first he was delighted that Katherine wanted to invite Jenny, but now he wasn't so sure. As he turned onto Highway 50 he mused about Katherine's indispensable part in his life, and his attraction to

Jenny. While Katherine was like an expensive red wine, smooth and smoky, Jenny was like a fine champagne, sparkling and clear. He couldn't keep sampling both. It was pleasant and pleasurable, but he felt uncomfortable.

He yawned—it had been a long week—and decided to grab a quick cup of coffee to re-energize before meeting the others. He pulled across two lanes of Highway 50 to park in front of the neon sign of Joe's Diner. His Jeep was the only car in the lot. He imagined it would fill up later. There were no other customers inside, either, and he sat down on a stool at the counter and ordered black coffee.

Looking around the place, David felt like he was in a time warp. The booths had red plastic seats, and an old jukebox sat next to the hallway that led to the restrooms. The records were probably all Elvis, Johnny Cash, Frankie Lane, and Harry Belafonte, with a few Beatles, Chubby Checker, and Frankie Valli and The Four Seasons mixed in.

The waitress was dressed in a uniform to match the 1950s decor, right up to the tiny hat that sat precipitously on top of her graying hair. She looked tired and the wrinkles etched in her face suggested that she was several years past retirement. An apron covered the lower half of the outfit indicating that she cooked as well as served. She splashed coffee into a heavy porcelain cup with a green line around the rim and set it in front of him.

"Good coffee," he said after he took a sip.

She gave him a weak smile and asked, "Where you headed?"

"Out of the Washington bubble into the real world," he said, holding the cup in both hands.

"Well, you came to the right place," she said, and gave a small brittle laugh. "It doesn't get any more real than this."

He glanced at her face and wondered what stories lay behind her wrinkles. Putting down the cup, he said, "Let me ask you a question. Say I was your senator. What would you want to say to me?"

She laughed. "If you were my senator, you wouldn't be here."

He nodded in acknowledgment. "Seriously. Tell me."

She leaned back on one of the black lids of the ice cream freezer and folded her arms. "I'd ask why I should vote for you."

"Okay," he said. "Then what would it take to get your vote?"

Looking at him thoughtfully, she decided to answer him straight. "What would you do to make my life a little easier? And to make Maryland a better place for my children. They're grown and have families and are struggling, too. And don't give me any empty promises. I've got no retirement to speak of. I'll be working till I drop."

She said it matter-of-factly, without a note of challenge in her voice.

David nodded and sipped the coffee in silence. He couldn't imagine what to say to her that would make a difference, which got him wondering how many other people were living in circumstances he knew nothing about? His mind flashed back to the first time he talked to Darlene in the restaurant, and he had a sudden intuition about what to do. He had to meet his constituents where they lived, let them tell him what was on their minds, and answer their questions as best he could. He needed to run an old-fashioned grassroots campaign, reaching working people like her in the rural areas of Connecticut as well as in the cities.

The waitress gave him a suspicious look. "Why'd you ask? You're not one of those public opinion survey guys, are you?"

David grinned. "No...I am running for senator in Connecticut."

He wiped his mouth with a paper napkin. Then he reached into his pocket, pulled out his money clip, and put a twenty-dollar bill on the counter. Standing up, he held out his hand to her and said, "Thank you...?"

"Maria," she said, smiling almost shyly as he shook her hand. "David Madison."

As she took the twenty and started for the cash register, he said, "Keep it. You've given me an idea."

He started to leave but she said, "Wait a minute." She filled a paper cup from the coffeemaker, snapped on a white plastic lid and handed it to him over the counter. "Good Luck."

He smiled. "I'll be back to see you in November and tell you how it turned out."

&

When David pulled up to the pier of the Annapolis Yacht Basin Marina, he came upon an impressive sight. He had expected John Ralston's yacht to be sizable, but the 175-foot motor yacht was more like a luxury liner. Its long projecting bow, massive yet sleek hull, and clean white lines, made the *Ingot* one of the most beautiful boats he'd ever seen. With its four decks and helipad on top it looked like a small cruise ship.

As David got out of the Jeep, he gave an involuntary whistle.

"Was that for me, or are you just impressed with the ship?" Katherine said, walking toward him with Grant.

"Both," he managed to get out as Grant tackled him. David gave him a hug, then grabbed his brown leather briefcase and travel suitcase from the back of the Jeep. "Have you been on board yet?"

"Yes," Katherine replied and gave him a quick kiss on the lips. "I've been here since this morning getting things ready. You're in stateroom number four."

Grant burst out, "Mr. Ralston wants to give me a helicopter ride before you leave!"

"To make up for giving up his weekend with you," Katherine explained. "You can take him back to the Langleys afterward."

"That's very nice of John," David said. "Where is our host?"

"Flying my dad here. They've been powwowing about campaign finances."

"Let's go on the boat, Dad," Grant said excitedly, pulling on David's arm.

The three of them walked up the ramp together.

"Most of our staff is here already, but some of them have gone to check out the Historic District. The captain said we'll be leaving at seven. They'll be back in plenty of time."

"And the Garretts?" David said nonchalantly, trying not to show too much interest.

"The senator called. They'll be here by five, too." Katherine glanced at him but gave no indication of how she felt.

She led them down a corridor to David's stateroom. The walls shone with polished teak and the marble bathroom matched the sense of luxury.

"Does this meet with your approval?" she asked him facetiously as he set down his suitcase.

He laughed. "It's a bit roomier than the cabin in our boat in New Haven this summer."

She faked a kiss at him. "That was cozier."

Grant bounced on the bed. "This is neat, Dad. Is this where you're going to sleep tonight?"

"Yes," Katherine said, extending her arm toward Grant. "Let me show you the rest of the boat."

She escorted them up a narrow stairway to the wood-paneled main salon, which was furnished with comfortable, cream-colored sofas arranged around a large marble and glass coffee table. Beyond it was a matching, formal dining area with fresh yellow roses in a crystal vase on a sideboard. Off to one side was a work table with computers, printers, a shredder, a whiteboard, and other office equipment. A polished mahogany grand piano stood nearby.

"This is where we're going to hold our meetings," Katherine said.

They followed her up an elegant, suspended staircase to the next deck and an intimate, warmly lit lounge. The interior bar, with its rich, creamy upholstered barstools, matched the upholstered easy chairs. As Grant jumped up on a barstool and spun around, David mused how different it looked from the cheap red plastic and chrome barstools in the diner.

"This is where we'll relax," Katherine announced like a tour guide.

She went to a sliding glass door that opened automatically as they continued out onto another teak deck and up an exterior circular staircase to the sun deck, open to the sky. A large spa at the stern and larger plunge pool faced a lounging and casual dining area and a shaded bar beyond. Past that and above the bridge was the helipad.

The sound of a helicopter approaching caught their attention and they looked up. The rotors became louder until they reached a roar as it hovered directly above the yacht.

"It's going to land on the boat!" Grant cried excitedly.

"That's John and my father arriving from New York," Katherine shouted.

Grant held his hands to his ears as the black Eurocopter, with lines as sleek as a race car, descended and stayed suspended for a moment before it touched gently down on the helipad.

Ralston waved from the window to them. As the rotors slowed he got out and held the door for Senator Cunningham to climb out and motioned to Grant and David to come to him. Still holding the door open he yelled to the pilot making a circular motion with his hand. "Take them up for a spin."

David picked up Grant, carried him under the slowly rotating blades, and placed him inside. Then he shook Ralston's hand and tried to shout something above the din.

John pointed to his ear and mouthed, "Later."

David climbed inside and buckled Grant in. He settled in his own seat and the pilot handed him a headset. David watched Ralston slam the door shut and run off, bent low, the draft from the rotors blowing his suit, tie and hair wildly until he reached Katherine.

Then the helicopter took off, ascending quickly.

Watching, Katherine said, "Thank you, John. Grant will love that."

He took her arm and headed to the bridge. Ducking inside, he said a few words to the captain. Then he continued on with Katherine climbing a level down to the master suite. It was considerably larger than David's stateroom, more like a luxury hotel suite with a king size bed, a comfortable sitting area, a bar, and closet space galore.

Ralston watched Katherine's awed reaction and opened a door to an adjoining room. "Let me show you my inner sanctum."

Katherine stepped inside and caught her breath in amazement.

The room looked like an investment banker's dream. A row of flat-screen monitors mounted on one of the walls displayed talking financial heads, muted, and electronic ticker-tapes running at the bottom of the screens. Clocks hung above them with labels below each, identifying the major cities that had stock exchanges—New York, London, Tokyo, Hong Kong, Shanghai and Sydney.

Soft light bathed a central U-shaped desk and leather chair. Three computer monitors sat at the apex and volumes of bound corporate prospectuses and reports were stacked at the sides. Unlike David's desk, everything was neat as a pin.

Katherine walked around the room. "So, this is where you disappear to."

"Yes," Ralston said, catching her glance at the clocks. "The markets never sleep, my dear."

"Do you?"

"There is always someone awake in my company headquarters in the new World Trade Center, watching the screens. It's like the bridge on this yacht. If the captain isn't there, a surrogate takes the helm. His eyes went from a screen to her. "As you can see, I make it a point to combine pleasure with business!"

"I always thought it was the other way around," Katherine said, only half-teasing.

"To pleasure, then," he said, grinning. As they walked to the sitting area, he added, "At some level, business is always personal, isn't it?"

Taking one of the chairs, she replied, "I wouldn't know about that."

Joining her in an identical chair across the coffee table, he said, "It's the same in politics. I know you hate Bradley Coyle with a passion." He gave a knowing nod. "Hate can be a powerful motivator."

"So can love," she retorted.

He smiled. "Are you still in love with David?"

Katherine flushed. Was she so transparent? Or was he just fishing? She decided to deflect his query and laughed. "Well, as long as we're getting personal," she said, glancing at the office door, "Is money the only thing that you're in love with?"

Ralston saw the challenge in her eyes. He liked the intimacy of their repartee. "You didn't answer my question."

"You didn't answer mine."

"All right, I'll go first," he said, grinning. "So far, yes."

"Then you're missing the most important thing in life."

"Love is encumbering."

She gave a breathy laugh. "Perhaps you haven't experienced the real thing." She knew she was pushing back hard but took the chance to press ahead. "Someday you'll tire of all your toys, even the living ones."

"You underestimate me," he said, more seriously.

"That remains to be seen."

"So it does. You still haven't answered my question."

"Haven't I?" She rose. "Now, if you'll excuse me, I have some prep before everyone arrives."

Ralston stood up, an amused expression on his face. "Very well. To be continued. I have some work to finish myself. Let me know when everyone is on board."

He acknowledged her with a nod and watched her leave.

After David and Grant finished the helicopter ride, they went to the Langley residence. Grant bubbled over with excitement to the point that the others hardly could get a word in edgewise. Laura Langley finally waved goodbye to David with a smile, releasing him from any obligation to make small talk, and ushered Grant inside the house.

When David reached the pier, he met up with his assistant campaign manager, Julie Hansen, and his field director, Bill Hamilton, from his congressional reelection campaign. They were returning from their visit to the historic section of Annapolis. David liked them both and appreciated their different qualities. Julie was a firebrand who led with her emotions in contrast to Bill, a cool, calm strategist, who analyzed his opponent's weaknesses and exploited them mercilessly. Both were supremely competent, and David was glad to have them on his team.

They went aboard together and a steward directed them to go up to the sun deck. As they emerged from the elevator, David saw that everyone else had assembled. He looked for Jenny and saw her engaged in conversation with Eric Lundstrom, Ralston's financial assistant.

Before he could go to her, John greeted them.

David shook his hand and said, "Thank you again for letting me take Grant on a helicopter ride. It made his day."

"Think nothing of it," Ralston replied. "Now that you're here, we can depart."

He motioned to the purser to inform the captain. Soon, a triple horn blast came from the bridge, and all the passengers went to the port side rail and watched the ship drop her lines.

David took the spot next to Jenny and said, "Hello. Thanks for coming." When her expression of surprise turned somber, he quickly added, "I'm sorry you missed Grant. He said to tell you, 'Hi'."

"So am I. We must have gotten our signals crossed," she replied, but her quick glance toward Katherine suggested that she did not believe for a moment it was a mistake. Then she relented. "I'm glad I came."

David relaxed and gave her arm a squeeze.

The *Ingot* left the harbor and headed north toward the Chesapeake & Delaware Canal. Katherine herded all the passengers on deck into the lounge to kick off the retreat. She waited until they had settled comfortably in their chairs and two waiters brought the drinks everyone had ordered. Then she gave the floor to David.

He had been standing at the glass door to the outside, watching. Now he walked slowly to the head of the room, taking a moment to look each member of the small group in the eye.

Then he began, "I was going to give a quick pep talk so we could relax and socialize this evening before getting to work tomorrow morning. But I've had an idea that I want to share with you and get your feedback." He hesitated for effect, watching their bodies grow alert, and continued, "I don't think we can beat Bradley Coyle with a conventional campaign. We need something different and unexpected that captures the voters' imagination and rocks him back on his heels."

The silence in the lounge made clear that he had their attention.

"The helicopter ride with Grant gave me an idea. I want to barnstorm Connecticut by helicopter—fly it myself. If I make four or five stops a day, I could hit every small town in the interior of the state, then hold rallies in the evening. What do you think?"

Senator Garrett's face lit up. "A whistle-stop campaign by air. I like it!"

Katherine joined in. "I think it's a brilliant idea." She put a hand on David's shoulder. "We can get local news coverage and use social media—twitter and blogging—to raise your national profile, and the national media might even pick it up."

But Julie frowned. "There's a huge risk if it comes off as a publicity stunt."

"They can call it what they want," David responded, "I'll be talking to the voters. I think it's a bigger risk if we run a conventional campaign. That's what Coyle expects."

Julie nodded. "But we can't let this turn into a circus. No press releases, except before each stop. No advertising, except in the local papers to bring in the crowds. Let the small-town newspapers pick it up and spread it."

"It might even bring in more young voters," Keith Wilson, data and media guru, contributed. "The Millennials will love it!"

"Once there's movement in the polls with all the publicity it will generate, we'll be able to attract more donations," Senator Cunningham said with enthusiasm.

Susan Holiday, the finance director jumped in. "You're talking about a grassroots campaign that can raise small amounts, but, multiplied by the numbers, it adds up. They become invested in you."

John Ralston turned to Eric. "You'll need to coordinate with Susan on the fundraising."

"Then we all agree?" Katherine asked.

They all answered Yes! in unison.

Then they broke into teams, chattering among themselves to start figuring out the details. Some drew their chairs closer together, others stood up and congregated at the bar.

David, noticing Jenny looking left out, clapped his hands. When he had their attention again, he said, "I have other announcements we need to include in our plans. Jenny is opening the Garrett farm to a horse program for veterans during the summer."

"That's wonderful!" Julie exclaimed.

Katherine mused, "We could have a press conference on the opening day with the vets, and David can explain how the program works."

John Ralston chimed in. "If it would help kick off the program, I could set up a polo exhibition at the Middleburg Club."

"I'd prefer to do it quietly," Jenny said in a restrained manner. "Otherwise it would definitely come off as a publicity stunt."

"No, it wouldn't," Katherine insisted, "It's too good an

opportunity to pass up for David's campaign."

Resting her elbows on the chair arms, Jenny entwined her fingers and said more firmly, "I don't want to do that. David will get plenty of publicity from the barnstorming, or you can do it with some other project that's been established and proven its success."

"If it works somewhere else, it will work here," Katherine said emphatically.

"No!" Jenny's raised voice surprised everyone. She noticed their startled expressions and resumed more softly, "Let's not fire all of our cannons upfront. Let's save this for later to keep the momentum going once I've tested it."

Senator Garrett came to his daughter's rescue. "There are a number of unknowns—both from the perspective of the horses and the veterans. I think we better take our time until we know it works."

Katherine smiled at him. "I yield to your judgment and experience on this, Senator," effectively hiding her annoyance with Jenny.

"Either way we can't lose, upfront or later," Bill Hamilton said. "David should visit the program once it's on its way, without the fanfare."

Keith picked up the ball. "Then, when the press finds out on their own, it could never be mistaken for a publicity stunt."

Katherine added, "It will make you look even better, David." She reached over and touched his arm, and turned to Jenny and said, pointedly, "Maybe you have some other ideas for the veterans' program."

Jenny smiled, all innocence. "As a matter of fact, I have. There are art therapy organizations that use drawing, painting and sculpture with veterans who have undergone stress in combat." She looked directly at Katherine. "I'd like to try a program and assess its merits. Would you be interested?"

Katherine recovered quickly. "Of course, but as you pointed out yourself, we need programs that are tested and verified. I'm sure you understand."

"Of course." Jenny turned to David. "What do you think, David?"

"I can tell you from my own experience that painting can have a profound effect on a person."

"Then it's settled," Jenny said to appreciative murmurs.

No one but her and Ralston noticed the darts in Katherine's eyes.

"These are all great ideas. We should make a schedule of when to implement them," Julie said.

"Why don't we nail down all the details tomorrow," David interceded. "For the rest of this evening, the umbrella is up as far as any campaign matters are concerned."

Just then the purser came over to John Ralston and whispered in his ear.

"Perfect timing," Ralston announced and stood up. "Dinner is served in the dining area on the main deck."

∽

After a breakfast buffet on the sun deck the next morning, everyone, except Jenny and Ralston, reconvened at eight o'clock. Bill Hamilton spread out a map of Connecticut on the table with circles around towns with local airports, as they began addressing specifics.

At some point, David let the pros and Katherine deal with the details. He would look at the plan they came up with later and make suggestions and adjustments as needed. He went topside where Jenny was sunning in a bikini. She wore large, dark brown sunglasses. An open paperback lay on a small table next to her deckchair.

When David took the chair next to her, she sat up. "How's it going?" she asked.

"Very well. Everyone's fired up with ideas. Aren't you going to join us?"

Jenny slipped her glasses down her nose and looked at him. "This is your and Katherine's campaign. There's not anything that I can contribute except tension."

"I'd like your input."

"Not in the meetings with your staff. You need to come together. That's the purpose of this cruise. I would only get in the way."

"Once this campaign starts we won't see much of each other."

"I'm sure that will please your chief of staff and campaign manager," she said, with a little edge in her voice.

David ignored her tone. "It won't please me, Jenny."

"Then do something about it, David." It sounded harsher than she intended. "Katherine treats me like I'm a political novice. She doesn't act as though she's just your chief of staff."

"What do you mean?"

Jenny pushed her glasses up and looked at the endless expanse of the ocean. "It's difficult sometimes because I know the two of you have been intimate," she said more softly, "She seems to say it with her eyes, 'I've slept with him and have a prior claim.'"

David's expression was doubtful.

In response, Jenny continued more vehemently, "She flaunts it. You can't just disappear for five months with her."

He tried to appease her. "I'll get back to D.C. for votes and committee hearings every so often. I'll bring Grant out to the farm with me."

She stared at him closely.

"What's the matter?" he asked.

"I've been here before, David. Others who made promises…" She left "that they didn't keep" unspoken between them.

He looked around the deck, feeling helpless. "This isn't a good place to have this conversation. Can't we discuss it some other time when we have privacy?"

"You're right'" she relented. "But we'll have to do it soon."

⤝

The rest of the day was taken up with meetings to map out all aspects of the campaign. The younger staff welcomed the input of the two senators, seasoned political combatants, and grew closer and more enthusiastic about their chances. David and Katherine participated with a watchful eye.

He saw Jenny only at dinner. She was gracious and pleasant, but there was no opportunity to spend any private time with her.

When David went to his stateroom, his mind was a whirlwind of plans and ideas. But he kept going back to his conversation with Jenny and her demand to discuss their future together. He tried to go to sleep but couldn't, thinking one moment about Jenny, the next about the campaign, and then about Katherine. Finally, he got up and went to Jenny's stateroom door. There was no light in the crack under it so he headed to the top deck.

As he walked toward the railing, a familiar female voice came out of the darkness. "Out on your usual four a.m. prowl?"

David looked over toward a row of empty deck chairs where Katherine sat in the shadows. "I didn't see you there. Can't sleep either?"

She shook her head. "Too much on my mind."

He moved closer. "It's our last chance to catch our breaths."

"Your barnstorming idea was brilliant," she said. "It will change the whole dynamic of the campaign. You've fired up the staff. We can really make hay with publicity."

David nodded. "Bradley won't know what hit him."

They listened to the foaming wake for a while. At last, Katherine broke the silence between them. "It's a bit awkward with her here, isn't it?"

"Only if you make it so."

"The two of you were missing for a while." When he didn't respond, she asked, "Have you slept with her?"

His head snapped toward her. "Now you are making it awkward."

"I just wondered how we compare."

"Kathy, I can't believe you said that."

She gave a slight laugh. "Neither can I."

As she shifted in the lounge chair, her robe dropped aside exposing one leg and most of the bare breast above. She slowly pulled the robe to cover her nakedness as though it didn't matter.

David noticed.

She walked over to him and opened the robe pulling it around him, pressing her naked body against him. He hesitated a moment too long and she kissed him softly and said, "But it's all right because I know the answer, darling."

He watched her walk to the door in her bare feet and disappear inside. He rubbed his furrowed forehead and ran his fingers through his hair.

The rest of the journey went without a hitch. The staff worked well together, inspired by David's pep talks, working constantly, sometimes well into the night to finish plans. Katherine and Jenny avoided further conflict, even when the discussions turned to how to best include her programs for veterans.

Katherine planned a party for the final night on board. Wine and liquor flowed freely and everyone had a good time. As they entered the Long Island Sound, the backdrop of the shining lights from the distant homes along the Connecticut coast provided a special touch. Confident that David was well on his way to winning the Senate seat, everyone let loose like celebrants at Mardi Gras before Lent when the real work began. The party lasted until well after midnight and all participants, satiated with good cheer and a sense of accomplishment collapsed into their beds.

The following morning's disembarkation was hectic, and David stopped at Jenny's stateroom and tapped on the door. Jenny opened it, her bag in hand. "Oh, David, I overslept."

A steward came up the corridor for her bag. "Your car and the senator are waiting at the ramp."

David handed him her suitcase. "Tell them she'll be right there."

When he left David said, "I just wanted to kiss you goodbye and tell you that I'll see you in a week at the Langleys for Grant's birthday party. Can you be there?"

"Of course."

"I haven't forgotten. We can talk then." He gave her a quick, hard kiss. "See you in a week," he said, and was gone.

CHAPTER 43

The tedium of the first week of campaigning was relieved by the diversion of flying again. It was early in the morning at the Tweed-New Haven airport. David followed the mechanics rolling the *Spirit of Connecticut* into a private hanger for refueling and a maintenance check.

As he went over to the helicopter, he saw Katherine coming to him through the huge hangar doors with a seductive strut and a bright smile on her face. *It was like old times,* he thought. How often she had met him that way in the hanger after a day of flight training at Whiting Field Naval Air Station near Pensacola. While he was in training there, she would come down most weekends from Washington, and they'd spend days at the beach and nights in an old motel, oblivious to everything except each other.

She came up to him and kissed him on the lips. "I saw on my calendar that Sunday is Grant's birthday. What do you want me to plan?" David hesitated for an instant, before answering. "I just got a call. Laura Langley is planning a party for him at the Smithsonian Zoo," he said. "Laura and Edward will bring Grant in from Annapolis."

"What a nice idea. We need to be there for the hearing on Monday morning. We can fly down after the rally in Bridgeport on Saturday night. That's perfect. I know just the present I'll give him."

David smiled uneasily. He had neglected to mention that the party was Jenny's idea and that it was she who had called.

Sunday morning was bright and clear, perfect for a five-year-old's birthday party. As David walked past the two lion sculptures nestled in the vegetation at the entrance to the Smithsonian National Zoological Park, he felt a pang of apprehension. He was looking forward to seeing Grant and Jenny again but wasn't sure how she and Katherine would get along.

Jenny's instructions were for everyone to meet at the wild animal carousel. By the time David got there, all the others had arrived already and stood around engaged in conversation. He didn't sense any tension among them and relaxed as Grant greeted him with a hug.

After casual hellos—pecks on the cheeks for the three women and a handshake with Edward Langley—they each selected an animal to ride. Grant picked the leopard, while Katherine and Jenny flanked him on the giraffe and big white stork, respectively. David rode the zebra in front of them, and Laura and Edward Langley brought up the rear occupying the high-backed wooden seat with a kangaroo on each side.

As the carousel started to turn the animals began to move up and down to the calliope music of "Turkey in the Straw." Glancing over his shoulder occasionally, David noted Grant's jubilant expression and thought, *Nothing can spoil this day.*

Afterward, they went to one of the party rooms. The walls were painted with animals in false window frames as though they were looking in from the outside. Jenny had placed the wrapped presents on a side table. Each had an animal sticker with the name of the person who gave it.

"C'mon Grant, you sit in the place of honor," Katherine said, touching the back of the chair at the head of the table. She placed a safari hat on Grant's head and sat down to his right, gesturing for David to take the other side.

Jenny smiled sweetly, but there was resentment in her eyes as she took the seat next to David. Edward plopped himself down next to

Katherine as Laura paraded in with the birthday cake she had baked for the occasion and set it down in front of Grant. It had heavy chocolate frosting and five lit candles in the middle. As if on cue, an elephant trumpeted in the distance.

"That's quite a fanfare," Edward Langley said, and they all laughed.

Grant closed his eyes tightly, made a wish and blew out the candles to a round of applause. Then Katherine cut the cake and placed each slice on a small paper plate and passed them around the table.

David took a bite, groaned with pleasure, and said, "This is sinful," earning a smile from Laura.

"What did you wish for, Grant?" Jenny asked.

He smiled broadly. "Another helicopter ride."

"Well," David chuckled, "there's no doubt that that wish will come true, since I leased one for the campaign. You can go back with me and fly to some campaign stops."

"Can Jenny come with us?"

"Jenny's not a part of the campaign," Katherine intervened, "but I'll be there." She wiped the chocolate frosting from Grant's cheeks and asked, "Which present do you want to open first?"

"Jenny's," he said bouncing up and down on his chair.

Katherine got up, hiding her irritation, and found a box with a gazelle sticker. She put it down in front of Grant and stood while he tore off the paper and opened the black lid.

"Gee, a new riding helmet!" he said excitedly. He removed the safari hat and put it on his head. "How do I look, Jenny?"

"Like a real horseman!" Jenny said.

"Like you and Dad!" he exclaimed.

Katherine took the helmet off and put it back in the box.

"I want to wear it all day, Aunt Katherine," Grant protested.

"You can wear it after we go on the safari," she said and put the safari hat back on him. Then, she brought the rest of the gifts to him.

Everyone watched as he oohed over the bedtime storybooks from his grandmother, aahed at the jigsaw puzzle from his grandfather, and gave a high-five to his father for the aquarium. Then he clapped his hands in delight over a big watercolor pad, with brushes, and a watercolor pallet that Nancy Sullivan had sent.

"Now this is from me, Grant," Katherine said and passed him a large box.

"What is it?" Grant said eagerly.

"Your Dad can help you open it."

When Grant had torn the wrapping paper off, David helped him pry open the box with a picture of a sailboat on the side.

"Wow, Aunt Katherine. This is really neat!"

"It's a model sailboat that operates on batteries," Katherine said. "You can work the rudder by remote control, and sail it by catching the wind."

"Wow!" he exclaimed again.

"When you come up for the helicopter ride with your dad, I'll take you to a place where you can sail it."

"This is the best birthday ever, Aunt Katherine!"

Watching the proceedings, Jenny kept up a good front, but she was churning inside.

"There's lots more," Laura said as a zoo attendant came in and announced that he was ready to start their safari tour.

As they went outside, Katherine took Grant's hand and led the way. Grant skipped between her and the guide full of questions while the others followed behind. They strolled past the panda exhibit, on to the Kid's Farm where Grant petted a donkey, and to a compound where two elephants were wading in a pool. To Grant's delight, they sprayed water from their trunks into the air.

By the time they got to the big cat displays where lions and tigers lounged lazily in the sun on rocks and sandy ground, Katherine had no interest in going further. "We need to get back to the office, David," she said.

"You go ahead, I'm staying. This is Grant's day," he replied.

Looking at her watch, she stood there for a moment as if debating with herself. Then she said, "We need to prepare for the hearing."

David stood his ground. "I'm as prepped as I'll ever be. You go."

"Okay," she answered with a touch of irritation, then turned to Jenny. "It was nice seeing you again." She thanked the Langleys perfunctorily, gave Grant an exaggerated hug, and left.

Grant took Jenny's hand and they all went to the monkey house where baboons were climbing along ropes overhead and chimpanzees clowned for the visitors. By the time they circled back to the panda area, Grant was getting tired and kept yawning.

"Time to call it a day," Edward suggested.

When Grant nodded, David knelt down and hugged him. "I'll pick you up next week as soon as I can arrange for you to help me on the campaign."

Yawning, Grant asked, "Why can't Jenny go on the helicopter with us?"

David smiled kindly. "We'll do it later. I promise."

Jenny kissed Grant's cheek. "It's okay, Grant. Daddy promised."

She and David waved as they left. Then, they walked over to the Panda Café. It was near closing time and there were no more people in the outside dining area. While David went in to get a couple of coffees, Jenny sat at one of the tables overlooking the panda exhibit. As she watched the pudgy, black and white bears stuff themselves with bamboo shoots, she thought, *Deceptively cute*, and her anger at Katherine's behavior rose to the surface.

When David joined her and set her coffee in front of her, Jenny asked pointedly, "When did this 'Aunt Katherine' thing start?"

David could tell she was miffed. Katherine had upstaged her all afternoon. He tried to keep the conversation light. "He calls Nancy Sullivan, Aunt Nancy."

"Nancy doesn't fawn over him."

"Yeah, it was a bit much."

"A bit? Even Laura was annoyed. Katherine took over as though it were her own party..." She put her elbows on the table looking directly at him. "I love Grant. He's your son, and I know how important he is to you. But I'm not going to compete for his affections as a way to your heart. I won't do that to him."

When David remained silent, she went on. "Every summer when I came home to my father from boarding school there was another woman, pretending that she cared about me, trying to get through me to my father.... Like Katherine's doing with Grant."

"Grant isn't the issue," David said quietly.

"No, he's not. Katherine is. She spoiled the day for everyone but herself."

"Grant enjoyed it. Wasn't that the point?"

Jenny rolled her eyes. "Her point was to tell me...no, to show me...and everyone else...that I'm not the only one in the picture with you."

"You know I had to invite her, Jenny," David pleaded. "She suggested a party. You'd already planned it. You have to understand. She plays a part in my life that began a long time ago. Right now she's irreplaceable."

"I understand that, David. I'm just beginning to wonder in what place she's irreplaceable."

He ignored her challenge. "I know it's difficult, but the important thing is that the party here at the zoo was a wonderful idea and pleased Grant beyond any party Katherine would have planned. Don't think that's lost on me."

Jenny expelled a deep breath. "Are you still sleeping with her?"

He let an uncomfortable silence build. Then he said softly, "I'll always be honest with you, Jenny."

She settled herself. "I've told you. I've heard that before."

"You don't believe me?"

"Not yet."

"Then I'll have to convince you."

"Why don't you start by answering my question?"

"All right. The answer is 'No,' Jenny. I'm not sleeping with her anymore."

She'd gotten the response she wanted but felt somehow diminished by having asked for it. "I apologize for asking the question."

"In that case, there's a quiet little seafood place near the National Cathedral. I want to take you there for dinner."

She smiled, remembering their first dinner together. "Only if they have trout."

He grinned back at her. "That's why I picked it."

CHAPTER 44

Bradley Coyle looked up from his desk with irritation as Bob Boyd, his chief of staff, plopped a copy of the *Voluntown News* in front of him. Above the fold was a large photo of David Madison looking out of the cockpit window of a helicopter with a banner headline, "MADISON TO BARNSTORM STATE."

"What is this?"

Boyd scratched his head. "He's leased a helicopter and is flying it all over the state. Check out the name on the side of the chopper."

Bradley squinted at the photograph. "The *Spirit of Connecticut?*" he read. "You've got to be kidding me!"

"And below the name, it says, 'Made in Connecticut.'"

"Why, that son of a bitch! He hasn't done a thing to promote jobs in Connecticut! That's what I've done for the last five years!"

Boyd leaned over the desk, picked up the paper, and read out loud, "David Madison, vying for the U.S. Senate seat held by incumbent Bradley Coyle, kicked off his election campaign yesterday at the Voluntown Airport. A sizable crowd welcomed the congressman as he stepped off his helicopter–"

"Where in hell is Voluntown?"

"It's one of the easternmost towns in the state, almost in Rhode Island, population two thousand six hundred," Boyd informed him and continued reading. "The former Marine pilot landed his Sikorsky helicopter, the *Spirit of Connecticut* to a cheering crowd. Madison plans to crisscross the state over the next few weeks."

Bradley grabbed the newspaper from him and looked at

the picture again. "Oh for chrissake, what kind of a hokey-assed publicity stunt is that?"

"One that could build popular support," said Boyd impassively. "There are over two-dozen public and private airports in the State, not to mention plenty of places where a helicopter can land. This is serious, Senator."

Tossing down the paper in disgust, Bradley said, "I'm not about to slog through a bunch of dairy and tobacco farms in the hinterlands, Bob, trying to pick up a few votes."

The intercom buzzed and a pleasant female voice announced, "Mr. Finch is here. He and his team are waiting in the conference room for you."

"Thank you, Doris, and get me a cup of coffee." Bradley turned to Boyd. "Who asked for Finch?"

"I did," Boyd replied, "Our campaign manager is supposed to know this was coming. We need Finch to develop a counter-strategy. Pronto."

Bradley rolled his eyes in exasperation, but he got up and followed his chief of staff out of the room. Boyd was good at his job. If he was concerned, Bradley knew from experience it was time to pay attention.

When they entered the conference room, Harvey Finch and his team sitting on the other side of the mahogany table stood up. With his thin lips and restless eyes that took in everything in his surroundings he always reminded Bradley of a nervous ferret. Finch was about 10 years older than him and a seasoned veteran of many campaigns. He had been one of the reasons Bradley had breezed through the previous Senate run. The people to either side of him were a hefty, mature Hispanic man, responsible for coordinating media relations, polling and research, and two young women, a blonde and a brunette, who were new. Bradley, assuming they would be doing the grunt work, found them pretty but not attractive enough to merit a second glance.

"You remember my staff," Finch said with a high, reedy voice. "This is Jorge Guitierrez and—"

"Of course," Coyle waved off the introductions. "Please sit down." He tossed the newspaper across the table. Jorge glanced at the headline as he slid it toward Finch. The two women sitting opposite him craned their necks to get a peek at it, too.

Finch didn't bother. "I've seen it."

"Well, what do we do about it?"

"Nothing. Madison is wasting his time."

"You're sure." Coyle looked for confirmation to the other faces at the table. "Follow the numbers," Finch said decisively. "You won last time with over sixty percent of the vote from the cities, both along the coast and inland. Don't get distracted by this publicity stunt. Stay focused on where the votes are."

Coyle turned with a triumphant smile to his chief of staff, as if to say, "I told you so."

Boyd countered, "Madison's getting free press, and he'll get it every time he makes a stop. As other local TV stations pick it up, the story will go state-wide, if not national."

Finch gave him an annoyed look. "We'll flood the State with ads. There's no need to follow Madison around. It would make us look weak."

He turned to the two women. "Put together an ad campaign that counters every article that's published locally about Madison. Big full-page ads with photos like, 'Senator Coyle at work while David Madison plays hopscotch.' Always say 'Senator Coyle,' and never say 'Congressman Madison,' always 'David Madison.' Then hit him again across from the opinion page. Make sure another ad goes there. Those little newspapers will love the money."

He paused to let the blonde woman writing his directives on her legal pad catch up. Then he continued, "And let's shoot a TV spot that drives the point home. We'll blanket the local stations during the news hour."

"Thank you, Harvey," Bradley said magnanimously. "Full steam ahead! There is plenty of money in the kitty." He rose from his chair to indicate that, as far as he was concerned, the meeting was over. As Finch and his team filed out of the room, he eyed the brunette from behind with appreciation as her skirt shifted provocatively with each step.

When they were gone, Boyd said, "This may just be a little brush fire now, but if we don't nip it in the bud, it will develop into a firestorm we can't control."

Irritated that his chief of staff was still harping on the issue, Bradley said, "Don't worry, I'll get Stephanie Jordan to make Madison look like a fool for pulling that stunt."

But every day the headlines got more pointed and the crowds grew bigger at each stop David made. After his third stop, the story went national on television, with pundits on both sides of the political spectrum debating whether it was a brilliant campaign strategy or just a crass attempt to hog the spotlight.

David's advance team did a bang-up job, making sure he was always met by the local press, hungry for stories and happy that their small communities were now getting attention. The local newspaper clippings began to pile up on the corner of Bob Boyd's desk, each with a picture of David in his flight suit talking earnestly to people in the town he was visiting, with the helicopter in the background and *Spirit of Connecticut* prominently displayed.

In his stump speech, David hammered Coyle for being asleep at the wheel or worse. He pointed out that Connecticut was in the poorest financial condition of the fifty states. Even though it was relatively small in size and population, three of its cities were ranked among the 25 most violent in the nation. Taxes were high, yet the infrastructure was falling apart and wages were stagnating. The State was losing people and one of the largest companies was moving out. David kept making the connection that the government had betrayed its constituents, just as had happened with the veterans.

It was a litany of disastrous policies coming home to roost, many instituted by the governor, but David laid all the blame at Coyle's doorstep. He painted his opponent as a man out of touch with the people, only concerned to satisfy his wealthy friends and donors who would further his political ambitions.

The unflattering image started to stick. Whenever Coyle set foot in the halls of Congress, reporters dogged him, shouted questions after him, and asked him to respond to the most recent of Madison's accusations, putting him on the defensive.

Things took an unpleasant turn at a dinner party held by Bradley and Helen at their posh Greenwich Estate overlooking the Long Island Sound. It was an important social gathering of Connecticut's power elite that included politicians, corporate bigwigs, and business owners and their spouses.

Everything went smoothly until Governor Morris made an ironic remark to Harvey Finch about how Bradley's opponent in the Senate race, characterizing him as an elitist, was beginning to rub off negatively on his "elitist" friends. Stung, Finch responded less than politely. It took Helen's considerable skills as hostess to smooth things over. Bradley rose to the occasion, spending the rest of the evening exuding confidence to reassure everyone that this was a mere bump in the road and that his reelection was a foregone conclusion. By the time the last guest left, he was gratified that, due to his efforts, the party had turned out to be a success after all.

Later, as they were getting ready for bed, Bradley approached his wife as she was seated at her antique vanity removing her make-up. He tightened the belt of his silk robe and rested both hands on her shoulders. "Thank you, Helen. It was a lovely dinner event."

Her eyes met his in the mirror. "I don't know why you insisted on having Harvey Finch and his wife here with the governor, Speaker of the House and President of the Senate. They were completely out of place."

He dropped his hands and plunked down in a chair by her side. "Because I needed him here. Everyone is getting super paranoid about this election. For the life of me I can't understand why. I'm still way ahead in the polls."

"David Madison is doing something different. He isn't playing by your rules, and that scares them."

"Scares them?"

"Yes. You may be ahead, but you're slipping in the polls, and they think you're in denial."

"What makes you think that?"

She turned around and faced him. "Their wives, my dear. You can see it in their eyes. They're looking at you like, maybe you won't be here next year. They're not confident and relaxed. Neither are you. You heard Governor Morris. He's getting dragged into the campaign because of Madison's criticism of the state economy and it worries him."

Bradley scoffed. "He isn't on the ballot for another two years. Besides, Madison's party has half the registered voters we have, and—"

"—And there are more independent registered voters than we have," Helen cut in. "That's your Achilles heel, and the Governor's." She picked up a pearl-handled brush and began stroking it through her hair.

Bradley didn't contradict her. Madison's ability to turn the tables on him was disconcerting. It had never happened to him in an election before. The problem he faced was that his old techniques of attacking and vilifying his opponent weren't working. Helen was right about that. Her political instincts were always incisive.

Helen took his silence as concession. "Madison has ignited a populist audience, tarring you as an elitist, out-of-touch politician," she said. "Hiding behind your incumbency will do you no good. You're answering David Madison with ads instead of confronting him directly. Your television floozy has been just as ineffective in exposing his publicity stunt for what it is."

Bradley exploded. "I'm sick and tired of you bringing her up whenever we have a disagreement!"

Helen ignored his outburst and answered calmly, "I'm just being realistic. I want to change my address to 1600 Pennsylvania Avenue. If you play it safe, you'll end up losing both the White House and me."

She went to pull back the coverlet from their king-sized bed and fluff the pillows on her side. As she got under the sheets, she said, "Good night, Bradley. Think about what I have said."

The coolness of her voice doused any fiery comeback he might have considered. He got up and walked out onto the balcony. The pool light was still on and he could make out the tennis courts beyond. When the bedroom light clicked off behind him and his eyes adjusted, he looked out over Long Island Sound and the halo glow of New York City in the far distance.

He loved the view both during the day and at night. Truth be told, the estate was Bradley's real trophy when he had married Helen after her husband died. It had been in the Branson family for nearly two centuries, and the name was as fixed in the minds of the Greenwich residents as the stones of the old colonial mansion and the wall that surrounded it. But someday it would be referred to as the Bradley Coyle Estate, home of the President of the United States.

He stared out at the Great Captain Island light in the near distance, flashing green every five seconds. It had done so for over a hundred years. As he pondered it, it seemed to count off the seconds of his life, like a long, unconscious heartbeat. He had no time to lose. With the election a little over three months away, he had to make every moment count. Whatever happened, the light would keep flashing, but would he be there to see it? If he didn't win, Helen would make good on her threat for sure.

There was no way he was going to give all of this up.

He went inside and climbed into bed, molding his body to Helen's back, and whispered. "You're right, dear. Time to get the knives out."

CHAPTER 45

Flying past Mystic Seaport in his Sikorsky helicopter, David radioed his approach to Wychwood Field, the small airport to the northeast of the city. As he headed for the airstrip, he was delighted by the number of cars parked on both sides of the road, and the ample crowd of spectators lining the turf runway waiting for him. The news of his progress across Connecticut was getting out and his campaign was gathering momentum.

He touched down on the field near the small building that served as control tower, airport offices, and arrival lounge and killed the engine. Waiting for the rotors to slow to a gradual stop, he looked at the waving arms and smiling faces and was pleased to see Coast Guard Academy cadets and uniformed Naval personnel from the New London Submarine Base among them.

As he climbed out of the cockpit, the members of his advance team waiting near the building, hustled to his side. Julie arrived with photographers, TV cameramen and reporters in tow. Melissa set up a camera of her own to record the event and stream it on Facebook Live. Robert brought a small cooler and handed him a bottle of water. They were working with the efficiency of a pit crew at a racetrack, and David thought with pride what a good job Katherine had done organizing and training them.

He stepped up on one of the struts of the helicopter from where he could see over the crowd. When he was comfortably balanced, Julie passed him a wireless microphone.

His booming, amplified shout, "Hello, Mystic, Connecticut!" quieted the throng.

David waited until he had everyone's attention. Then he said, grinning, "I know that you all just came out to see if I can really fly this thing."

Laughter swept the crowd.

He pointed to the name painted on the side of the chopper. "This machine was invented here and I call it the *Spirit of Connecticut* because it represents the resourcefulness of all of you who live in the Constitution State." He paused for a moment. "But you've been short-changed for the last six years by someone who lacks respect for that resourcefulness and doesn't care about you. Bradley Coyle has stood idly by as we are losing population from our State, industries are deserting, taking your jobs with them, and a financial crisis looms. You did not create this mess. The politicians did who care only for themselves. They're responsible!"

A cheer rippled through the crowd.

"But it's up to you to send them a message. You have the power to throw them out and replace them with people who will work for you. If you elect me senator, I promise I will always be on your side and fight for your interest, not for those of the Washington elites and their wealthy cronies."

The applause was resounding as David continued, "I also want to address the veterans who have come out today." A cheer went up among the uniforms. David waved his hand to them in greeting and continued, "The VA does not serve you as it should. While the politicians have excellent health care, they have left you waiting in line for months on end. Well, the waiting is over. We will restructure the VA to give you the best medical care available. I will fight to appoint a special commission to make that happen, and I won't rest until the work is done! That is a promise."

When the thunderous cheers subsided, one of the reporters

shouted out, "Congressman, what do you say to Senator Coyle's accusations that you are just exploiting the veterans to advance your own career?"

David's eyes flashed. "I don't answer to Bradley Coyle," he said, sweeping his arm over the crowd. "I answer to these people."

"And what are the people saying?" the reporter prompted in an effort to get a better quote for his story.

"They're saying that they're fed up with Washington." David raised his hand to his chin. "Up to here! And I agree with them. Being a veteran myself, I know from first-hand experience what they are going through."

David stepped down from the helicopter strut and went over to the reporter. The badge on his lapel read, "Paul Andrews— *Hartford Times.*" He looked straight at him. "Well, Paul, why don't we ask one?"

He led him to a soldier in a wheelchair in the front row, dressed in fatigues and holding a sign, "Please don't forget us." Holding out his right hand, David spoke into the microphone, "I am David Madison, and I'm asking for your vote, because you, and all who served with you, will either be forgotten or remembered. At one time, I was one of the forgotten, and I'll never forget how it felt, or forget you."

The veteran grasped his hand, shook it and said into the mic, "I'm Jim Butterworth, and I'm pleased to meet you, sir. I did four tours in Afghanistan."

"What happened to you?"

"I lost my legs when a roadside bomb went off."

David nodded in understanding. Then he motioned toward the reporter. "Jim, I'd like to introduce you to Paul Andrews from the *Hartford Times.* Would you please tell him what your experience has been with the Veterans Administration?"

The soldier shifted awkwardly in his wheelchair and looked up at Andrews. "The military always took good care of us, but since I got discharged it's been a different story. I've been waiting three months for an appointment to get my prosthesis adjusted."

David said into the microphone, "Jim, I promise you, and every soldier here and in the nation, that I will do everything I can to change that. And we will win that war, too."

He shook Jim Butterworth's hand and returned to the helicopter without a glance at the reporter. Back on the strut, he waited for the crowd to calm and said, "I'd like to ask you veterans to serve with me to fight a new war. It's a battle for the neighborhoods of our cities. Here in Connecticut, Bridgeport, New Haven, and Hartford are in the top twenty-five for highest crime rates in the country. Bridgeport ranks fourth highest!"

A murmur swept through the crowd.

"Yes, that's right, the fourth-worst crime rate per capita. But we can change that, with your help. There are twelve-thousand of you veterans in this State, and that's a big army. We will set up organizations in Bridgeport, New Haven and Hartford utilizing successful methods by veterans' groups from other major cities to bring boys and girls out of gangs and off the streets. It's time to break the cycle of violence and poverty. We can do it! But not with Bradley Coyle in office! Elect me, and we will fight that war together and win!"

The cheers went on for a long time.

For the next hour David shook hands and talked with members of the crowd, listening to their concerns and answering them. Then he got back into the helicopter and lifted off to fly to Hartford to take the shuttle to Washington. Looking at the receding crowd below him, he felt heartened and energized. He was finally doing something that mattered.

CHAPTER 46

Gathering by the stables at Middleburg, Jenny and four veterans watched Jack Bowden demonstrate how to put the bridle on a horse. She realized how fortunate she was to have him help with the Vets With Horses program. When she'd asked him to join her, he immediately agreed. After flying to Texas together to observe a successful Horses for Heroes program, they had decided to start small. He had picked four gentle horses—Red and her mare Fanny remained in the barn; they needed expert handling. She had found four veterans willing to give the program a try.

A Vietnam War veteran with an easy-going, down-to-earth manner, Jack Bowden had developed rapport with the men quickly. They were more than halfway through the initial eight-week program, matching the vets with horses, having them groom and feed them, and learn all the equipment and how to adjust it on the horses they had chosen. Actual riding would come in the next session.

At first, the men had felt intimidated by the large animals, but by now all four had grown comfortable enough to begin forming a bond. One of them, Jesse, had taken to his horse so quickly that he asked if he could come on Saturdays as well. He had no immediate family and Jenny, sensing his loneliness and isolation, had agreed.

She was pleased to observe a gradual change take place in the lives of the vets, manifesting in their enthusiasm and dedication. She saw it also in the relaxed, upbeat expressions in the eyes of the wives and children that sometimes came with them.

Compared to the arts program for vets she was running at the

National Gallery, it was slow going, though. For some it seemed like they forgot during the week what they had accomplished and when they came the following Sunday had to start as if from scratch. For the first time Jenny had an inkling of what it must have been like for David in the depth of despair, and the effort it must have taken him to climb out of his emotional abyss.

Of course, the men came to the horse farm only once a week, whereas the participants in the painting program quickly agreed to three evenings a week. There were some talented members in the group, even those with severe physical limitations due to injuries they had sustained during their tours of duty.

As she watched Jack demonstrate how to put the bit into a horse's mouth, her cell phone rang. She muted it and looked at the screen. It was David. With the campaign in full swing Jenny hadn't seen him for several weeks. They had made plans to get together three times, but he had canceled abruptly as more events piled up on his calendar—donor meetings, press conferences, speaking engagements, and flights on his helicopter.

As Jenny walked off, she touched the screen and brought the phone to her ear. "I hope this is the future senator from Connecticut calling to tell me he's finally found the time to come and spend some time with me," she said.

She heard David clear his throat. "You must have read my mind. I'm coming down for a vote on Friday. Can I bring Grant to the farm on Sunday?"

She strolled along the dirt drive leading to the stable entrance. "Yes. But if you cancel again, I'm not going to vote for you."

He chuckled in response. "I am crushed. Especially since you're not a resident of Connecticut and can't vote here."

"Well, if I were, I wouldn't," she said facetiously. "You owe me."

"I wish I were with you right now."

His voice sounded intimate, as if he were right next to her and she relented. "I see you're moving up in the polls. You must be doing something right."

"I have a great staff. They're really fired up. They love the Sikorsky and have come up with a new ad slogan, 'Keep looking up. You may see your next senator. He's looking out for you.'"

"Corny," Jenny said, entering the stables. The humid, musty air inside enveloped her. Red whinnied from his stall further in.

"Yeah, but it's working. It's the perfect counter to Bradley Coyle's attack ads. People are tired of that. As long as I keep flying, he loses in the polls. My staff is betting on how many stops it takes to gain yet another point in the polls."

"That's wonderful."

His voice became soft. "I've missed you, Jenny."

She sat on a bale of hay in front of an empty stall, sighed and said, "I've missed you, too. But we're both busy. The vet programs take up a lot of my time, but there is good news: The arts program is really taking off!"

He responded to the excitement in her voice, "I'm glad, Jenny."

She leaned back against the stall. "Which reminds me, some of the vets are so good, I'm organizing an official showing of their works at the end of the program. My friends Cybil and Bill Seaton have agreed to hold it at their art gallery in Georgetown on M Street. We haven't set a date yet, because I wanted to check with you. I'd really like you to be there."

"Of course," he said immediately. "Let me coordinate with my campaign schedule, and we can set a date for when I'm back in the capital."

Jenny absentmindedly teased a stalk from the bale and rolled it between her fingers. "I want the opening reception to be a night for the veterans, not a campaign stop."

"Makes sense," David agreed, "I know from personal experience how nerve-racking a showing can be."

"That's why I'd like you to speak about how art affected your own recovery. It will mean a lot to the veterans coming from you."

David hesitated only briefly. "I can do that."

"There's one more thing."

Laughing, he said, "You're running up quite a tab today, but okay. What is it?"

Jenny took a deep breath. "I'd like to include one of your paintings and auction it off. Proceeds would be used to keep the program going." This time, there was a definite pause at his end and she grimaced anticipating his No.

When he answered, he sounded nonchalant. "It's all right. All for a good cause. Just pick one from Frank Gannovino's gallery catalog and have him send it down from New York."

"In that case," she said happily, "you're forgiven."

But David canceled their Sunday get-together at the farm again, although he apologized profusely, and he promised to be at the gallery opening "come hell or high water." Jenny believed him, that it wasn't because she had asked him for his painting, *Rescued*. But now, in the middle of the opening, as she walked past it displayed on an easel on a small, low platform, a realistic depiction of a pilot floating in the ocean waving toward an approaching helicopter, she wasn't so sure. David was late and hadn't called to say why. It wasn't like him.

She stood in the middle of the gallery and tried to cover her trepidation with a confident smile, but the vets were tense, self-consciously standing by their paintings, each in a separate space walled off on three sides, an instructor next to them.

Unbidden, Katherine came to her mind. She had taken every precaution to keep them at ease, but were they ready? She wondered if she had jumped the gun and pushed for a public showing too soon in an effort to show David how important she could be to him. To prove to him that she was as competent as Katherine.

The artists had started as a group of mixed talents, twenty men interested in art, and she had built on that interest to exorcise feelings they couldn't express in words. The majority, she felt, weren't ready yet, but she asked if she could just exhibit their work, and they had agreed.

The Seatons had gone all out with the installation. They had dedicated one wall to all of the vets who did not feel ready yet. The others each had their separate spaces. She also had the instructors there to assist by making introductions, helping to lead the conversation and explaining the art.

Everyone, Jenny had made clear, was to watch and make sure no veteran was left out. But what if some of the paintings that released the anger of the artist onto the canvas as a catharsis, went unsold—how would that affect the artist's fragile self-esteem? For a moment she felt that she might have made a mistake. She had risked so much on this showing and she began to worry that its failure could set them back. Maybe it was just the jitters. But this was no time to second guess herself.

Jenny saw a man standing in front of a painting by Sam Oliver, the most gifted artist in the group. Sam had been in the army on several tours in Iraq, including the original invasion and refused to talk about his experiences. But his large canvas of a horse rearing, its face contorted, eyes blood red and bulging, and mouth foaming was a study in unbearable anguish. Most people were taken aback, even repulsed, by its visceral emotional power and moved on quickly. This man seemed transfixed by it, however. As Jenny walked over to him, she noticed Oliver standing off to the side, observing, a troubled expression on his face.

"Hi! I'm Jenny Garrett, from the National Gallery," she introduced herself. "Welcome to the Veteran's Art Show."

The man barely acknowledged her and continued to ponder the painting. Holding a hand to his chin, he said, "What can you tell me about this?"

Instead of answering, she asked, "What do you see?"

He continued to study it. "The details are magnificent, the power in the horse's muscles, the darkness of the background as the horse emerges from it." Then he took a step back, as if evaluating it in its totality. "Of course, the anguish is palpable, but what I see"—he turned to her for the first time—"is the release of pain."

Oliver stepped forward. "I'm the artist," he said softly. "You're the first person to understand that."

Jenny squeezed his arm and slipped away, leaving him and the man to talk further.

She gave a smile to Scott Sutherland and his wife in the next exhibit area. His three small canvases of birds had attracted a sizable crowd. A quadriplegic, he could only move the thumb and index finger of his right hand. While he was able to maneuver his wheelchair, he didn't have the strength to hold a paintbrush. So, he clamped it in his teeth and produced miniatures of songbirds, patiently and meticulously finishing their feathers with a brush of only one hair. The effect was almost physical: Jenny always wanted to touch them. Now as Scott sat in his wheelchair next to his paintings, people peppered him with questions, and he seemed to warm to the attention. It was the beginning of a new career, Jenny was sure.

In the next space, several young women studied a painting by a vet who went by the name of Forrest whose face was covered with shrapnel scars. He never told Jenny whether Forrest was his first or last name. He was hard to get to know, too. His entire platoon had been killed in an ambush. He was the only one who survived and he withheld friendships like a hand of cards he wouldn't play.

His painting was titled, *The Bear*, although it only depicted a bird's eye view of fish swimming in a tranquil stream. But if you let your mind go, eventually you'd see the ferocious face of a black bear reflected on the water looking back at you. Jenny was amused the first time she saw it. She laughed, and Forrest, who never smiled, had looked at her in surprise. From that day on, he had started to open up bit by bit, although she still didn't know his full name.

Forrest was watching the young women with interest.

Suddenly, one of them jumped in fright, took several steps backwards, and pointed at the canvas. "I see him!"

Her friends, who didn't yet, looked at her in puzzlement.

Jenny saw Forrest grinning. She caught his eye. He winked at her and she winked back.

Then she felt a hand on her waist.

"Flirting again?" David's voice caught her by surprise.

She turned to face him, relieved that he was there. "Yes. Does it make you jealous?"

"Only the paintings," he said. "These guys are good."

"Come on." She took his arm. "There's someone I want you to meet."

She led him across the room to a group that had formed around a young man in battle fatigues sitting in the artist's chair. The dog at his feet was a mongrel, part German Shepherd, and lay with his chin on the floor with watchful eyes that missed nothing.

"They're inseparable," she whispered. "If it weren't for Rufus he wouldn't even be here today."

When the other patrons moved on, Jenny introduced David to Peter Reed who stood up and shook hands with an infirm grip, his eyes shifting away.

David looked over Reed's shoulder at the painting of the dog. "That's him?" David nodded down at the dog on the floor.

Reed opened his wallet and showed David a small snapshot of a soldier carrying a half-starved, stray dog, one arm around his chest and the other around his rump, his four legs dangling. Then he pulled out another photo, in which Rufus was sitting on his haunches while children were gathered around him, petting him. "That's him with some Iraqi kids."

"Well done," David said and stroked the dog's head.

A well-dressed, middle-aged woman came up and studied the

painting, then looked at Reed. "I love the expression in his eyes," she said. "Do you think you could paint one of my Fifi? What would you charge?"

Reed seemed uncertain, but the woman paid no attention to him. She opened her purse and extracted a photo of a Chihuahua whose ears were bigger than its face. "Here she is. Give me an idea."

After scrutinizing the picture of Fifi, Reed said, "I don't know. She's small. How about five hundred dollars?"

The woman smiled. "If it's as good as yours, I'll give you twelve hundred."

As they shook hands, Reed looked like the beneficiary of a surprise birthday party.

David gave the dog a final pat and said, "Excuse me, I'll catch up with you later, Peter." He turned to Jenny. "It's going well."

But Jenny was distracted by the sight of Katherine entering the gallery with three men in tow. One seemed to be a reporter. Another had a camera with a large lens hanging from a strap around his neck. The third was carrying a black television camera with an audio attachment on his shoulder.

Jenny's fingernails dug into David's arm, "What is she doing here?"

"Who?" David looked toward the door.

"Katherine!" Jenny whispered through gritted teeth. "With a reporter, photographer, and TV cameraman." Her eyes bore angrily into him. "You and I agreed that this wouldn't become a campaign photo-op, David!"

"Wait a second, Jenny," he called after her in confusion. "I knew nothing about this!"

But Jenny was making a beeline for Katherine and her crew. She planted herself in front of the cameraman and said, "No video recordings! This is a private affair!" Then, she took Katherine by the arm and pulled her away from the crowd. "What are you doing? I had an understanding with David."

Katherine yanked herself free and adjusted her jacket. "I'm trying to win an election. This is too good an opportunity to miss. It's as much for the veterans as for the campaign."

Jenny wanted to wring Katherine's neck but forced herself to speak calmly, "No TV. You can have the photographer take pictures if the artist agrees, but make sure the reporter includes the names of every vet exhibiting—every one! This is their story, not David's! Play it any other way and I will let the Coyle campaign know that you crashed this event uninvited and exploited it for political gain. Just imagine what they will do with that story."

"You wouldn't."

"Try me!"

Katherine looked at Jenny, calculating the odds. Her rival was livid but controlled. She opted not to find out if Jenny was bluffing. For the benefit of those watching, she said, "Deal!" and shook Jenny's hand as if they were simply negotiating a purchase. "Now, if you'll excuse me."

When Katherine returned to her crew and whispered to them, the television cameraman shrugged and left. The veterans accepted Jenny's presence as approval and began to enjoy the attention. The photographer kept snapping away. Jenny made sure no artist was left out. Then she arranged to get copies of the photos that showed each individual artist next to his paintings. They would make fine graduation gifts.

When they had finished, Jenny stepped onto the raised platform next to the easel displaying David's painting. She formally introduced each of the veteran artists and reminded the visitors that their works were for sale. Then, she called on David to join her.

When he stood next to her, she said, "This is David Madison. He did this painting, which he has donated for auction to help us expand the Arts Program for Vets. Many of you know that he is running for the U.S. Senate from Connecticut, but that is not why he is here tonight. Before entering politics, David was an up-and-coming artist whose paintings were exhibited in New York. Like all of the artists here, he is a former veteran. But he can better tell you himself."

As David took the microphone, all the people that had gathered around the platform applauded. "It's true that I am running for office," he said. "But when I returned after two tours in Iraq, I needed a lifeline to get back to civilian society. Painting and the mother of my son provided that, and I am grateful to all three. I could bore you with the details, but tonight is not about me." He gestured toward the veterans and their paintings on the walls. "It's about these talented artists and all they have done on our behalf and continue to do by sharing their creativity and inspiration. My small contribution here is a way of saying 'Thank you' to them."

Some of the vets began applauding, then the rest of the spectators joined in. After David stepped down, Jenny started the auction with an opening bid of $1,000. A number of patrons joined the bidding, and the painting finally sold for $5,000. It was bought by a man for his VFW post, where it would hang with other paintings he had purchased.

By the time Katherine and her crew left, the main group of patrons departed, too. When the show officially ended David, stayed on, continuing to talk with the veterans. To his surprise, he got into a number of conversations about his technique—brush strokes, the benefits and challenges of different materials, and his approach to his subjects. He answered as best he could and found he actually enjoyed the exchanges.

Then Bill Seaton announced that all of the paintings that had been offered for sale had found purchasers to a round of applause.

David congratulated each of the veteran artists and thanked the Seatons for everything they'd done.

Then he kissed Jenny on the cheek and said. "I need to get going."

"I have to help clean up," she said regretfully.

As she walked him to the door, he stopped and faced her. "Look, Jenny, I'm sorry for what happened with Katherine."

"I am, too, David. But thanks for all the time you spent with the vets. It means a lot to them."

"It means a lot to me, what you're doing."

"There's still a long way to go," she said after a deep breath. "Some of them weren't ready for this yet and weren't here, but once they see that the painting they reluctantly let me exhibit sold, they may come around." As he nodded, she added. "And thanks again for contributing your painting."

He grinned mischievously, "Well, now you know why I didn't become a painter. You only got five-thousand for it."

She smiled. "I think that was the fault of the auctioneer, not the artist."

"I'll call you after the committee hearing. It would be nice to have lunch before I leave for Connecticut."

"I'd like that," she said and gave him a quick kiss on the lips.

But as she closed the door behind him and watched him cross the shiny wet street, she saw him get into Katherine's waiting car. It quickly pulled away, its wipers, like flashing eyelashes, seeming to give Katherine the last word.

CHAPTER 47

As Katherine pulled into traffic, David began admonishing her. "What you did tonight was completely out of bounds." She acted contrite. "I understand. I'm sorry. But it's the subcommittee hearing tomorrow that I'm worried about right now," she said.

David was immediately on the alert. He knew her well enough that she was not just trying to deflect his anger. "How is the subcommittee vote looking?" he asked.

"It will be close. I'm worried about Bill Jenkins."

David straightened, surprised. "The congressman from Indiana? He's been in favor of the commission from the get-go. Why do you think he'd be a problem?"

"Just a hunch. He wouldn't look me in the eye the last time I ran into him."

"Your instincts are rarely wrong."

He pulled out his cell phone and tapped in a number. When there was no answer, he said, "Hey, Bill, it's David Madison. It's a little after ten. Give me a ring, will you? I'll be up late."

He ended the call and turned to Katherine. "If he doesn't call back tonight, I'll corner him in the House dining room in the morning. What time's the hearing?"

"Ten."

"Alert your father, Senator Garrett and Smithson. This may require a full-court press."

He closed his eyes and relaxed, but the gnawing feeling overtook him that an important cornerstone of his election bid was about to crumble.

ᦥ

David reached the Capitol by 8 a.m. the next morning, feeling on edge. Jenkins had not called him back, and he'd hardly slept, counseling with Garrett and Cunningham late into the night. When he got to the House Members' Dining Room and saw Jenkins seated with Stan Forsman near the large rococo mirror and console table, he was certain that he had a defection on his hands.

He took a table across the room under the fresco of George Washington receiving the message from Cornwallis asking for negotiation at Yorktown. He waited for Forsman to leave, then took his coffee over to Jenkin's table. As he sat down he said calmly, "Bill, you're about to make a fatal mistake."

Jenkin's receding hairline showed perspiration and he looked harried. His eyes darted nervously around the room, as if he was concerned that others were taking notice of them being together. His fleshy lower lip pushed forward made it appear that he was sulking.

"Don't try to twist my arm on this, David," he said with forced determination. "I've made my decision."

"I'm not going to do that; I'm going to save your congressional seat."

"Is that a threat?" Jenkins said defensively, nervously toying with his coffee spoon.

"Of course not. It's advice."

"I can make my own decisions."

"Letting Bradley Coyle pressure you through his surrogate into changing your vote isn't making your own decision. This isn't about anything but the veterans and doing the right thing for them. There are too many voters in your district who will vote against you if you side against the vets. Don't go there. You'll lose, Bill."

"Why are you calling *me* out?" Jenkins pouted. "I'm not the only one who is voting against this."

"Because you were going to vote in favor until Coyle got to you. He's merely using you against me for his own political ends. He's not thinking about the vets. He's not thinking about you. He's thinking only about himself. Don't make the same mistake."

Jenkins didn't reply, and David noticed his forlorn expression. "What did he promise you? He threatened you, didn't he?"

Nodding anxiously, Jenkins admitted, "He said he'd primary me and ruin my career if I vote in favor of the commission. He'll do it, too. I'm barely hanging on in the polls as it is."

"All the more reason to vote your conscience!" David ran his hand through his hair. "Bill, you voted for those men and women to go to war. They did. Some of them came back maimed in body and spirit. You owe it to them. You could save a lot of lives. I'm asking you to do the right thing."

Jenkins turned away from David, toward the heavy gold mirror resting on the marble top of a massive table with huge claw feet. He looked as if he felt its oppressive weight on his shoulders. "Coyle could become president," he said.

"I wouldn't bet my career on that one." When Jenkins didn't respond, David fixed his eyes on the frightened man. "Okay...you want to make a deal? Here it is. You vote 'Yes' and I'll campaign with you; Senator Garrett and Senator Cunningham will campaign with you. You're in a working-class district. Most of your constituents stand by the military. You vote against the vets and they'll punish you for it. You stand with us and the vets, and I'll do everything I can to help you win. And you won't stand alone against Coyle."

"Is that a promise?" Jenkins looked like he was ready to clutch at any lifeline offered.

"It's more than a promise," David said with resolve. "It's a guarantee."

Jenkins studied David for a moment, a glimmer of hope in his eyes. He stood up, cracking a small smile and said, "You drive a hard bargain, Madison."

David breathed a sigh of relief. *Crisis averted*, he thought.

CHAPTER 48

As Jenny and David walked down the steps of the National Gallery toward the Mall, she said, "It's such a beautiful fall day, let's not eat in a restaurant. I love the smell of the leaves, the crispness in the air, the color. It'll be gone soon. I don't want to miss it."

"Sure," David said mechanically.

She thought she was over the previous night's confrontation with Katherine but was dismayed that he didn't mention anything about it. "You seem preoccupied. What is it?" she asked.

As they walked on, down Madison Drive toward the Washington Monument, David answered, "I was just thinking about what you said: That it'll be gone soon. You don't want to miss it. Old memories...ghosts."

"It's too beautiful a day for ghosts." She grabbed his arm and squeezed it. "C'mon. You've been gone for a month and I missed you. Let's not waste a moment."

They headed toward the shiny truck of a street vendor. The aroma of hot dogs wafted from under the awning shading the small kitchen inside.

"How's Grant?"

"He's fine. The Langley's are taking good care of him."

"Are you going to see him before you go back?"

"I have to be in Hartford tonight."

She gave him a disapproving look.

As they reached the street vendor's truck, David asked, "What would you like?"

"I'd like you to cheer up."

He ordered two hot dogs and two Cokes.

Trying again, Jenny said, "I've got some good news. When I talked to Frank about the painting he sent down, I convinced him to do another show in his gallery: contemporary American artists that I think are talented. We're going to display your paintings along with three other artists."

David didn't respond to her enthusiasm. He took the bagged food and they walked on.

Jenny had enough. She stopped and confronted him, "What is going on with you?"

"The subcommittee hearing this morning," David began dejectedly. "Bradley Coyle got to Bill Jenkins whose vote I counted on, and I lost. There will be no special commission to investigate the VA."

"Oh, David, you've worked so hard on this."

She took his hand as they walked on in silence until they reached a bench looking at the Washington Monument. They sat in silence for several more moments.

Then Jenny ventured, "Is there nothing you can do?"

"No, it's dead for this term. Coyle's managed to take away my biggest asset in the campaign—the veterans. I told them what I'd do and failed."

She laid her hand on his arm. "I understand how you feel. But that's politics, David. Don't take it personally."

"Not take it personally? Isn't that how you've taken politics all of your life?"

Stung, she withdrew her hand. "It's not the same thing."

"Then what is it?"

Jenny let the question hang in the air for a while before saying softly, "It's about you and Katherine."

"What? You can't be serious!"

"She is affecting how you view things and how you act."

David looked bemused. Then he said dismissively, "Katherine has nothing to do with this."

"Katherine has everything to do with this," Jenny retorted. "Every time I try to make something happen for you, she tries to mess it up. Like last night. Did you talk to her about how inappropriate her behavior was?"

When he didn't respond, she continued more vehemently, "You didn't do anything about it did you?"

"What can you possibly expect me to do, Jenny?" he flared up. "She's the most experienced person on my staff. I give her a lot of latitude. Besides, the vets ate it up. They felt like celebrities. What could be better for them?"

Her eyes narrowed. "That isn't the point. It could easily have caused a setback for some of them." She took a deep breath. "What I expect, David, is that you are on my side and honor your promises to me."

His eyes flashed. "At least I follow through on my commitments."

Shocked by the accusation, she protested, "And I don't?"

"You abandoned the veterans' program at the farm and did a gallery showing instead. Did you think if I don't win, I will go back to painting?"

Jenny responded with fire in her eyes, "Is that what this is about? Who told you I abandoned that program?"

"Katherine said your father told her. I expected better of you, Jenny."

In an instant, her voice became frosty. "I see. Then you owe me an apology."

"For what?"

"For believing what someone else said about me without checking with me first."

"Okay then, why did you do it?"

Covering the hurt she felt, Jenny said with an edge in her voice,

"Katherine omitted one important detail. Some of the men in the program thought they were falling in love with me. I couldn't help them personally. So, I decided to help Sally Simmons instead. We're working to expand the program to locations near every regional VA hospital, which includes Connecticut, by the way. Jack Boden will run the program until the end of the summer."

After a long pause, David said, "Jenny, why didn't you tell me this?"

"Because on a beautiful day, in the brief time we have together, all you can think about is losing to Bradley Coyle, and how I betrayed you and the vets, and take Katherine's side."

"Oh, Jenny...," David said helplessly and reached for her.

But she got up and stood like someone balancing on uneven ground.

"I know how committed you are politically, David. I'm not so sure about your commitment to me. Perhaps we need some space from each other. I certainly do."

"Jenny..." But she turned on her heels and hurried off to the museum. She didn't look back.

David had an impulse to go after her but knew better. He picked up the unopened lunch bag and dropped it into a nearby trash container as he walked away.

CHAPTER 49

Jenny didn't sleep well that night. She kept fretting about the side of David she hadn't seen before—short-tempered, irritable, and unkind. She had hoped her news about his artworks would please him and felt hurt that he hadn't appreciated her efforts on his behalf. Art could be what would help him keep his bearings, but he kept rejecting her efforts to help him realize that. The fact that he seemed more sympathetic to Katherine's point of view instead of her own made her want to shake some sense into him. Then she had a terrible thought: *What if he was more like her father and the previous men in her life who became irrationally angry when she confronted them?* She began to wonder if she and David were too different from each other after all to develop a long-lasting relationship. It pained her to consider the possibility that he did not feel as deeply about her as she felt about him.

As the night went on, the recurring thoughts made her miserable and increasingly angry. She just wanted to get away from him and Katherine and the whole bloody political mess of Washington—the duplicity, the distrust, the lies, the philandering and the two-faced culture of self-aggrandizement.

When dawn came, the diffused light lifted her mood somewhat. She dressed in her riding clothes and went down to the stable. Fanny and Red stood next to each other in their separate stalls, and she rubbed their foreheads, whispering softly. The sun inched its way above the horizon as she fed and curried them. Then she impulsively saddled Red.

As she rode the chestnut thoroughbred toward the pond, she remembered how Red responded to David with a sense of trust that he gave to no other rider except herself. In her world, that counted for a lot and she considered the possibility that she was overreacting. David was under a lot of pressure, as she knew from her father's campaigns, and she had ambushed him with the news of the exhibition. Perhaps she was not giving him the benefit of the doubt—but the feeling in her gut still said that she needed space.

As she and Red stood quietly overlooking the reflections of the willow trees on the water, it reminded her of the time with David, and she impulsively turned Red's head, simultaneously kicking him with her heels and headed toward the Middleburg Club. By the time she reached the polo fields the mist had lifted and she recognized the two players exercising their ponies—John Ralston and Tony Mangione.

She rose up in her stirrups like a jockey that had just finished a race and they stopped as she approached. When she dropped back into the saddle, the three horses stood nose-to-nose.

John Ralston removed his helmet and made a partial bow. "Good morning, fair damsel," he said with exaggerated gallantry. "What brings you to these pastures at this hour?"

Tony tipped his helmet. "What a pleasant surprise."

"I didn't expect to find the two of you here," Jenny said, smiling. "I thought you were in Europe, Tony."

"We're playing in a match this weekend before we head to San Diego for a sand polo exhibition and then to Palm Beach and Argentina for the winter season," Ralston explained. "He's picking out which of my horses to ride in the match."

Tony eyed Jenny appraisingly. "I understand that you used to play. Why don't you join us?"

Jenny held up a hand waving off the suggestion. "It's been a while. I couldn't even pretend to keep up with you."

Ralston chuckled as if he knew better. "You can ride Jasmine, your favorite of my ponies."

Tony grinned. "We'll promise to take it easy on you."

She looked from one man to the other, her competitive nature aroused. Why not? Perhaps it would take her mind off her woes. "All right, you talked me into it."

"That's the spirit," Ralston said.

As they rode to the stable to switch mounts, Jenny turned her attention to Tony. "How was your summer in Europe?"

"It is always pleasant to go back there. The pace is so much different. People are busy, but not like here. Everyone in Washington is so obsessed." He caught her involuntary glance at John Ralston and continued, smiling, "What is your obsession, Jenny?"

Jenny evaded his attempt at easygoing intimacy. "Right now, it's polo."

She kicked Red and they followed her to the stable where they selected mallets and mounted fresh horses.

When they rode back to the center of the field, Ralston tossed the ball into play a little toward Jenny and she smacked it hard in the direction of Tony's goal, then rode after it. Tony reached the ball ahead of her and sent it back toward her goal. They circled back and raced side by side. He knocked the ball forward ahead of them. When he relaxed for a moment, Jenny pushed Jasmine against his horse's shoulder, thrust her leg against his and her elbow into his side while hitting a backhand. Then she made a quick turn back toward his goal.

Surprised, Tony circled, but instead of pursuing her he just watched, admiring her form and confidence as she sent the ball through the goal. *How else had he underestimated this woman?* he wondered. Her poise in the saddle, her apparent love to match wits and test him was a side of her he hadn't seen before.

John Ralston came up next to him. "I told you she played before."

"Not like that, you didn't," Tony said, smiling in admiration. "You coached her well."

"She's a natural on a horse. Been riding since she was a kid. I just taught her the fundamentals. She doesn't just watch a match now— she studies and analyzes it. She doesn't shy away from telling me when I've made a mistake."

They watched her posting toward them, her lean figure emphasized by the tight jodhpurs.

"My kind of woman," Tony said.

Ralston's eyes narrowed for a moment.

As they continued to practice, Jenny played as though each race for the ball was of serious importance, attempting to ride off the two men in turn, more often than not succeeding.

When John Ralston sent the ball toward one of the goals, she and Tony raced after it. He let Jenny move ahead, but as she swung her mallet he reached across his horse, leaning almost off of his saddle and hooked it, then spun on a dime and sent the ball toward the opposite goal. Jenny turned just as fast and headed back downfield. She reached the ball before it crossed the line and struck it between Jasmine's legs in a perfectly timed shot. Surprised, Tony roared with laughter.

Meeting Jenny at the goal line, he said in a serious tone, "That was a beautiful shot. You would have had the crowd on its feet." With a twinkle in his eye he added, "I give in."

Her face was flushed with excitement and pride as she slapped his arm, playfully. "Liar. I know you let me win. But I forgive you. This is just what I needed to let off some steam."

As John Ralston rode up to join them, he asked her. "Why don't you play with us in the match this afternoon?"

She laughed in turn. "Not a chance. You two wouldn't be so forgiving in a real match."

Tony pushed back his helmet with the tip of his mallet and rested it on his shoulder "Then, why don't you just come to cheer us on?"

Jenny looked at him thoughtfully before she dismounted. "Thanks, but I need to get as far away from Washington as I can for a few days."

Tony swung his leg over his horse's neck and slid to the ground next to her. "Then how about joining us next weekend in San Diego at the Hotel Del Coronado Beach Polo event?"

Jenny studied him for a moment, his handsome face boyish and eager in anticipation. Intrigued, she said, "I have a friend who lives in San Diego. We used to ride the equestrian circuit together when we were in college. She's been asking me to come visit."

Tony liked this attractive, energetic woman and pressed his advantage. "You can't get much further away from the pace of Washington than San Diego."

Jenny considered his offer. This might just be the break from David she needed. She looked back at John Ralston for support. "Will you be going?"

"Wouldn't miss it for the world. You'll love it, Jenny." He nodded in approval.

Tony jumped in. "Then it's settled."

"Well," she said brightly, "I could arrange a few days off."

CHAPTER 50

Harvey Finch and Bob Boyd were seated on the sofa in Bradley Coyle's study at the Greenwich mansion like two schoolboys watching the headmaster pace in front of his desk. They were all dressed in their tennis whites, waiting for Harry Morgan to arrive. It was a ritual that Coyle held every Saturday morning with different invitees each week. After the tennis there would be a breakfast buffet by the pool with Bloody Marys. Finch knew what was bothering his boss and waited, resigned, for the inevitable explosion.

"Did you see the *Bridgeport News* this morning, Harvey?" he asked testily.

Coyle reached for the newspaper on his desk and adjusted his glasses to the photo on the front page which showed David Madison, Lance Donovan, and a well-dressed black man in a business suit in front of a school building. "Who is this...," he squinted at the caption, "...Pastor Jeremiah Robinson?" He snapped the back of his fingertips against the newspaper.

"He's a popular black preacher in a black neighborhood in Bridgeport who makes the local news a lot," Finch replied in his higher than usual nasal voice. "I'm surprised you haven't heard of him."

Coyle barely contained his impatience. "Why in hell would I know some black preacher in a Bridgeport ghetto?"

"Well, he's a bit of an activist."

"A bit of an activist? He's either an activist or he's not. What the hells' going on?"

"Robinson's a former Gulf War veteran, became a pastor when he got out. He has a big congregation. And he's a tough, no-nonsense guy. He regularly denounces gangs and started a charter school in the neighborhood. Even the drug dealers stay clear of him. Apparently, Madison and Donovan are bringing in vets to get a program going there—like Donovan did in Chicago. They had a big rally yesterday with–"

Coyle cut him off. "I can read, Harvey. What I want to know is why we didn't know about this." He looked over at Boyd. "And what are we going to do about it!?"

"That's what we were discussing before you came in."

"Well, I'll tell you what we're going to do while you're thinking about it," Coyle burst out. "We're going to hire hecklers and guys in ski masks, break windows, and start a full-scale riot. This veterans bullshit has gone too far!"

Finch and Boyd both remained silent. They knew they had to let Coyle rant for a while.

"This son-of-a-bitch Madison!" Coyle sputtered." First, he helicopters all over the state badmouthing me and now he gets in bed with some black preacher in my black voter base..."

"He's running a classic grassroots campaign," Boyd ventured.

Coyle turned to him. "Okay, we'll play his game. Announce a new program with federal funds that I propose to clean up the ghettos and address the poor conditions in Bridgeport. That preacher will come begging me for funds...."

"Senator, if I may." Finch's reedy voice came back in its usual range.

"Yes. Well?!" Coyle said more composed.

"This is a warning flag, nothing more. We don't want to overreact. What this tells us is that you have to get out of Washington, like I've been saying. Advertising and TV appearances aren't enough. We need to be on the ground and in front of the voters like Madison's doing. We need more rallies—get coverage from there. Like he's getting it. You need to be on the front page of the local papers."

Boyd nodded in support.

"Okay, adjust my schedule. But I want hecklers at every campaign stop of Madison's—every one...and veterans in uniform on the stage behind me at my rallies."

"Got it," said Finch.

Coyle tossed a look at Boyd who was getting up, hoping the meeting was over. "Well, what do you think?"

Boyd stopped and said, "All politics is local."

Pursing his lips, Coyle said, "While I'm localizing, dig up some dirt on Madison."

At that moment Harry Morgan walked in, his spindly white legs showing. Waving his racket, he said, "Tennis anyone?"

Relieved laughter broke the tension. "Perfect timing, Harry," Coyle said, as he put an arm around him and they all walked out to the tennis court.

&

From her solarium on the second floor adjacent to the master bedroom, Helen Coyle heard the thwocks of the tennis ball being batted back and forth, punctuated by occasional cursing and yelling of the players. She hated to leave basking in the sunlight, but it was time to check on the kitchen staff to make sure brunch was ready and put the final touches on the Bloody Marys, her signature drink that was the envy of her social set because no one else was able to duplicate it.

She disliked it when Harvey Finch and Bob Boyd visited, even if they had a good reason. Finch was common, if not vulgar, and she tolerated him because he was one of the best operators in his business. Boyd was effective enough as Bradley's chief of staff, but had the charm of a potted plant.

Harry Morgan, on the other hand, was always amusing. He had

a deceptively acerbic sense of humor, deceptive because you could never be sure if he meant his barbs, and his inherited wealth and breeding gave him easy entrée into the higher circles of society. When she had engineered his acting as a decoy to divert attention away from Bradley's relationship with Stephanie Jordan, she had an ulterior motive as well. She wanted to see how Harry would perform with a young, attractive woman on his arm, and he was acquitting himself nicely. While remaining a model of discretion, he relished being the talk of the Washington scene.

Satisfied that the buffet was flawlessly set out on a linen-covered table in the pool area, she dismissed the servants. Then she added her secret ingredient to the Bloody Mary pitcher and poured herself a drink. Tasting it to make sure it was up to snuff, she watched the men finishing up their tennis match.

From Bradley's strutting she gathered that he and his partner had won. Helen loved his drive and ambition, but she worried about his flaws and was not above hedging her bets. David Madison was proving a formidable opponent, a hard nut to crack. If Bradley came up short in the Senate race, she might take on the Senate Majority Leader as a more advantageous paramour.

She poured four drinks and set them on a silver tray for the men as they arrived. "So, who won today?" she asked pretending interest.

"Harry and I," Bradley crowed, grabbing a Bloody Mary. "His serve saved my neck."

The Senate Majority Leader took a glass as well, shrugging with practiced modesty. Boyd didn't care who won the match, but Finch looked on sullen-faced, still irritated that Bradley always called any close shot in his own favor. He took a glass and gulped the contents down. He would be glad when the campaign was over.

"There is more in the pitcher over there," Helen remarked drily, handing Boyd the remaining tumbler. "Help yourselves to brunch."

It was their cue to go ahead and eat, and Bradley made a beeline for the table. Normally, Helen would have left, but she took Harry aside as the others were occupied at the buffet.

As they stepped under a shady arbor, Harry took a bite from the celery stick and pointed the remainder at Helen. "You always make the best Bloody Marys, Helen. When are you going to give me the recipe?"

Helen grinned. "When you marry Stephanie Jordan."

Harry burst out laughing. "Then your recipe is safe."

"Don't underestimate yourself, Harry. If you can manage the Senate, you can manage her."

"Managing is a lot different than marrying."

"Marriage is all about managing."

"If you say so." He gave her an amused, knowing look. "I'm managing the situation rather well and enjoying it, but if I try to change the arrangement, it will go sour."

Helen grinned. "You are nothing if not a politician."

He acknowledged her compliment with a nod and took another sip.

Turning serious, she asked, "How's Bradley's game?"

Harry understood what she was really asking. "He was tense and overly aggressive all morning, like he was smashing the ball at the devil. It's getting personal with him."

"Do you have any doubts?"

"Not yet. But when you let your opponent get inside your head you start making critical mistakes. I think you need to get involved in the campaign. Bradley can't afford any fatal errors. At the same time, he needs to take some chances. The old tactics aren't going to work. Not with Madison, and Cunningham behind him."

Helen finished her Bloody Mary. "I know."

CHAPTER 51

On the flight from Washington to San Diego, Jenny contemplated the far-off clouds and felt morose. David's lack of trust still upset her. She felt like the distance between her and David was greater than the miles that separated them. His tenacious desire to battle against the arrogance, ignorance and pettiness of the Washington establishment was as important to him as his wartime service had been. It was an admirable quality, she had to admit, but it belonged to another world, not hers. She didn't want to wage a war, she kept telling herself. There was no beauty in it, only destruction and, ultimately, desolation. She wished that she were more successful getting him to see that his artistic side could help temper the uglier aspects of politics, but her efforts had paled in the face of his ambition and near-obsessive determination to defeat Bradley Coyle.

An involuntary shudder took her mind off what had happened, and she thought about what lay ahead—the promise of being worshiped by a debonair, international polo star, if only for a while. Even better, she'd spend time with an old, trusted friend who would provide a safe harbor for the duration of her stay.

It had been a year since Jenny had visited Allyn—too long an absence—and she was looking forward to reconnecting with her and, perhaps, getting her perspective on things. After all, she was the closest thing to a sister Jenny had, both physically and emotionally.

Once again, David and his quixotic political quest invaded her thoughts and she shook her head to dismiss them. Instead, she pictured Allyn's five-year-old twin girls, Barbara and Brenda. How much would they have grown in a year?

Before long the flight attendants announced the start of the descent into San Diego Airport. The landing and deplaning went smoothly, and the transition from the air-conditioned interior of the building to the outside was a pleasant surprise—balmy weather, a good ten degrees warmer than Washington.

Rolling her carry-on bag behind her, Jenny spotted Allyn waiting curbside next to her white SUV. To Jenny's surprise, her hair was platinum blond. They hugged and Jenny held her at arm's length to get a better look.

"Time for a change," Allyn said in response to Jenny's amused expression.

"It becomes you. Maybe I should do the same."

Picking up the luggage and depositing it in back, Allyn said, "That can be arranged. My hairdresser is a genius."

As Jenny slid into the passenger's seat, she asked, "How are the girls?"

"Anxious to see you."

"Me, too."

Allyn got behind the wheel, pulled away from the curb and expertly negotiated the lanes leading to the airport exit. When she settled into the flow of traffic, she relaxed and asked, "So who's the guy?"

Jenny laughed. "What makes you think there's a guy?"

"You're here, aren't you? A year and a half ago it was John Ralston. When you were in New York, there was that corporate lawyer, what's-his-name, who couldn't hold his liquor. And before that, the banker whose swelled head was bigger than the balloons at the Macy's Parade."

Jenny wrinkled her nose. "Are you questioning my taste in men?"

Allyn said dryly, "I'm hardly one to talk. But, except for

John, yes."

Opting for deflection, Jenny said, "What's going on with you and Jim these days?"

Allyn sighed. "Not much. I got the farm, the girls, the horses and my independence. He went for big boobs, barely out of diapers. By the time he wised up, it was too late." She gave another sigh. "At least he takes the girls on weekends twice a month."

"Sounds like he's the one who lost out."

Allyn nodded, then swept her blond hair back, as if to dismiss her ex for good, and changed the subject back to what really interested her. "So, you were about to tell me about the guy."

Jenny laughed, admiring her persistence. "I told you when I called. John Ralston and a polo player friend of his asked me to come down for the sand polo tournament on the beach at the Coronado Hotel. I just needed a break, and I wanted to see you. It's been too long."

"So tell me about the polo player, then."

"His name is Tony Mangione."

Allyn's hands tightened on the steering wheel as she glanced at Jenny. "The ten goaler? Since when did you get into the fast lane?"

"Washington is the fast lane," Jenny reminded her.

"Well, this is where the fast lane winters."

"It's not winter, so I'm pretty sure I'm safe." Jenny stretched her arms over her head. "I want to relax and spend quality time on the beach."

Allyn smiled. "We can do that."

By the time they entered the equestrian community where Allyn lived, they had caught up on everything else—what was happening with Jenny's job at the museum, how their respective parents were doing, and news about former classmates with whom they kept in touch. As they turned into the drive lined by white paddock fences and palm trees, Jenny felt a sense of relief from the burden she'd been carrying.

She looked at the horses lazily grazing in the green pasture and said, blissfully, "I'd forgotten how beautiful and peaceful it is here."

Pulling up to the "farmhouse," which looked more like a country estate, Allyn grinned. "You've also forgotten how the twins can change that in an instant."

As if on cue, the bang of the front screen door broke the serenity. Two girls rushed toward the car, their faces radiant. Jenny barely managed to get out of the SUV and kneel before they raced into her arms, almost knocking her over.

Untangling herself from their embraces, she scrutinized them. "Now, let's see...." She patted one head, pretending to be uncertain. "This is Barbara...hmm." Then she touched the other with confidence. "And this is Brenda."

"No, no!" they shouted, then giggled and trumpeted in unison, "That's backwards!"

"Are you sure?" Jenny said, acting confused. "You wouldn't be playing a trick on me, would you?!" and was rewarded by squeals of delight. "I'm really Barbara," Brenda said, trying to heighten the deception. Jenny enjoyed the familiar game. Although most others—friends of the family and strangers—could not tell the two girls apart, Jenny had no difficulty. With her artistic background and training she could discern the slight differences in their appearance and personalities. Barbara always had a sparkle in her eyes and was a tad more aggressive, while Brenda wrinkled her eyebrows unevenly when she was thinking.

"I know what I'll do," Jenny teased, "I'll call you both Miss B. That way I'll never be wrong."

Brenda frowned. "Then how will we know who you are talking to?"

"You'll just have to guess, Miss B," Jenny said.

The other girl squawked indignantly, "No, no, I'm Barbara."

Jenny touched her nose. "Indeed, you are. And I love you both!

No matter which is which." She stood up putting an arm around each of their shoulders and walked with them to the front porch steps.

As they came through the front door, they were met by a heavyset woman who exclaimed, "Buenas tardes, Miss Garrett. It is nice to see you again. Mister Ralston called. He said he couldn't reach you on your cell phone." She looked at the twins. "Dinner in fifteen minutes. You'd better wash up."

"Thank you, Maria," Jenny said, then she looked over at Allyn for help.

"I'll call him," Allyn offered. "He wants to take us out to dinner tonight. I told him you'd probably want to rest, but John's not one to accept 'No' for an answer."

"Jenny grinned. "Tell him we'll see him tomorrow. I'm spending the first evening and day with my favorite twins. They'd be hurt if I didn't. John will understand."

"He's taken a room for us at the hotel that we can use to change for the different events for the next three days."

"That's just like John," Jenny smiled. "Mister thoughtful."

The three-day weekend at the Hotel Del Coronado sand beach polo event officially opened with a skydiver dressed as a polo player descending from a prop plane overhead. An American flag fluttered from the parachute wires as he floated down to an upright soft landing on the sand beach in front of the hotel while one of the house bands played the Star-Spangled Banner.

Jenny joined Tony and John for the kick-off event, the Porsche Road Rally through the streets of San Diego. The cars left the starting line near the hotel at twenty-minute intervals, and rotated three drivers. When Tony and John's third polo partner didn't show up in time, Jenny volunteered to drive the last leg.

John started out with precision and measured speed at curves and corners like the experienced Lamborghini driver he was. For the second leg, Tony pressed the Porsche 911 as if he was determined to use every one of the five-hundred horses under the hood. Finally, Jenny brought them home with a competitive spirit both men admired, but she missed a few gear changes that cost them the win. Still, it was a respectable showing, and a fitting beginning of a whirlwind weekend in which the festivities never seemed to end.

Then the tournament began with a parade of the polo ponies. The teams each had three players, instead of the normal four since the area marked off for the matches and bordered by low, wooden boards was about one fifth the size of a regular polo field. Instead of the hard, plastic ball that would get buried in the sand, an inflated ball about half the size of a volleyball was used. Matches consisted of seven chukkas, or periods, of seven minutes each.

Watching the first round, Jenny felt that the sand polo wasn't a real test of the players. With the goal markers closer together, the horses never went full out and the contestants treated it more like a carefree social occasion. In real competition, the players and their mounts traveled at speeds as high as 35 miles an hour and the plastic ball whizzed past at 100 miles per hour. This was just an excuse for having fun.

The first round of polo matches concluded with a champagne reception under a huge tent afterward. It was an occasion to dress to the nines, mostly in fun, and Jenny relished gussying up in a world gone casual in almost everything else. To her surprise and amusement, a number of the men were dressed in white dinner jackets, colorful, patterned bow ties, and Bermuda shorts, called surfer's shorts here. Times had changed, she thought, since the game was founded in India in the mid-1800s and brought west by the British. At least the players still dressed the same, even as the spectators' fashions changed.

As Jenny walked with Allyn, John and Tony through the sand toward the Coronado, she found its red roof, turrets, cupolas, and white wooden exterior reassuring. Apparently, they had remained unchanged since the luxury hotel opened its doors in 1888. They had dinner on the terrace of the 1500 Ocean restaurant, watching the sun set over the Pacific, with sailboats silhouetted against the descending, red solar disk. Its disappearance below the horizon was the signal for the entertainment to start in the Babcock and Story Bar, named after the original owners.

Tony was charming and attentive, and kept his eyes on Jenny like a mesmerized hawk. At first, Jenny was not amused by what she considered excessive adoration, but she soon discovered that she actually enjoyed being cherished with such undisguised attention. He was a surprisingly skilled conversationalist, capable of talking about a wide variety of topics. She also appreciated that he didn't try to force himself on her and seemed content to act as her gallant escort.

When they got home, Jenny and Allyn stayed up talking. Sensitive to her friend's moods, Allyn refrained from asking any more questions about her love life. She'd wait until Jenny was ready to talk. Instead, she unburdened herself about how angry and hurt she felt about Jim's betrayal and rejection. "I walked in on him at lunchtime unannounced, and he was screwing one of his young nurses on his office desk," she said in a voice dripping with bitterness.

Jenny didn't know what to say.

"The worst thing is that it's all made me feel unsure of myself... and unattractive," Allyn continued and burst into tears.

Jenny went over, put her arms around her, and said soothingly, "I understand, but you know that's not true. You just need a little more time and you'll get over it."

"I'll be an old maid by then."

She wrinkled her eyebrows just like her daughter Brenda, and Jenny burst out laughing. Allyn wanted to keep frowning but started to giggle. Before long, they were both laughing.

Helping her friend felt good to Jenny and made her doubts

about herself and David seem trifling and far away.

⌀

Immersing himself in his campaign, David waited several days for Jenny to cool down, but when he called her she didn't answer her cell phone. He tried the National Galley several times and learned that she was in San Diego. Figuring she was at the art museum there, working, he didn't give it much thought, although her not answering when he called and left her a message bothered him.

When David thought about their little spat, he felt that he'd had some justification to be irritated. Why did she continue to harp on him pursuing art, especially when he was in the middle of a campaign that consumed just about all of his attention? At the same time, he felt guilty about not thanking her for the veterans' art show. It had gotten good play in the newspaper as a feature article in the Sunday edition and shaved another point off Bradley's lead. Instead, he had wrongly accused Jenny of giving up on the horse program with the vets.

David waited for the right moment to confront Katherine. Over lunch at a campaign stop, he said casually, "I heard that Jenny didn't abandon the Horses for Heroes program at the Middleburg Farm, just moved the venue and put Jack Bowden in charge."

He saw Katherine stiffening, which told him that it wasn't just a mistake on her part, but a deliberate deception. "It's not like you not to get your facts straight," he said.

Rallying, Katherine doubled down and said, "As far as I'm concerned, she did abandon the program. At least that's what I heard."

Although her explanation rang hollow, David let it go, having made his point.

Katherine played along, determined to be more careful in the future. In the meantime, she was upbeat knowing that she had managed to get Jenny out of town.

David, on the other hand, was more downcast. He wished Jenny would return his call so they could straighten things out. He tried reaching her once more but got the recording to leave a message. Hanging up without leaving one, he couldn't help wonder if something had gone more wrong than he'd initially thought. But there was no time to deal with it.

Jenny was enjoying herself, caught up in the excitement of the polo tournament, cheering John and Tony on to success. The last day, at the conclusion of the final chukka, the victory ceremony took place on a platform to the side of the beach. John and Tony, the winning team, held up the Cup, and a gaggle of press photographers kept snapping photos. As John and Tony came down from the platform, Jenny stepped between them and gave each a lingering kiss on the cheek. The picture of her and Tony made the *San Diego News* the next day.

At the big celebration in the hotel ballroom afterward, the star polo players preened for their high society fans and trawled for interested partners to hook up with. Jenny relished being courted by a number of admirers and contributed stories of Washington intrigues to the lively cocktail conversation while keeping an eye on Tony and challenging him to pay more attention to her.

Allyn watched the sexual gamesmanship with wry amusement. Still feeling the sting of her ex's betrayal, she was not ready to join in the fray. She circulated and made pleasant small talk. Eventually, she needed a break and strolled out to the veranda for a breath of fresh air.

When she noticed John Ralston following her, she said, "Escaping from the testosterone-saturated atmosphere, John?"

Ralston smiled as they walked to the white, wooden railing and balusters that lined the veranda.

"It's been an enchanting few days, John, just what Jenny needed."

"I think you're right," he replied. "She and Tony seem to be hitting it off."

Allyn leaned back against the railing post. "I don't know. I think maybe she's running away from something...someone. Do you have any idea why?"

He shrugged uncomfortably. "Washington."

"No...it's definitely someone. And don't tell me you don't know what I'm talking about."

John placed both hands on the rail and stared out over the ocean. "His name is David Madison. He's running for the U.S. Senate from Connecticut. I thought they were the perfect match. Now I'm not so sure."

Suddenly, Allyn realized what Jenny wanted from Tony—a thorough distraction. Lying idly on the beach would only have encouraged her to brood about what was bothering her. "Tell me about Tony Mangione," she said. "What does he do when he's not on horseback, besides trying to seduce Jenny?"

John gave her a sidelong glance. He had known Allyn for a long time. She was a kind person, but since her divorce, she didn't have many good words for handsome men.

"Tony's not a bad guy," he said. "He has a horse farm and a vineyard in Argentina, in Mendoza not far from Cordoba where he raises polo ponies. I've bought several of them. But it's the vineyard that impresses you most. The rows of grapevines seem to go all the way to the snowcapped Andes mountains. One of the most beautiful and peaceful places I've ever been to. And his Malbec wine is excellent. I've got several cases of that, too. Jenny could do worse."

"She has." Allyn smiled knowingly. She wrinkled her brows like one of her daughters. "There's something most people don't know about Jenny. Everyone sees the surface—the exquisite appearance, the upbeat personality, the lively mind. She's as quick as a cat and loves the mental fencing. But there's something deep inside that no man has reached yet."

"Do you think that Tony can?"

"I doubt it. Jenny is drawn to beauty, but she treasures it most when it connects to something beyond herself in an almost spiritual way. That's what attracts her to art and why she loves it so much. Whoever can touch that part of her and bring it out will have her heart."

John stared ahead, thoughtfully. "Maybe it isn't either of them."

Allyn nodded. She let him have a moment of introspection, then tapped his arm. "So, what about you? Anyone tickle your fancy? Or are you going to remain a bachelor forever?"

He hesitated and looked at the moon. Then he said, "Not planning on it, Allyn. It's just that the right woman hasn't come along yet."

The day after the tournament ended Tony invited Jenny for a night out at The Argentine nightclub in San Diego, and she accepted. The place was atmospherically dark and the softness of the lights gave a romantic ambiance to the dance floor, where couples moved with supple steps to lively tango music. The band, consisting of a piano, guitar and bandoneon, played with passion and abandon. From time to time a female vocalist in a sinuous black dress sang, giving the couples on the dance floor a break.

The owner who took them to a table nearby greeted Tony like a favorite customer and brought them two glasses of wine without any prompting. Jenny followed Tony's lead and swirled the dark red liquid and absorbed its aroma for some time. They clinked glasses, and Jenny took a sip. It was an exquisite Malbec.

"Yours?" she asked.

Tony nodded and gave a little shrug.

"If you're trying to impress me, it's working," Jenny said, giving him an approving look.

His eyes lambent, trying to envelop her, he reached for Jenny's hand and led her to the dance floor. Taking her in his arms he began slowly to give her the feel of his lead, gliding forward as her foot slid next to his. Their calves brushed briefly as she met his strides. His hand confidently pressed her back, directing her, guiding her, communicating his next move.

It was all improvisation. She responded to his commands, and her counter triggered his next move. Their contact was a momentary caress, as their chests came together, their thighs touched, and his arm reached completely around her back to her opposite side almost, but not quite, touching the side of her breast. They tangoed in silence, unconscious of everything except the invisible connection between them.

The more they danced, the more her confidence grew and she teased and parried his demands with her own quick leg and foot movements. Finally, his hand guided her leg around him, and he bent her over backwards. Her hand clutching the back of his neck, she let him dominate, trusting him to take care. He held her for a tantalizing moment, then brought her back up and they continued.

Jenny felt jubilant, enclosed in his arms but inexplicably free. He invited her into his domain, she accepted, then abruptly escaped only to draw him to her in a ballet of mutual seduction. The music became a part of her, and as it intensified, she felt as if she was drawn into a vortex of passion. Nothing else mattered. Time disappeared. There was only the present.

When it was over she awoke as from a dream. He leaned in slowly and kissed her. She felt his lips, his arms on her back pulling her toward him.

Responding, her lips caressed his, then his cheek until they touched his ear, and she whispered, "Again."

∽

It was almost four a.m. when Jenny returned to the farmhouse. The light was on upstairs in Allyn's bedroom. She had awakened at three-thirty and when Jenny wasn't there she couldn't get back to sleep. Jenny quietly walked up the stairs and tapped on her door. She barely heard Allyn's voice. "Come in."

Allyn was sitting up in her bed, leaning against the pillows, an open book in her hand. She took off her glasses. "How was it?"

Jenny smiled, swaying dreamily. "Heavenly." She collapsed into the cushioned side chair, slipped off her shoes, propped her legs up, and leaned her head back. "Intoxicating."

Putting a bookmark in her paperback, Allyn said, "I heard that before with what's-his-name."

"This is different. He couldn't tango like Tony Mangione in a million years."

Allyn rolled her eyes. "You aren't falling for that, are you?"

"And he didn't have a horse-breeding ranch and vineyard in the foothills of the Andes, as far from Washington as possible."

Allyn placed her book on the bedside table. "You're kidding, aren't you?"

"Why would I kid about a thing like that?" Jenny replied fervently. "I love horses, I love wine, and I love the tango."

"How much wine did you have?"

Jenny smiled. "I don't remember. It was Malbec from his own vineyard and it tasted divine." She added dreamily, "You know Tony's interested in art."

Allyn scoffed, "The only reason he is interested in art is because women are naked in so much of it."

"Can't you say anything nice about Tony?"

"He looks great in those tight polo pants."

Jenny looked down at her fingernails. "He's invited me to come to Argentina. John Ralston's going to pick out another pony, and I could go with him."

Allyn gave Jenny a penetrating look. Then she said, "What about David Madison?"

Jenny's face flushed red instantly, then turned into a rigid mask. In a tight voice she said, "Ancient history. Like the rest of Washington. To hell with it all!"

Patting the bed next to her, Allyn said, "You don't mean that. Come here."

Reluctantly, Jenny got out of the chair and slumped on the bed. A plaintive cry escaped her lips. "Oh God, Allyn, I'm so confused!" She grasped her friend's hand. "I enjoyed myself tonight for a change. It was like Tony lifted a weight from my shoulders. I don't know where it could go with him, but it would be fun. Life shouldn't be serious and sensible all the time." She started to sob. "I don't know what to do."

Allyn put her arms around Jenny and drew her close until her tears subsided. "I think you needed to get away, even if it's just to find out that there's someone you can't get away from.... So tell me about this David Madison guy."

CHAPTER 52

The late-afternoon sun shone brightly in the heart of downtown Hartford. A sizable crowd had assembled in the meadow facing the stage of the Performance Pavilion in Bushnell Park to hear David Madison speak. It was a mixed group of mostly young and middle-aged working people and families—white, Hispanic and African American. Many had brought blankets and folding chairs to sit on, just as at musical and theatrical events. A few reporters were hovering around the edges.

The introductory campaign rally orations had just finished, and cheers erupted in small pockets of the crowd as David stepped up to the podium, waving. He let the accolades for him build as he looked out over the crowd.

When they started to quiet, he began, his voice amplified by loudspeakers carrying far beyond the meadow. "When the pastor Horace Bushnell stood on this spot in October of 1853, this was a slum of leather tanneries, livestock pens, garbage dump and crowded tenements where poverty and crime reigned. Reverend Bushnell described it as 'hell without the fire.' But he had a vision for a better future and, with the support of the people of this city, it was transformed."

He paused for emphasis. "Now I am asking you to help me transform this city and this State again."

From the back, Paul Andrews, a reporter for the *Hartford Times*, watched the speaker and the reaction of the audience. What a change from the fledgling days of the campaign when David first stepped off the Sikorsky helicopter in Mystic, Connecticut. He had already been compelling, if somewhat tentative, but now his voice rang out with confidence and conviction. He had an assurance that came from practice and experience, and it augmented his natural sincerity and passion.

Andrews was surprised that he found himself responding to what David was saying. The professional in him appreciated how deftly David wove together a call for new leadership with the concept of creating partnerships among government, businesses and universities. Offering relevant details and statistics, David made his case for how technology, science, and innovation, along with cutting-edge manufacturing and training would create jobs and a new prosperity. It was not a new idea, but David made it sound exciting and roused the hearts of his listeners.

Cheers went up from the crowd, louder and more unified than at first.

David went on about rebuilding infrastructure, using skilled labor that was the pride of the State, and the cheers grew louder. Paul felt an energy that, as a veteran of a number of political campaigns, he had not experienced at those events. David inspired his listeners and offered hope based on concrete proposals, not just more pie-in-the-sky promises. But he also challenged them to become active participants in creating a better future for themselves. It was Kennedyesque in its youthful charisma, and Paul felt himself getting caught up in the enthusiastic response of the audience.

As the crowd continued to roar its approval, Paul noticed a sudden movement out of the corner of his eye. From the rear of the park a dozen or so men approached. They were dressed in dark clothes and wearing ski masks to disguise their faces. Fanning out in back to surround the crowd, they began booing and shoving people from behind.

Paul pulled out his cell phone and clicked on the camera app to record what was happening.

Some of the hecklers lit firecrackers and threw them into the crowd. The popping and crackling sounded like gunshots. Pandemonium broke out. People panicked, screamed, ran into one another, tripped over sitting spectators trying to get up, and ran off in all directions. Parents grabbed their sobbing children. Some tried to help up friends who'd fallen and had been trampled on.

On the stage, David dropped down behind the podium. Campaign workers shielded him, and a park policeman helped him to safety.

Paul tried to stay clear of the chaos and keep an eye on the agitators. Having caused a panic, they tried to blend in with the crowd. He followed one who tossed his mask in a park waste receptacle and jogged toward Union Station. Paul retrieved the mask and stuffed it into his back pocket. When the troublemaker disappeared into a bar by the station, he went after him, removing the press badge that hung from the strap around his neck.

The Pig's Eye Pub was dimly lit and mostly empty, awaiting the rush of the crowd from the rally. Paul followed the thug past the red felt pool tables into the men's washroom.

He took a place at the urinal next to him and glanced over. If he expected a battle-scarred hooligan, he was mistaken. The young man next to him was soft-faced and clean-shaven. Paul figured he'd come from Hartford University. As they finished and went to the sinks to wash their hands, Paul decided to take a chance.

He pulled the mask from his back pocket so that the heckler could see it and stuffed it into the used paper receptacle by the door and said, "I'm in Sigma Nu. How about you?"

The young man smiled. "Theta Kappa. How much they give you?"

"A hundred bucks," Paul guessed.

"Shit, man, I got two hundred."

"Son of a bitch," Paul yelled in pretend anger. "Where can I find the bastard?!"

The young man guffawed. "He's one of my fraternity brothers." Seeing Paul's face darken, he offered, "Hey, let me treat you to a beer."

Paul sighed and said. "Sure. Why not? I could use one."

❧

The following morning a front-page article in the *Hartford Times* under Paul Andrews' byline revealed that the protesters had been paid by someone linked to the Coyle campaign. Of course, the senator vehemently denied that he or anyone on his staff had anything to do with it. Harvey Finch demanded that the paper retract the accusation, but the publisher stood by its coverage.

David was finishing breakfast in his hotel suite when Katherine arrived. She handed him his schedule for the day along with a copy of the *Times*. "Yesterday's disaster has turned into a win for us," she said, beaming. Bradley shot himself in the foot. He must be getting anxious that you're gaining on him."

David quickly read the story. "You know who Paul Andrews is, don't you?"

"The reporter from your fly-in campaign at Mystic you had the run-in with. You must have impressed him."

"Nice to know someone from the press is doing his job."

"It gets better. I just got a call from a *Washington Post* reporter this morning. The national feeds are picking it up and it'll be 'Breaking News' on CNN, Fox News and MSNBC in no time!"

Her face clouded. "You know, if Bradley is resorting to dirty tricks when you're starting to catch up in the polls, what is he going to do when you surge ahead? We better be prepared."

"What do you mean?"

"You will need a protection detail."

"Aren't you a bit paranoid?"

"Better to be safe…"

"I'm not going to hide behind a bunch of rent-a-cops," David insisted, tossing the newspaper on the table. When it landed, a copy of the front section of the *San Diego Union-Tribune* slid out, the picture of Jenny kissing Tony Mangione prominent above the fold. As David took a closer look, he felt a stab of pain, followed by a jolt of anger.

"What's this?" he asked with eyes flashing dangerously, "Why did you put this in here?"

"John Ralston and Tony Mangione won the Polo Tournament in San Diego. They made the front page," Katherine said off-handedly, trying to hide the nervousness she felt. "I thought you could congratulate John when you see him again." She hadn't expected her gambit to provoke such a ferocious reaction and quickly added, "He called from San Diego and proposed an idea for a campaign fundraiser."

David forced himself to remain calm. "What does he have in mind?"

"He wants to throw a bash on his yacht for the muckety-mucks in Fairfield County that usually come out for Bradley. We could anchor it in Greenwich, where he now lives in his wife's mansion, to rub it in."

David couldn't help but grin. "I'd like nothing better than popping Bradley's balloon in his own backyard."

Katherine, happy to be back on safe ground, said, "We could anchor off his estate. That would deflate his ego a bit."

"And pump out the waste as the tide goes in?"

"David!" She slapped his arm playfully, pretending to reprimand him.

His look told her that he was only half kidding.

As he got up to go into the bedroom for his tie and suit coat, David glanced at the picture of Jenny and Tony again. He didn't take it with him.

CHAPTER 53

Nursing a glass of bourbon, Bradley Coyle stared out of the window of his hotel suite in downtown New Haven. The rain pelted the street below. He couldn't hear it because of the sound-proof glass, but the streams of water running down the window pane told him that his outdoor rally would be a bust. He wished they'd booked an alternate indoor venue, but the forecast had been for perfect weather. This was one of those freak summer storms no one could have anticipated.

At least the weekend wouldn't be a total loss. Stephanie was coming up from Washington. He checked his watch and frowned. Her flight must have been late.

There was a knock at the door. Bradley checked the peephole, then let in Bob Boyd and Harvey Finch. Pointing to the bar, he said, "Fix yourselves a drink, and tell me what the hell's happened to my poll numbers since the Hartford thing backfired."

Harvey exchanged a worried glance with Boyd. Taking the bottle of bourbon, he started to fill a glass and said reluctantly, "It cost us five points."

"Jesus Christ, Harvey!"

"We're still ahead of Madison by a comfortable margin," Harvey said defensively, as he topped off his glass.

"This guy must have a magic boomerang," Boyd chimed in. "Everything we throw at him comes back against us."

"It was just bad luck that the reporter saw what happened and decided to play boy scout."

Joining Finch for a refill, Bradley said, "Harvey, every time something goes wrong, you claim it was bad luck. That's an excuse, not a reason. The only thing that's bad luck is the weather right now. No one can do anything about that, except we should have had an indoor venue."

"Senator," Harvey began, "you said—"

Bradley interrupted. "You're supposed to be the expert. The hecklers should have been more careful and better prepped. If we're going to play dirty, let's do it right, not just a bunch of college kids running around. This fraternity party lark cost us five points instead of gaining five, for chrissake."

He glared until Harvey lowered his eyes. Then he walked back to the window. The rain continued to come down in sheets. He shook his head in disbelief and took a gulp of bourbon. Then he rounded on his chief of staff and said, "I hope you have better news for me, Bob. Have you dug up anything on Madison?"

"Not yet," Boyd said cautiously. "I'm working on it with someone at DOJ, but he has to be careful. We can't be caught digging up dirt on your opponent there."

"Well, hurry up, Goddammit!" Bradley snarled. "Get me something, anything! I want those points back—with interest!"

There was another knock at the door.

"I'll see who it is," Boyd said, using the opportunity to escape Bradley's wrath.

When he opened the door, he was dumbfounded. A bellman was standing in the hall holding a travel bag and a small suitcase, and behind him, Stephanie Jordan.

She was just as surprised to see him, but recovered more quickly. "Hello, Bob," she said blandly.

"Hi Stephanie." Her presence unnerved Boyd. He pulled back, giving Finch a warning glance.

Bradley had seen Stephanie, too. In the heat of the moment, he'd forgotten that she was on her way. Bad timing—he hoped it wouldn't ruin his day completely. He reached into his pocket, found a five-dollar bill, and held it out to the bellman. "Just put the bags here in the entryway."

The bellman did as he asked, took the money, said, "Thank you," and left.

By then Stephanie had stepped into the room and realized that Finch was there, too. She normally avoided him whenever she could; she didn't trust him. Mechanically, she said, "Hello, Harvey."

His nod to her was perfunctory, too.

As they stood around awkwardly, she suddenly felt cheap, like an unwanted call girl. They all knew about her relationship with Bradley "unofficially" and ignored it, but face-to-face in his hotel room with her luggage, there was no pretending anymore. Why hadn't Bradley warned her? So long as they kept their rendezvous discreet, they could always claim that she was there for an interview.

"What can I get you?" Bradley said as though she were one of the boys.

"Make it a martini," she answered curtly.

She nervously twisted her three-carat diamond ring. How could Bradley be so careless? Had he forgotten it was the anniversary of the day they'd met? It made her wonder if he really was serious about her or simply using her.

"We're just discussing the campaign strategy," Boyd said, trying to relieve the tension. "You might have some advice we could use."

"I'm a journalist, Bob. I'm not supposed to take sides," Stephanie said. It came out harsher than she intended. The fact that she had once dated Bob made her feel like she was playacting. They were normally candid with each other, but now they were caught in an awkward charade.

"Maybe I should go down to the bar until you're done," she said.

"No need," Bradley said, as he handed her the drink. "We've finished for now."

He glanced at the window and addressed Finch. "It's still raining.

Cancel the rally and we'll go directly to the dinner at the Hilton and the President's speech. I don't want any hitches there, Harvey. He's doing me a favor, not that he doesn't owe me." As he ushered him and Boyd out the door, he added, "Let me know if Air Force One is delayed and you have to change anything with the welcoming party on the tarmac. The mayor will be disappointed, but what the hell can we do?"

Bradley closed the door behind them and took his time locking it. He expected a blast of anger from Stephanie at any moment.

It came with both barrels. "How could you have put me into such a compromising position? Bob is one thing. He's an old friend. But Harvey Finch, that snake! Feed his suspicions all you want, but inviting him to join us in your hotel room when I'm staying here is too much! If our relationship comes out in public, I will lose my job!"

"The front desk was supposed to call me," Bradley said apologetically, making up an excuse. "I left instructions not to be disturbed until I had finished with Harvey and Bob."

He marched over to the phone self-importantly and hit a button. "This is Senator Coyle," he said in a tough tone, "What are you people doing down there? You were instructed to call me before sending anyone to my room. How do I know who's coming up here? It could be some lunatic. Tell the manager if this happens once more, I will never set foot inside this hotel again."

He slammed down the phone and looked at Stephanie to see the effect his performance had on her. When he saw that it had made no impact, he approached her with a hangdog expression. "I'm sorry, honey. It wasn't my fault. Let's enjoy our time together. You'll meet the President with the press members after the dinner, then we'll come back here."

That finally coaxed a smile from her. She put her arms around his neck. "I couldn't wait to get here. I knew you had something special planned."

"Planned? What do you mean?"

"You flew me out here for something special. I'm glad you remembered."

"Remembered what?" he asked, confused.

"It's our anniversary!" Her voice rose an octave. "Why else did you bring me here?"

The phone rang just in time. He took her wrists, removed her arms, and went to pick it up. "Hello?" he said, all charm. Suddenly, his eyes widened. "Helen?... What?... You're downstairs?!"

Stephanie watched him roll his eyes as he listened.

"Yes, Helen, I told them not to give out my room number," Bradley said officiously. "I don't want to be disturbed. I'm on a conference call with Bob Boyd and Harvey Finch." He added in a tone of bewilderment, "What are you doing here, Helen? I thought you didn't want to be involved in the rally." He grimaced. "Oh, the President's secretary called, and asked that he be seated next to you...I understand...I do..."

His helpless glance in her direction made Stephanie's heart sink. So much for their anniversary celebration.

"Look, Helen, why don't you tell them to send your bags up to the presidential suite and I'll meet you in the bar in ten minutes... There is nothing the matter with me. I just need to finish this call. I'll see you in the bar...Helen?...Helen?"

He smashed down the phone. "Shit! She's coming up," he yelled, panicking. "You have to get out of here!"

Stephanie's eyes became reptilian slits. "Actually, this would be a great time to finally have it out with her."

"Like hell," he said, desperate. "I told her the presidential suite. This is the honeymoon suite. I planned a romantic evening for our anniversary after I introduced you to the president to arrange a private interview. It was to be a big surprise. Now Helen's ruined it."

Hands on her hips, she said, "I don't believe you."

"You have to. I'll make it up to you, I promise!"

Stephanie appraised him like a praying mantis contemplating

another insect. Then she said. "OK. I want that one-on-one interview with the President of the United States." She waited until he nodded in agreement, then turned toward the door.

"Wait!" he said. "You might meet Helen in the corridor or the elevator. Go down the fire stairs, and take your bags."

"What?! You want me to–"

"Look, just wait in the stairwell for ten minutes, then check into another room. I'll take care of the bill."

"Bradley!"

"I know, I know! I've chosen you! That's our engagement ring on your finger!" He almost yelled. "Now go! Before she realizes she's in the wrong suite!"

"When?"

"The day after I win the election. But I won't be able to do that if you don't go right now."

He dragged her suitcases out the door and scrambled down the long corridor.

Stephanie, still irked, stalked after him. He yanked the door to the stairwell open, and shoved her luggage onto the landing.

When she caught up to him, he gave her a quick peck on the lips. "I'll make it up to you, Baby."

"You'd better."

"I promise."

He shut the door behind her, breathing heavily, and rushed back to his suite.

CHAPTER 54

The Gold Coast of Connecticut juts down into New York State like the tip of a finger dipping into the water of Long Island Sound. With the highest concentration of wealth in the nation—billion-dollar hedge-fund managers, Wall Street titans and plenty of old money, it features some of the State's most beautiful and exclusive real estate.

The sun had just set in the distance when David flew the *Spirit of Connecticut* along the coastline, pointing out the waterfront mansions to Katherine sitting next to him. They were headed to the special fundraiser on John Ralston's yacht, looking the part, with David wearing a black tuxedo and Katherine dressed in a red taffeta Chanel gown cut diagonally across the front, exposing one shoulder.

Ralston had chosen the marina of the Delamar, a luxury hotel on Greenwich Harbor, as the point of departure. His 175-foot yacht occupied nearly a third of the long boardwalk. By the time David circled the ship, it was dark, and floodlights from the dock bathed the white hull of the sleek, four-deck ship in a romantic glow. Guests crowded the railings on the two open decks, pointing and waving at them.

David expertly set the helicopter down on the helipad atop the ships' bridge. As he waited for the rotors to stop he reached across Katherine to unlock her door. "Are you ready for our grand entrance?"

She kissed him lightly and straightened his black bow tie.

"You look like a movie star about to walk out on the red carpet," he said.

Katherine felt a flicker of triumph. This would be her evening as much as his.

One of the ship's officers came out on the landing deck and opened Katherine's door. He wore a crisp, white naval uniform. As she took his hand and stepped down, her dress blew up above her knees and she clutched it with her free hand.

David jumped down on the other side and joined them. As the officer escorted them inside to the elevator, Katherine squeezed David's palm. "We are lucky to have John in our camp."

"I am lucky to have you," David said and was rewarded with anther affectionate squeeze.

Going down in the mahogany-lined elevator, David felt a pang of anxiety. "At least I won't have to give a speech," he ventured. "I just hope I remember all their names."

Katherine beamed at him. "Just be yourself and you'll do great!"

But when the elevator doors opened to the main salon, Katherine's smile turned into a scowl. "What's she doing here?" she snarled under her breath.

David was stunned, too. Next to John Ralston, hands extended to greet him, stood Jenny. She wore a flowing white chiffon dress, and her hair was pulled back into a twist with streaks of white highlights. The sparkling diamond earrings drew his eyes to her face. She looked breathtaking.

John Ralston, enjoying his confusion, said, "Welcome, Congressman. I believe you know your hostess for the night."

In a daze, David shook John's hand, then Jenny's. "I'm surprised to see you here," he managed to get out.

"I thought your campaign might need a little help," Jenny said, smiling pleasantly.

"There's no question about that," David replied, his mind spinning. What was she doing here? She hated politics. Had she

303

forgiven him? What game was she playing?

Katherine recovered more quickly. "Jenny, how nice to see you! I thought you were still in San Diego." Before her rival could reply, she kissed Ralston's cheek and continued smoothly, "You are so generous to do this, John."

Ralston looked admiringly at Katherine. "It was Jenny's idea."

David felt as if he were reeling from another blow. Jenny seemed to enjoy his bewilderment and offered no help.

"Well, now that the guest of honor has arrived, we can shove off," Ralston said, and nodded to a waiting steward. Admiring the white skin of Katherine's exposed shoulder, he continued, "You look gorgeous, my dear. Red is definitely your color."

There was a gentle rumble from below, and the *Ingot* started to move away from the dock. Some of the guests applauded, others cheered and went out on the open decks to watch as the yacht headed into the Long Island Sound.

Ralston offered Katherine his arm. Although she was reluctant to yield the field to her rival, she couldn't very well be rude to their host. She dipped her head in appreciation and allowed him to lead her outside where a band played jazz and dance music under the star-filled sky.

The black-tie affair was gearing up. Well-groomed men in tuxedos and their wives, displaying colorful designer gowns and sparkling jewelry, mingled in the ornate main salon. Waitresses circulated with trays of caviar canapés and other fancy hors d'oeuvres, while waiters glided among the attendees offering champagne and taking drink orders.

One approached Jenny, and she declined, using the opportunity to break the stand-off between her and David. "Let me introduce you to someone you need to know," she said.

She took his arm and steered him toward a well-tanned, middle-aged man standing at the lavish buffet table. David recognized Arnold Anderson, the TV station owner from the photo Katherine and he had looked at together during the extensive background prep they'd done for all the important people on the guest list.

Anderson, swirling his glass of Scotch was waiting for the chef to carve him a slice of rare filet mignon.

Jenny put her hand on his arm. "Arnold, I'd like you to meet David Madison."

Anderson eyed her appreciatively. David felt irritated. His reputation as a playboy with a penchant for young women preceded him. He wondered how Jenny knew him. Connecticut was not her bailiwick.

Raising an eyebrow theatrically, Anderson said, "So, this is the famous congressman who wants to unseat Bradley Coyle?"

Jenny smiled. "Yes, and he will do it—with your help.... I'll leave you two to discuss how."

Anderson gazed after her and grinned "Quite a dish, Senator Garrett's daughter." He turned to David. "I understand that Bradley isn't taking kindly to your challenge."

David suppressed his annoyance. "Neither would I."

"Personally, I'd like to see him lose."

Surprised, David replied, "Personally, so would I."

Anderson chuckled. "Then we're in agreement. He hasn't done a goddamn thing for the State. You have solid proposals." He raised his eyebrow again, a habit David found annoying. "But what makes you think that you can make anything happen to bring jobs back? That's the governor's job." He took a swig of his Scotch.

"I think Washington and the state need to work together on this," David said.

"So what would you do?"

David had prepared for that question and launched into a full-scale assault. "We've got one of the most highly educated labor forces in the country. Boston has Harvard, but we have Yale. We're only an hour from the money capital of the country. Knowing that Anderson was a big baseball fan, he added, "What we don't have is the Red Sox," and watched the eyebrow go up again. He continued with passion, "We're driving young workers away with our tax policies and lack of technology companies. As the white-collar economy grows, we need local job training programs. Add to that federal programs to rebuild infrastructure. I'm not just talking about spending the money on pie-in-the-sky corporate cronyism. That's Coyle's way. He's buying votes with the taxpayer's money."

"Do you really believe you can change that?"

"Yes, but it will take your support—both during the campaign and after."

David held his stare until Anderson broke into a smile. "I like your enthusiasm." The eyebrow rose dramatically. "Now, if you can get the Red Sox to move..."

"I'll see what I can do about that," David said, grinning. "But no promises."

Anderson laughed. "Have Katherine come see me next week. She and I will work up something on your behalf."

David wanted to thank him, but Anderson gestured to the other guests and said, "Have at it while I enjoy this exquisite filet mignon. You've got your work cut out for you." Then he turned to the buffet table as if David didn't exist.

Strange bird, David mused, as he searched the crowded main salon for Jenny.

His eyes lit on Katherine speaking to an older couple seated at one of the tables. She signaled him to come over. He recognized the man and woman before she introduced them. Josh Baird, a small wiry man, was the legal counsel for a multinational manufacturing company headquartered in New York. He and his wife Ellen were big opera supporters and attended opening nights at the Met whenever they could.

"Come and join us," Josh said expansively as Katherine vacated her chair and moved on to another table.

David sat and the Bairds looked at him eagerly. Hoping to

forestall any conversation about opera, a subject he knew nothing about, he said, "Tell me how your son Arnie is doing at the Air Force Academy."

Ellen brightened. "Very well. Thank you for asking."

Frank nodded in appreciation. "You do your homework, Congressman." Before David could make light of it, he continued, "Actually, you got my attention when you pulled that stunt with the helicopter and flew all over the state. Nice touch arriving here in it!"

"Our son was impressed, too," Ellen chimed in. "He told us anybody who can do that is a candidate we should definitely vote for."

David smiled. "Since when do parents listen to their children?" and earned a good laugh from both.

"A good thing, too, considering the music he likes," Ellen said still smiling.

With a sinking heart, David realized where the conversation was heading, and he looked around for help. Just then Jenny magically appeared and joined them. She deftly negotiated the world of opera singers, composers and conductors, and the upcoming season and new productions at the Met. All that David had to do was nod at appropriate moments.

He was about to express his gratitude, but all of a sudden Katherine was at David's arm. "Excuse me," she said to the Bairds, ignoring Jenny, "I need to steal David away for a few moments."

"Of course," the Bairds said in unison. As David rose from his chair, Ellen took his hand. "So good to talk with you. I'm delighted that you love opera as much as we do. Arnie will be thrilled to hear we met you."

"Give him my best," David said courteously and nodded to Josh Baird.

He didn't have time to check on Jenny as Katherine whisked him away. "You'd better stick close to me," she murmured and took him to the deck below and a new group of guests.

For the rest of the evening, Katherine didn't leave his side, taking him from lounges and main rooms to after decks. They worked their way through the crowd of movers and shakers like a pair of veteran campaigners. David's visual memory allowed him to easily match the photographs he'd studied with the faces of the people he met and lace each encounter with a personal touch. Katherine supported him by interjecting comments that helped him tailor his remarks to the interests of the people before him. She kept him so busy and engaged that he hardly noticed what a tight rein she had on him. He saw Jenny only in passing. Whenever he caught her eye, she smiled pleasantly at him but moved on to another guest.

Finally, he excused himself to use the restroom. But he went out on the rear upper deck searching for Jenny, and a bald-headed man in his fifties waylaid him. He looked trim and had the bearing of a former athlete. Tennis came to David's mind, as he recognized Mark Silverman, one of the biggest investment bankers on Wall Street.

The man looked like he had a drink too many. He laid his hand on David's arm with familiarity and asked, "What do you think of the fiduciary rule, Congressman?"

David decided not to mince words. "I am in favor of it," he said. "Without it, the financial industry will lose what little integrity it has left after the 'too-big-to-fail' debacle. Who can the small investors trust without some regulations in their favor?"

Silverman looked taken aback. "But what about the increase in costs for the investors, the very people you're trying to protect," he said, wrinkling his brows.

"Don't you think that competition would solve that? The clients need protection. Look what happened with Wells Fargo. They opened over two million false accounts to meet quotas and get bonuses. In any other profession, you'd lose your license for that."

"That was a stupid thing to do. It gave us all a black eye,'" Silverman said, stiffening.

David grew a little strident. "Three trillion dollars in retirement assets is a huge temptation, especially when you're dealing with vulnerable retirees. If your clients don't come first, who does?"

Before Silverman could take offense, Jenny suddenly appeared. "Who's giving whom a black eye?" she asked playfully.

Silverman replied good-naturedly. "I suppose I'm giving myself one."

David mouthed "Thank you," over Silverman's shoulder as Jenny extended her hand. "I'm Jenny Garrett. I understand your daughter is entering Smith in the fall. She'll love it there."

Silverman looked surprised. "I hope so. It's costing me plenty. He looked pleasantly at Jenny. "Did you go there?"

"Yes. It's a wonderful education if you take it seriously and don't get too caught up in the social scene."

Silverman smiled. "Perhaps you could meet with her sometime and talk some sense into her." He squinted at Jenny. "You're Senator Garrett's daughter, aren't you? We haven't met before..."

"I've just been talking with your wife, Gladys. She told me about your art collection. I'm eager to see it."

When Silverstein looked oddly at her, David interjected, "Jenny's a curator at the National Gallery in Washington."

"Ah, I didn't know that. No wonder you hit it off with Gladys."

"Yes, we did. But I'll let her tell you what we've cooked up herself," Jenny said mysteriously. "Now, if you will excuse me..."

Silverman looked after her. "What a lovely young woman." He inspected his empty glass. "Let me refresh this. What were we talking about?"

David decided to steer the conversation to a topic he knew Silverman would enjoy. "How did you like the U.S. Open tennis tournament this year?"

"Never miss it. Or Wimbledon, for that matter." The banker peered at David with renewed interest. "You play?"

"I did, in college."

"What is your ranking?"

"It's non-existent. I haven't played for years."

"Why do I get the feeling you're being modest?"

"Because I've found it to be a good approach. Just like overdelivering on what you promise."

Silverman nodded in approval. "Those are wise principles that don't only apply to tennis."

As they walked to the buffet, David saw Jenny circulating among the guests, the perfect hostess. It was a side of her he hadn't seen before. Her stepping in to lighten the conversation between him and Silverman and the Bairds when things got awkward meant she was attentive to him, and it intrigued him.

Just then the band announced "last dance" to the disappointed groans of many of the guests. A look to the starboard side told David that the *Ingot* was heading back up the harbor channel to the hotel dock. He decided it was time to take the bull by the horns and ask Jenny to dance with him.

But as he made a beeline for her, an attractive, blond woman intercepted him and said, "I haven't had a chance to meet you yet, Congressman. I would be delighted if you did the chivalrous thing and asked me to dance." She spread out her arms and opened her hands. The view afforded by her low-cut black dress was a bit distracting. David figured it was intentional.

Recognizing Silverman's wife, David smiled charmingly. "That was my intent, Mrs. Silverman, but I assumed you were already taken."

She threw her head back as she placed one hand on his shoulder. "Are you sure you aren't a diplomat instead of a senator? And please, call me Gladys."

David laughed as they started to move with the music. "Actually, Gladys, I'm neither yet."

She was at least twenty years younger than her husband, looking like a former model or actress—a trophy wife David supposed.

She was a good dancer, making up for his inexperience by easily matching her steps closely to his. Once they found a congenial rhythm, she purred, "I understand you are a painter."

David grimaced. "What did Jenny tell you?"

She batted her eyelids. "Do you do portraits?"

"That was in a former life. Besides, portraits are too dangerous for a politician. If they don't flatter enough, I'll lose votes."

"I'll tell you what," she countered. You paint my portrait, and Mark will make it worth your while. That's what this party is all about, isn't it? Deals and donations?"

"I suppose so," David said, enjoying the banter. "I'll tell you what. If I win the election, I will."

"I'm going to hold you to that. You know, Jenny is your biggest promoter. She's collecting votes faster than you can say 'Senator Madison.'"

David maneuvered them to the side of the dance floor away from the dense crowd. "What did she say about me that was so convincing?" Gladys held his eyes long enough for him to realize that he'd been too eager. Then she relented, "Just that you're a man of integrity. You can be counted on to do the right thing, not necessarily the expedient one. She wants to see you elected, but she won't fawn over these billionaires. I think she'd be at home anywhere, because she knows who she is. I haven't met many women like her in our circles. It's refreshing."

"You can tell all of that in one evening?"

"That and a lot more." An impish smile started to play on her lips. "For one, she looks at you whenever you're not aware of it." The smile broadened. "So does she." She nodded toward Katherine who was trying to get his attention, gesturing that she was going downstairs and for him to follow.

David flushed. Were his romantic affairs that transparent that every woman at the fundraiser knew?

Gladys seemed to read his mind. "Don't worry, not everyone is as perceptive as I am. The secret is safe with me," she reassured him.

"But let me give a bit of advice. Being pursued by two beautiful women who are in love with you is a more dangerous minefield than politics."

He realized that he had underestimated Gladys Silverman. She was anything but an ornament on her husband's arm to display his financial prowess and success.

To change the subject, he swept his hand across the room and asked, "Will they support me?"

Amused at his discomfort, Gladys replied, "I can tell you this much. They all want to be on the side of the winner. They understand that making a donation is an expected quid pro quo for these functions, or they wouldn't be here. Last round, they went all in for Bradley Coyle. This time, they'll contribute to your campaign, too, just to cover themselves. A handful will go big for you. I'll make sure you'll get the lion's share of Mark's support."

"I'm flattered."

"Just remember that when you paint me," she said, pointing to two women a good 10 years younger than her. "I want to look like them."

As the music stopped, she took his hand and led him to where Mark Silverman stood at the railing, smoking a cigar. He was watching the *Ingot* maneuver to dock. He nodded to David and put his arm affectionately around his wife's shoulders.

A blast from the ship's horn announced that the yacht was close to docking. Crew members stood at the lower deck ready to toss lines to their counterparts on the boardwalk below.

Silverman said, "David, it was a pleasure meeting you. We'll say 'goodnight' now, if you don't mind. We'd like to be among the first to disembark, and we need to thank John for this lovely party. Shaking David's hand, he added, "We'll see you again soon, I'm sure."

"Yes," Gladys said, winking at David over her shoulder. "At the Fairfield County Hunt Club."

They disappeared in the crowd before David could ask what she meant.

As the dance floor began to clear, each guest shook David's hand and thanked him warmly. He studied their demeanor, but couldn't tell which ones would support him.

The band began to pack up their instruments and equipment, a not-so-subtle sign that the party was over. David looked down to the boardwalk. There was a line of cars waiting at the bottom of the gangway. At the back of the main deck, Katherine stood next to John Ralston and said goodbye to the guests as they disembarked. A few were a bit unsteady, and crew-members assisted them to their limousines.

David was surprised not to see Jenny there. He went to the rear of the upper deck and stood at the railing. The twinkling lights from the Long Island coastline across the water looked like a band of glistening jewelry.

Suddenly, he heard a soft voice behind him. "David."

He turned around. Jenny stood framed in the entrance to the lounge, a vision of soft femininity.

They faced each other awkwardly across the deck, neither knowing where to begin.

Finally, David said, "Why are you doing this, Jenny?"

She took a step toward him. "Isn't that obvious?" When he hesitated, she sighed and said, "Oh, David, sometimes you're so dense."

He stiffened. "The last time I saw you was in a photograph in the San Diego newspaper."

Her eyes flashed. "And just what have you and Katherine been doing? She's been looking daggers at me since the two of you arrived."

He let it go and murmured, "I've missed you, Jenny. I shouldn't have let you walk away angry. I tried to reach you repeatedly, but your father said you'd left town. I didn't know when I would see you again."

She took another step toward him. "Well, here I am, David."

He felt a flutter in his chest, as he slowly moved toward her. "You're all I want, Jenny!"

"Are you sure? What about Katherine? You can't have both of us anymore. That's where I draw the line." Her voice was deep and throaty.

"I know."

"That's an inviolable condition."

"She's a part of my past, Jenny. You are the future." He stepped up to her and cupped her face with his hands.

They were about to kiss when Katherine called up from the deck below, "David, are you up there? We're having a nightcap. Come join us."

Jenny, overcome with the absurdity of the timing, started to giggle.

"Just a sec," David called down.

He kissed her softly and she responded eagerly.

Then she put her hand against his chest and said, "We better go down."

They ambled arm-in-arm to the elevator, like two children who had misbehaved. On the way down, Jenny used David's handkerchief to wipe her lipstick from his face and straightened her dress.

When the door opened onto the main salon, John Ralston and Katherine were relaxing in a comfortable seating nook. Two brandy snifters sat on the table before them.

Katherine's eyes widened in surprise. Then a look of anguish crossed her face—her evening in shambles, her world collapsing. "Well, that was quite the party," she said tight-lipped, willing herself to remain calm.

Ralston got up and went to the bar, saying, "Yes, and I understand congratulations are in order."

Katherine's head snapped toward him in shock.

Pouring two brandies, he continued, unconcerned, "You really impressed Gladys Silverman, Jenny. She said that you and she are going to hold a rally at the Fairfield County Hunt Club."

"Yes," Jenny said, smiling at David, as Ralston handed them the glasses. "An old-fashioned, vote-getting affair with families and games and horseback events."

"Brilliant!" John exclaimed. "You're a lucky man, David."

"Yes," David said, distractedly.

Katherine's pained, accusatory look made him feel anything but.

CHAPTER 55

Bradley Coyle's campaign headquarters was located in a storefront on Chapel Street just southeast of the New Haven Green. He sat in the conference room with his feet up on the conference table next to the remains of a half-eaten Egg McMuffin. His fingers drummed impatiently on the arm of his vinyl-covered chair.

The chimes of the carillon in Harkness Tower at Yale University rang in the distance, reminding him that he had an hour before his meeting with Arnold Anderson to bring him back into the fold. A number of his TV stations had aired positive stories about David Madison and his "exciting vision for the future of Connecticut." Bradley would have to remind him who paved the way for his most recent license applications at the FCC.

Bradley looked at his picture on the campaign posters, all smiling and radiant, hanging on the gray wall across the room; but he felt anything but pleased. In fact, he was livid. He knew he should go into the outer office and give a pep talk to the staff and volunteers, but he didn't feel like it.

There was a knock on the door, and Boyd and Finch walked in. Bradley had come to think of them as the infernal duo—whenever they arrived together, there was hell to pay. He removed his feet from the table and growled, "What the hell is going on?"

His chief of staff and media advisor traded worried glances. Boyd raised his hands to ward off an attack. "Let me explain–"

Bradley cut him off. "I feel like I've been knifed in the back,

Bob. I saved the asses of those bastards on the gold coast during the crash and this is how they repay me? With a fundraiser for Madison on John Ralston's yacht cruising by my own backyard?"

"Senator," Harvey Finch interjected, "that's all part of the game. They donate to Madison's campaign as an insurance policy on the remote chance he wins. You know that. It's par for the course. They only give a fraction of what they give you."

"Excuse me, Harvey, but I had to find this out from Helen and her hoity-toity friends! Do you know how this makes me look?"

Finch said amiably, "When you win it won't matter. All will be forgotten. We're well ahead in the polls."

Bradley gritted his teeth and leaned over the conference table. "That's what you always say, Harvey, every time Madison beats us to the punch. First, he pulls that stunt with the helicopter, then Hartford, now this. I'm sick of playing catch-up. We should be out in front crushing him like a cockroach. I want action, not reaction!"

Finch glanced at Boyd and gave a slight nod.

Bradley narrowed his eyes. "What? What is it?"

Boyd stepped closer. "The lawyer from the DOJ may have found something."

Instantly alert, Bradley said, "Yes?..."

Boyd waited for effect until his boss became impatient. Then he said, "Madison has a love child."

Finch joined in, "Apparently he had an affair with a young girl a while back, got her pregnant, but never married her."

Bradley pulled back in astonishment. "He fathered a bastard kid?"

They both nodded, grinning.

"Do you have proof, or is this just a rumor?"

Boyd answered, "The lawyer is going to overnight us a copy of the birth certificate for Grant Madison. He says it lists Madison and some woman with a different last name as the parents." He paused dramatically before continuing, "There is no record in Washington that they were married. The lawyer checked."

Bradley started to move around the table. "Are you sure about this?"

"Yes, there...is...no...marriage certificate!" Boyd said emphatically. "The woman that gave birth to his son died shortly after, but they were never married."

Bradley smiled broadly. "That self-righteous bastard."

"This could be a game changer," Boyd said happily.

"Stephanie Jordan can reveal it on MBS Television on her nightly show." Bradley started to pace. "I can see it already"—he stopped and held up his hands like two brackets—"BREAKING NEWS! David Madison has Love Child!"

Then he noticed Finch's skeptical look. "What's the matter?"

"We need confirmation," Finch said impassively. "The kid was born in Washington, D.C., but we need to check all of the nearby states, and Connecticut, for the marriage certificate. We don't want this to blow up in our faces."

Boyd, looking annoyed, interjected, "You're right. Check it out. Make sure this one's airtight."

Finch almost looked relieved. "Of course. We'll do that."

Bradley pointed his finger at him. "And let me know right away. I can't wait to set this in motion.... That sanctimonious hypocrite."

The intercom buzzed. A female voice announced, "It's your wife on the line, Senator."

Bradley picked up the phone. "What is it, Helen?"

Boyd and Finch stared straight ahead as they waited.

"What?!" Bradley exclaimed. "I can't believe it! When?"

Boyd and Finch looked at each other—here we go again. Bradley slammed the phone down and turned on them, his face red with fury. "Gladys Silverman is holding a rally for Madison's campaign at the Fairfield County Hunt Club." He looked angrily at Finch. "So much for these Wall Street friends of mine not being traitors." He banged his fist on the table. "Get the story out now!"

"No!" Finch jumped up and shouted, forgetting himself. "We have to be dead certain! Jordan will not run the story without iron-clad proof!"

Bradley's eyes were wild, shifting around the room as if he were looking for something to smash.

"When is the rally supposed to happen?" Boyd interceded. "Next weekend," Bradley answered between clenched teeth.

"That's in three days!" Finch exclaimed.

"No, I said next weekend, not this weekend. Next weekend, Harvey."

Finch expelled a deep breath, composing himself. "Well that gives us time to nail the story down," he said. "If it checks out, Jordan can go with it on Wednesday. With Madison on the defensive, people will either bombard him with questions, or they won't bother going. The Silvermans might even cancel the rally. Senator," he added meekly, "I didn't mean to raise my voice–"

Feeling magnanimous, Bradley forestalled any further apology. "That's perfect! Glad I got a rise out of you for once, Harvey. I guess it isn't just ice water flowing in your veins."

CHAPTER 56

As David exited the Merritt Parkway onto Black Rock Turnpike, Grant looked at the red and yellow-gold leaves on the maple trees and shifted impatiently in the back seat.

"Hang on, pal. Just five more miles," David said, steering the yellow Jeep lazily with one hand, the other resting at the open window. He pointed to a gaggle of geese heading south, flying in their distinctive V-pattern, another sign of the approaching change of season.

Grant barely glanced at them. "I can't wait to see Jenny," he said eagerly.

David nodded. He felt the same way. Since the boat party, he had managed to speak to her briefly on the telephone. They had exchanged endearments, but that didn't make up for the time spent apart. He hoped they would find a quiet spot, after checking out the Hunt Club for the rally, and spend some time alone together.

Soon they drove along a reservoir and David pointed to a boat ramp where people were putting kayaks into the water. Grant noticed that there were kids his age among them, waved, and was happy when they waved back.

The air was Indian summer balmy, with hardly any breeze, perfect for a Saturday of family fun. David was glad he had brought him along on the spur of the moment. Grant was enjoying his stay with the Langleys, but the promise of Jenny and horses trumped any interest in going to a movie or museum with his grandparents.

Watching Grant bouncing in his seat with anticipation, it

occurred to David that his presence might make the afternoon go by more easily. He expected some tension and awkwardness between Jenny and Katherine, although he hadn't seen any signs of jealousy on Katherine's part. Since the boat party, she had been warm and professional as always. He hoped that it wasn't just the lull before a major storm.

Before long, they reached Westport and the low wall of loosely stacked gray stones separating the green polo fields of the Hunt Club from the road. Farther back were several white-fenced equestrian riding arenas and matching stables with green trim. The horse weather vanes on top of the shingled cupolas were motionless.

David hoped the weather would be just as clear and warm for the rally the coming weekend as he steered his yellow Jeep up the maple tree-lined entrance drive. He pulled up next to John Ralston's black Lamborghini parked by the clubhouse entrance, its top down. The country air was suffused with the smell of the last hay cutting, and a wisp of smoke rose from the chimney of the clubhouse stone fireplace.

Gladys, Katherine and Jenny were all sitting on the porch in short white tennis skirts. John Ralston dressed in old-fashioned, white tennis slacks sat among them. Waving happily, they looked like a *Saturday Evening Post* cover by Norman Rockwell.

"There's Jenny!" Grant crowed. He jumped out of the Jeep, raced up the steps, nearly bowling over Gladys, who was coming down to greet them.

Jenny barely had time to get out of her chair before he flung his arms around her. She looked for a moment at David, her eyes shining. Then she disengaged and crouched down to say hello.

Meanwhile, Gladys walked over to David and said, "I'm glad you brought your son." Then she gave him a peck on the cheek and whispered, "Beware, the witches of Greenwich." She slipped her arm into his. "I'm claiming you as my tennis partner, so there will be no disputes."

David grinned. "You may regret that. I haven't played in ages."

"Don't worry, this is just for fun. I hope you have a good backhand, though. Mine's no good."

"Then we're both in trouble."

Jenny introduced Grant to Gladys, and John Ralston shook his hand man to man. Katherine said hello, outwardly friendly, but fuming inside. She had looked forward to David's arrival. But he brought Grant, and now Jenny had an even bigger advantage. The boy obviously adored her.

Katherine greeted David with a quick kiss on the lips, "We thought maybe your Jeep broke down, partner."

"I've already claimed him for tennis," Gladys butted in, pleasantly. "We're going to mix it up. You'll be John's partner, and Jenny will play with Mark, when he gets here."

Katherine felt irritated but didn't let it show. At least Jenny wasn't playing with David.

Before she had a chance to say anything, Gladys took charge. "We'll take David's Jeep for a tour of the grounds." She looked up at him. "Do you mind?"

"Not if you don't," he said, glancing over at the Lamborghini.

"I don't." She squeezed his arm. "Yours has character." She climbed into the passenger seat and tousled Grant's hair. "Grant, you sit up front with me and your father. Jenny told me that you like horses. You can visit them when we get to the stables."

He clambered up and let Gladys hold him between her knees. As he stood looking out the windshield, he nodded his head up and down enthusiastically.

John jumped in back and reached down to help Jenny and Katherine into the Jeep. When they settled in, he sandwiched himself in between and spread out his arms behind them. "Drive on," he said.

"Enough room back there?" David looked over his shoulder to see.

"Perfect," John said. "Like three anchovies in a tin can."

"If that's a reference to my vehicle," David quipped, "I take exception to that."

John smiled, "I'm not complaining."

David jerked the Jeep back in reverse causing Jenny to slide forward, grasping his shoulders. She stayed in that position, to make more room for John, holding onto David as he shifted into first gear. She gave him an affectionate squeeze. He hit the gas pedal in surprise and the Jeep lurched forward.

"Whoa," Grant said, eyes shining.

John kept his arm around Katherine. "I hope he didn't fly the helicopter like that," he said, giving her an affectionate look.

"Where to?" David asked.

Gladys pointed to the polo field where some of the club members were practicing. "We'll have large, white tents set up along the sidelines for the barbeque picnic," she said.

Leaning forward so that her head was beside David's, Jenny indicated an open area and said, "This is where you can land the helicopter. You can do photo-ops in front of it with the families."

Next, they drove past the indoor riding arena where the equitation would be judged, and on to the outdoor riding ring where the jumping would take place. "You can award the ribbons, David, if you'd like," Gladys said. "The reporters from the local papers will be here and will eat it up."

"I'd love it," he said, warming to the idea of being involved and not just giving speeches.

When they got to the stables Jenny announced, "This is where Grant and I get off." She leaped down easily and walked around the Jeep to take Grant's hand and help him to the ground. "We're going to see the horses."

Grant looked back at Gladys. "Thank you," he said. "Are you coming, too?"

"We'll meet you back at the clubhouse when you are done," she said and blew him a kiss.

Katherine rolled her eyes. As far as she was concerned, Gladys and Jenny performed this overblown display of affection for Grant only to score points with David. It further annoyed her that he seemed to be completely taken in by it.

The tour of the grounds continued with a look at the dark green clay tennis courts.

"How many teams will be in the tournament?" David asked.

"Eight. You'll present the trophies in the late afternoon," Gladys said. "Normally Mark and I would play, but of course we'll be busy." On their way back to the clubhouse, Gladys swept her hand in the direction of an empty meadow. "Here we'll have a carousel, inflated bouncing equipment, badminton, volleyball and pony rides."

"This reminds me of a State Fair," John quipped. "All we're missing are the pigs and the apple pie contest."

"I'm sure that could be arranged," Katherine mocked.

John gave her a forgiving glance, "For what it's worth, I think it's a home run."

By the time David stopped the Jeep back in front of the clubhouse, Jenny and Grant were walking up from the stables.

Flushed with excitement, Grant raced ahead and called out, "Jenny brought Red and Fanny May with her, Dad! Will you go riding with us?!"

Katherine saw David's surprise and delight. If only she could wave a magic wand and make Jenny disappear. Ignoring her, she said, "Thank you, Gladys. You've been just wonderful to sponsor this event and pull it all together so quickly. It will be a great rally."

"We were lucky that the weekend was open. Once I booked it, Jenny did the rest."

"I think this will be the first campaign rally I'm really going to enjoy," David said, smiling.

Jenny and Katherine locked eyes. Jenny held her look just long enough to score a point.

Jumping down from the jeep, John Ralston said, "I think that goes for everyone." He reached for Katherine's hand and, helping her down, announced to the others, "We'll meet you at the courts. We need to stretch our legs."

As the Jeep pulled away, he turned to her. "Katherine, you're letting your feelings show. It's not like you to be petty. You totally ignored what Jenny has done."

"Petty? She had her paws on him the whole time!" Katherine stomped off down the path.

Catching up to her, he admonished, "You're like two college girls fighting over the same guy. It's beneath you, Kathy."

Hearing him call her by her nickname brought her up short. He was right. The last thing she wanted to do was advertise her jealousy to everyone out in the open. But how could David not see that Jenny was just an interloper, a passing fancy, nothing like the partnership they had built together?

As they continued walking, she looked up at John. "How good are you at tennis?"

He answered, "Let's just say I'm a polo player."

By the time they reached the courts, Mark Silverman had arrived. He and Jenny were just starting to play against David and Gladys. Grant was watching in the bleachers trying to bounce a tennis ball on his racket.

John greeted him with a light punch on the shoulder. "I challenge you to a match, Sport," he said lightly.

Grant jumped up. "Okay!"

They walked to the court next to where the doubles match took place while Katherine remained in the bleachers and watched.

Standing at the net, John lobbed a ball across to Grant who smashed it back, causing him to duck just in time. He came back up, surprised, and said, "Maybe we should play polo instead."

Grant snorted with laughter. When John positioned himself at mid-court and lobbed another ball over the net, Grant hit it past him to the open side of the court.

John shook his head and called to Katherine, "It appears that I am overmatched. Help!"

She left the stands and went down to the court.

In response to Grant's next return, John whiffed his racket at the ball, intentionally missing it. "There's something I don't understand," he said with a puzzled look. "If I can hit a small white ball with a mallet head this big"—he cupped his hands in a small circle—"why can't I hit it with a big tennis racket?"

"Maybe you should try it on horseback," Katherine suggested, causing Grant to have another fit of laughter.

John feigned further dismay. "I concede and yield to the lady in the white skirt," he said as he gave Grant a high five from the other side of the net.

By the time he returned to the stands, Katherine had accepted her assignment to play with Grant good-humoredly. Watching them John felt a warmth inside for both. As the two laughed together, he thought how gracefully Katherine moved, and how she seemed to enjoy teaching Grant how to meet the ball with the face of his racket and move his feet into position. And she claimed she didn't like kids!

On the adjacent court, David and Gladys were getting trounced. Mark Silverman was a foxy tennis player. His placements and drop shots kept catching David off guard, and Jenny was playing like she had just stepped off the court at Smith College. She kept drilling shots from the net right at David or at his feet, and took shameless advantage of Gladys' weak backhand.

After a while David's serve hit the groove. He charged the net before Mark took his drop shots, returning them out of Jenny's reach. Gladys stroked her forehand with a smooth consistency, scoring winners down the line. They managed to make it a contest, but in the end both their backhands failed them and they lost the set. Jenny raised her racket above her head triumphantly and did a little victory dance.

At the net, Mark placed his hand on David's shoulder. "I trust you'll fight for your Senate seat with as much passion and panache, and I'm sure you'll win that contest."

David shrugged. "I hope so."

Mark waved his racket toward John Ralston and called out, "Your turn."

John stood up in the bleachers, shook his head and waved him off. "When God created polo he should have stopped there. The horses do all the running, and I just swing the mallet. I'll leave the running to you all," he said good-naturedly. "I'll see you at the bar."

Mark looked over at Katherine as she and Grant approached. "You can take Gladys' place," he said.

"I'm going back with John," she said. She had spent enough time on Jenny's turf and was not about to add to her defeat on the tennis court. She'd concede that match and make up for it in the future, at a time and place of her own choosing. Let Jenny and David take Grant riding. They couldn't get into mischief with him along.

CHAPTER 57

I t was dark when Stephanie finished her broadcast and caught the Metro to the Alexandria King Street station. She could have taken a limo, but she felt like being among ordinary people for a change. Wearing a baseball cap low on her forehead, she did not worry about being recognized. Besides, most of the other passengers were tired, on their way home from work, too, and did not pay much attention to their fellow commuters.

As the Metro car door opened she stepped out, looking directly ahead at the George Washington Masonic National Memorial. She paused for a moment. Illuminated on the rise overlooking Alexandria, its pathway lights winding snakelike up to the top of Shooter's Hill, it stood like a sentinel watching over the city. For a second she wondered what George Washington, the man, had been like. One of the few national leaders ever to give up power voluntarily, he insisted on retiring after two terms as U.S. President, leaving a legacy as a wise and genuine statesman.

She thought of Bradley Coyle and his raw hunger for office. After the debacle in New Haven, he had left apologetic messages on her cell phone that became increasingly desperate because she refused to pick up. When she finally relented, he was suitably contrite. The bouquet of 24 red roses awaiting her at the TV station when she arrived that Monday morning helped, too. They were a pleasant surprise, she had to admit, even without an accompanying card; and she had enjoyed the envious looks from her co-workers, as well as the flood of swirling rumors about who her secret admirer might be.

She walked down King Street to her new apartment building and took the elevator to the eighth floor. When she entered her apartment, she dropped her briefcase and purse by the door, stepped out of her heels and shrugged out of her light trench coat, then walked out on the balcony in darkness. The lights of Washington D.C. on the other side of the Potomac River sparkled. The irony that they hid a great deal of lies and double-dealing did not escape her. At times like this, when she was exhausted from the weekly grind, she envied those who had simpler tastes and did not lead a double life in order to claw their way to success.

Her reverie was broken by the ringtone of her cell phone. For a moment she thought of not answering, but then gave in and retrieved it from her purse at the door. Flipping on the apartment lights, she recognized Bradley Coyle's number on the touchscreen and sighed. She was tempted to let it go, then found herself hitting the speaker button.

Heading into the kitchen, she said, "Hello, Bradley," and placed the phone on the counter by the stove.

"What's wrong? You sound a bit blue?" His voice seemed to penetrate the room, trespassing on her solitude.

"I just got in." She opened the refrigerator door, took out an opened bottle of Chardonnay, slipped out the old cork, took a glass from the cupboard above and filled it almost to the top.

"How are you?" he asked. "You sound far away."

"Tired."

"Too bad I'm not there. I could cheer you up quickly."

She took a sip from the glass and slumped down in the nearest easy chair, leaning her head back and closing her eyes. She knew how he meant it. He saw everything in terms of himself. "How's the campaign going?"

"That's what I'm calling about," he said.

She sighed. "You only call me when you want something."

There was silence at the other end. Stephanie took another

swallow and decided she didn't want to get into an argument. "So what do you want me to do?"

"Break a new story on Madison." He sounded relieved and eager.

"What is it?"

"Madison has a love child."

Stephanie sat upright and set the wine glass on the coffee table. "Who's the source?"

"We don't want to get into that. Just use the old, 'undisclosed source,' or 'someone connected to his campaign.'"

She got up, suddenly wide awake, and walked to the balcony glass door, seeing mostly her own reflection. "So Madison has another child?"

"No, it's the same kid. Grant or whatever his name is. He never married the woman. The kid's a bastard."

"So what happened to the mother? He's raising the child, isn't he?"

"That's because she died giving birth."

Stephanie started to pace. "So, let me get this straight. David Madison got a woman pregnant. She died giving birth, and he is raising the child on his own?"

"He never married her, Stephanie. It's your scoop."

She returned to her chair, biting her lip. "And what about the boy?"

"What about him?"

"It will be plastered all over the newspapers and television. 'David Madison Has Love Child.'"

"That's Madison's problem. He's the one who screwed her."

"How old is the boy? Five?"

"I don't know. What difference does it make?" Bradley started to sound exasperated. "Madison created the problem for the kid. You're just reporting it. The guy is running for senator and the voting public needs to know what a charlatan he is."

She retrieved her wine glass and went to the kitchen counter.

"Did you or Finch come up with this?"

"Bob Boyd did, and Finch and I agree."

"Has it occurred to you that you are making a huge mistake?"

"What do you mean?"

She turned speaker mode off, brought the phone to her cheek, and said softly, "In the eyes of a lot of women, Madison will look like a hero and most men won't care."

"They will if we spin it right." His voice became nasty. "Righteous war veteran, family man and all that crap!"

Stephanie took a long swallow. "Find someone else."

"What?"

"I said, 'Find someone else to leak your story.'"

After another long silence, Coyle asked, "You won't do it?"

"No."

Another pause.

"You're making a big mistake, Stephanie. There are plenty of journalists that will be happy to have this scoop."

She cradled the phone between her shoulder and cheek and walked, bottle and wine glass in hand, to the easy chair saying, "You're right, there are. I'm just saying that I won't do it, and that you'd better give it careful thought, because it could backfire—again."

She sat, propping her legs on the cocktail table.

"You're serious, aren't you?" Bradley sounded more puzzled than angry.

"Dead serious. Don't do it, Bradley. For your own sake."

A pause. "Okay," he said reluctantly. "So come up for the weekend."

She finished the wine. "Stephanie, are you there?"

She leaned her head back and felt a trifle dizzy. "No, I'm with George Washington, two hundred years away."

"What is that supposed to mean?" he said gruffly. "Call me back when you come back to reality."

The line went dead.

Stephanie went to her bookcase and found a paperback of Ron Chernow's *Washington: A Life*. She poured what was left of the bottle and settled into the chair. She was about to open the book when the phone rang. It was Bradley again. She sighed, but accepted the call.

Bradley's voice was bright and energetic, as if their previous conversation hadn't happened. "So when are you coming up?"

"Bradley," Stephanie said heavily, "I just need the weekend to myself."

"I miss you, you know."

"You're busy with the campaign. Ask Helen about what I said. Just don't tell her I said it."

"You're sure I can't change your mind? I want to make it up to you. There will be a room waiting."

"Bradley, not this weekend." She glanced at the thick book in her lap. "I just want to be alone with Washington."

He mistook her meaning. "Washington isn't everything it's cracked up to be...but okay." He ended the call.

For the first time that evening, Stephanie smiled.

CHAPTER 58

The weather for the Hunt Club rally couldn't have been better. There wasn't a cloud in the sky when David landed the *Spirit of Connecticut* at ten o'clock sharp. From the air it had looked like the entire Hunt Club membership and many of their friends were there to greet him. The white picnic tents were in place at the sidelines of the polo field, and the grass between the tents, and the road outside the stone wall were lined with cars— Mercedes, BMWs, Lexuses, and a few Bentleys. The large number of SUVs indicated that a lot of families with children had come as well.

There were so many kids that David couldn't exit the helicopter for some time. All the children wanted to have their picture taken, sitting on his lap in the *Spirit of Connecticut*. For a while, he felt like a 21st-century Santa Claus who had arrived in the modern equivalent of a sleigh.

At last, he made his way to the clubhouse and remembered John Ralston's comment about the event being like a state fair. Sure enough, there were banners with "MADISON FOR SENATOR" stretched at intervals along the white fences between Stars and Stripes bunting, and the Connecticut State flag fluttered in the breeze below the Star-Spangled Banner on the clubhouse flagpole.

Horses with braided manes, and riders in black helmets and jackets pranced in the paddock area. Banners and bunting hung from the fence around the tennis courts, too, as white-clad players competed in the first round of the mixed doubles tournament. The heated swimming pool was filled with families and children. It was like a Fourth of July celebration in September.

David looked for Jenny, but before he could find her, Katherine greeted him and hooked her arm in his. She kept David on schedule throughout the day. She was always at his side, like a wife with her campaigning husband, making sure he arrived for each event at the perfect time. David caught a glimpse of Jenny overseeing the equestrian judging, but Katherine whisked him away, so he didn't even notice her waving to him.

Mark Silverman introduced them to the high rollers of Wall Street who hadn't been on John Ralston's yacht. While Katherine entertained them like a seasoned hostess—she had something personal to say to each of them—Mark took David aside to meet Robert Jensen, a philanthropist whose private foundation funded charter schools. Jensen saw himself as the Andrew Carnegie of education, endowing schools and putting his name on them throughout the country the way Carnegie had done with public libraries. Having made the introductions, Mark returned to Katherine and the other guests.

Jensen was fascinated with David's notion of blending inner-city education and the skills of war veterans. Realizing that there wasn't time to go into details, David invited him to visit one of the proposed projects in New Haven, and Jensen promised he would.

Later, Jenny came up to take David to the awards ceremonies for the riding competition and the tennis tournament. Katherine deftly interposed herself, grabbed his hand and did the honors. She handed each ribbon to David as he presented it, leaving Jenny with the job of making the announcements at the microphone.

Jenny was somewhat irritated, but decided to let it go.

But then Katherine did the same thing when it came time to award the trophies at the tennis courts. Gladys made the announcements and Jenny stood by, feeling left out. It didn't help that David seemed oblivious to Katherine's usurping her role.

Adding insult to injury, a woman next to her turned to her

and said, "They make such a beautiful couple, don't they?" Then someone asked, "Are they married?" and someone else chimed in, "If they aren't, they should be."

When the festivities drew to a close in the late afternoon and David got ready to leave in the helicopter, a crowd gathered around the *Spirit of Connecticut* to send him off. He gave a short speech about how much he had enjoyed meeting everyone and hoped that they would give him their vote.

He acknowledged the Silvermans and Jenny for their sponsoring the event, and nodded to her, smiling. Just then, Katherine rushed up, and put her arm around him. She reiterated his message by calling out to the crowd, asking people to vote for their futures and the future of their state. Then she turned into him, pressed her body against his, and kissed him like a bride about to leave the wedding reception.

Surprised, David responded instinctively. He pulled her tight and kissed her back. The crowd cheered wildly, and the longer they cheered the longer the kiss lasted.

Jenny saw him yield to Katherine. To her he looked like a passionate groom anticipating his wedding night and she felt like a stake had been driven through her heart. The blood drained from her face, and a cry of anguish escaped from her mouth. She turned and fled the scene like someone running away from a disaster threatening to engulf her.

Katherine got into the helicopter. David kept waving as he climbed in. Startled to see her sitting beside him, he said, "You're going with me?"

She smiled and waved to the crowd and kissed him again. "You bet."

David scanned the crowd for Jenny, but didn't see her. He had no choice but to follow the expected protocol.

The helicopter lifted off as they both waved to the crowd. All that was missing was the tossed rice.

CHAPTER 59

Jenny sat at her desk in the glass conservatory of her studio looking at a scrapbook. The large window faced toward the stables and a white fenced pasture of the farm where Red and Fanny May were grazing. The lone maple tree in the center of the pasture, protected by its own circle of white fencing, had lost most of its leaves. It looked as depressing as she felt.

When she had bolted from the Hunt Club, with her horses in tow, she had driven through the night, crying and wanting to escape the pain that had pierced her when she saw David respond to Katherine's kiss, but it gnawed at her heart the whole way. Now it was more of a dull ache and, while she was exhausted from the trip, she felt too wound up to rest.

A sigh escaped her as she turned a page in the scrapbook with the picture of a young woman not much older than herself—it was her mother. The resemblance to Jenny was evident.

There was a knock at the door.

Jenny looked up distractedly and called, "Come in."

Senator Garrett entered, trying to appear nonchalant. "David called—several times," he said. "Why haven't you returned his calls?"

"I've been busy," she said vaguely.

The senator eased himself into the flowered chintz armchair near her desk and looked around. "I haven't been up here in a long time," he said. "I'd almost forgotten how much I always enjoyed being here with you." He added, sensing her mood, "Even if it wasn't all that often; not often enough."

She kept looking at the scrapbook with her back to him. "I haven't forgotten."

He scanned the wall of her own framed drawings. "You always had a knack for art. I never understood why you didn't pursue painting yourself."

She gave a slight laugh. "My talent was underwhelming. I'd rather be overwhelmed by real art."

"And whose is this?" He pointed at the large painting of a seated woman dressed in a soft white gown, her hands resting together comfortably in her lap. "It's lovely. The woman looks a bit like you. The eyes."

He got up to get a closer look. He glanced at the signature in the bottom right corner—D. Madison. Although taken aback, he decided not to say anything.

As he turned to her, Jenny said in a dull monotone. "I bought it some time ago at a gallery in New York. It's called, *Lady in Waiting*." Her face showed no emotion. "But I'm not waiting anymore."

The Senator slipped his hands into his pockets and walked over to her. "Jenny, what's going on?"

She responded bitterly. "He's in love with Katherine. He always was."

"How can you say that? That's not been my impression."

"I just know."

He put his hands on her shoulders. "I think you're wrong about that, Jenny."

She refused to look at him. "Well, I must be wrong then, since you're the expert on philandering."

The senator stiffened and pulled back. He had thought that that was all in the past, if not forgiven, then at least accepted. What could have possibly happened with David? He recognized the picture of her mother in the scrapbook.

A rush of anguish overcame him as he remembered the fatal accident. He took a deep breath and gently said, "Jenny, I know that it was my fault. I'm the one responsible. I'm the one who has to live with that—not you. But please don't make the mistake of confounding my character with David's. He is nothing like me."

Jenny looked up at her father. "He made a promise to me and so did I. He didn't keep his, and I'm keeping mine. It's over."

He grasped her by the shoulders. "Jenny, this is the man that is taking on the establishment!" He felt her head shaking in disagreement, and tried to make her look at him. "It isn't love for Katherine that I see in his eyes when we've all been together. It's you."

Her head stopped shaking. "You're taking his side—just like a man!"

"No, my dear, I'm on your side, trying to help you see that you're making a terrible mistake!"

Her eyes narrowed. "You're not in a position to judge! I didn't have a choice when I was born, but I have a choice now! So leave me alone!"

He continued contritely. "I know, I know, I've made more than my share of mistakes, I just don't want you to do the same. You're the kind of woman he needs, Jenny, and he's the kind of man you need. If it doesn't work out, then I'll understand. But you've always been a fighter. Instead, you're closing yourself off and staring into your past, feeling sorry for yourself. That isn't the girl that grew up in this room—the girl pulling on the oar with determination." He turned her toward the *Lady in Waiting*. "Look at the woman in that painting. You bought it for a reason. It said something to you. What was it?"

She looked at it for a moment, then reluctantly said, "Contentment. Something I've never felt."

"What is she telling you now? To quit or to fight?"

Her eyes flashed. "She's telling me that I can never find contentment with the man who painted her."

Senator Garrett sighed deeply. "No one else can give you that.

You have to find it within yourself."

She struck out at him. "Those are fine words, Senator. But you should have taken your own advice."

As he stood there helpless, at a loss for words, she turned away and closed her eyes. There was a long silence. When she looked up he was gone.

She started to run after him but stopped at the closed door. She went back to her desk and, after a final look at the page of the scrapbook, closed it. Then she opened a drawer and removed a piece of stationery with the name Jennifer Garrett at the top.

'Dad," she wrote, "Forgive me for what I said." Her left hand held her forehead, and her fingers ran into her hair as she continued writing. "I'm leaving for a while. I have to get away. I have to sort things out."

CHAPTER 60

David sat in the passenger seat of the Reverend Jeremiah Robinson's army surplus Humvee, with Lance Donovan in back. They were driving along Dixwell Avenue in New Haven's Newhallville neighborhood. There were small stores interspersed with two and three story residential homes that had large front and side porches. It was a sunny afternoon and looked deceptively peaceful, with no signs of the gangs that made this one of the city's high crime areas.

They were on their way to meet another minister to talk about starting a pilot veterans' program, but David had a hard time focusing. While the Reverend drove on, citing crime statistics that he already knew, David's mind kept wandering back to Jenny.

She had not returned any of his increasingly desperate phone calls. The last time he spoke to her father, the senator had discouraged him from running after her. "There are more issues than reason could resolve," he had said—whatever that meant—but it paralyzed David with the feeling he could do nothing about it. He realized that he had gotten carried away with Katherine at the rally in the heat of the moment and the enthusiasm of the crowd. It was his fault, he knew. If only he could talk to Jenny and explain, but she was on her way to San Diego, and he couldn't very well abandon the campaign.

The Reverend Jeremiah pulled up in front of a storefront church along the sidewalk, and David shook himself to regain focus. As they got out of the car, he saw four young men lingering on the street corner. They wore sneakers, T-shirts and baseball caps, and their arms were covered with tattoos. They offered no greeting, but looked at David with barely disguised interest. He knew word would spread quickly through the neighborhood of the presence of a white visitor.

When they entered the church, the musty smell of stale air greeted them. A tall, slim man came out of the office next to the congregation room where folding chairs were stacked against the walls.

"I'm Reverend Oscar Meade," he said.

The Reverend Jeremiah made the introductions. As David shook the minister's hand, he noted the short graying hair, the narrow clean-shaven face and the penetrating eyes.

Reverend Meade was almost as tall as David, and next to Jeremiah, who was five-foot-nine-inches with shaved head, he looked even taller. They were both dressed in black suits but Meade's clerical collar differed from Jeremiah's gray, V-neck sweater and bright red tie.

Meade's serious demeanor contrasting with Jeremiah's jovial energy would have led one to believe that the two had nothing in common. But they had developed a friendship at seminary together, and both were committed to changing the conditions of their impoverished and underserved communities.

The Reverend Meade ushered them all into his office whose walls were covered with dark panel board. A photograph of Martin Luther King, Jr. hung behind the desk. There were framed certificates as well—a law degree from Howard University and a Doctor of Divinity from the University of Chicago.

As David sat down at the meeting table in one of the wooden chairs, he noted the framed picture of Abraham Lincoln on the opposite wall. They settled in and looked at one another expectantly.

The Reverend Meade cleared his throat and said, "I understand you are interested in starting a program here with veterans, similar to what Mr. Donavan has launched in Bridgeport and done successfully in Chicago. In return, you'd like our help with your election campaign."

David smiled. "I'm glad you don't mince words, Reverend. And, yes, that is what we have in mind."

Meade nodded. "Yes. Well, we have the same problems as Bridgeport with gangs, school dropout rates, and high unemployment."

"Twenty-five percent," David said, nodding.

For the first time, the hint of a smile crossed Meade's lips. "You're well informed."

The Reverend Robinson interjected. "Even many of those who are employed work in low-skill jobs at low wages. They lack training and education. We believe that can be changed."

"Yes," said Meade. "There is an old high school building just a block from here that has been empty for several years. We have a contract to purchase it and want to renovate it, turn it into a trade school."

Robinson jumped up. "Why don't we check it out?"

David looked at Lance who nodded his approval.

On their way out of the building, David noted that the youths were still at the corner, but as he, Lance, and the two clergymen walked in the other direction, he saw that more people had come out. They were sitting on the stoops and front porches of the houses and looked out of the ground floor windows, making no bones about checking him out.

The building up ahead was three stories tall and made of dark, red bricks blackened by years of smog and lack of cleaning. It looked like practically every other high school from the first quarter of the twentieth century in the industrial towns in the northeast. It was a recognizable anchor to every community, and David immediately saw the merits of using the old structure.

He looked up at the first-floor windows, some of them with broken glass panes, others boarded up with plywood and said, "Can we get inside?"

The Reverend Meade reached into his pocket and pulled out a key. They walked over to the sandstone entryway, where double metal doors were fastened with a heavy chain around the handles. He opened the large padlock, and the chain rattled as Lance removed it.

As they entered the building, the air was heavy with the odor of rotten food and urine. They walked down the dim central hallway, the floor littered with broken plaster from the deteriorating ceiling and huge flakes of paint peeling from the walls.

"It's amazing how quickly man-made buildings deteriorate," David said.

"With a lot of help from vandals," Lance added. He looked into one of the rooms through the broken glass pane in the door. "It probably would be cheaper to demolish it and replace it with a new one."

Reverend Robinson shook his head. "There's value in preserving these old buildings. They give the neighborhood a sense of history. That's one of the things we want to teach—what came before and the character of the men and women who built it—following in other people's footsteps."

Meade added, "I used to go to school here. This was Mrs. Lehman's class. She taught math."

David's respect for the reverend doubled. Here was someone who was working every day to make a difference in his community.

When they reached a room with long wooden tables, Meade said, "This was the old shop. There used to be lathes and saws. They were the first things to go, but we could revive it. Let me show you the room upstairs we could use for your veteran's program."

David saw the hope on Meade's face, but it was Jeremiah who jumped in enthusiastically. "This is going to be our first project in New Haven. We're going to build a charter trade school come hell or high water. A year from now you won't recognize this place."

"A year?" Lance's eyes widened. He gestured toward David. "We have to get this man elected now, Jeremiah."

"That can be done," Jeremiah said, "but you need to have an election office here and a groundbreaking now."

"Look," Lance said earnestly. "I'm all in favor of a pilot program here, but you're dreaming if you think we could pull it off that quickly."

"We can." He shook off the skepticism. "Meade and I have laid the groundwork—plans, contracts, even some of the staffing." Jeremiah looked at David. "You wanted a job training program? Well here it is. We have an unlimited, unemployed workforce here. All we need is the money."

Lance glanced at David as Jeremiah continued with determination. "I understand that winning a Senate seat costs $20 million, on average. Think of what we could do here with just a fraction of that." He nodded toward David. "If you can find the money for us, we will do a groundbreaking in a week on the project from a campaign office in the building next door."

David hesitated, looking over at Lance. "Let's see the building."

The two pastors led them next-door, and Reverend Meade unlocked a steel gate at the storefront that lent the building the appearance of a jail. There were bars on every window and plywood behind them instead of glass panes. The ubiquitous litter crowded into the doorway and along the empty street like fallen leaves.

Lance pushed the door open and the stench of urine reeked from the opening, more powerfully than at the school. "Are you sure you think we should open a campaign office here?" he asked.

"I've got people who will fix that," Jeremiah said, unconcerned, as they walked inside. "I've smelled worse coming out of Washington."

Lance looked skeptical. "Do you honestly think these people will vote for David? If they even vote at all?"

"Yes, I do," the reverend said confidently.

"But what could we do in less than two months?" Lance countered.

"That," the reverend said, "is why you need to have an election office here, and a groundbreaking now. It'll bring in the votes."

Lance continued to look dubious.

The Reverend Meade turned to David. "You have no reason to trust us. We could just be blowing smoke, but we've been living in the community all our lives, and we know what we're doing. We don't make empty promises. That's what your opponent's been doing. He's been buying votes with taxpayer's money for years, with no improvement in the community. We've got to show them the way out. If they know someone is actually working for them, not just their vote, someone they can believe in, and something concrete like this project, we'll win them over. But not with promises. They don't believe that anymore."

Shaking his head, Lance said, "I've worked in these kinds of neighborhoods before. It's a painstaking, lengthy process. You can't change it overnight."

"Yes, it is, Lance," Meade concurred. "But it begins with the first step. If they see that, they'll believe."

Looking at the broken light fixtures hanging from the ceiling and the debris of broken shelves and empty boxes, David mused, "A broom and a power washer and some paint could fix this place up in four days. Even if I didn't win the election, it would be worth it."

"And the money?" Meade asked.

David turned to him. "That will not be a problem, so long as you're willing to call it The Robert Jensen Charter Trade School." In answer to Meade's puzzled look, he continued. "I don't make empty promises either. If I can raise the money for my campaign, I can raise it for this project. Get it cleaned up and we'll bring someone out who, I'm confident, will put up the money."

Meade held his look for a moment longer and nodded. When they shook hands, Jeremiah smiled and said. "Four days is all we need."

By the time they left the building and locked up, a small crowd had assembled across the street.

Jeremiah took David's arm and said, "Come, let's introduce you to your new constituents."

David took a deep breath and switched into campaign mode. But as they started to cross the street, they heard the roar of a souped-up car engine. The group of people began to disperse immediately, as an old, black Buick convertible came barreling around the corner toward them.

Jeremiah yelled, "Watch out!" in a terrified voice.

He and David jumped back. The air seemed charged with electricity and everything went into slow motion. There were several bursts of gunfire.

David felt as if someone punched him in the chest, followed by a searing pain. He pressed his hand over the spot. Looking down, he saw blood seeping between his fingers. His knees sagged and he crumpled to the ground, hitting the sidewalk hard.

Unable to move, his face pressed to the concrete, he saw a black dot crawling from a crack in the sidewalk toward his face. He thought of Jenny and how much he wanted to see her again. He realized that he was watching an ant crawling. Then there were vague faces above him, calling out to him. He tried to respond, but no sound issued from his mouth.

CHAPTER 61

Jenny walked briskly through the concourse at Reagan National Airport, pulling her roller carry-on bag behind her. She was so determined that she didn't notice the unusually quiet and subdued atmosphere rather than the usual bustle. But when she reached the gate for her flight to San Diego, there were people gathered around the television news monitor high up on the wall. She heard a woman gasp, "Oh my God!" and saw a man shaking his head in disapproval.

A banner notice flashed across the bottom of the screen—ALERT! BREAKING NEWS! U.S. CONGRESSMAN SHOT!

Jenny joined the back of the crowd and asked a man in a blue business suit in front of her, "What happened?"

"Congressman David Madison's been shot!"

Her face blanched and she took his place as he moved on.

She heard the male news anchor on the screen say, "Congressman Madison has been rushed to Yale New Haven Hospital. The seriousness of his condition is not yet known."

Jenny felt a stab in her chest and swayed for a moment. Then she turned and rushed toward the Admirals Club, her carry-on bag dragging behind her. She took the elevator up, wishing she could will it to go faster. She dug in her purse and, when the door opened, hurried to the agent and thrust her ticket toward her. "I have to change my flight to New Haven! I need to get there as quickly as possible!"

The attendant took her ticket and looked at it, "Certainly,

Ms. Garrett."

As she started to type, Jenny caught her breath.

A reporter on the TV monitor in the lounge was reporting on the shooting. "The Congressman is in critical condition, hospital sources say. The Reverends Jeremiah Robinson and Oscar Meade, and a companion, Lance Donovan, all staunch supporters who accompanied him were unhurt."

Jenny closed her eyes. "Oh my God, please don't let him die!" she whispered under her breath.

"Ms. Garrett?" the agent caught her attention. "There are no direct flights. The next plane leaves at 5:45 with a stopover in Philadelphia, arrival time in New Haven 10:05 p.m."

Grasping her forehead, Jenny thought feverishly. "What about Hartford? I can drive from there."

The agent typed into her computer again. "There's a non-stop flight at 2:45 that gets into Hartford at 4:12." She looked up at a series of clocks on the wall behind her console showing the times of key cities. "You can still make that, but there will be a 200 dollar change fee."

"I don't care. Just get me there!"

Bradley Coyle was sitting at a small desk in his suite at the Quinnipiack Club in New Haven going over the dinner speech he was to give in a few hours when the phone rang.

It was Harvey Finch. "Turn on your TV, Senator," he announced. "You won't believe this. David Madison has been shot."

Bradley put the phone on speaker, fumbled with the TV remote on the desk and finally managed to punch it on. A picture of an ambulance with red and blue flashing lights filled the screen. Behind it, the entrance to the emergency room at Yale New Haven Hospital was visible. The BREAKING NEWS banner beneath read, "Congressman Madison critically wounded in apparent drive-by shooting."

There was a knock on the door and Bob Boyd rushed in. Seeing Coyle looking at the TV, he said, "You've heard."

"Unbelievable!"

They watched together as Stephanie Jordan appeared with two talking heads in the picture next to her. They were speculating on the implications for the election. The legal expert weighed in that, if David Madison were to die, Bradley Coyle might remain in office, be re-appointed by the governor, or would have to stand for a special election.

Bradley muted the sound, smiling grotesquely, then called toward the phone. "What do I do, Harvey? Should I head over to the hospital to show my compassion?"

"We need to hold a press conference," Boyd said.

Finch's voice sounded deliberately calm. "No, I wouldn't do anything yet. The last thing we want is for you to show up and have to stand around waiting."

"Yes," Boyd said. "We need to hold a press conference, make a statement of some kind. Suspend the campaign."

"Not until we know where things stand." Finch retorted.

"We've got to do something," Boyd argued. "Otherwise, it will look like we're pleased that Madison got shot."

Bradley chuckled. "Well, aren't we?"

Speaking with more intensity, Finch said, "This has to be handled with class and restraint. Above all, you want to look presidential here. It's a great opportunity, but we have to pick the right moment. Then, when you walk in, the press and photographers will already be there, scrambling for a word from you."

Bradley started to pace. "I think we should issue a preliminary statement now. You know...I am shocked...my heart goes out to him and his family...blah, blah, blah...I'm suspending my campaign for the time being. Our thoughts and prayers are with him."

Bob chimed in, "That's good. Then, once we know, you go to

the hospital and do an informal press conference. That way you can tailor what you say to how delighted you are for Madison's survival, or how sad for the tragic loss."

"Okay," Finch agreed. "We'll handle it that way. Bob, can you pull together the immediate announcement? I'll put together two versions for the press conference at the hospital—whether he lives or not. We have to move fast to capitalize on this. Get the limo ready."

A broad smile filled Bradley's face. "Maybe our luck has finally changed and the son-of-a-bitch will die."

Katherine was alone in the small private waiting area of the Yale New Haven Hospital. It had been two hours since they had rushed David into the operating room. Unable to sit still, she paced, wringing her hands. From time to time she stopped to look out the window at the gathering crowd and satellite trucks. Then she'd turn away repeating, "Please, God, please, don't let David die."

Suddenly, the door burst open and her father strode in with John Ralston close behind. "How is he?" Senator Cunningham asked as he embraced his daughter.

"I thought you'd never get here," Katherine burst out. "He's still in the operating room."

Her father's presence calmed her, and she let him lead her to a couch. Just then, a nurse came in. The senator took her aside, and John Ralston sat down next to Katherine, putting his arm around her.

"He has two gunshot wounds and lost a great deal of blood," the nurse said quietly. "A doctor will be in shortly with an update. I'll tell them you're here."

The senator thanked her as she left and went over to a service table with a large thermos of coffee. He raised his eyebrows at the others and they shook their heads. He drained what was left in the thermos into a paper cup, and then took a seat across from them.

They waited in silence for a while, each consumed with their separate thoughts.

After a while, John Ralston looked at his wristwatch. "Jenny took a flight to Hartford. By now she should be on her way here," he said. "I'm flying the Langleys and Grant up from Washington in my jet."

He got up. "I'll pick them up at the New Haven airport and get us some decent coffee."

As he left, Katherine got up, too, and stiffened. "What is Jenny Garrett coming here for? I thought she abandoned the campaign and went to California."

"I'm sure she changed her plans when David was shot," the senator said. Noting Katherine's defiant expression, he moved toward her and added, "Katherine, don't say something you'll regret."

She rounded on him angrily. "She made her choice and walked out."

"You did that once, too. You had a second chance. But it didn't work out."

Her eyes narrowed. "Yet."

"Katherine, if it hasn't happened by now, it will never happen."

She shot him an incensed look. "Whose side are you on?"

The senator took the last sip from his coffee cup and set it carefully down on the side table. "David's."

She turned her back on him. "I will never give him up."

"You may not have a choice, my dear."

"He isn't going to die."

"That's not what I meant. You're tired. You can't keep going on like this. You hardly sleep during the campaign...and now this."

She whirled on him. "He's mine. Even if he dies."

A pained look crossed her father's face. "You're exhausted, my dear. You don't know what you're saying."

Katherine dropped into the sofa, covering her face with both hands, and started to sob, her body shaking.

The senator sat down next to her and held her close until she regained her composure. "You have to let go," he said.

She shook her head emphatically. "He will always be mine."

CHAPTER 62

John Ralston waited by the security entrance with a uniformed guard. When he'd called Jenny again, she was within minutes of the hospital. He'd told her to avoid the main entrance where a small army of reporters was camped out, waiting for the latest news. His cell phone beeped and he checked the screen for a text message just as Jenny drove up in her rented Ford sedan.

He opened the passenger side door. "Hello, Jenny."

Jenny looked up at him anxiously, "Anything new?"

He shook his head and got in beside her. "No. Nothing has changed." He strapped himself in. "Grant and the Langleys should get to Tweed-New Haven Airport in about twenty minutes."

As Jenny pulled away from the curb, she said, "It's nice of you to bring them in on your plane. Grant wouldn't have understood if he'd gone to the Baltimore airport and learned about David the way I did. It was such a shock."

He directed her to the Oak Street Connector and I-95. They rode in silence for a while.

As they crossed the Q Bridge to East Haven, John said softly, "Katherine's extremely upset."

"Aren't we all?" Jenny shot back, keeping her eyes on the road.

"I'm just warning you. She isn't herself."

"Right now, all I'm concerned about is a little boy and his father— not Katherine."

John Ralston sighed and said gently, "We all are. Let's just keep our attention on who matters—David."

353

Jenny relented. "You're right. I'll keep praying for him."

John nodded. "If prayers will save him, we have two pastors out in front of the hospital holding a prayer vigil."

They reached the hangar just as the small, white Learjet with its turned-up wing tips taxied off the runway and headed toward them.

"Put on a strong face," Jenny said, as it came to a stop 20 yards in front of them. The cabin door with built-in stairs opened and slowly descended.

Grant's head popped out of the door first. When he saw Jenny, he let go of Laura Langley's hand, bolted down the steps, and ran across the pavement to her. She knelt down and caught him in her arms.

He held on to her and burst into tears. Between sobs, he asked in a small voice, "Is my dad going to be okay?"

She felt a lump in her throat. "I hope so," she said and drew him close to her again. As he calmed a bit, she asked, "What did your grandparents tell you?"

"That he got hurt and the doctors at the hospital are taking care of him."

Jenny held him by the shoulders, looked him in the eyes and said, "Your daddy is a Marine, isn't he?"

Grant nodded eagerly.

"Well, marines are fighters and courageous, and your daddy has the best doctors trying to help him get well."

"But will he be okay?" His eyes searched hers.

Jenny reached out and touched his cheek. "I believe he will."

Grant straightened manfully. "I want to be a Marine someday," he said.

Jenny smiled. "There will be plenty of time for that. Let's go to the hospital."

By the time they joined the others, John Ralston had introduced himself to the Langleys. Edward stood next to him, his face drawn.

Jenny hugged the Langleys.

As they walked over to the car, Jenny handed John the keys and got in back with Laura Langley. Grant sat between them. Edward Langley took the passenger seat, and John settled in the driver's seat.

Looking at the Learjet, Grant told Jenny, "My dad could fly that plane."

John looked at her in the rear-view mirror, then at Grant. "I'm sure he could," he said and drove off.

The trip back to Yale New Haven Hospital was quiet. But as they approached the entrance, they passed the satellite trucks and television newscasters crowded before the main entrance.

When they got to the security gate at the side, Jenny said, "You all go on ahead. I want to show Grant something. Call me if there's any news."

Leaving the others to head to the back elevators, she took Grant by the hand and they walked to the gift shop near the main entrance. Grant let go of Jenny as he saw the stuffed animals in the window and hurried inside. He examined each one and settled on a small teddy bear. Jenny bought it for him, along with some coloring books and crayons. Then they went to the cafeteria.

It was an hour later when they arrived in the waiting room. The Langleys were sitting next to each other with their eyes closed, holding hands. Grant went over to them and they admired the teddy bear and his drawings.

Senator Cunningham stood up and kissed Jenny solemnly on the cheek. Katherine, tight-lipped, nodded to her and went to the window. Jenny gazed after her for a moment, then joined Grant and the Langleys.

Looking out at the reporters in front of the hospital, Katherine said bitterly, "Those vultures. They can't wait for a tragic story." She glanced at John Ralston. "I thought the doctor was supposed to come in and inform us about David's condition."

"If nothing else," John replied, "it means he's doing all right. No news is good news."

The sterile white room fell silent. The minute hand on the clock on the wall moved with agonizing slowness.

Around 9 p.m. a nurse came in. It was Nancy Sullivan. "I have good news. He is okay. The doctor is on his way to give you the particulars."

As if on cue, the surgeon, still in green scrubs, arrived. There was a hushed silence as he cleared his throat, then smiled. "Congressman Madison is out of danger. He is in intensive care and will not regain consciousness for some time, but he should be fine. We removed the bullets and repaired the damage."

Katherine buried her face against her father's chest. "Thank God!"

Jenny's eyes filled with tears. Laughing and crying at the same time, she knelt before Grant. "Your Daddy's okay."

He jumped up and down and hugged the Langleys. As Jenny rose, John Ralston put his arms around her and held her for a moment until she regained control.

Over her shoulder, he announced, "I've booked rooms for everyone for the night at the Omni up the street."

Jenny held on to him. "I need to leave," she whispered in his ear.

He took her off to one side of the room. "Are you sure? Hasn't this changed anything?"

"It distorts everything. He's okay. That's all I need to know right now."

"Then take my plane to San Diego."

"I've changed my mind. I'm going back to Washington."

"Then it will take you to Washington," he insisted. "You'll be there by midnight. Otherwise you'll have to stay overnight here."

"You're too good to me."

"Nothing's too good for you."

She hugged him and then the Langleys, while Senator Cunningham queried the doctor about further details. "We need to talk to the reporters. Please come with me."

Jenny sat down next to Grant. "I have to go now," she said tenderly. "You'll see your daddy tomorrow morning."

His face dropped. "Do you have to go?"

"Yes, I have to. But I'll see you again soon. You tell your dad, 'Hi,' for me in the morning, and that I'm glad he's okay."

"We all need some rest," John Ralston declared. "I'll drive you all over to the Omni, and drop Jenny at the airport."

As everyone started to leave, Katherine touched John's arm to hold him back. "You go ahead without me," she said.

John gave her a startled look. "Katherine, you must get some rest."

She shook her head. "I'm not leaving him."

With a concerned look he said, "I'll send for a nurse on my way out."

"Thank you. All I want is to see David."

A few moments later, Nancy Sullivan came in. "I understand you want to visit David. I'll take you there," she said. "He's been moved into recovery, but it will be a while before he wakes up."

She led Katherine down a corridor into a dimly lit room. When she pulled back a curtain, revealing David lying in a bed, the sight of his pale face and stone-like appearance frightened Katherine for a moment. The intravenous feeding tubes projected from under the bed covers to bags filled with liquid hanging from a stand above his head. Monitoring instruments registered his vital signs with low beeping sounds at regular intervals.

Nancy left quietly as Katherine pulled the stiff, high-backed chair over to the bed and sat down. Resting her arm on the bed, and her head on her arm, she listened to the beeping sounds, like a repetitious metronome, and drifted off to sleep.

She awakened some time later when David began to stir. In the semi-darkness it took her a moment to realize where she was.

Then she heard his voice calling softly, "Jenny...Jenny...Jenny."

She rested both of her elbows on the bed, her fingers entwined in her hair, her palms covering her ears as she tried to deny what she had heard, shaking her head defiantly. After a moment she leaned toward David's face and said, "It's Katherine, darling, I'm here."

His eyes opened and he started to smile. "Jenny?" Then he recognized her and his face fell.

It broke her heart. Desperately, she whispered, "No, it's Katherine, darling, Katherine."

CHAPTER 63

J ust after noon the next day, Bradley Coyle's black limousine slowly worked its way through the crowd and pulled up at the front entrance to the hospital. As he was about to enter the lobby, a flock of reporters descended on him.

They thrust their microphones at him and Bradley raised his arms to quiet them. He began with Harvey Finch's prepared speech. "I want to say how relieved I am that Congressman Madison has survived the brutal attack while he was on the campaign trail. As much as anyone wants to win an election, no one would wish such a tragedy on one's opponent. As you know, I have suspended my own campaign for the time being. I hope you will all join me in praying for the Congressman's speedy recovery."

With Bob Boyd and campaign aides running interference, Coyle ignored the questions reporters tossed his way and swept inside. As he led his entourage to the elevators, the director of the hospital, a middle-aged man with distinguished gray temples, greeted him warmly.

"So good to see you, Senator," he said shaking Coyle's hand. "Let me take you upstairs to the Congressman's room."

"Thank you, Trevor. It's been a while." Coyle replied, matching his charm.

"Yes, the hospital fundraiser two years ago. Your eloquent speech made a big difference."

Bradley beamed with pleasure. As the elevator doors closed he asked, "How's he doing?"

"Better than expected. He's a true soldier."

"We're all grateful," Coyle replied.

When they reached the floor of patient rooms, the director took Coyle and Boyd to the nurses' station and introduced them to a woman in a crisp white uniform. "This is our head nurse, Nancy Sullivan. She has been personally in charge of the congressman's recovery and knows everything about his medical condition. I'll leave you in her capable hands."

"This way, Senator," Nancy said briskly. "The Congressman's son and in-laws have been visiting with him."

Bradley barely gave a nod and followed her down the hall. There was very little activity on the floor. Bradley recognized David's room by the security guard stationed outside. As they got closer, a small boy came out followed by an older couple.

Looking back, the boy bumped into Bradley and dropped the teddy bear he was carrying.

"Whoa," Bradley said good-naturedly and bent down to pick up the toy. "And who is this handsome young fellow," he asked.

"That's Reggie. I'm sorry I ran into you."

"That's quite all right," Bradley said, holding the bear out. "You must be Grant."

"Yes," Grant replied.

But as he reached out for the bear, Bradley pulled it back, causing Grant to miss. He continued to dangle it in front of him and play keep away until Grant shouted in frustration, "Give him back!"

Surprised, Bradley started to laugh, then realized everyone was staring at him. The older couple glared with stone-faced disapproval, and the nurse looked like she wanted to strangle him. Even Boyd was unable to hide a pained expression. When Bradley quickly handed the bear over and tried to make it up by patting the boy on the head, Grant drew back as if bitten. His grandparents surrounded him protectively. As they walked past him, Bradley heard Grant whisper to the woman, "I don't like that man!"

He almost turned to say something nasty but thought better of it. Not a good time to make a scene. He shrugged it off, gestured to Boyd to follow him, wrapped his knuckles on the open door, and walked into the room as if he owned it.

David was sitting up in bed. He seemed tired but more fit than Bradley would have liked to see. Katherine hovered at his side. To Coyle's surprise, there was someone else standing nearby, a tall, athletic, well-tanned man. It took Bradley a moment to recognize John Ralston.

After Katherine made introductions, Bradley sat on one side of the bed and faced David. "You look good, all things considered," he said, grinning.

David smiled back. "No one looks good with a couple of bullets in their side."

"You're pretty good at stopping bullets. What is this, the third one?"

"Yes, but you're the only one who seems to be counting," David quipped.

Bradley leaned in and whispered so only David could hear, "Too bad it didn't hit two inches over."

David's smile disappeared in an instant. He held Bradley's gaze for a long moment. Then he said, with steel in his voice. "Thank you for suspending your campaign, but don't bother on my account. I'll be back soon enough to take your Senate seat and torpedo your presidential ambitions."

Bradley sat back, startled, but recovered quickly. "Did you hear that, Boyd? The gloves are off again! Well, speedy recovery!" He rose and nodded to the rest of the people in the room. "John, good to see you again. Katherine, always a pleasure."

Then he stalked out, eyes blazing, with a baffled Boyd in tow. He brushed past Nancy and the guard and moved so quickly toward the elevators that his chief of staff had a hard time keeping up.

Inside the room, Katherine broke the silence that had settled in the wake of Bradley's departure. "What did he say to you, David, that made you so angry?"

He shook his head. "It doesn't matter. Get the brain trust in here. We've got to strategize how to beat that son-of-a-bitch."

Nancy waded in. "Oh, no you don't. You need rest. Now. Everybody out!"

That brought a smile to David's face. "Okay, Nancy, you're the boss."

"And don't you forget it," she chided with a twinkle in her eyes.

As John Ralston was about to follow Katherine out, David called to him, "Give me a minute before you go, will you, John?" He looked pleadingly at Nancy.

"Oh, all right. Five minutes," she assented and left the room, closing the door behind her.

David rubbed his forehead as if to clear away a migraine. "Grant told me that Jenny was here last night and left. Do you know anything about that?"

John hesitated, then leaned against the bed with his arms folded. "She was at the airport on her way to San Diego when she saw the news of what happened to you and came as soon as she could. Once she was certain you were all right, she left."

David leaned back into the pillows and closed his eyes. "She believes I'm still in love with Katherine, doesn't she?"

"Afraid so."

David opened his eyes and said plaintively, "But I'm not and she won't let me explain. She doesn't return my phone calls. What should I do?"

John cleared his throat. "I'm probably not the best guy to ask. Women aren't exactly an open book to me."

Laughing ironically, he said, "I understand, John. But put yourself in my shoes. What would you do?"

After thinking for a moment, John said, "Get on with my life, I'd win the Senate seat, and hope for the best."

David blinked. "Well, that's hardly reassuring, but–"

Just then, Nancy came in with a small paper cup of pills and a glass of water. She gave John Ralston a stern look. He held up his hand. "I get the message."

She waited until he closed the door and David swallowed the pills. Then she sat in the chair by the bed and said solemnly, "I need to talk to you about something. It may come as a shock to you."

CHAPTER 64

Roused by Coyle's visit and Ralston's admonition, David held meetings all the next morning. Between doctors' visits, he strategized with Katherine and his other political advisors in person and by telephone. He discussed reaching out to other donors with the Silvermans, funding the charter trade school with Robert Jensen, and the Bridgeport veterans' program with Lance Donovan.

Nancy hovered and finally put her foot down. "Time to rest!" she insisted and all but muscled the Reverends Meade and Robinson out the door.

But as she started to change his bandages, David pleaded, "I want some time with Grant. Would it be all right for him to spend the afternoon with me? He is leaving to start kindergarten the day after tomorrow."

"I suppose so," Nancy relented, while cutting off the old bandage. "So long as you stay in bed." She began sanitizing the wound with alcohol. "The Langleys need a break. They have many old friends here in town I'm sure they'd like to visit. I'll call them. That way they'll know I approve."

"One other thing." David winced as he held up his arms and she wound a new bandage around him. "There's an art supply place on Chapel Street across from the Yale campus. I've known the owner for quite a while. Would you mind asking Steve Coleman to send over a sketch pad and sketching pencils?"

"I'll take care of it," Nancy said and gave him a peck on the cheek.

An hour later there was a tap on the door. Then Grant ran into the room and jumped on the foot of the bed. "Hi, Dad!"

Laura Langley followed him and took David's hand, patting it like a doting mother. "You look much improved," she said. "A shave and you'll be as good as new."

"It takes more than a few bullets to stop a marine," Edward Langley said, joining her. "Come, Laura, remember we're going to leave David and Grant alone this afternoon."

David smiled at him gratefully. When they had left, he nodded toward a small table and chair that Nancy had brought in earlier and suggested, "Why don't we both make a picture?"

Grant's eyes lit up as he saw the crayons and paper and settled in quickly.

David watched him closely for a minute, then reached for the pad and pencils on the side table. He'd have to find a way to thank Steve. He had sent the art supplies right over—no charge.

He decided to draw Grant who was completely absorbed. As he started to sketch, he was struck by the irony of the situation. Here he was doing what Jenny had asked him all along: to make time for his artistic side. Outlining the shape of Grant's head, he considered how much it mattered to have a good subject, someone he loved with all his heart. That reminded him of Darlene and how his paintings had brightened when she entered his life. Her love for her unborn child had enveloped him, too, even though his feelings for her had never been as strong as they were for Jenny. Yet he had not let Jenny affect him as deeply. Perhaps that is why she doubted him and had run away.

David continued sketching, smudging occasionally with a fingertip for shading, until Grant finally looked up.

"What are you drawing, Dad?" he asked.

"Come and take a look."

Grant ambled over to the bed and leaned his chest over his folded arms, holding himself up as his legs dangled off the floor. As

David turned the sketchpad toward him, he exclaimed, "It looks just like me!"

Smiling, David asked, "Do you like it?"

Nodding eagerly, Grant replied, "Can you draw one of Jenny?"

David hesitated only a moment. "Sure I can," he said and folded the drawing over the sketchpad to a blank page. He patted the bed. "Sit up here and help me."

Grant climbed onto the bed and plopped down beside his father. He watched intently as David, with easy wrist motion, shaped her face and eyes. Longer strokes created her hair, and crosshatching at her cheeks and below her neck added a sense of dimension.

Grant's eyes lit up with pleasure as Jenny's face began to emerge. "Dad," he looked up at David, "It's like you're bringing her to us!"

If only I could, David thought, as he kept sketching.

"She's pretty, isn't she, Dad?"

"Yes, very pretty."

"Do you love her as much as I do?"

David looked at Grant. "How much do you love her?"

His son stretched out his arms as wide as he could. "This much."

David set the sketchpad down on his lap and spread his arms apart. "I love her this much."

Grant laughed. "That isn't fair. You have longer arms!" He paused and became serious. "When I grow up, I'm going to marry her!"

David pulled Grant's head to his chest. "My love for you will never end, whatever may happen," he whispered. "You know that, don't you?"

"Sure, Dad."

"Always remember that." David released him and winced.

"Does your side hurt?"

"No, it's okay." David picked up the sketchpad. "Shall we finish it now?"

Grant nodded. "I can't wait to see her again."

Neither can I, David thought.

∾

When Katherine arrived the next morning with the day's schedule and carrying a small suitcase, she was surprised to see David at the window.

"I want to get out of here as soon as I can," he said. "I'm tired of the view of the parking garage."

"Your butt is showing, you know," she said without humor. "Not that I mind," she continued, all business, "but you have a full schedule this morning, and your guests might, so I brought you a robe."

"The Langley's left with Grant this morning. He needs to start school."

"Good." To herself she thought, *Good riddance.* She put the suitcase on the bed and opened it.

"So what's on the agenda?" David said absentmindedly, as if to make conversation.

As she withdrew a robe and pajamas, she replied, "Reverend Robinson and Reverend Meade at nine o'clock to update you on the progress of the campaign office on Dixwell Avenue." She looked up at him. "I'm still not sure it's a good idea to go back there."

"I want to restart the campaign there." He became more animated. "Remember, lightning never strikes twice in the same place."

She hung the robe in the closet and took his shaving kit to the bathroom. "It's a brilliant strategy, but have you ever seen the Empire State building during a thunderstorm?"

"That's because of the lightning rods."

"Well, isn't that what you are?"

He went over to the bed, picked up the pajamas and went to the bathroom door. "Kathy...don't argue. Besides, you like the idea because it's a smart political move."

"You're right," she said, walking past him.

He watched her for a moment, then went into the bathroom.

Katherine called after him, "I scheduled you for an interview with *The Connecticut News* for this afternoon. The crew will start setting up the TV cameras at one o'clock. The whole thing will run on the local news, with excerpts going to the national and cable networks, so say something witty."

"Like what?"

"Like, you still have six lives left." As she closed the suitcase, she noticed the drawings on David's bedside table. The one on top showed a colorful airplane done in crayons, obviously Grant's work.

"We've got to come up with something better than that," David muttered from the bathroom.

"I will. I want to do a couple of run-throughs with you this morning." She picked up the stack and leafed through it.

From the bathroom, she heard, "Christ, I look like death warmed over."

Katherine smiled. "In a way you are. But there will be a make-up artist, so don't worry."

Then she saw the pencil sketch of Jenny and froze. She felt a stab of pain. David must have done it from memory, yet it looked so lifelike. She closed her eyes for a moment to regain control. When she opened them, she saw David looking at her from the bathroom door. He was dressed in his pajamas.

"Grant asked me to draw her," he said softly.

Katherine forced herself to smile. "You must do a sketch of me sometime."

He was about to answer her, but afraid of what he might say, she put down the sketches and quickly went on. "Let's talk about the interview. I don't want you to announce the Newhallville office yet."

He frowned. "But I just said—"

"I know you did, but I want to hold it back."

"Why?"

"Because," Katherine explained, "I want it to be a surprise when you appear there with the two reverends. It will be another opportunity for a poll rise and will knock Bradley back on his heels."

David settled himself on the bed and smiled, "And seriously piss him off. He was so hoping I wouldn't make it."

Katherine sat in the chair next to it, opened her briefcase, and pulled out some papers. "Here is the itinerary for the interview, and a list of some questions and answers I've prepared. If he gets off message, you can pivot to any of them."

She noticed David was staring off toward the windows. "David, are you listening?"

He looked back to her. "Something about pivoting."

"David, stay with me. You don't want to mess this up."

"It must be the medication," he said, refocusing on her.

She didn't think it was.

CHAPTER 65

A taxi pulled up in front of David's bungalow in New Haven early on Sunday morning. The driver got out, looked around the quiet street, his breath fogging in the crisp fall air. Seeing no one, he walked up the path toward the front door and rang the bell. He waited for some time. When David finally answered, the driver handed him a business card and motioned with his head toward the cab.

David looked at the card, then at the cab, and followed the driver to the street. When the rear door opened, he slid inside while the driver busied himself polishing the windshield and headlights.

Stephanie Jordan held the collar of her blue, wool coat and knotted scarf tightly around her neck, as if she wanted to conceal her face.

"Ms. Jordan," David said with guarded formality. "Since I got shot, a lot of people want to talk to me, but you're the one I would have least expected. If you're hoping for an interview, I suggest you get in touch with my communications director."

"I'm sorry for surprising you like this on a Sunday morning," Stephanie replied. "But I'm on my way to the airport, and there's something you need to know."

David glanced out the back window to see if there was an unfamiliar car parked farther back, but the street was empty. "Did Bradley send you?" he asked calmly.

Stephanie gave a hollow laugh. "Hardly. I came to warn you about something."

David wondered if the woman he knew to be Bradley's mistress was trying to set him up. He decided to play. "What is it?"

"Bradley Coyle has some personal information concerning you and your son that he's about to leak to the press."

David looked at her intently, studying her for signs of lying. "Which is?"

"That you got a young girl pregnant and never married her. That you had a son who lives with the girl's parents."

His eyes narrowed. "Why are you telling me this?"

"Because I believe involving a child is crossing the line. Until now, they have been off-limits in political battles. This is hitting way below the belt."

"Did he ask you to reveal this in your newscast?"

"He did, but I refused. Harvey Finch will leak it to a newspaper reporter in such a way that it can't be traced back to his campaign, and make sure it will become national news. I'm sorry."

David thought for a moment. "When is this supposed to happen?"

"Tomorrow, so it can land the day after."

He nodded to himself. Then he looked at her. "Does that mean you're no longer with him and supporting his campaign?"

Stephanie stared ahead and her carefully composed face fell, revealing a look of exhaustion, disappointment and pain. Recovering, she said, "Yes, we're done. I would appreciate it, though, if you kept my name out of whatever it is you're going to do."

David extended his hand toward her. "I can't promise that, but thank you. You've done a courageous thing, Ms. Jordan."

"Not really. I couldn't live with myself if I hadn't." She took his hand. "Good luck."

Bradley was having breakfast in his suite at the Quinnipiac Club when the telephone rang. He looked at his wristwatch. Who would be calling this early? He went over to the bar and picked up the receiver of the French phone.

It was the concierge downstairs. "A Mr. David Madison is here to see you."

Surprised, Bradley asked, "Is he alone?"

"Yes."

He wondered what David was up to. Perhaps he should call Boyd to witness the meeting in case things got messy, but curiosity got the better of him and he decided against it. He would face David on his own. "Send him up," he said.

Mystified, Bradley went to the mini-fridge, took out a small can of tomato juice, poured it into a glass and added the contents of a tiny gin bottle. He tasted it and added another bottle. Then he made a second drink, stirred both, tossed the swizzle stick on the counter, and carried them to the coffee table. Sitting down on the sofa, he imagined that he could still smell a trace of Stephanie's perfume and was momentarily distracted. They'd argued once again about Helen. Why couldn't women just enjoy themselves without always pushing for a permanent state of affairs? Annoyed, he took a big gulp of his cocktail.

Eventually, the doorbell rang. Bradley put on his best smile and, drink in hand, walked over to open the door. Seeing David stand there with a serious expression on his face, he said expansively, "Well, to what do I owe the pleasure of this visit?"

"Are you alone? I want to meet with you privately." David's intense voice surprised him.

"I'm having breakfast. I've got a meeting in an hour." Watching David looking around the room and noticing the breakfast table set for one, he added, "You haven't caught me with anyone, if that's what you're thinking." He followed David into the room and picked up the other Bloody Mary and held it out to him. "Your favorite morning beverage, as I recall."

Ignoring the drink, David said, "I didn't come here for chitchat."

"Very well." Bradley gestured to a chair opposite the sofa. "Suit yourself." Raising his glass toward David, he continued, "To the taxpayers!" Then he seated himself and asked, "So what is it that brought you here so early? Have you decided to concede?"

David looked at him calmly. "I understand that you're preparing to leak something about me and my son."

Bradley blinked and tried to conceal his surprise, but his mind was racing. How did he know? Who told him? He took another sip to buy time and said, "What makes you think that?"

"Let's not be coy, Bradley. I know what you're up to, so you might as well stop trying to deny it."

Leaning back casually, his arm resting on the back of the sofa, Bradley tried for petulant outrage. "That's quite an allegation. I don't know where you get your information, but I have nothing to do with it."

David leaned back, "We've known each other for a long time, Bradley, and I know what you're capable of. But children are out of bounds, and you know it! Don't do it."

Bradley frowned. David's contention echoed what some of his advisers had counseled. He decided to hold fast. "I know nothing about any leak. What are you talking about?"

"I'm talking about your attempt to smear me and my son."

"Okay," Bradley countered, "Let's say, for the sake of argument, that I had some kind of information. What could you do about it? What's in it for me, not having it run?"

"Nothing, other than to appeal to whatever shred of human decency you have left."

Bradley's nostrils twitched. "You're talking about the so-called moral high ground. But you're a charlatan who impregnated a young girl. How old was she? Eighteen?"

David leaned back. "So you're admitting now that you know all about it." He paused and tried to reason with him. "You're attacking a five-year-old boy. Would you do that to your own son?"

Caught in a lie, Bradley's face hardened. "You're the one who brought this on the boy, not me."

Realizing that Coyle was digging in, David hesitated. Then he said, "If you want to play hardball, then let's play hardball. If you leak the information about Grant, I'll make sure the world knows about your relationship with Stephanie Jordan. I'm sure people will be happy to ask about the ethics of going to bed with someone in the media you're feeding stories to."

Bradley smirked. "You tried that once before when you ran for Congress against Edwards and I caved then, but not this time. This time I go to the mat. I'll deny it, and the media will cover for me. You won't get away with it."

Getting up, David brushed off his pants disgustedly as if cleaning dirt from them. "We'll see. I won't release it if you keep what you have on Grant and me under your hat. Let me know by the end of the day. I'd prefer to defeat you fair and square."

As he walked to the door, Bradley called after him, "Don't wait up. If you don't hear from me, you'll know my answer. Just remember, you're peddling rumors. What I've got on you are hard facts."

When the door closed Bradley hurried to the phone and punched the buttons to reach Finch.

CHAPTER 66

The emergency meeting of David's brain trust was in full swing at his bungalow in New Haven. Not only had Coyle called David's bluff about Stephanie Jordan, he and Finch had managed to make the revelations about Grant being illegitimate sound as sordid as possible. The media labeled it as 'The Love Child Scandal," and Bradley relentlessly hammered away at David for being a hypocrite who talked family values for everyone but himself. His smear campaign had taken a heavy toll. The gap between them in the polls, which had been negligible days earlier, had widened once again to nearly 10 points.

David sat at one end of the kitchen table opposite Senator Cunningham with John Ralston and Senator Garrett facing Katherine on the sides. Their faces were tired and drawn from fielding endless questions from reporters and trying to counter Coyle's character assassination machine. There was a nervous tension in the room.

David seemed distracted, letting the conversation swirl around him, but inside he was seething. He wanted nothing more than to wring Coyle's neck. How could he ever explain it to Grant?

"Our poll numbers are still dropping," Cunningham said. He looked over at his daughter. "We need to do something to stop the hemorrhaging."

"What about the Reverends Meade and Robinson?" Garrett asked. "Would they stick their necks out?"

Katherine shook her head. "Personally, they're supportive, but I doubt they'd go public."

"And the Langleys? They've known about this all along and have been fine with it," Garret persisted. Laura Langley could make an appearance with David, make a statement about how David's been an exemplary father. It could create a wellspring of sympathy."

"Couldn't we get the papers to run spreads of photographs of David with Grant together at different times," John Ralston chimed in. "When he was holding him as a baby...later with him on the helicopter."

Senator Cunningham shook his head. "That won't change the narrative enough." He looked at his daughter. "What do you think, Katherine? We have to find a way to counter the national media outlets and Twittersphere."

Katherine twisted a pencil around her fingers. "We have to go on the offensive, turn the tables on Coyle."

"How do we do that?" Garrett asked.

"Leak the story of Coyle's mistress," she spat out. "Let him defend whispering national secrets to a news anchor while screwing her."

Surprised by her outburst, the men shared furtive glances.

Abruptly, David spoke up. "You're all missing the point. I'm the one who has to deal with this. I'm not going to send out surrogates to fight him. It's my election to win or lose."

Katherine's eyes flashed angrily at him. "Really! You've been sitting there stewing, while we're all trying to save your campaign. A lot of people have poured time and money into this. You didn't get here by yourself, and you're not going to get out of it by yourself."

"Katherine, I created this problem, and I'm the one who has to fix it."

"And how are you going to do that?" Katherine clenched her fists and got up. "You keep playing the Lone Ranger, and you'll blow the election. You created this mess in the first place."

David's voice rose. "And what do you want me to do?"

"Admit it, you can't fix it yourself," she challenged, advancing on him. "Admit, just once, that you need someone else in your life."

"And what would that accomplish?"

"I don't know. Make you a real man, not just some macho solo flier who turns tail when things get rough. You made a mistake a half a dozen years ago. That's the real truth, and you can't deny it!"

Stung, David jumped up and shouted, "That's not the real truth! The real truth is that I'm not Grant's father!"

He froze, and the others with him for what seemed like an eternity. Senator Garret got to his feet and faced David. "Then who is?" David hesitated, but having opened Pandora's box, there was no way back. "Bradley Coyle," he said.

The ensuing silence lasted even longer.

Finally, Ralston said, as if expelling a breath, "I don't understand."

David walked to the window and, with his back to the others, started to explain, "Darlene was pregnant when I met her. I rented a room to her in my boarding house just off the Mall after I got back from Iraq. I was suffering from PTSD and she helped bring me back from the edge."

You could hear a pin drop as he went into the details of their relationship and the confusion that resulted in his name being mistakenly placed on the birth certificate after she died, and his decision to become Grant's father without knowing who the real father was.

When he was finished, everyone sat in shocked silence.

Then Katherine said, almost to herself, "Bradley Coyle did that while he and I were married."

He nodded. "Yes."

"That son-of-a-bitch!"

"And you knew nothing about Grant's paternity five years ago?" Senator Garrett asked.

"Nothing."

"Then how did you find out?" Senator Cunningham asked.

"Nancy Sullivan was the nurse in the maternity ward at the time and Darlene told her. She swore her to secrecy, but Nancy broke her promise when she saw Coyle in the hospital with Grant and revealed it to me as I was recovering from the gunshot wounds."

When Katherine spoke, she sounded different from before, a steely anger in her voice. "What you're saying is that Bradley set off a bomb for you and it is about to explode in his own face."

"Not quite," David said. "I'm not going to let Grant find out that I'm not his father and that Bradley Coyle is. It would be devastating."

Katherine's eyes widened. "I'll tell you what will be devastating. If you lose to Bradley and let him get away with it."

"I won't do it." David looked at her with determination in his eyes.

Her voice rose in intensity. "David, this will assure your election. If you don't use it, you will go down in defeat. It's that simple."

"I'm telling you, Kathy, I won't do it."

She grabbed his forearm with both hands. "Don't you see what you're doing? You're handing the Senate seat to Bradley on a golden platter."

"I'll defeat him in another way."

"What other way? There isn't another way."

"Then I'll lose, won't I?"

Senator Cunningham got up and implored David, "Coyle's lobbed a grenade at you. You've got to throw it back at him! You've got to!"

As David shook his head Senator Garrett joined in. "David, we can't let Coyle win," he said with emotion. "That's why we put you up for his seat. There's too much at stake."

By now, all but John Ralston stood around him.

Katherine said casually, "Grant's young. He'll get over it with time."

David gave a harsh laugh. "And the Langleys? What happens

when they find out that I've misled them all these years about being Grant's father, and that it's Bradley, of all people? No. I've done this for their daughter and for Grant. I made a promise to myself then and I'm going to keep it."

Katherine looked at Ralston. "John, don't just sit there, reason with him!"

He shook his head. "This is out of my league. I'm a financier, not a politician. It's David's call as far as I'm concerned."

Her eyes burning with fury, she confronted David, "Are you going to be a chickenshit like Bradley, or grow some balls and give him what he deserves?"

David answered forcefully, "I'm sorry. My mind is made up!"

The color drained from Katherine's face. "Then I'm done with you, your campaign, your life!"

She spun on her heel and stormed out, slamming the door behind her.

David looked after her, deadpan.

Senator Cunningham took his coat from the back of the chair and put it on. "She's upset, it will blow over," he said reassuringly. "Think about it, David. Another day won't be the end of the world."

Senator Garret placed a hand on David's shoulder for a moment, then followed Cunningham out.

David looked at John Ralston, who finally stood up. He held David's stare for a moment and said, "You've got to do what you can live with for the rest of your life. You don't owe me anything."

When he left, David stood alone in the room, rigid as a stone pillar.

CHAPTER 67

Bradley Coyle sat in the back of his limousine, his mind racing. He felt like his head was about to explode. He'd just finished the video Finch had sent to his cell phone of Katherine Cunningham appearing on Stephanie Jordan's show.

"That bitch!" he shouted. "After all I've done for her! Not even a heads-up."

A throng of television crews and reporters greeted the limo as it pulled up to the curb in front of his New Haven campaign office. As the driver opened the back door and Coyle emerged, the crowd surged forward, jostling and pushing. Soundmen stuck their shotgun mics with furry muffs in his face. Cameramen with video recorders held high above their heads stood behind them while reporters peppered him with questions.

"IS IT TRUE THAT YOU ARE GRANT MADISON'S FATHER?"

"ARE YOU GOING TO TAKE A DNA TEST, AS THE MADISON CAMPAIGN HAS CALLED FOR?"

"DID YOU DEMAND THAT DARLENE LANGLEY HAVE AN ABORTION?"

The driver tried to run interference and muscle ahead through the pressing horde while the questions came at Coyle like bullets from an assault rifle.

"ARE KATHERINE CUNNINGHAM'S CLAIMS TRUE?"

"ARE YOU GOING TO RESIGN?"

Coyle almost took the bait and started to lash out in anger, but Boyd behind him yelled, "No comment!" and propelled him onward. As they ducked into the office, Boyd bringing up the rear, the reporters kept lobbing questions after them. Inside, they were met by a cacophony of ringing telephones. They made their way past the desks of tight-lipped campaign workers who gave them fearful sideways glances. Finch was waiting in the conference room. Boyd shut the door, reducing the clamor to a muffled roar.

Coyle rushed to the bar, poured himself a glass of Bourbon and downed it in two gulps. Coughing, he poured himself another and sat down on the side of the mahogany table, staring in front of him in a slow burn.

Finch gave him a hard, evaluating once-over, then eyed Boyd who shrugged helplessly. He started to pace and strategize, talking to Bradley but not looking at him. "Okay, Senator, this is bad, beyond bad. The video's gone viral, and there have been calls for your resignation already. But we can deal with this."

Boyd, incredulous, mouthed, "How?"

Ignoring him, Finch continued, "We'll issue a denial. Right away. This is obviously a politically motivated attack, a disgusting, desperate ploy. They're ten points behind in the polls with a week to go!"

Boyd asked, "What about their demand to take a DNA test?"

Coyle flared up. "I'm not going to do it!"

Finch turned to him. "That's right. Under no circumstances. We can't let them dictate the terms. We have to counterattack."

Bradley said, venomously, "Katherine is the one to talk. She had an affair with David Madison while we were still married, and now she's running his campaign and making wild accusations!"

"That's good, that's good," Finch said with rising excitement. "We can use that against her."

Boyd chimed in, "And the party's behind you. They don't want to lose the Senate seat."

Bottom line," Finch said, "all we need to do is to muddy the waters and hold on for a week. We can weather this storm."

Suddenly, the door flew open without warning, and Helen Coyle charged in. She marched past Finch and Boyd and faced Bradley across the table.

The blood drained from his face. "Helen! What are you doing here?"

"Is it true? Are you the father?!"

Finch and Boyd looked at each other and slipped out of the room together.

Bradley started to rise. "It's a shameless smear campaign against me, Helen."

"Don't lie to me, Bradley!"

The venom in her voice drove him back into his seat. He swallowed and said petulantly, "What do you want me to say? You knew I was no saint when you married me."

"Take the test and we'll find out."

"I can't do that, Helen."

"Why not?"

When Bradley remained silent, Helen leaned over the conference table, her eyes boring into his. "So it's true—the affair, the paternity, the demand for an abortion, the abandonment. All of it."

Bradley looked away. "They can't prove a thing."

Helen groaned. "You think they didn't orchestrate this carefully? Katherine on that TV show, shilling for Madison so he wouldn't come off as a callous bastard regarding his son. Do you really think they don't have a credible follow-up? You can't just stonewall your way out of this. This will finish you."

"You've got to stand by me, Helen," he pleaded hoarsely. "We will get through this if you stand by me."

When Helen straightened, her demeanor had changed. It was as if a curtain of ice had descended between her and Bradley. She said quietly, "You've been getting away with this disgusting behavior for so long that you think there are no consequences, but eventually there are." Her voice cut like a shard of glass. "We're done. Don't come home, don't try to call me, and don't send your sycophants to try to persuade me otherwise. You've put your head in the noose by yourself, and you're going to swing alone."

She turned and stalked out of the room, leaving the door open.

Bradley looked after her with a murderous expression on his face. Then he balled his fists and bellowed like a gored bull.

CHAPTER 68

I t was late at night. Aboard John Ralston's Learjet, David looked out into the murky mist of darkness. He was exhausted from dealing with Katherine's unexpected resignation from the campaign and her subsequent release of the Coyle story. That had set off a chain reaction whose shock waves radiated through the media and Twittersphere.

Projecting a sense of calmness he did not feel, he treated it all as a military firestorm and rallied his troops, reassuring his campaign workers that this was all good news. His appointment of Julie Hansen, his communications director, as his new campaign manager helped. Fortunately, Katherine had left behind a playbook of to-dos right up to election day, the victory party, and the acceptance speech. He'd found it significant that she had not bothered to draft a concession speech.

As soon as the barrage of emails and phone calls asking for comments on the Coyle revelation ended, David called Edward Langley in Annapolis. He asked him to take Laura and Grant to a hotel. John Ralston had booked them a room already to escape the relentless onslaught of reporters who would soon be camped out on their lawn. Then he huddled with Senator Garrett to work on an official statement to be released first thing the next morning. Now that Katherine let loose the dogs of war, he would follow them to victory.

David wondered what Jenny was making of all the turmoil. God, how he missed her.

The cockpit door opened and John Ralston came out trailed by a pretty female flight attendant. He whispered to her, and she went to the bar and galley station to fix them drinks. Ralston sat down opposite David in a matching padded leather chair that made a regular airline seat look like an upholstered plank.

"We'll be airborne for about an hour," he said. "We're flying along the coast to the Bay Bridge Airport near Annapolis. It's by The Inn at the Chesapeake Bay Beach Club where the Langleys are staying. Edward Langley will pick you up."

The flight attendant set two drinks on the table between them and returned to the cockpit with coffee for the pilots. David figured it was a fine single malt Scotch and, when he took a sip, he was not disappointed.

He felt a sense of relief. "John, I can't thank you enough," he said.

John nodded as they each took another sip.

"Have you heard from Katherine?" John asked softly.

"Only what's on TV." David set the glass onto the table. "How could she do this to me, John?!"

John waited for David to go on, and he did. "Apparently, she's dragged Nancy Sullivan into this now, too! She gave her name and number to Stephanie Jordan. Nancy called me to confirm that I was okay with her going public with the details. She was actually quite eager to do it. I told her to go ahead and tell the truth. What's done is done, and now we have to see it through to the end. I don't think that winning the election is enough for Katherine now. Nothing short of destroying Bradley will do."

"I think you're right about that," John said. "My impression has always been that Katherine is an all-or-nothing person."

"Yeah," David said, with a bitter laugh. "We didn't have to go nuclear to win. I believe I could have won without it."

John shook his head. "That's speculation. Katherine believed Coyle had a winning hand. Why take the chance? After Nancy goes on the air, whether he refuses a DNA test or agrees to take it, he'll be finished either way."

David took a gulp of Scotch. "I can't forgive her for this. It wasn't her call."

"No one's asking you to. Not even Katherine. She's made her decision and she knows she has to live with it."

John got up and retrieved the bottle from the galley, holding it out to David with a questioning look. As he poured more Scotch, he remarked off-handedly, "Maybe sometimes we take people so for granted that we forget who they are. I've known from the moment you introduced us how self-willed she is."

David gave John a quizzical look. "What makes you say that?"

"She has so much invested in you and the election. Think about it. You have been her life, her whole purpose. Aside from her father, what friends does she have? She's put all her energy into you, and now she sees you slipping away with Jenny."

"That doesn't justify what she did."

"No, but it does explain it."

"I've never thought of you as perceptive about women, John."

"I'm not. I'm a ruthless financier, and Katherine's a ruthless person about anything she sets her mind to. So we can understand each other. You're not. You march to a different drummer. I believe in what you're doing, but I would never want to go down that path myself."

"So you love money. That's not so bad, if you make it ethically."

"No. But that's where Katherine crossed the line. Her problem is that she's got you under her skin. She'd do almost anything to get you elected, even defy you."

"Even to the point of destroying our relationship?"

"She didn't lose anything she hadn't already lost. I think she knew that. Maybe it was her way of getting back at you for not loving her." He took another sip of Scotch, then resumed, "She got her revenge on all of her men in a twisted sort of way. You, Coyle, even her father. His dream of her being part of a Washington power couple is shattered, too. And she's left with nothing, not a good place to be."

"I can't forgive what she's done. Grant's at an impressionable age. Revealing that Coyle is his father is unpardonable!"

John said gently. "Give it time. Maybe you will, maybe you won't. In any case, it's time to move on, for both of you."

Almost inaudibly, David said, "I do love her, but not in the way she wants."

John nodded. "Then maybe she needs someone who can." He paused before continuing, "Now you've got to think about Grant."

David looked up at the curved ceiling in silence for a moment, lost. Then he lowered his head and whispered, "What in God's name am I going to say to him?"

John smiled. "You'll figure it out. You're his father."

CHAPTER 69

As the Learjet taxied toward the small administration building for private air traffic, David could see a car waiting outside in a cone of light with someone standing beside it. His heart leapt. Could it possibly be Jenny? But as they got closer he recognized Laura Langley, her arms wrapped tightly against the cold.

When the plane came to a halt, David again thanked John Ralston, who wished him luck. Then he gingerly descended the exit staircase created by the lowered cabin door. The gap to the ground caused him to misstep, and he winced at the pain radiating from his chest, a reminder of the bullets he'd taken.

Laura's face looked pale and drawn as he approached. "Grant knows nothing about this yet," she burst out. "I thought you'd want to tell him in your own way. I'm so completely unnerved by all these revelations. It's a terrible mess."

As David embraced her, he said, "It never should have happened."

She held onto him for an extra moment. When she released him, he opened the driver's door for her and walked around the car, getting in on the passenger side. She sat behind the steering wheel motionless, her hands in her lap, and stared straight ahead, making no effort to start the engine.

"I wanted to talk to you alone, David, before the turmoil begins," she said. "John Ralston told us that it was Katherine who let the story out. That you were against it."

"It wasn't her call. She shouldn't have done it."

"Edward is devastated, too. To think that Grant is Bradley Coyle's son and that my own daughter...it's almost more than I can deal with. I've come to see Grant as your son, with your qualities, and to discover this...and how we blamed you...I don't know what to say..."

David turned to her. "He is my son. Don't ever think of him any differently. Darlene made her choices and we just have to accept that. But she refused to sacrifice Grant to Coyle's whims. That was also her choice. She was his mother and I became his father, because that is how she and I wanted it."

Laura grasped his hand. "Oh, David, my one consolation is that in the end she chose you."

"I'm glad she did," David said.

She gave him a final squeeze, then straightened and took a deep breath. "What are we going to tell Grant?"

David instantly felt at a loss. "I was hoping you might have some ideas," he ventured.

Smiling at him regretfully, she said, "Not really." She turned the ignition switch and the engine came to life. As she pulled onto the highway, she added, "This is new territory for all of us."

Nodding in agreement, David changed tack. "I know one thing. We have to keep the press away. Can you and Edward stay with him here until after the election?"

She glanced at him. "Certainly, but then what?"

"Then we'll see," he said, more confidently than he felt.

They stayed quiet for the rest of the drive, lost in their separate thoughts.

When they arrived at the hotel and parked, Laura turned to David, looked him in the eyes, and said simply, "Thank you."

David gave a small smile of acknowledgment. It was but a brief moment of grace for him because as soon they entered the lobby and rode the elevator to the top floor, he felt his gut clench. He took a deep breath when Laura inserted the key card, opened the door to their suite, and stepped inside.

Before he knew what was happening, Grant rushed up and grabbed his hand. "Dad," he crowed excitedly and pointed to an adjoining door. "I have my own room!"

David laughed. "If you wouldn't mind sharing, we can bunk together tonight."

"Sure!" Grant jumped with delight.

Nodding toward the connecting room, David said, "Go get into your pajamas, and I'll be in in a minute to read you a story."

As Grant skipped into the bedroom, David looked up and saw Edward Langley standing at the windows. He moved awkwardly into the light and stammered, "David...I...I..."

David said, "Let me just get Grant to sleep. We can talk then," and was rewarded with a grateful smile.

He entered the room, which had two queen-sized beds. The light between them was on, and Grant was bouncing up and down on his bed.

"You aren't asleep yet?" David kidded.

Grant giggled. "I've been waiting for you to read me a story about Winnie the Pooh and Tigger."

David closed the door and sat down on the bed next to Grant. He reached over to the night table and picked up the thin, dog-eared children's book. "It looks like you've read this a few times before."

"Grandma gave it to me. She reads it to me every night."

Rippling the pages with his thumb and glancing at the pictures, David said, "Good old Winnie the Pooh. I remember him."

"Did your mommy read it to you?"

"No," he shook his head, "I was an orphan." He looked at Grant. "Do you know what an orphan is?"

"Sure. Someone who doesn't have a mommy and daddy."

"That's right, but everybody has a mommy and daddy when they are born. Even Pooh and Tigger, even though their parents aren't there. But Pooh has so many friends in the hundred-acre woods that they are like his family."

"I was real scared when you were hurt," Grant admitted reluctantly. "I didn't want you to go to heaven to be with mommy. No one could take your place, Dad."

"I've always been your dad since the day you were born, and I always will be. You'll never forget that will you?"

"Sure."

"Promise?"

"Promise!"

"Okay then."

Grant became pensive. "What was Mommy like? Do you think she was pretty?"

"Very pretty."

"As pretty as Jenny?"

"Almost."

"I wish Jenny could be my mom," Grant said hopefully and looked up at David. He rolled over onto his side, his elbow resting on his pillow, his head on his hand. "Why don't you ask her to marry us?"

"You'd like that?"

"Sure would."

David hesitated. "We'll see." Then he said, "Let's read about Tigger." He held the bed covers so that Grant could slide under them.

As he pulled them up to his son's chest, Grant raised his arms for a hug. He held onto David's neck for a long time. When he finally let go, David read until Grant's eyelids kept closing and he fell asleep. Then David closed the book and set it back on the nightstand. "Good night, son," he whispered.

But instead of leaving the room David went over to the windows and looked out at the Chesapeake Bay Bridge lights crossing the black expanse of water. He called Jenny's cell phone, but there was still no answer. When her voicemail came on, he ended the call. No point in leaving yet another message among the myriad others he'd sent, which she hadn't returned.

He thought about her angry silence, then Katherine's angry and hurt betrayal. The victory that would soon be his felt hollow and came with too big a price. He looked over at Grant fast asleep and quietly went out.

As he entered the living room of the suite, Edward Langley handed him a snifter of brandy.

"Please sit down, David," he said.

As David complied, Edward remained standing and started to pace nervously. "What I want to say," he began, "is that I am very sorry. When I think of all that I said about you when we first met, I had no idea what the truth was—that it was Darlene's fault, not yours. I've thought a lot about what I did to drive her away and into the arms of a lecherous, rich, spoiled–"

David shook his head. "It wasn't her fault, or yours. Bradley Coyle was the culprit, although I didn't know that at the time." He registered the deep, angry sadness in Edward's eyes and continued, "Darlene was one of the sweetest people I ever met. She was going through a terrible struggle herself, and yet she helped me come back to life. If it weren't for her, I wouldn't be here today."

Edward shook his head. "You're giving her too much credit."

"Bradley Coyle tried to destroy their baby, but Darlene remained steadfast to the end, and Grant will grow up to be a fine young man because you are his grandparents, and we will never forsake him. He is Darlene's and yours, and mine."

Tears began to well up in Edward's eyes and he covered them with his hand. "I didn't love her enough," he said. "I didn't know how little time was left."

"Whether you did or not," David said, "you've loved her son like your own. There is no shadow on Darlene. She was the one who followed her conscience, something that you and Laura gave her."

Laura Langley came up to her husband from behind and put her arms around him. "We have to live for today and we have to live for the future, Edward. The past is gone and we just have to accept it, and move on."

He nodded and sighed. Laura guided him to the sofa and they sat down next to each other, holding hands. To David they seemed like two ancient teenagers whose unspoken love for one another forged an unbreakable bond. The three of them continued to talk, sharing memories of Darlene and favorite stories about Grant. At some point, David excused himself, pleading tiredness and a long day ahead.

"Let's have breakfast together tomorrow morning, the four of us," he said and went back into Grant's room.

Walking up to the window he looked at the bridge lights and the dark waters below again. Their steady glow was the same as before. Nothing had changed.

He took out his phone and punched in a number. When he heard the call being picked up at the other end, he said, "Katherine, it's David. I need your help."

CHAPTER 70

The next morning Jenny sat in her office at the National Gallery, looking at museum catalogs to plan a new exhibition. Having spent a nearly sleepless night, she had a hard time concentrating. The revelations on the news about Grant and David not being his real father kept chasing thoughts around in her head.

Her emotions vacillated between anger and hurt. Had David ever intended to tell her the truth? What other important secrets had he kept from her? How could she ever have fallen for such an untrustworthy man?

She shook herself to clear her head and started to get back to work when the telephone on her desk rang, startling her. She received an even bigger shock when the receptionist announced that Katherine Cunningham was there to see her.

"I'll be right out," Jenny said. She stacked the catalogs into a neat pile to calm herself. What in the world did that woman want from her now?

By the time she walked into the reception lobby, she had regained her composure. She saw her rival standing at the tall windows looking out at the Mall and walked up to her. "Katherine?"

The woman who turned and faced her looked haunted and exhausted. "Is there somewhere private where we can talk?" she said.

"What's it about?" Jenny asked, puzzled.

"Something you need to know," Katherine said.

Jenny hesitated. This wasn't the right place to have a conversation. "We can go to my office."

Katherine picked up her coat and leather attaché case and followed Jenny through the rotunda down a broad staircase to the lower level, then to a hallway and a door marked "Staff." When they got to her office, Jenny removed a stack of art books from a chair and said, "Please sit down."

But Katherine kept looking around at the posters from exhibitions. Her eyes were drawn to the one painting hanging on the wall, a horse with his neck stretched down to touch a dog's nose titled *Friends Forever*. She walked up to it and was surprised to see "Madison" signed in the bottom right corner. Glancing at Jenny, she walked to the chair facing the desk.

As she sat down, she said, "I never thought that his paintings were very good. Obviously, I'm right since it's been put here in the basement."

"This is where living artists start. At the bottom," Jenny replied testily, taking her own seat. "The National Gallery only displays paintings by artists that have stood the test of time." She fixed her eyes on Katherine's. "But you're not here to discuss David's artworks."

"You never wanted him to go into politics, did you?" Katherine countered.

"I don't see how that's relevant," Jenny shot back.

"What's relevant is that he did."

"I think I had him figured out quite well. I knew he had a mercurial side, or should I say fickle, and that he was driven enough to do anything to get elected. But I never imagined he would stoop so low as to sacrifice a five-year-old child on the altar of his ambition."

Taken aback by Jenny's tirade, Katherine appraised her warily. Seeing both her anger and her desperation, she said deliberately, "If you must know, David had nothing to do with the release of the story about Bradley Coyle's fathering Grant. In fact–"

Jenny quickly cut her off. "What does that have to do with me?"

"Perhaps nothing, perhaps a great deal. You'll have to decide once you know the whole story."

Stone-faced, Jenny leaned back in her chair. Then her eyes narrowed. "Did David put you up to this?"

"As a matter of fact, he did," Katherine replied, and a small smile played about her lips. "He thought I was the only one you'd believe." For a moment she relished a feeling of superiority.

Jenny was mystified. "Why would he ever think that?"

"Because I'm the one who released the Coyle story against David's wishes."

This time, Jenny was speechless. Her eyes darted around the room as she tried to work out the implications. At last, warily, she said, "I still don't know why you're telling me this."

"Because I owe him, and I want him to be happy. He deserves it!"

Katherine opened her attaché case and pulled out the sketch David had made of Jenny and put it on her desk. "I've known him a lot longer than you, and in all that time he has never drawn a picture of me."

Jenny looked from the drawing to Katherine, bewildered.

Katherine closed her case and stood up. "He will be waiting for you at the Vietnam Memorial Wall at three o'clock."

Taking her coat, she walked to the door. Then she turned back and said, like a champion relishing an empty victory, "Head to head against me, you never stood a chance. But he doesn't want me. He loves you."

Before Jenny could react, she swept from the room, leaving Jenny sitting alone in her chair, staring at David's drawing of her.

≪

David looked out at the Wall, 144 polished black granite slabs, inscribed with more than 58,000 names, forming a boomerang-shaped wedge with one arm reaching toward the Washington Monument and the other toward the Lincoln Memorial. He tightened the collar of his trench coat against the gray, chilling afternoon. It reminded him of the day when he found Darlene, and he looked up at the sky almost expecting snowflakes to begin falling.

Nothing had changed at the Vietnam Veterans Memorial in the five years that had passed, except that more names had been added of those killed and missing in action. But for him everything had changed. He had replaced his battle fatigues with a blue suit and his field jacket with a trench coat. He was about to become a U.S. Senator, he had a son he loved as dearly as life itself, and he had found a purpose that gave meaning to his actions.

Was it enough?

He looked at his watch. It was ten minutes past three. Jenny was late. He started to feel panicky. What if she didn't come at all.

Then he heard a familiar voice behind him, "Hi."

He turned slowly and there she was, standing before him, a small, tentative smile on her lips.

"Why did you want to meet here?" she asked softly.

He pointed at a nearby bench. "This is where I met Grant's mother, Darlene. I want you to know the whole story of what happened here five years ago."

Jenny looked at the Wall. "I've never been here before," she said.

"I used to come here often, both before and after." David's voice had a melancholy tone. "It felt like a fitting place to remember my fallen friends. Then I met Darlene. I didn't know until afterward that she had cancer. She battled it long enough for Grant to be born. To my mind, she died a hero."

Jenny remained silent. She felt overwhelmed by the spiritual impact of the place. She had been to Arlington National Cemetery before, but there was something up close and personal here, people touching the names, some solemnly bearing witness, some weeping, their own reflections in the mirror-like granite making a connection between the living and the dead.

David said tenderly, "Let's walk."

They made their way past the people who spoke in whispers to their loved ones, past the Three Soldiers statue and the pole whose flag, like an eternal flame, never stops flying; and on to Constitution Gardens until they reached the pond. Jenny sat down on a bench and looked toward the Washington Monument in the distance, lost in thought.

David joined her and said, "The reason I wanted to get elected is because of this place—not for the money or the power. I hope you can understand that, Jenny."

Jenny took his hand in both of hers. "I realize that now, David, especially since you were prepared to risk everything you've worked for to protect Grant." She squeezed his hand. "Have you told him that Coyle is his father?"

David looked away at the ducks swimming in the pond. "Not yet."

Jenny's voice was full of compassion. "He can't comprehend it now, David. He's too young. You're doing the right thing, keeping him away from the media so he won't find out yet. When the election is over, it will all be forgotten. Then, when he is older you can tell him. Until then, build his confidence in your love, so that there is no one who can replace you."

David turned back to her. "There is someone," he said.

Her eyes found his. "David, there is something I must tell you."

He tensed. "What is it?"

She hesitated for a moment and finally said, "The night of the opening at Frank Gannovino's Gallery I bought the *Lady in Waiting*."

David was stunned. "But...but Frank sold it to an older man."

"No, he sold it to me through an emissary."

Comprehension dawned on David's face. "It was you...and all this time...? Why didn't you tell me?" he said, dismayed.

"I had no idea that I'd ever see you again, much less fall in love with you. Then, when we had dinner that night at the Middleburg Club and you told me that you were an artist I realized who you were." She went on fervently, "I never thought I'd marry a politician and I tried to convince myself that I had to end our relationship...

but I couldn't!" The words kept pouring out as if a dam had broken. "And then, Katherine...I was so hurt...thinking what a cad you were. And when it looked like you'd sacrificed Grant for your own political ambitions, I thought I was right in the first place, and how stupid I'd been to trust you." She started to choke up. "But now I find that you were protecting him, a child that wasn't even yours!"

He put a finger to her lips to stop her. "Nothing could make me happier than to know you have it," he said, smiling, "except if you would marry me. We belong together, Jenny—like the painting. I love you more than I ever thought I could love anyone."

As he drew her close he slipped one hand into his pocket and withdrew a small, dark blue box. He took her hand and placed it in her palm, closing her fingers around it.

She opened her hand and stared at it in amazement.

"I told you that night that I would marry the woman who bought the *Lady in Waiting*. Will you? Will you marry me, Jenny?"

When she snapped the lid open, the large natural white pearl in a stunning setting took her breath away. "Oh, David, it's so beautiful!" she exclaimed. "How did you know I didn't want a diamond?"

David grinned. "You told me once that a diamond is a cold stone. A pearl starts from a grain of sand as an irritant that slowly builds over time into a beautiful creation by a living thing."

She slipped the ring on her finger. "Like the beautiful life we will create together from a prickly beginning."

As he leaned in to kiss her, she pulled back. "Did you get Grant's approval?"

David chuckled. "He told me to ask you to marry us."

Jenny smiled. "Then you can tell him I accept."

CHAPTER 71

The morning after the election the sky was clear blue with no clouds in sight, and David and Jenny flew together from Connecticut to the Baltimore airport. They rented a limo to take them to the Langleys and Grant in Annapolis.

On the way, they made a slight detour and stopped for a cup of coffee at Joe's Diner. When Jenny asked why, David said, "I made someone a promise."

Inside, the place was as empty as the last time David had been there, but the waitress recognized him right away. She blinked as if she couldn't believe her eyes.

"Hello, Marie," David said.

"Hello, Senator Madison. I didn't think I'd see you again." Her eyes teared up but her smile was radiant. "I've been watching you on TV. I just knew that there was something special about you. Congratulations on your victory."

"Thank you. You know you had something to do with it."

She waved him off. "What can I get you and your lady friend?"

"Oh, how rude of me. This is Jenny, my fiancé."

Jenny said, "Hi, Marie, it's a pleasure to meet you."

Marie leaned toward her. "The pleasure is all mine. You're marrying a fine man, even if he is a politician."

Laughing, Jenny put her arm around David's waist. "I know."

David grinned. "Can we get two cups of coffee to go?"

Marie smiled and got busy. "Coming right up," she said. "Of course, they're on the house."

❧

Back in the limo, David told Jenny the story of meeting Marie on the way to John Ralston's yacht and how his conversation with her gave him the idea to barnstorm Connecticut.

They talked about the demise of Bradley Coyle. Helen had divorce papers served on him just before his concession speech and he ended up addressing an almost empty convention center, a broken man, devoid of power and any semblance of self-respect.

In contrast, David's victory party, which took place in the ballroom of the Omni Hotel in downtown New Haven, was packed with boisterous celebrants. Much of the evening felt like a dream he only remembered in snatches—Jenny by his side; his acceptance speech being met by wild cheers; Katherine standing in the back, watching; John Ralston spotting her and moving to join her; balloons and confetti filling the ballroom air.

When they arrived at the Langleys, Edward came out the front door onto the porch and hurried down the steps. He grasped David's hand, pumping it vigorously. "Congratulations, Senator," he said, beaming.

"Not until I'm sworn in," David replied. "But I like the ring of it."

"Speaking of rings," Jenny said cheerfully and extended her hand as Laura came down the steps to join them.

Laura admired the ring and gave Jenny's hand a squeeze. "I was so happy when I heard that the two of you had become engaged. I'd been hoping this would happen ever since I met you."

As the chauffeur placed their bags on the porch, Grant charged out the door, almost bumping into him, and shouted to David, "You won, you won, you won!" He leaped down the steps two at a time and into David's extended arms.

"We both won!" David said, holding him tightly. "Jenny is going to marry us."

Grant's eyes became large as saucers. He raced over to Jenny. "Is it true, Jenny? Really? For real?!"

"For real, Grant," Jenny said with a big smile.

Edward went over to Jenny and gave her a kiss on the forehead. "I'm so glad that you'll be a part of our family." With his arm around her he led the way up to the porch and into the house.

Inside, they went to the living room. Grant snuggled with Jenny on the sofa as David and Laura sat in comfortable armchairs opposite each other. Edward went to the fireplace and put another log on the fire.

David noticed the bare space above the fireplace. "What happened to the painting over the mantel?" he asked.

"I took it up to my bedroom to make room for a new one." Laura said, eyeing David. Then she turned to Jenny. "It was a portrait of my daughter holding her baby. David painted it for me one Christmas, and I've never been able to thank him enough for it."

"May I see it?" Jenny asked.

Laura smiled. "If it's all right with you, we'll go up later and I'll show it to you. But, right now, I just want to enjoy sitting here with my new daughter, and her son."

David had caught Laura Langley's not so subtle hint, and her implication of a new beginning. David would commemorate that beginning in a painting of them all together.

The warmth of the fire, the smell of the smoke, the aroma of hot cider and turkey wafting from the kitchen brought a smile of contentment to David's face. Everything that he had missed in his past and everything that he now loved most was in this one room.

He looked over at Jenny conversing with the Langleys about renting a house in Annapolis so that Grant would be near them. Grant's little hands were grasping her arm and his head was tipped against her, contented just to be close to her, and that's how he decided to paint them.

For the first time in David's life he felt like a whole person.

◈

If what we call love doesn't take us beyond ourselves, it is not really love.

— *Oswald Chambers*

ACKNOWLEDGEMENTS

This was the first journey I took with fictional characters as companions. Our adventure together took several years and, like most such undertakings, it had its rough patches, unexpected surprises, and moments of pleasure and delight.

There were others who helped make the journey possible and I want to thank them for their affectionate and unwavering support. Chris Angermann, my editor, was a lifeline when I got bogged down, offered nourishing advice, and pointed out road signs that opened up additional paths to explore.

My son, Curtis Alexander, a writer in his own right, provided special insights and direction as well.

Susan Angermann, who read the "journal" of the expedition in various incarnations, gave valuable suggestions.

Carol Ann Ohlers, a retired York University librarian, proofread the final version with meticulous attention to detail.

Lisa Monias, of South River Design Team, who gave so willingly and generously of her expertise.

Ed Maxwell gave invaluable behind the scenes support.

And with me always was Jackie, my wife and muse, encouraging, inspiring and helping me to stay on course.